programmes. She

..., studying PPE at Balliol College

...onal Relations at St Antony's College. She lives in London with her husband and two sons. *Acts of Omission* won the Paddy Power Political Novel of the Year award 2014.

## Praise for *Acts of Omission*

'Terry Stiastny proves herself a skilful prose stylist and a connoisseur of telling details . . . The neatly drawn cast of spies, journalists and politicians orbit each other with compelling stealth . . . Stiastny writes locally but thinks globally, and the result is impressive' *Guardian*

'An intriguing political spy thriller from a former BBC reporter . . . Stiastny brings all her experience to bear in this sinuous story . . . A spirited portrait of the murky skulduggery that inhabits modern politics' *Daily Mail*

'A thriller of rare intelligence' *Saga*

'A convincing picture of Westminster in the 1990s' *Woman Magazine*

'Stiastny cleverly entwines historical fact with fiction . . . not simply a good work of fiction, but an ode to the history that inspired it' *We Love This Book*

'The recreation of the atmosphere of late '90s London is excellent as is the impression of the fast regenerating city of Berlin' *Promoting Crime*

# Acts of Omission

## TERRY STIASTNY

JOHN MURRAY

First published in Great Britain in 2014 by John Murray (Publishers)
An Hachette UK Company

First published in paperback in 2015

1

A CIP catalogue record for this title is available from the British Library

Paperback ISBN 978-1-444-79431-1
Ebook ISBN 978-1-444-79430-4

Typeset in Bembo by Palimpsest Book Production Ltd,
Falkirk, Stirlingshire

Printed and bound by Clays Ltd, St Ives plc

John Murray policy is to use papers that are natural, renewable
and recyclable products and made from wood grown in sustainable
forests. The logging and manufacturing processes are expected to
conform to the environmental regulations of the country of origin.

John Murray (Publishers)
Carmelite House
50 Victoria Embankment
London EC4Y 0DZ

www.johnmurray.co.uk

For Thomas and Maxi

History had a slow pulse; man counted in years, history in generations.

Arthur Koestler, *Darkness at Noon*

# I

*London, November 1998*

THE FIRST HOUR of the morning was the worst, when all the mobile phones on the shelves began to ring. Steve needed a strong cup of tea to help tune out the cacophony of ringtones: the ones that sounded like phones were supposed to; the ones that trilled; the ones with that irritating up-and-down song. But by nine o'clock the batteries started to go flat, and you heard hopeless, dying bleeps. Then it went quiet, and he could read the paper. The phones were one of the things that made the job more tiresome than it used to be.

He was surrounded by the detritus of London life, all the objects carelessly left behind in the backs of thousands of black taxis. It was late November and it had been raining for days. There were dozens of umbrellas lying furled on the shelves, smart black umbrellas with polished handles, cheap folding umbrellas with broken spokes, colourful golf umbrellas with advertising slogans. There were shelves of hats and coats and gloves, and bags of unclaimed shopping. As Christmas drew nearer there would be the remnants of shopping trips and office parties: shiny bags full of gift-wrapped presents; bunches of wilting flowers; discarded items of clothing that weren't the kind you'd normally remove in a cab. He had to unwrap the presents, for security reasons, but it wasn't a job he looked forward to. At first it had been a guilty pleasure to open them, as though the presents were meant for him. But doing it every day felt like perpetually spoiling surprises, ruining birthday after birthday.

Steve's main pleasure at work now was matching the customer to the item that they'd come to look for. After seventeen years at the Lost Property Office he prided himself on his ability to take an educated guess about the person who approached the counter. Who were they, and what had they lost?

So when the second customer of the day walked in, Steve appraised him as usual. A young man, somewhere in his late twenties. He would have appeared tall if he hadn't hunched his shoulders in so closely. He was in a fading black raincoat, and he was soaked. His fine hair was darkened by the rain to a shade of wet mouse. So either he'd come for his umbrella, or he never carried one and had got lost trying to find his way here. He wasn't someone who could afford to take taxis everywhere. Steve could tell that from the shoes, which had soaked up the rain like school blotting paper.

His skin was pale, and he looked as if he'd had a run of sleepless nights. There were dark circles under his eyes, far too dark for someone that age. He still bit his fingernails. This wasn't a man who spent a lot of time outdoors.

This was all normal. Young people these days were so careless, they didn't value their stuff; everything could be replaced cheaply. Life was just one big insurance job. So the boy must be looking for something that mattered to him, something worth the journey to an unfamiliar part of north London at half past ten on a Thursday morning, in the rain, when he should probably have been at work. One of those bloody phones, then, or a computer. But the thing that Steve noticed above all else, and what he'd tell people later, was that Alex Rutherford had looked genuinely afraid.

He put down the newspaper and looked at the young man across the heavy wooden counter.

'I'm looking for my laptop, please.'

Steve mentally chalked up another successful deduction. He was wasted on this.

'Where did you lose it then, sir? And when?'

'Between the City and Pimlico,' he told Steve. The boy was shivering, and his waterlogged sleeves left damp, rainy patches on the woodwork. Steve couldn't help but think of him as a boy, though he evidently had a job. 'Late last night – or maybe early this morning.'

'Where exactly in the City, mate?'

'Somewhere near Liverpool Street. Or could have been Moorgate. Does that help?'

Steve was warming to this bloke. He looked like he needed a hot meal and a warm drink. He was obviously suffering from a killer hangover, and he could tell he wasn't the kind of kid that usually did. And most important, he was polite and trying to be helpful, and didn't talk to him like his time was worth money and Steve's wasn't.

'I'll have a look for you. Can't promise it's here, though. If the driver was working nights, he might not have brought it in yet. Might take a day or two.'

Alex had spent most of his morning so far going over and over in his head what had occurred the previous evening. He knew the sequence of events, and the gaps in it, would matter. How he was going to have just one quick, quiet drink after work, meeting James from college in a pub somewhere near Liverpool Street Station, but then James was swept up into a noisy group of colleagues from the bank, and Alex had allowed himself to be swept along with him.

Alex had been floundering out of his social and financial depth with these confident guys in their expensive suits and laundered shirts, who enjoyed the feeling of putting their new credit cards behind the bar and ordering champagne. When he had explained that he was just a junior civil servant and couldn't really run a tab, they pitied him and offered to pay for his drinks anyway. No one was interested in what he did; he was nothing in the City and he didn't matter. If they asked him more, he would have told them he was something to do with data analysis, that the work was mostly spreadsheets. He'd had that kind of conversation before; they would commiserate with each other about the dullness of spreadsheets and decide to talk about something more interesting. No one asked anything: that was a relief. He drank gratefully but too quickly, on an empty stomach.

He'd left the office with his laptop because he had work still to do, something that needed finishing. The laptop had been under the table in the pub, and he'd certainly taken it to the wine bar after that. He'd surfaced in the morning, late and groggy, shaved clumsily, and rushed to leave. He was putting on his coat when the thump of realisation hit him, a thump that landed in both his queasy stomach and his tender head at once. The laptop wasn't there, next to his work bag, where it should have been.

As Alex put his keys in the pocket of his raincoat, he had found a book of matches there, with the name of the wine bar on it, something Spanish. For an instant, he wondered why he had a matchbook, although he didn't smoke. Had he been smoking? The bar's phone number was on the matchbook, and he turned back from the door to call them. The woman who answered the phone, just when he had been on the point of hanging up, said she hadn't seen any computers. The pause after he'd asked her to look again wasn't really long enough to be sure that she had checked.

When he'd left the bar, he recalled, not entirely sure where he was after following the others down narrow streets and away from the offices where the lights still burned, he'd made his way back towards a main road and hailed a cab. He'd remembered trying to stick his arm out confidently, so that he'd be noticed when he shouted 'Taxi!' It's what the guys at the bar would have done. It was raining, and the orange cab light was reflected in the puddles. The taxi braked hard and came to a halt in a deep pothole, splashing him. Alex climbed in the back and hoped that he wouldn't throw up before he got home.

Now the man behind the Lost Property counter was telling him he might have to wait a day or two as though forty-eight

4

hours wouldn't matter. Two days was a long time. He was already going to be in more trouble than he had ever been in before. Alex tried to stop himself shaking as the man shuffled slowly down the aisles of belongings. He paused for a second and looked back over his shoulder.

'Does it have your name on it? Your company?'

'No,' Alex replied. 'Afraid not.'

The thickset, balding man shook his head in disbelief, and continued. He passed a shelf of walking-sticks and crutches, and turned left by the pushchairs. Alex thought that it must be harder to lose a pushchair.

One black vinyl computer case looked much like any other. The bag that the man brought back to the counter now had a brown cardboard luggage tag tied on with string, with a date and a place; he dumped it on the counter with heavy hands. Alex winced slightly at the thud, imagined delicate electronics shifting out of place. He couldn't be sure until he opened it, but the very anonymity of the bag was promising. He unzipped the case and lifted the cover. There was no name inside, no manuals or pieces of paper shoved into the pockets. That was also good.

Alex switched it on, and the computer whirred very slowly into life. The screen didn't give anything away at first, but soon the familiar page of warnings appeared, full of baleful threats about inappropriate access. That was what he wanted to see. He reached into his trouser pocket for a small grey plastic fob. Holding it sheltered in one hand, he waited for the string of numbers on the fob's tiny screen to change. They had never taken so long before. He tapped in the new series of numbers. The screen lit up, and Alex's face in the reflected blue glow shone with a certain relief.

'It's yours then, mate?' the man said.

Alex nodded. 'I need to check something else though.'

He reached to the side of the laptop and clicked open the disk drive. The tray slid out slowly. It was empty.

'There was a disk inside,' he whispered. 'An important one.'

The lost property man looked sympathetic, but said they didn't check things like that when they got something handed in.

There were forms to fill in, and details to give, far more details than Alex was comfortable with. He had broken the most basic of rules, the rules they taught you in the first week. He'd never broken the rules before, neither these nor any others. So maybe if you only did it once, maybe since he'd got the laptop back, the worst wouldn't happen; but he couldn't be sure of anything any more.

Alex said goodbye to the man behind the counter, and left him to his sports pages. He went out of the building and crossed the road. He kept walking, heading back in what he hoped was the direction of the office. He managed to get around the corner and onto Pentonville Road before he was sick in the gutter.

# 2

THERE WAS A stern notice at the top of the steps leading down into Durbar Court: no red wine was to be taken onto the marble courtyard. The waiter and the waitress who flanked the broad white steps balanced silver trays, the glasses on them filled in a palette of yellow tones: pale champagne, white wine, orange juice. The champagne glasses were being clutched from the trays most quickly. Other waiters hovered in the courtyard, refilling the glasses. The hum of conversation rose from the sunken floor, floated over the balustrades surrounding it, and up to the galleries around with their polished red-granite columns.

Ian Phillips had chosen this party over the others he could have attended. This was the season of receptions and he had a poker hand of invitations to pick from. It wasn't just the Foreign Office canapés or the surroundings; there were bound to be people here with something worth knowing, something he could use.

He looked around the courtyard for someone worth speaking to. Scanning the horizon, he was alert to the ebb and flow of the room around him. His height allowed him to spot his prey while others, shorter and less fortunate, were confronted with only shoulders and elbows. He edged towards a woman near him who was intercepting a young waiter as he walked past with a tray of bacon-wrapped sausages.

'It's too soon,' Hester Bradbury began, holding the cocktail stick like a weapon.

'Too soon for what?' Ian Phillips wondered whether she meant too soon to be having Christmas drinks; decided instead that she meant too soon after the funeral.

'The funeral was last week,' he prompted, as Hester chewed the sausage and twisted the empty, pointed stick between her fingers.

Hester shook her head. 'I don't mean that.'

She wouldn't be hurried. Hester had been in and around Parliament long enough to know what Ian was after. She would get there in the end, she would say just enough and no more, and it would be in her own time. As she chewed, Ian called to mind the adjectives that were customarily attached to Hester's name: the redoubtable, strident, feisty senior MP Hester Bradbury. They were adjectives that went with women, as a rule. Men were heavyweights, big beasts. The words would have fitted her just as well, he reflected, but call Hester either of those, in print or to her face, and you'd get a punch to the jaw. She insisted that she was a chairman of her committee. 'I am not a piece of furniture,' she had once intoned to Ian when his newspaper's new style guide had specified that she was a chair. Hester shifted her weight from one foot to the other and adjusted the shoulders of her orange jacket.

Ian knew that this was the game. He took another sip of his champagne. In his mind, he had a pencil hovering over a notebook. He slowed down.

'Terrible news about Colin, of course. Such a shock.'

'Terrible,' Hester agreed. Ian wasn't as shocked as he made out. Nor was she. Colin Randall had drunk too much, and everyone had known it. Still, no one ever expected a friend to be gone so suddenly. If it could happen to Colin, it could happen to many of the people now happily accepting refills to their glasses in the echoing courtyard. Colin wouldn't have held with the champagne at the party; he would have asked loudly why there wasn't any beer, before draining the white wine.

Hester Bradbury had given the eulogy at the cold grey stone

church that looked out over the edge of the moors. Ian had sat a few rows back, listening to her resonant voice that carried easily to the last pew. She had recalled how delighted and proud Colin Randall had been to become a government minister at last, having spent decades as a mulish backbencher, and how well he often hid the pride and delight. She reminded the congregation of his stubbornness, his half-mocking complaints about the ornate buildings where he was obliged to work. Colin had enjoyed being prickly. There had been gentle acknowledging laughter from the dignitaries in the front pews; they hadn't stayed long afterwards. The large black cars waiting outside the church had swept them back down the motorway. This was to be expected, as were the subdued discussions that had already started as to who would succeed Colin Randall in his enviably secure seat. Some of the mourners had been noticed wandering around the town later, taking a circuitous route back to the station and looking in the estate agents' windows.

'How's Jill bearing up? And the children?'

'Remarkably well, from what I've heard. A lot of people are rallying round. The freezer's overflowing with shepherd's pies.'

Ian nodded again, encouraging her on.

'I meant it's too soon for Lucas. He isn't ready for it. He hardly knows his way around.'

Ian Phillips was inclined to agree. He found it disconcerting to have become a veteran journalist so soon, and to find himself now surrounded by Members of Parliament who were scarcely older than his own children. His hair had gone grey early: at first he had welcomed the gravitas; now, with that and the glasses, he just felt old. He only knew Mark Lucas slightly, knew that he wasn't quite one of the youngsters. At least Lucas had actually had a job that wasn't just working for another politician, unlike half of them. He'd made documentaries, some of them really not bad, pretty cutting stuff. Then become one of those go-to people for a quote on modernising government, the kind of person who signed worthy letters to newspapers. But Ian still doubted whether it was wise to make someone a minister when their main qualifications seemed to be a plausible manner and the ability to greet people in a variety of foreign languages. Wasn't that what the Foreign Office had expensively trained diplomats for?

He shrugged. 'But that's the way it's going, isn't it? What can we oldies do?'

'Speak for yourself, Ian.' Hester bristled, but then laughed. 'He should have paid a few more dues, they all should. This place will eat you up if you don't really know how it works. They think it looks easy, but they don't realise anything worth having takes a lot more work.' She paused for another sip of wine. 'He'll come a cropper.'

Ian lodged her words in his mental notebook, and prepared to make his excuses, so that he could scrawl the comments in shorthand into the real notebook he kept in his inside breast pocket. This was not anything yet, not in itself, but he never knew when it might be.

'You couldn't fault Colin for that,' Hester added as a final thought. 'He'd worked for this all his life. He drank after a hard day, sure, but they found him dead at his desk, collapsed over his red boxes.'

Ian made his excuses and started to move on, looking around for a waitress to top up his glass. He detected a shift in the pitch of the chatter, as though everyone at the party had changed the subject of their conversations at once. Ian saw that others were looking towards the entrance steps, and followed their gazes.

The perception of power caused a shift in the room; people swirled like iron filings on a sheet of paper over a magnet. The Foreign Secretary was descending the steps, smiling and shaking hands. Advisers fanned out around him, guiding him towards the people they thought he ought to speak to. Mark Lucas followed a few steps behind. He paused to accept a glass of champagne, then stood for a moment, looking around at the atrium, and down to the people below. He drew his shoulders back, breathed deeply, and took a careful sip from the glass before he stepped forward into the crowd, his hand and his face open in one greeting after another.

Ian Phillips held back slightly. He didn't feel the need to rush forward and be one of the first to greet the new minister. In fact, it would be better if he wasn't too keen. Ian would wait to be approached. For a while, he watched, seeing how newly acquired power had burnished Mark Lucas. Lucas seemed taller and more confident already; he held himself straighter now. His smile was broad, but in his eyes there was a faint and endearing look of disbelief, as though he too was surprised that he was here. He looked as if he, and not just his better-cut suit, had been recently dry-cleaned and was fresh from the plastic wrapper. The guests hovered in his orbit, waiting to catch his eye. As Mark met each one, he shook hands intently, and his hazel eyes held their gaze just long enough. He exchanged a few words with each and, for those few seconds, they had his full attention and left with the conviction that they mattered. Between greetings, Mark pushed back the thick lock of brown hair that flopped forward over his brow; it added to his eager, boyish look. Good-looking, without, so far as anyone knew just yet, being sleazy. That, at least, was the view of the younger women Ian had asked about him; he noticed they smiled slightly when he put the question.

Lucas caught sight of Ian on the edge of the circle that had formed around him. He broke off gently from a chat about the Christmas holidays, and held out a hand. A gap formed in the circle, and Ian stepped forward. Lucas's handshake had a warm, dry grip. It was a good handshake, Phillips thought. Up there with the best ones.

'Ian. Lovely to see you. I enjoyed your last column. Not sure you're right about where our policy is going, though. But you do have a great turn of phrase.'

*Lovely to see you*, Ian noted. Gliding over the fact they had scarcely met beyond a brief chat in a corridor, talking as though they knew each other well. Ian was reluctantly flattered, and drawn in. The conversation turned from foreign policy to football, and Lucas moved on, with a vague promise of lunch when the diary allowed.

As he watched the back of Lucas's navy jacket move away through the room, Ian felt the thump of a heavy hand on his shoulder. There weren't many people the same height as him, and even fewer who greeted him like this.

'Theo. What are you up to?' Ian stepped back slightly, retrieving the portion of his personal space that Theo Sadler had appropriated.

'He's good, isn't he?' Theo always seemed as though he was sharing a confidence, even if he was just telling you the time.

'Is he? Hard to tell, at this stage.'

'Yes. Good talker, very presentable. We like him. He'll go far.'

'We' meant Downing Street. Theo always seemed to be excited by the novelty of speaking on behalf of the whole institution. In particular, he left his words open to the interpretation that they stood for the innermost thoughts of the prime minister, bestowing favour way beyond his pay grade.

'Some people think it's come a bit quickly for him,' Ian observed.

'No, no. We need to bring on good people as soon as we can. There's a lot of, well, dead wood's not the phrase.'

'It certainly isn't.' Ian grimaced, remembering Colin Randall.

'I didn't mean that. But Mark knows his stuff. And the stuff he doesn't know yet, he'll pick up.'

Then Theo too started to pick holes in Ian's latest column. He was clumsy where Mark had been gracious; he recited lists of statistics that this was not the time or the place for, berating Ian for not having checked his facts. Ian tuned out; he started to wonder instead whether there was time for one last drink, and whether he should get the Tube home or claim for a taxi.

The Rover pulled up outside the narrow terraced house and Mark Lucas got out of the rear door. He was still getting used to this; he couldn't quite hide his excitement at having a car and a driver to take him home. The wooden shutters in the front window were closed, but a warm reassuring light shone through the gap above them. The driver handed him two red leather ministerial boxes. They were heavy and still hardly scuffed.

As Mark opened the door, he could hear the fractious sounds that indicated Emily still hadn't managed to get Jack to sleep. He dropped the boxes in the hallway, took off his shoes and raincoat, and went upstairs. Emily was trying to detach Jack's pudgy, clinging fingers from her neck and hair and to put him down in his cot. His feet, encased in their blue Babygro, braced themselves against the bars.

'No,' Jack protested with the fierceness of having just discovered the word and its power. 'No bed.'

Mark reached into the cot and held out a limp stuffed pig of greying pink with a damp, chewed ear.

'Bedtime, Jack. Here's Piggly. Piggly needs a cuddle.'

'No Piggly. No, Daddy.'

He looked across to Emily to see what more he could do.

'Why don't you read to Bella?' she said.

Bella had left her room to see what was going on. Mark bent down to scoop his daughter up in his arms and return her to bed.

'You're not still awake too?' he said gently.

'Jack was being noisy,' Bella replied.

'What story would you like, Bella? How about *Bear Hunt*?'

'*Bear Hunt* is for babies. I am nearly five.'

'Well, which story should Daddy read you, then?'

'I don't want stinky Daddy to read me a story, I want Mummy.'

'Mummy is putting Jack to bed, and he's being a bit silly. Which story shall we read?'

This was a situation where the powers of persuasion and diplomacy that he could usually muster didn't work. Bella was her mother's daughter; she could summon an imperious manner and a look of injured pride in the same way. Mark stroked her blonde hair where it curled in to her neck, and tried to soothe her. In the next room, Jack was howling loudly against Emily's song. Emily finished another repetition of the lullaby and her footsteps moved towards the landing. Jack screamed again.

'Mummy!' Bella had heard her too. 'I want Mummy to read me a story!'

'Daddy's reading the story tonight.' Mark rummaged through the pile of books near Bella's bed. The stuffed toys were lined up in serried ranks on the shelf. Eventually, Bella conceded that Daddy would be allowed to read one of her books, as though she were granting him the greatest of favours, far greater than that of the Queen making him a Minister of the Crown. Bella, too, could withdraw her favour just as quickly.

Goldilocks fled from the house, and the three bears contemplated their broken furniture and their cold porridge. Mark closed the book, and tucked Bella under the duvet. She allowed herself to be kissed, and curled up. Jack was screeching intermittently now. Mark wanted to open the door and see his son, but he knew it would only make matters worse. In any case, he would probably wake again in the night, and Emily would be more than happy for him to go up and try to settle the boy again.

He crept down the stairs to his and Emily's bedroom, took off his tie and hung his suit jacket in the wardrobe. He swapped his navy trousers for the old pair of jeans that lay on the chair. The buzz of the champagne and the accolades had worn off. Earlier in the evening it had all felt effortless. Now he ached with tiredness from the work that it really required, like the legs of a swan after a day of appearing to glide on the surface of a river.

Mark was turning to leave the room when he remembered to unclip his pager from the belt of his suit trousers, to take it downstairs. A couple of days ago there had been an unfortunate moment when he'd heard a buzzing, late at night, from under a pile of laundry and wondered blearily what it was. It hadn't been anything important, that time. The little dark-grey plastic case was a reminder for him as much as anything that he was needed, and he cradled it in his palm.

Emily stood in the basement kitchen, reheating pasta sauce. The sleeves of her old sweatshirt were pushed up to her elbows, and she stretched a pale arm out as she stirred with a wooden spoon. The street lamp outside cast its light through the railings above and towards the dining table. She turned towards Mark.

'Are they asleep?'

'Nearly. Bella will be. Jack's still complaining, a bit. But he'll go off.'

'Wine?'

'No, thanks. I've got to work.'

Water came to the boil on the hob and Emily rattled pasta into the saucepan.

'How was your day?'

'It was pretty good. The party was good. The rest of it was fine.' Mark paused for a moment, remembering that this was home, and this was private. 'It was terrifying. Still terrifying.'

'Why?' Emily's response was usually to find out the facts first, and empathise later. It was partly her professional training, but it was a training that fitted the way she looked at the world. Mark hadn't had a chance yet to stop and work out why it felt so overwhelming. He was less than a week into the job and still wondering if it had been someone's mistake. He occasionally thought he might get a phone call, a polite word from an official saying they were terribly sorry, but there was another MP called Lucas and the call had been meant for him; that Downing Street's switchboard was usually very reliable but regrettably, in this instance, a dreadful error had been made.

There wasn't another MP called Lucas. He had even checked the internal directory, just to be sure.

'It's the place itself. I still turn the wrong corners and end up in some department to do with an obscure bit of the Middle

East, and they look at me strangely and say "Can I help you, Minister?" I have to stop myself looking around to see who they're talking to. Then I remember it's me. It's the pillars and the staircases and the sheer weight of all the history. I think I'd be fine if I was in some sixties block with grey walls and cubicles and I could just feel it was an ordinary job.'

'If it's just about the architecture, you'll learn that. Even the prime minister probably had to ask someone where the Downing Street loos were on the first day. You won't even notice it after a while. You've just got to keep playing the part: you'll convince them.'

Emily extracted a tube of pasta from the salty water and bit into it, to test whether it was ready. She pushed a wavy strand of blonde hair away from her face, and efficiently lifted the saucepan towards the sink to drain it. Mark envied her equanimity, the way she was always so grounded. He watched from his chair as she moved athletically across the room; her frame was as taut and wiry as it had ever been. She ran: she said it cleared her head of the huge binders full of intellectual property contracts to be negotiated and the minutiae of the lives of small children. Long muscles showed on her arms as she poured the cloudy water away. She tasted the sauce one last time, and mixed it with the pasta.

'Do you think I can do it?' he asked, wanting to be reassured.

'Of course you can. It's not a question of not understanding it, or not being up to the job. They couldn't have picked a better person for it than you. And my day was fine, thank you,' she observed with an eyebrow raised as she brought the bowls to the table.

After supper, Mark took the boxes laden with documents up to the small room at the back of the house that they had made into a study. There were Emily's law tomes on one side of the shelving; his eclectic collection of history, politics and French novels on the other. On the windowsill, behind the computer monitor, a cube of perspex with a metal shape inside reminded him that he had once won an award for a documentary he'd made. He told himself that this was why he was putting himself through it all: it was fine to make searing pieces of television that would make people sob for a few minutes and then change the channel, even if the work did get a few headlines and a prize awarded at a smart dinner, but that was just observing. Now he could make decisions, now he could change things. A few initials and comments on the papers inside the box and something would happen.

He thought of his father's first response when he'd phoned him last week to tell him that he'd been promoted: 'Heaven help us.' Mark had to remind himself that the brusqueness was only the top layer, a conditioned reflex. It would have been his mother who would have told him at once how proud she was. For all his mother's Englishness, her reverence for manners and correctness, she had usually been the one to express her emotions. His father sometimes had to be reminded to say the right thing and now there was no one to remind him. He lived quietly with his books and his routine at the college, disappearing so far from the modern world that he was startled when the phone rang at home. He could go for days without talking to anyone if he didn't feel like taking dinner in hall: that feeling occurred often, when the weight of small talk seemed oppressive. His pride in his son ran deep but had to be dowsed for, like an underground stream. Only once had Mark seen it break the surface dramatically and in public: when Mark had sworn his affirmation as a Member of Parliament, Anthony Lucas had stood in Central Lobby and sobbed huge tears into a red spotted handkerchief.

Mark heaved the first lead-lined box onto the desk, took a deep breath as he saw again the gold lettering that read 'Minister of State, Foreign and Commonwealth Office' above the keyhole, and unlocked it.

# 3

THEY WERE SUPPOSED to be meeting her at the station. Anna looked up at the clock on the platform whose bright yellow numerals flipped over, showing her that the train had arrived on time. It had been two hours since it had left the grimy arches of St Pancras, two hours she should have spent on research, on thinking about the questions she needed to ask, but she had instead divided her time between reading the less serious stories in the papers, attempting the crossword and staring out of the window. Two hours in the wrong direction, away from everyone rushing towards London, accompanied only by a group of lawyers whose heavy cases of documents blocked the aisle, discussing with a worrying lack of discretion the case they were about to argue in court. The station was a low, modern building that felt as though it was away from the centre of town. A multi-storey car park stood opposite; warehouses near it were being hollowed out for redevelopment. New places never revealed themselves at their best from the railway station. It was always the back end of town, the tradesman's entrance. Anna was looking at the map on the outside wall of the station building, trying to get her bearings, when she heard the car horn behind her.

A young man unfolded himself from a small red car that had just pulled up. She recognised him from the newspaper cuttings: he was the candidate. They'd asked her who they should be looking out for. Look for a woman with shoulder-length brown hair, medium height, about five foot six, wearing a dark-red coat, she'd told them. She hadn't said to look for the scruffy woman, the one with newsprint and the ink from a leaky biro on her fingers, the one with a stain on her coat where her coffee had spilled as she rushed to catch the train. All of that would have been more accurate, though less concise.

'You must be Anna Travers.' The candidate bounded over to her with a loping step. Anna realised that a description had hardly been necessary: she was the only woman standing outside the station looking as though she wasn't quite sure where she was, certainly the only one carrying an overstuffed bag with newspapers and photocopied cuttings protruding from it. 'John Lander. Good to meet you.'

He had a bony handshake and a slightly forced grin. John Lander was the ideal candidate for the seat, the one who would make everyone happy as long as he didn't screw up in some unforeseeable way. He was someone who had only just slipped through the net at the last election, missing his chance out of modesty and the feeling that he wasn't ready for it. Later, as people had taken their seats in Westminster, who had surprised even their own parents, let alone their agents and their future whips, by being elected, others had determined that he shouldn't miss that chance again. He had the perfect Westminster credentials: a job in a think tank and good connections, combined with a legitimate claim to come from the constituency he wanted to represent.

Anna had seen the reports in the local paper about his selection; she knew that the first stop for all visiting journalists was likely to be the butcher's shop that had been founded by John's grandfather, with 'Lander and Sons, Family Butcher' above the door. Bad puns that she knew the subeditors would take out were already running through her mind. Local boy makes mincemeat of the opposition . . . no, stop it. It may have been a colour piece, but she wasn't a sketch writer. This wasn't one of those stories that was going to make a big splash: John Lander would have to have fathered and abandoned illegitimate triplets with the woman who ran the sweetshop next door to the butcher's to lose the seat. Colin Randall had bequeathed him a healthy majority, and his campaign's only worry seemed to be the low turnout that a frosty February by-election would bring. Her editor had said that this was about taking the political temperature – how was the government doing? Had the novelty worn off? When she wrinkled her nose in response, he reminded her forcefully that this was how democracy worked, and that if you didn't care about the small stories in the small places, there was barely any point in covering politics at all.

John Lander held the rear door of the car open for her.

'Sorry about all the mess. Just move the leaflets onto the floor.' The hatchback was easily ten years old; there were huge red posters in the boot with 'Lander' on them in large yellow letters. Some were on boards attached to long wooden stakes. There were *Vote Lander* stickers in the rear window and the side windows. Bundles of leaflets lay on the rear seat: hundreds of John Landers smiled out from them, each with the same eager grimace; John with his wife and baby; John in front of the butcher's shop, pointing up at the sign; John visiting a local school. In the car's footwells there were discarded crisp packets and empty chocolate wrappers. By-elections ran on junk food and nervous energy.

Anna heaped the leaflets on top of some clipboards and moved them to the side, easing herself into the back seat. As Lander climbed back into the driver's seat and pulled the car's tinny door shut, Anna noticed the other passenger in front. She leant one elbow on the back of the passenger seat and stuck her arm through the gap between the seats to introduce herself and shake hands. As she did so, Mark Lucas turned around to look at her and their heads clashed. They both sat back again with awkward laughter.

'Oh, hello. Sorry,' Anna began. 'I'm Anna Travers.'

'Mark Lucas. Are you just up from London for the day?'

Anna mumbled something apologetically about how she didn't have long, that she had to see as much as she could in a short time.

'That's fine. We'll show you around. It's all going very well.'

'I'm doing sort of the view from the ground, you know.'

'Ah yes. In the best traditions, of course.' Mark looked towards her again as Lander made a second attempt to start the car. The ageing engine wasn't dealing very well with the cold and the ignition sputtered. 'But we might have a bit more for you than that, if you don't get too early a train back.'

He now had Anna's full interest. For her, meeting one rising star was already a bonus for the day. As it did too often, her imagination began to dance away with her. Mark Lucas would be her best source, she would be his confidante. He was going places, and with him as her best contact, she would follow in his wake. And he would now introduce her . . . to whom? He could only mean that someone important was coming up for a visit. By the time the car pulled up outside the butcher's shop, Anna had promoted herself by several job titles and was writing imaginary exclusive splashes, all based on her acquaintance of only seconds. She was easily charmed.

She was jolted back from her reverie by the phone buzzing in her pocket. She still wasn't quite used to having a mobile phone and often missed calls. It was Andy, the photographer, who was driving up and already complaining about the town's bloody useless and incomprehensible one-way system. She passed him over to John Lander, who gave him directions towards the butcher's. So he really was a local boy.

In the meantime, before the glory, she would have to do her real job. She dutifully went into the shop. It was pristine, with rosy pink chops lined up precisely on display in the window. Generous, glistening strings of sausages, flecked with green herbs, were coiled around each other. The walls still had the same white tiles they would have had in John's grandfather's day. There were obliging, grandmotherly customers who were happy to chat to Anna about how they remembered John as a boy, coming in on a Saturday morning to help in the shop. They were less forthcoming about his politics, though. She struggled to get them to talk about the government; they would vote how they had always voted, which was great if you were John, less great if you were trying to find a pithy insight into grass-roots democracy.

Anna looked up from her shorthand notes about the cost of bacon and the disappearance of beef on the bone to find that Mark Lucas was having to mediate in a burgeoning dispute between Andy the snapper and Edward, the master butcher. Edward was the epitome of a traditional butcher. He was solid, dressed in his white overalls and a blue apron, and his hands were enormous and as fleshy as the meat he hacked into with his cleaver. Andy had become marginally less grumpy when he arrived at the butcher's and saw that there were some shots that might work. He'd stepped behind the counter with his camera and started shooting over Edward's shoulder, the motor-drive whirring. Andy directed the candidate to lean over and talk to the butcher. John adjusted his rosette, leant in, and turned to look down the barrel of the camera, smiling the nervous smile.

'Not like that,' Andy snapped. 'This isn't the local paper now. Look at him. Talk to him. Ask about a good roast for Sunday.' Edward had taken this in good part, pointing towards a large leg of lamb, but he'd drawn the line at Andy resting his lens on the display counter and trying to shoot arty views through the curved glass vitrine.

'Get that camera off my meat!' he boomed. 'I don't know where it's been. And you're bothering my customers.' There was only one customer left in the shop, as Andy was just pointing out when Mark stepped in.

'Maybe if you didn't put the lens on the counter? I'm sure you won't get camera shake. And best not to argue with the man with the meat cleaver.' Andy pulled his camera in protectively towards his chest. Mark turned to the butcher. 'He'll only be a couple of minutes. I think we've nearly got everything we need. I might be back later for some of that lamb. It looks wonderful.'

Anna wasn't certain whether this was the former television producer in him speaking or the current diplomat, but either way it seemed to work. Professional honours were satisfied. They went back to the car.

Their next stop was a windswept housing estate on the outskirts of the town. The sun still hung low over the horizon. A couple of local volunteers met them at the entrance to a cul-de-sac. They'd been waiting for a while and were starting to shiver. The clipboards and the leaflets were retrieved from the back of the car, and the volunteers were pointed in the direction of the right doors to knock on. John and Mark conferred with them in low voices over the clipboards. Anna was sure they were explaining who she was, and pointing out a few door numbers to avoid so that she didn't overhear aggrieved and unhelpful rants about local politics and the state of the potholes.

As they set off past low walls and up front garden paths, Anna trotted to keep up with Mark. Her hands were cold, and as she delved into her bag she realised that she'd lost her gloves somewhere on the way. Still, you couldn't write with gloves on. They reached the doorstep of a house where the doorbell played a long tune and where a large dog barked far inside, but there was nobody home. Mark pushed a leaflet through the letterbox and they heard the rumble of heavy paws down the hallway, followed by a ripping and a chewing.

'They're not one of ours, anyway,' Mark shrugged. 'If the dog hadn't ripped it up, the owner would have.' It was the first time he'd said anything that wasn't entirely predictable since Anna had got off the train.

'How's it really going?' Anna asked, sensing a chance to find out a bit more that wasn't in the script. Although she was new to this kind of story, she already had a weary sense of having heard it all before: that all was to play for, that we can't take anything for granted, that every vote counts and nothing's decided until polling day. John Lander had been pleasant enough, when she interviewed him outside the butcher's, but she didn't get anything from him except how proud he was of his hometown and the usual platitudes about local schools and hospitals.

'Well, we can't take anything for granted.' Mark must have seen her roll her eyes and he laughed graciously. 'Are we off the record?'

'If you like.'

'We can't take anything for granted, but we sometimes do. We were taking this place a bit for granted, because Colin was so well loved. They didn't have to do anything here. There were no up-to-date canvass lists or anything until a couple of weeks ago. John's good, of course, he'll make a great, hard-working MP, but he needs to plug away at it.' They moved on to the next house, where an elderly lady shuffled slowly to the door away from her television. She was hard of hearing, as they could tell from the way the volume blasted out of the front room. She was not pleased to have her favourite quiz show interrupted, but she said John Lander could count on her vote. She took a leaflet and went back to the TV.

'The others have moved in over the last couple of weeks. You hardly saw them at all, at first, but the last few days they've sent more people up. They had a minibus-load of MPs here on Tuesday. In fact, I think they can fit all their MPs in a minibus these days.'

Anna laughed, and scribbled the line down. 'Go on, you can have that last bit,' said Mark, amused at his own joke. 'From me.'

Mark continued, 'Which is why we've got the boss coming up later. It's supposed to be local media only, so John can get a handshake and a picture or ten with the big man. But I'm sure they won't mind if you drop by. Give me your number and I'll call you when I know exactly where.'

This made the prospect of spending the rest of the afternoon with the candidates who had little chance of winning more palatable for Anna. She even had to go round to meet the man who was standing to save the local open-air swimming pool. Percy Gainsborough was a local character, who swam in the pool every day that it was open, from March to October, and she'd had to make many phone calls to arrange to meet him outside the pool, even though it was closed for the winter. She only hoped he wouldn't arrive in his trunks and swimming hat.

Mark rejoined the canvassers, and Anna went over to talk to Andy, who was leaning against the bonnet of his car, bored now of taking pictures of activists silhouetted against the low sun, and looking like he wanted nothing more than a cup of tea and a bacon sandwich.

'Can you stay? There's a big visit. The prime minister. I'm not really supposed to know about it.'

'I know about it. I'm already doing it.'

'What do you mean?' Anna was instantly deflated.

'Ian Phillips is on his way up. He's got a big sit-down interview with the PM and I'm shooting it. Moody portraits of the PM, Phillips looking even more pompous and self-important than usual. Moving the furniture and the plastic flowers round in the banqueting suite of the hotel. You know the sort of thing.'

The light was already fading when Anna said goodbye to Percy Gainsborough outside the shuttered swimming pool and started to walk back towards the town square. Despite her misgivings, she had found him quite an endearing man, someone with a genuine belief who was fighting something everyone else knew was inevitable. Under the light from a shop window, she took her phone from her pocket with numb fingers. There was a missed call, from the number she'd saved as 'Mark L mob'. When Anna rang him back, she could barely hear his voice. He was whispering in a crowded room.

'Can't talk. He's just arrived. The Crown Hotel. It'll be easy to find us.'

'I don't think I'm supposed to be there. One of my colleagues has come and he's invited, not me.'

'I'm sure no one will mind. Got to go.'

Two police motorbikes had pulled up, one on either side of the Georgian portico of the Crown. The police officers stamped their heavy black motorcycle boots to avoid losing the feeling in their toes. Anna pulled her shoulders back and marched through the front door, knowing that the more you looked like you were supposed to be somewhere, the less likely anyone was to stop you. Hotel staff hovered in the lobby, looking nervous.

'Are you for the function room?' a manager asked helpfully. 'Just that way. Most of them are already there.' Anna nodded and hurried along the corridor.

John Lander's name was pegged out in white plastic letters on a red velvet board at the door of the suite. Anna made to walk into the room, but her way was blocked by a blonde woman in a black suit and a blue shirt, carrying a clipboard. Behind her, Anna could see local dignitaries milling about between gilt-framed chairs.

'Are you accredited?' the clipboard woman snarled. Anna announced the name of her paper, expecting it to be an automatic entry ticket.

'No.' She was implacable. 'This is local press only. It's not for you.'

'But I was talking to Mark Lucas earlier, and he said I should come.' The name-dropping didn't work either. Anna looked into the room, to see if she could catch Mark's eye, but his attention was focused entirely on the prime minister, who was posing for smiles and handshakes with John Lander for the local photographers.

The woman glowered even more fiercely.

'And surely your editor should have told you that one of your far more senior colleagues is covering this. It's his story.'

'Yes, of course I know that. I'm doing a feature. We're working together,' Anna bluffed. She caught sight of Ian Phillips, deep in conversation with another equally tall, dark-haired man. They were laughing conspiratorially. The other man looked across to the doorway, as though he had sensed the presence of someone unwanted. The blonde woman looked back at him for help and he wandered over. She turned her back on Anna and stretched up on her high black shoes to whisper to him.

The man looked Anna up and down. She thought she recognised him, but he made no show of recognition in return. Clipboard girl, who was even younger than Anna, turned back.

'Definitely no. Sorry.' She wasn't in the slightest bit sorry. She was enjoying wielding the power of excluding people.

Anna wasn't going to fight her way in. She tried not to show the humiliation she felt as she walked back along the hotel's patterned carpets, and held her phone to her ear with a concerned expression as though she'd been summoned away urgently. As she wandered around the square, looking for somewhere to eat, she consoled herself that she wouldn't have got much, that the most she could have hoped for was another formulaic line about what a great MP John Lander would be, which Ian Phillips would get anyway. But there was no denying that staying in the room and getting the quote would have been better than eating greasy chips in a dingy cafe, and coming home without it.

# 4

A LEX HAD BEEN invited to attend the meeting, at an address he didn't recognise near Whitehall. That it was an invitation was a polite euphemism: there was no option to decline it. He walked there, on a blustery December day, the plane trees along Millbank shedding the last of their leaves. The low sunlight caught the Houses of Parliament, and he noticed how the clean sandy stone made it brighter now than when he'd passed the sooty buildings as a child.

He took the back route, away from Parliament Square, that led him through a stone archway into the precincts of Westminster Abbey. He wanted to hold on to any moment of tranquillity he could grasp before what was coming next. In the quiet offices, the church buildings, the classrooms he passed, the morning routine went on as usual. It was too early, and the wrong time of year, for the tourists. Alex did not have time to stop and take it in; soon the clock chimes made him realise he had to hurry, and the rush of traffic as he emerged onto Victoria Street startled him.

The building was one of those you hardly noticed. It backed onto the park, and passers-by naturally looked instead towards the cultivated view: at the neatly tended flowerbeds; at the pelicans and the geese on the lake, and behind them the fountain, and Buckingham Palace. Normally, Alex would have been fascinated to discover another of the buildings that belonged to the days when his world was really secret, but this was not the moment for historical curiosity either.

They were expecting him. Graham sat in a windowless room below ground level, behind a desk that looked as though it had been retrieved from storage; it was old and wooden with a green leather blotter, edged in gilt patterns, sunk into the top. There was no computer, no phone. In the corner, an electric heater blew out intermittent gusts of dusty air. On the wall was an insipid watercolour of a rural landscape. Next to Graham sat a grey-haired woman who Alex thought he recognised, but couldn't quite place.

This was Graham as Alex had never seen him before. He was no longer genial and languorous but terse and impassive. Graham gestured to Alex to sit. Alex hung his coat on the back of the chair and complied. Graham shook his head slightly, as if to say he was disappointed in him. He looked down at the buff cardboard folder that lay open on the desk, then slowly poured himself a glass of water from the jug on the desk. There were only two glasses. Neither was intended for Alex. He'd heard of 'meetings without coffee' – a phrase people at work knew denoted a bollocking. This was a meeting without even water.

They began with the moment that he'd left the office on that Wednesday evening. He did know, didn't he, that it was a breach of the conditions of his employment to remove material from the office without authorisation? Alex nodded. He was prepared to concede that without argument. And had he sought any prior authorisation from his line managers? No. Were there any extenuating circumstances that meant he felt his actions could have been justified? Alex said something that didn't come out very clearly about wanting to do some extra work, put in some extra hours on the research he needed to finish, a problem that was troubling him.

Graham raised one eyebrow. For a moment Alex could see again the charm of the man he dealt with every day, and felt briefly hopeful.

'Under other circumstances, Mr Rutherford, your diligence might be laudable.' Graham wrote a note in the file with his fountain pen; but then the dark look returned. Alex had another insight into the old world that he could have done without. This is what Graham must have been like when things were really serious; this was how he'd been in the Cold War, when there was a clear enemy. This was why he'd been so good at his job, and why people talked in the canteen in lowered voices about Graham Fletcher's reputation.

'I feel obliged to warn you, though I am sure you are already aware of this, that you are potentially in breach of the Official Secrets Act, which you of course signed as a condition of your employment. We obviously take any such breach with the utmost seriousness, and there is of course the possibility of bringing a prosecution under the Act.'

Alex shuddered. He had run through many of the possibilities in his mind: losing his job was the most obvious one, but there was also the chance of a trial, of prison. He hoped it wouldn't come to that, but he needed to prepare himself. Graham's careful, legal language reminded him of what he might face. He was still horrified by the prospect of being made public, a furtive, blurry picture on the front of the newspaper, the shot snatched as he arrived at court and tried to hide his face in his raincoat collar.

Graham moved on to what had happened on the Wednesday evening. He made Alex retrace his steps precisely from the moment he left the office. How had he got from Vauxhall to Liverpool Street? Where was the first pub? The bar? Who had he been with? As Alex answered as best he could, Graham drew a series of cubes in blue-black ink on the sheet of paper in the file in front of him. In each cube he drew a word in capital letters. Alex strained to see what they said, but couldn't quite make them out. He saw Graham link the cubes with arrows, some with question marks over them. Alex had rehearsed his story many times by now, each time with more details of the evening in place. Graham picked those memories apart again, finding holes where Alex had woven things together, making him unsure.

Then it was the woman's turn. She had a soft voice but her questions were, for Alex, even harder. She wanted to know about him and his feelings, him and his friends. Graham had started pulling at the threads of his story to unravel them; she seemed to want to unravel the threads of his own identity. She latched on to one small observation that Alex had made; that the bar was expensive, that the others were drinking champagne and offered to pay. How did he feel about that, she wanted to know?

'I felt a bit small,' Alex admitted. 'As if they were worth more than me, because they earned more than me.' She nodded, and wrote something down.

'And did you think they were?'

'No. I am – I was – proud of my job.'

Graham flicked his head up slightly at this. Though he'd given a good impression of being slightly elsewhere, buried in his documents, he wasn't letting any word escape him.

'So proud that you told them what you do – what you did?' Alex felt Graham's echo of his own shift to the past tense was ominous.

'No. I told them I was a civil servant, a junior civil servant. They really weren't interested at all. Didn't even ask which department. If it wasn't a bank they didn't want to know.'

'Do you have any money problems at all?' The woman returned to her questions.

Alex thought about this: no, he was in many ways very lucky. His parents had inherited the flat in Pimlico two years earlier and kept it, as an investment. Although he'd offered to pay them rent, they refused to accept it. So, unlike many of his friends, he could live in the centre of London, almost free, and walk to work. It was a place that he took small pleasures in; it was the top half of a white stucco terrace, and once he was past the fraying carpets and the pizza delivery leaflets in the shared hallway, it was his sanctuary. It was small, calm and orderly. It was enough for him for now, and for as far ahead as he could see. In five minutes, if he needed some space, he could be at the Tate Gallery, looking at the Turners.

Eventually Alex remembered where he had seen her before: this was the woman who had interviewed him when he was vetted. He couldn't remember her name, but then even if she had given one, that was probably the idea. He remembered the uncomfortable way that a very bland question made him, almost against his will, bring up answers to which he had never given much conscious thought. When Alex had first seen her, it was after a day of interviews and exercises. He'd answered maths papers and reasoning tests. He'd ticked boxes answering questions about how he reacted in difficult situations. One for strongly agree, two for somewhat agree, three for neither agree nor disagree, and so on. Alex's answers were always somewhere in the middle. He didn't feel that strongly about very much. That time, too, she had drawn him out, probing him gently on his family, his friends, his sexuality, his relationships. She didn't look like someone you would naturally confide in: she had a square jaw and thin, disapproving lips; but her gentle voice asked just the right things in just the right way. She was not someone you could embarrass, even if Alex had had anything to say that could have been embarrassing.

She wanted to know more about James: how they knew each other; why they kept in touch; how often they met. Alex thought that she must have known about James already. James Rycroft had seemed the perfect person to give as a character reference when he joined the service. There was nothing about him that was unorthodox. Good school, good university, all-round good fellow, unquestioningly loyal and straightforward and honest. Somebody to be trusted.

Their friendship was one that went in and out of season with the sports they played; they were closer in summer, when weekends drifted by on cricket pitches the way they had at college. In winter, rugby season for James but a sport that Alex didn't care for, they saw each other less often.

When James left university he had joined the bank, as had been expected of him. His father's recommendation had still counted for something, but was not nearly enough any more. The bankers were more impressed by James's natural air of captaincy, his string of sporting achievements, and his dogged capacity for hard work. They were now exploiting that last quality at the expense of the first two. One of the reasons Alex hardly saw James these days was that he worked so hard. He would stay in the office, hunched over spreadsheets, until the early hours of the morning. Sometimes he'd sleep in his chair and change into a clean shirt as the vacuums of the office cleaners hummed around him before a new working day began. He had acquired thousands of air miles from business trips that he kept telling Alex he would one day use for a long beach holiday, with no shoes and no news, sailing little dinghies on turquoise seas, but he never did. James, who'd always been straight-backed and muscled, now had aching shoulders from sitting at a computer all day, and the beginnings of a paunch from late-night curries at his desk. When he went to watch rugby now, it was in a hospitality tent with visiting clients, and he told Alex he wished he could have been standing on a cold touchline somewhere in the countryside instead.

She wanted to know where James went on his trips: was it Russia? China? The former Soviet states? Which ones? Alex genuinely wasn't sure. James rarely talked about it with him, except to complain about the cold weather and the hotel food. Alex glazed over with talk of mineral deposits and discounted cash flows in the same way James's colleagues had when Alex mentioned the civil service. How could you suspect James of anything? Alex wanted to ask. He's someone who still believes in institutions, in duty, even though he's twenty-eight and we're a year away from the twenty-first century. But it wasn't his turn to ask questions.

Alex shifted in his seat and wondered what was going to come next. It was Anna. He knew he'd told them all about Anna before.

'When did you last see Anna Travers?'

It was three years earlier, in March. Alex even knew the date. Anna was in London again and had wanted to see him. She'd tracked him down and sent him a postcard. It was a deliberately corny image that she'd picked up from a souvenir shop: a London bus; a red phone box; the Changing of the Guard. 'Greetings from London' on the front in red, white and blue. It was the kind of joke Anna loved, and they'd used to share. They had always sent each other the worst, the tackiest postcards they could find. In her familiar handwriting on the back, a flippant message asked him to show her the sights. Although he knew very well that Anna resorted to archness when she was trying to hide her vulnerability, the idea that meeting him was something mildly amusing still hurt.

The evening hadn't gone well. Anna was full of her new job and its excitements. She talked, far too fast, about the people she'd met and the places she'd been. She drank red wine quickly, refilling her own glass before his. She was convinced that she was going to be a great success; after all, she was now a reporter on a national paper, in London, and this was what she'd always wanted to do.

For a reporter, however, she'd asked very few questions about him. They'd gone to a restaurant near her office where the food was piled in elaborate towers on square white plates. When the pudding arrived, Alex had felt brave enough to ask her why she'd got in touch again now. It had been four years since they'd last seen each other; though her postcards from far-flung places had been frequent in the first year, they had petered out soon after.

Anna had pulled a spun-sugar decoration from her tiramisu and licked the end of it. Then she stared at the strands of sugar, rather than him, as she spoke.

'I don't know,' she hesitated. 'I just wanted to see you. I wanted to see an old friend. I have plenty of new ones, of course, but I still like you.'

'How do you mean, like?' Alex asked cautiously. He didn't enjoy, at all, the reference to all her new friends and the obvious implication they were somehow better, and more exciting.

'Well, as a friend, of course.' She picked up her spoon and dug it into the cream and sponge.

'No,' Alex replied with a firmness that surprised him. He motioned to the waiter for the bill. Now Anna looked up at him, hurt. She had not expected this. 'No. I'm not here for you to fall back on. You've got your new friends. Real friends don't treat people like this.'

Since then, he had only seen her byline in the paper. He'd looked for it, of course. Once or twice, more recently, there had been a picture of her above the articles, with an expression he recognised as the one she assumed when she was trying to be desperately serious, and taken seriously. She was obviously doing well.

He told the woman from the vetting department the exact date, but she seemed unconvinced by him, perhaps because he was so precise.

'Have you had any form of contact with her at all? Letters? Phone calls?'

No. Even the postcards had long since stopped. He'd kept the last one at the bottom of a wooden box on his bookshelf, where he almost never looked at it.

'Do you miss her?' This was one of those questions in that enticing voice that he had to answer truthfully.

'Yes. Yes I do. All the time.'

'But no recent contact?' she persisted.

'I've told you. None.'

It was nearly over. Graham showed him out, but didn't say anything friendly or encouraging. He was not to come back to work until they contacted him. He would be kept informed about the process. He would be well advised not to leave the country. Alex stopped himself from asking where they thought he might go: to a country that no longer even existed? These were no longer the days of George Blake vaulting the wall of Wormwood Scrubs and being spirited off to Moscow.

Alex had to wait to cross the road into St James's Park

for the Guards to ride by. The horses tossed their heads proudly. The silver breastplates of the Guardsmen caught the light. The hooves clattered on the tarmac as they turned neatly towards Horse Guards Parade. He remembered the postcard at the bottom of its wooden box.

As he sat down on the park bench, Alex was in tears. This park was a place for dead-letter drops and for meetings at dusk between men in grey flannel overcoats. People were supposed to say things like 'The tulips are blooming early in Leningrad this year' and exchange leather briefcases. This was a place for people who did things the way they were supposed to be done, the way he had always wanted to do things. And he was sure spies weren't supposed to cry.

# 5

ANNA WAS ALONE in the waiting room, considering the posters inviting her to spend a lovely family day out at local attractions, and deciding that she couldn't imagine anything worse. She was relieved to hear the sound of the train approaching, a sound that meant she was only two hours away from London. Out on the platform, her breath made clouds in the frosty air. The lights of the train and the prospect of dozing gently on the journey home were inviting. Anna tried to remember whether there was anything in the fridge.

She sat down, pulling her coat around her and tucking her cold hands into her sleeves. She was leaning her head against the window, closing her eyes, when she heard heavy, rushing footsteps and the sound of loud swearing behind her. A man who seemed to be all legs and arms flailed through the train door and into the carriage. Anna opened her eyes and gave him a grumpy stare. She was about to shut her eyes again when she realised that it was the man from the hotel, evil clipboard girl's colleague; even worse, he was moving to sit on her side of the aisle, throwing his rucksack into the overhead rack above, folding his coat and thumping himself down directly opposite her. He splayed himself out across the seat. Anna coiled herself in tighter, flinching away from him and pushing her folded arms further into opposite sleeves.

'Sorry about all that, earlier.' He had one elbow on the table now and waved a hand around. 'Today's all just been a fucking mess. Total shambles. Glad it's over.'

Anna made a non-committal murmur. She wished even more that she had something to read. A book, last week's *Economist*, anything, to avoid getting drawn into this conversation. 'Yes, well. It wasn't much help to me. Would have been no skin off your nose.'

'We have to keep these things under control. You'd have come in and be asking about whatever, stuff we don't want to talk about today. Can't have just anyone turning up.'

Anna couldn't let that one go.

'I'm not just anyone. I'm a reporter. And I was covering the by-election, which is precisely what you did want to talk about today, the whole reason he was there.'

'Well, we don't know you. And your man Phillips wasn't too keen to have your tanks on his lawn either.'

'For future reference, I'm Anna Travers. Anyway, how come they left you behind?'

'This was always the plan. He's going on to Chequers. Family time.' For the first time, he looked less than completely confident.

'So where's the woman with the accreditation list, and all the others?'

He changed the subject.

'Listen, it's been a bastard of a day and I need a drink. What are you having?'

Anna asked for tea, no sugar, grateful more for the few minutes of peace as he went to look for the buffet car than for the offer. As she watched his big frame move away down the train, she tried to remember why he seemed so familiar. The long limbs, the way he sprawled over the seat and the springy black hair formed a half-finished jigsaw puzzle. She turned her mind back to the piece that she would write up the next day; they weren't planning on running it until the weekend.

It was a train of thought about articles that she'd worked on being spiked that led her to the final pieces of the puzzle. As he returned from the buffet car carrying a brown paper bag, she remembered Theo Sadler's name. It was obvious that he didn't remember her at all.

He was one of those people who had seemed fully formed at university, who was just whiling away a few years gathering even more contacts and confidence before launching himself on a world that was certain to recognise his talents. Everybody knew who he was. When Anna timidly submitted some articles for the magazine that he edited, he rejected them in favour of those written by his many friends. She remembered his hand waving in the same dismissive way as he said that he really appreciated her efforts, that she must have tried really hard, but that her stuff wasn't quite up to the mark.

He was in an expensive suit now, with a red silk tie and a jacket that flashed glimpses of a colourful lining, rather than the faded T-shirt under a thick, checked shirt that she remembered. The expansive bluster and self-belief were all the same, though. Theo sat back down in the seat and took four quarter-sized bottles of red wine out of the brown paper bag. He lined them up against the train window, and they rattled as the train speeded up. He handed Anna one of two flimsy plastic cups, and began to pour the wine.

'I thought . . . tea?'

'You don't want tea. Have a proper drink.'

Theo took a large packet of crisps from the bag and ripped it open, spreading the flattened packet on the table between them. 'Here you go. Cheers.' He gulped a large mouthful of wine.

'Why was it such a bad day?' Anna asked. She thought that talking about himself was something that Theo had always done well.

'Badly organised. Not thought through. I mean, who wants to see him in some dingy hotel with a load of worthies? We should have been somewhere outside, playing football, at a school. Tried to find somewhere scenic, though it would have been bloody hard. And cold.'

Theo took a large handful of crisps. Halfway through the mouthful, he remembered something. 'You're not . . . working now? This is all very background. I don't want to read it somewhere.'

'Don't worry,' Anna replied. 'It's not all that fascinating.'

It started to sleet as the train flashed through the countryside, the names of the stations under sodium lights appearing and disappearing too quickly to read. Anna drank the wine less reluctantly as the journey went on, and Theo talked. She heard about how he'd got the job – he'd made his name as a researcher for another MP, had been poached by the leader's office before the election – and how he'd turned down a prestigious scholarship in America to work on the campaign.

By the time they reached the suburbs, Anna felt even more strongly that she'd missed out on a few years, the years she had spent in small countries and small towns. There had been Prague, a year and a half spent partly writing for an English language paper, partly spending long evenings in beer cellars with others who dreamt of being writers. Then there'd been the grim couple of years on local papers: she had nearly given up on journalism when she was sent out to knock on the doors of people whose children had died, but you had to do it, and you had to come back with the photo from the mantelpiece too. She had her copy shredded, sometimes physically, by a draconian editor who saw it as his role to disabuse university graduates of the idea that they could write anything. Her world seemed to have become smaller, not larger as it was supposed to have done. By the time she was back in London, she felt as though everyone else had moved on, further and faster, and was now to be taken seriously. They weren't playing at this any more.

This was not something she was going to tell Theo, who was unscrewing the top of another miniature bottle and had just started mapping out his own ambitions.

'It's only a matter of time,' he began. 'They need me now, of course. Couldn't manage without me. But next time a seat comes up that's in the right part of the country, I'll get it. I could have gone for this one, but they want me to stay in Westminster for now.'

The wine was gone by the time the train slowed through north London, and Anna felt strangely distant. Theo stretched himself out even further, and his legs bumped against hers under the table. She wasn't sure if this was intentional. She composed herself enough to remember to get his mobile number.

'Of course, you can always get me through the Downing Street switchboard. They can find me wherever I am. But here you go; let's do this again sometime, somewhere nicer. I'm Theo Sadler.'

'Yes,' said Anna, getting up from her seat, hoping that her unsteadiness would be ascribed to the movement of the train. 'I know.'

# 6

THE SMALL PLANE that had brought Mark Lucas from Brussels seemed to have transported him back to another age. The plane's propellers juddered to a stop; he climbed down steps that were rolled up to the aircraft door. They had landed through patches of thick fog that clung to the ground. He hoped he'd done a good job of not looking nervous during the clumsy landing.

The building had wings of its own, sweeping curves that gave him shelter from the cold air. Mark felt as though he should have been wearing a trenchcoat and a fedora. It was that sort of place: a place from films, a place from history. Inside, the arrivals hall was long and wide, and the milky light from the high windows formed rectangular patterns on the polished floor. Tempelhof Airport was enticing and frightening at the same time; somewhere that drew you in with its scale and elegance, before reminding you that it had a sinister past.

Mark was reminded that he was neither in a film, nor making one, by Louisa, from the private office, calling him over. She had rushed ahead to claim the bags from the conveyor belt, less concerned with history than with everything running smoothly. He snapped back into his here and now self, the one with a different sort of role to play. Mark held out his hand as he was introduced to a young man from the embassy who was there to greet him. Jeremy was formal, protective, and talked a bit too slowly, like someone looking after an elderly relative. Mark was becoming aware that although he still felt young, at thirty-five, his office meant he was expected to behave like someone far older.

'They call it the fork, Minister,' Jeremy explained, as they walked towards the waiting embassy car. He pointed out a curved, three-pronged concrete monument just outside the airport that looked like part of a motorway bridge lacking a motorway on top. 'It's a memorial to the Airlift. Everything in Berlin gets a nickname. Like the raisin bombers. And the pregnant oyster.'

'The what?' queried Louisa, as if wondering whether raisin bombers were some new security threat she should have been briefed on.

'The British and American planes in the Airlift,' Mark cut in. 'They dropped sweets and raisins for the children here when the Russians cut off supplies.'

'Nineteen forty-eight. Have you been reading up, Minister?' asked Jeremy, impressed but a little annoyed to have his expertise usurped.

'Not really. I've just been told some of the stories,' Mark replied. 'And it's OK to call me Mark. What's the pregnant oyster?' It seemed tactful to admit to something he didn't know.

As they were driven through what had been the West towards the centre of the city, it was hard to see either what kind of place it had been, or what it would become. Berlin was in a state of flux. Cranes rose over building sites. There were holes in the ground that could still have been bombsites, or the foundations of new buildings. This wasn't a part of town that Mark knew; these were the grubby and neglected bits of the old West that used to abut the Wall. Kreuzberg seemed a familiar name; he had a dim recollection of a strange bar with red brocade on the walls and candles wedged into beer bottles that he'd been taken to once as a student, before the Wall came down, though it was somewhere he could never have found again. He looked out from the back seat of the Rover as it cruised along a wide highway bordered by grey pebble-dashed apartment buildings, each one indistinguishable from the next. They crossed the canal and passed under a railway bridge as a bright-yellow train rattled overhead. As they neared the city centre, Jeremy decided to score another historical point.

'Minister, if you look to the left-hand side, you might be able to see a very interesting site. Probably different since you were last here.'

Mark could just about make out a patch of what looked like scrubland, a muddy, overgrown, cratered plot with a wire fence around it.

'That used to be the Gestapo headquarters. They've got a sort of museum there now. You walk through the ruins of the old cellars, where people were tortured.' Jeremy took a less than official tone for a moment. 'I've been. It's really quite disturbing. The place feels haunted.' He stopped himself again. Mark nodded and made a noise of indeterminate concern from the back seat, though he couldn't really see much across the oncoming traffic. It was the kind of noise that worked for most situations where you couldn't think what the right thing to say would be. Louisa looked perplexed by talk of haunted ruins. She thought they were supposed to be dealing with the future, not the past.

'And up here,' Louisa began, 'is this where the new embassy's going to be?'

'Yes, that's it,' Jeremy replied, happy to be back on less unsettling ground. This was in all the background briefings and was one of the things he was supposed to be talking about. 'Up on the corner. You'll get the official tour, of course, later on. It's going to be a great place to work. The design's all about openness.'

Mark let Louisa and Jeremy chatter away. He craned his neck around, getting a glimpse of the Brandenburg Gate as they arrived at the embassy's office on Unter den Linden. Britain's former mission to the old East Germany had a transitory feel, a place where the nameplate on the door kept changing to keep up with the world around it. The precise names of the buildings were sensitive here, but Mark had been assured that once the new embassy opened, there would be permanence again: a return to how things had once been, and were now expected to remain. It was the job of the people who worked here to remind him of the niceties and of the correct forms of expression.

They did that politely but intensely, in a long meeting over a sandwich lunch, around a table in one of the bland meeting rooms with blurry abstract art on the walls. Mark felt stale from the journey and the endless meetings before that, in Brussels; from sterile air pumped through office buildings that lacked windows. He ate a flaccid cheese sandwich and sipped weak coffee, and wished instead that he could have been left alone to find a strong coffee and maybe a beer in one of the new places he'd heard about in the old East. The noise of pneumatic drills hummed through the walls from outside, where the roads were being dug up and renewed.

They had his time planned out for him, minute by minute. There was the speech to give, to attentive students who would ask long, academic questions in perfect if wordy English; there was a tour of the new embassy, which now had walls and a roof but was some way from being completed; there was dinner at the residence with the ambassador and many prominent guests, whom it was important not to upset.

Most importantly, he'd been reminded both in London and in Berlin, were the meetings with his German counterparts, the ministers and officials who were his hosts. The relationship between the prime minister and the German chancellor was outwardly friendly but, he was told, rather a touchy one behind closed doors. They claimed to believe in the same things, had articles written under their names which constructed cumbersome frameworks for their friendship, but the truth was that they didn't really like each other. It was like a blind date where well-meaning friends had told them they'd have lots in common but there was no spark.

Mark's job was to remind people of all the things they had in common, and not to let the discord show. Look genial, smile nicely, don't say too much was, effectively, the brief. A word out of context, a word mistranslated by the press of one country or the other, and hackles could easily rise and it would be weeks of painstaking work on the part of the diplomats to soothe them again. There was a big meeting coming up in a couple of months, a summit. He was not to make it any harder than it need be, and ideally a bit easier.

Sir Malcolm Caudwell looked wrong in a yellow safety helmet. It made him conspicuous, as did the fluorescent high-visibility vest over his grey, chalk-striped suit. Although he was now a man with a public face, who was indeed the public face of his country, he was someone who had spent much of his career in back rooms and was still uncomfortable drawing attention to himself. He wore his grey hair slightly long, the fact of its grazing his shirt collar a tiny rebellion. As the new embassy was a building site, Mark had been asked with apologetic politeness to put on a helmet and a vest. He and the ambassador paused for photographs in what would become the building's lobby. Sir Malcolm looked around at the internal courtyard, which the architects' plans showed full of foliage and artwork, with a tree growing in the centre and smart people chatting to each other. There would be brightly coloured shapes jutting from the walls over the street, purple ovals and blue triangles, the building wearing its own high-visibility markings.

'Apparently this is all about being open to the outside world,' he began. 'One of my illustrious predecessors, before the last war, thought the building we had here was too dark and cramped.' They walked deeper into the shell of the future embassy, and climbed the stairs to a part that would be away from public view. 'Though I have to say, if he'd spent more time realising how bloody terrible everything was that was going on around him here, and less worrying about whether he had a sunlit office, then we might not have had to rebuild it from a hole in the ground sixty years later.'

Sir Malcolm stopped to check that no one was reading his lips, that no camera would accidentally record his words.

.'To me,' he whispered to Mark, 'it looks like one of those sorting boxes my grandchildren play with. You know, the ones with the holes that shapes have to fit into.'

Mark laughed, seeing what he meant.

'Though it's in a rather good location,' he replied, avoiding agreeing out loud.

'Oh yes, couldn't ask for better. It's practically part of the Hotel Adlon. If you'd asked me twenty years ago whether all this would ever happen, I'd have laughed at you.' Sir Malcolm looked through what would become an internal window, but was now a gaping hole, at the scaffolding and at the builders working on it.

'When did you first come to Berlin?' Mark asked. He could tell Sir Malcolm's history came from more than just a briefing note.

'The first time was the end of the fifties, beginning of the sixties. Before the Wall. We were based out by the old Olympic stadium, a long way west of here. Then much later, the late seventies. I seem to end up here every twenty years or so.'

'What was it like, then?'

'Rather grim,' Sir Malcolm said. 'It seemed as though it would last for ever, in those days. Lots of drinking with some very unpleasant Russians. One had to pour the vodka shots into the pot plants so that they ended up under the table before you did.'

'And what was your role, exactly?' Mark realised it was the kind of question one never asked, or had answered straight, but perhaps as a minister he would get a better response than he once might have done. 'Were you . . .?' Sir Malcolm knew perfectly well what he meant.

'Oh well,' he shrugged. 'Our friends the Russians certainly thought so.'

Louisa and Jeremy were about to rush them on through the rest of the building, but Sir Malcolm had been prompted to remind Mark of something that wasn't for their ears. He gestured them away with a quick flip of the hand.

'They – the Germans – will want to talk to you about some of the unfinished business from then. Around ten years ago, when the Wall came down, we seem to have acquired some of their old files. Don't ask me how.' Mark didn't. 'They're the indices to the lists of agents who were working for the Stasi in the West. They've been on at us to give them back. Truth and reconciliation and that sort of thing. Well, we'd really rather not.'

'But surely we should, shouldn't we?' Mark had read something about this. It was filed under one of the coloured tabs in Louisa's briefing folder, the ring binder that she carried with her everywhere so that she could flick through and give Mark the correct answer at any moment. Each coloured tab indicated a subject, a question Mark might be asked, and she provided him with the expected, approved answer. Sir Malcolm exhaled disapproval.

'Oh dear. You're an advocate of freedom of information, then?'

'It's one of the things I promised to do,' Mark replied. 'When I was elected.'

It was one of the issues that had made him cross the line, from journalistic observer to participant. He had found himself campaigning, signing letters, getting involved. Mark wanted to know things, he wanted other people to have the right to know things. Eventually, it had seemed that the only way to do that was to put himself out there and try to get elected, though Mark sometimes wondered how much the people who voted for him had really cared, how much they really wanted to know about the organisations that ran their lives.

It was the answer Sir Malcolm had been expecting. 'Yes, I suppose you did. I'm sure you'll realise, Minister, as you seem rather well up on the place, that there was a great deal of unpleasantness on all sides, and it's not necessarily best to be reminded of it all now. Sometimes what we don't know hurts us all rather less.'

Louisa and Jeremy were hovering nearby again. Sir Malcolm offered Mark a lift back to the embassy in the official car with the crest on the bonnet.

'Thank you, Sir Malcolm, but would you mind very much if I walked? I haven't been here in a long while and I just want to see a couple of things for myself.'

'Of course, of course.' The ambassador seemed to understand, but Louisa and Jeremy looked unsure.

'Minister – Mark – we'll need you back,' Louisa said, flicking through the folder and checking her watch. 'In half an hour. So that you can go through the speech and get to the venue.'

'I'll be there. Now get in the car with the ambassador and I'll catch you up.' Louisa took back his helmet and the hi-vis jacket and reluctantly let him go.

Mark turned left out of the building that was taking shape behind him and rounded the corner of the Hotel Adlon, now returned to its old plush velvet and gilt self, to see the Brandenburg Gate.

Last time he'd been here they were still selling fragments of 'Real Berlin Wall' along with the Russian rabbit-fur hats emblazoned with Soviet stars and the Gorbachev matryoshka dolls at dozens of little stalls strung out along the pavement. Mark had bought a chunk of concrete with some red spray-paint on it, not entirely believing the stamp on the plastic packet that promised its authenticity. It still sat on one of his bookshelves. The flea-market stalls had unsettled him: some of the stallholders were long-frustrated entrepreneurs, people who would always find themselves with something to sell, whenever and wherever they were. Alongside them were others he hadn't thought would thrive in the new world, elderly ladies in housecoats who were selling the contents of their attics and hoping that old boots, old army uniforms and out-of-date textbooks would seem like history to the tourists, artefacts of their lives that could bring them some money. He remembered looking at those old ladies and thinking of the people they had seen come and go here, of what they must have survived. Were they the same women who had stood here at the end of the war passing bricks pulled from the rubble from hand to hand to help rebuild their devastated city? They had lived through much worse than the free market in their time.

The only stall that remained was one selling sausages. Mark was drawn towards the smell of the grilling sausages, overlaid with the incongruous scent of curry powder. He had never quite understood the attraction of currywurst, but the man behind the stall, who looked Turkish, was serving up the sliced sausages slathered in reddish sauce to a queue of hungry customers. Mark ordered a bratwurst instead and realised that this was the first time all day he'd had to speak to anyone in German. There had been a bit of a discussion about that, not quite what diplomats euphemistically called a full and frank one. Mark had wanted to say a few words in his rusty but serviceable German on one of the public occasions; he argued it was only polite. There had been raised eyebrows and queries as to quite how good his German was, and then a shaking of heads as it had been decided that the risk of him making some politically sensitive howler was too great. Mark had protested that he'd heard the prime minister attempt his barroom French, and that his own German was certainly no worse. 'Yes,' he'd been told. 'But he's the PM. And even then, he ended up accidentally telling the French prime minister he fancied him. So best not, I think.' Mark's suggestion that he mention his family connections to the place were also greeted with pursed lips. 'Let's not make this all about you,' one adviser sniffed.

The stallholder pushed the sausage back and forth on the griddle before wedging it into a roll, the ends of the sausage protruding from the bread. He handed it to Mark, indicating the bottle of mustard on the counter with a grunt. Mark squirted mustard along the length of the sausage and handed over a few Deutschmarks.

He was briefly conscious that Ministers of the Crown weren't generally seen eating street food from a stall on official visits, but Mark didn't care. What was the worst thing someone could say about it, the worst picture caption? 'British minister enjoys traditional local delicacy', if you're the German press. 'Minister takes a turn for the wurst', if you're the Brits. No problem there. This was the only chance he would have to breathe the real air of the place and feel its ground properly beneath his feet, and he'd had to snatch it for himself.

There was even something different about the Brandenburg Gate. You couldn't miss the new buildings starting to rise out of what had been an almost open space – large placards around the square showed images of what they would look like – but suddenly Mark realised that the four copper horses that belonged on top of the gate, the Quadriga, had been returned. They'd been missing before, taken away for their most recent restoration, as they had often come and gone over the decades, harnessed to the whims of whoever was in charge and facing the way that power dictated. Now they reared up again in front of their chariot, as if about to charge east down the wide avenue ahead of them. Traffic rushed under the gate, drivers squeezing through the narrow gaps between the pillars.

Mark walked towards the Reichstag, still fenced off as a building site, with Portakabins dotted around the grounds in front of it. The sunlight reflected on the new glass dome that was still taking shape; a form that was more complicated than it looked, new and transparent on the surface, a coil of spirals and mirrors beneath. The opening ceremony for the building was not far away now, a date marked on a grid a few months in the future, when the German Parliament would officially belong here. It was still a capital in progress: all the German officials he was due to meet were spending their time half in one place, half in another. They wanted to meet him here to impress upon him the place it was becoming, rather than to have awkward meetings in emptying, fading Bonn, where the contents of their offices were already being packed into plastic crates and loaded onto removal lorries.

Mark had only seen the Wall come down on television, but those images were still as clear in his mind as if he had been here that November night and seen it for himself. He could see the people helping each other climb on top of the Wall, hacking at it with pickaxes, the looks of joyful surprise on the faces of the East Germans who could not believe that they were there, and that they were changing everything, and that no one was stopping them. He had felt close to them, those people in their badly made clothes and dreadful haircuts, wearing thin anoraks against a cold they no longer noticed in their longing to escape from their circumstances. He knew that had one tiny piece of human history gone differently, he could have been one of them.

Finishing the bratwurst and wiping mustard from the corner of his mouth, Mark realised he was expected back at the embassy. He tried to follow the embankment along the canal but found his way blocked by building works, with huge blue pipes snaking above the roads and carrying the groundwater away. He turned back, down Unter den Linden. He bought two cuddly bears in funny hats for Bella and Jack from a souvenir shop on the way, realising that he was unlikely to get another chance, and rushed along the street. Mark knew that Louisa would be fretting, but he also knew that a bit more stress would make her feel important, and give her the sense that without her to keep an eye on him, things would fall apart.

# 7

MARK FELT THAT it would have been rude to refuse the bacon and eggs that Lady Eleanor Caudwell offered him, but he noticed that his waist felt ever more constricted by his suit trousers, particularly after the heavy dinner of the evening before. But then, it wasn't every day that you had breakfast at the British ambassador's residence. This was how come, everyone said, you got into government and found yourself putting on an extra stone.

'We have terrible trouble with the boars,' Lady Eleanor said, as Mark took long sips of the strong coffee that she had poured for him from an ornate pot. He wasn't quite sure how to react to a comment like that, certainly not before his first cup of coffee of the morning had taken effect.

'The bores?' he repeated. Was this how the ambassador's wife usually referred to the diplomatic circuit? How had she tolerated decades of it? 'Well, I hope the dinner wasn't too awful. I enjoyed it, anyway.'

'Oh, no! The wild boars!' Lady Eleanor's pale skin creased into genuine laughter. She was younger than her husband by perhaps ten years. Her blonde hair was held back with a hairband this morning, and she wore a jersey of butterscotch cashmere. 'Berlin has had a real problem with them for the last ten years. All the big wire fences around here used to keep them in the old East. When the fences came down, the creatures decided that Western herbaceous borders were jolly tasty, so sometimes they crash in here. Plays havoc with the tulips.' She pointed towards the lawn, and the spring flowers emerging from the borders.

'Though they're rather tasty themselves, of course,' Mark pointed out with some relief.

'Yes, I've suggested that to the chef. Though for some reason my husband is a little reluctant to go after them with a rifle. I don't know why. He's a very good shot.'

'I can imagine,' Mark replied.

Mark helped himself to toast, spreading it with marmalade from a silver-lidded pot. He resolved that when he got back to London he would try running again, even though there seemed to be less and less time. He reproached himself again for his lack of discipline. Sir Malcolm entered the breakfast room, a folder full of documents under his arm. He poured himself a cup of tea.

'Is she telling you about the wild boars?' he asked. Mark nodded. 'I thought as much. I've spent enough of my career pointing weaponry at great bristly brutes round these parts. The great joy of this go-around is that it's no longer required.'

The room caught the morning sun through the tall French windows that were flanked by long green shutters. The residence was an elegant villa in the Grunewald, surrounded by tall trees, and it felt very far from the Berlin of roadworks and construction sites. Mark had signed the guestbook, which lay on a table in the tiled hall, in front of the framed portrait of the Queen. He felt the regal gaze as he wrote his name, and for a moment wondered whether she would entirely approve of him.

He looked at the much younger Queen, wearing a white gown with a blue sash. It's all chance, he thought, as if addressing Her Majesty, though he imagined one never said such things in such a way. This was a silent lese-majesty. You might not have been Queen. You might not have been British either. There's no such thing as destiny: it's decisions other people made long before they were aware that you would ever exist, chance things that happened that changed their lives and yours. He was here, and he was British, and he was a member of your government; anything else that might have happened if history had worked out differently simply didn't exist, and so didn't matter.

Mark was driven in the embassy car across the city from its western suburbs to its eastern reaches. From his comfortable leather seat, he watched the cityscape change. The first time Mark had ever crossed into the East he'd been a student and had bought a ticket on a slow bus with vinyl seats and a window that was wedged permanently open. His parents had been reluctant to let him go: his mother tried quiet persuasion, suggesting other options, somewhere sunnier; he and his father had a loud argument that ended in Mark slamming the door of his bedroom shut and refusing to speak to his father until he left. As he'd left home for the coach station with his rucksack, all his father would say to him was 'Don't talk to anyone. Don't trust anyone.' Mark had thought this a stupid comment. How could you go somewhere and not talk to anyone?

When the East German border officials called him over into a beige room inside their frontier post, after the coach had already waited for ages in the traffic jam at the checkpoint, he wondered if his parents had been right after all. He tried to remember who it was he'd travelled with, who he'd shot the glance at that he hoped meant 'send for help if I don't get back on the bus'. Dave, that was it. David Carter, the guy who'd sold the *Socialist Worker* in the high street on Saturdays, much to the chagrin of his father the Wing Commander. Dave had still been drunk on the beer they'd chugged down at the bus station and wouldn't have noticed if Mark had gone until it was too late. And would probably not have thought it was ideologically sound to rescue him anyway.

Mark had stood there in the draughty customs office in his denim jacket, carrying his rucksack, listening to the guards talk about him in gruff accents and trying not to let them see that he could understand them. He had decided that he would say he only spoke English, apart from *Guten Morgen* and 'please' and 'thank you'. There were several packets of cigarettes wedged into the bottom of the rucksack; Mark was wondering whether to pull a couple out as an offering, but had just decided against attempted bribery when they handed him his passport and sent him back to the bus. He had tried to sleep but the flickering fluorescent light over his seat had kept him awake most of the way across East Germany to Berlin.

No matter how well he knew in theory that things were different now, the reality never failed to surprise him. It had surprised him last time, when he'd been walking around the no-man's-land where the Wall had been, filming the one abandoned restaurant left standing and the burnt-out cars that had been discarded there, a great strip of emptiness that had been so fought over; it surprised him now, when that same strip of land was being hollowed out to be turned into shopping arcades and cinemas and casinos.

The six-lane dual carriageway down which the embassy car now drove headed east. It was newly resurfaced and looked as if it would keep going smoothly until it reached the steppe.

Ilse Bernau, his German counterpart, was meeting him at the museum, and as the car turned in to the courtyard of a forbidding, beige block, Mark saw the welcoming party already waiting for him on the steps of the former Stasi headquarters. Ilse Bernau was a petite woman who made herself look taller with high, pointy shoes. She had cropped blonde hair and sharply angled cheekbones. She stood with her feet turned out and her neck elongated in a way that made Mark think she must once have been a dancer or perhaps a skater.

'Mr Lucas. How lovely to meet you.' She spoke fluent English, with a slight American accent. 'I realise this is a bit unusual,' she explained as they entered the building. 'You'll have the opportunity to see some of the new government buildings later, over lunch, but we thought it was important for you to come here too.'

The corridors echoed as they walked along them. These days it could have been any slightly down-at-heel government building in any country. Frau Reinhard, the archivist who was in charge of his personal guided tour, was nervous and talking quickly. Ilse Bernau offered to translate, but Mark said she didn't need to.

'You speak German?' Ilse asked.

'Not as well as you speak English,' he replied. 'Where did you learn?'

'Yale. I had a scholarship. It was not long after the Wende and they wanted us Ossis to come. And I wanted to see America, because I'd never been anywhere but here.'

'Where did you grow up?' Mark was curious about her. She seemed like a woman who was progressing through her life at frightening speed, making up for lost time.

'Leipzig. I was at university when it all started, the demonstrations. We are the lucky generation, it came at just the right moment for us.' Mark made a quick calculation: she must have been younger than him, in her early thirties now, her early twenties then.

Frau Reinhard showed them into a large white room full of library stacks and filing cabinets. Towards the back of the room, other researchers were working in silence. She showed them a large glass jar standing on one of the cabinets. It looked like something from a laboratory; sealed inside was a square of dark-yellow cloth that looked like a grimy duster. Mark was just about to ask what it was when Frau Reinhard began what was obviously a well-rehearsed explanation.

She said that jars like these contained the scents of people that the Stasi wanted to be able to follow. Sometimes that meant stealing pieces of their clothing; sometimes it meant taking the scent from a place they'd been, a chair they'd sat on. The scents were kept in these jars in case they wanted to use sniffer dogs to track someone down.

Mark wondered whose stale smell was trapped in the jar he

saw; whether that person was even still alive, whether if you opened the lid any trace of them would remain. It made him realise how far the intrusion had come into people's lives; that nothing then had really been private, not even the smell your body left on your clothes.

'Did everyone have a file?' Mark asked, astonished at the scale of the archives he saw, even though this was only a small part of it.

'Not everyone,' replied the archivist. 'But very many people.'

'Even visitors to the country?' Mark was wondering whether his brief trips as a student would have meant that he was recorded on a card index somewhere.

'Not people who just came for short tourist visits, no, unless they were of special political interest. But many people who studied here, or had a more significant connection with the country. Everyone has the right to come and look for their file. But as you can imagine, it takes a great deal of time to find out whether such a file even exists.'

They moved on to where two young men worked at large Formica desks. Frau Reinhard spoke in a whisper now. She explained that they were piecing together files.

'We started with sixteen thousand sacks of documents,' she said. 'They had been torn up, shredded, by the officials when they left here. Now, we are putting them back together.'

Mark marvelled at the scale of the historical jigsaw puzzle, the seemingly endless task that faced the two quiet and patient men who sat there. He envisaged them growing old over their work, their eyes straining as they tried to match one shred of typewritten note to another.

'How long will it take?' he asked.

'Many, many years,' replied Frau Reinhard. 'We don't know even now.'

'And is it necessary?'

Frau Reinhard seemed bemused by his question. Mark wondered if he'd used the right word. Frau Reinhard looked to

Ilse for an answer, as though this was a question that required a calculated and political response.

'Of course,' said Ilse quickly. 'There are people whose whole lives may have been affected by what's in these sacks of paper. They have a right to know what happened to them, the same as everybody else. It's not their fault that it's their files that were destroyed. So it's our duty to give them that truth back.'

Mark realised, as he was shown along another corridor and into a suite of offices preserved exactly as it had been when the Wall came down, that this was the point she had brought him here to make. The office of Erich Mielke, who'd been in charge of the Stasi, was panelled with a wood that looked like plastic. There were net curtains at the windows and a bust of Lenin on the desk. The heavy phones had dials, and there were sets of clunky switches to flick if he'd wanted to call in his subordinates. It would have seemed as if he'd just stepped away for a minute, if it hadn't been for the absence of papers on the desk and the velvet museum ropes to stop people sitting in his chair. Ilse moved through this room uncomfortably.

'I don't like to stay here,' she said. 'I don't like the idea of being connected to this man in any way.'

'How were things for your family, then?' Mark asked cautiously.

'We were mostly fine, we were OK. What's the expression? We didn't show up, we were not people they noticed.'

'Under the radar?' Mark prompted.

'That's right, under the radar. Except me, for a while. They said I showed promise as a gymnast; I had good training but it also meant I had to make the right impression. Join the Pioneers and wear the red bandana, this sort of thing. But then I got injured and I was never going to be a great champion, so they stopped caring about me.'

'You must have been disappointed. About the gymnastics, I mean.'

'I was then. But now I know more about what happened to some of the other girls, I'm glad.' Ilse changed the subject, and took them into an adjoining room, brighter and less oppressive, to sit down. Their advisers pulled up seats and opened notebooks.

Ilse Bernau was direct. 'So now you've seen why it's so important to us that we can come to terms with our history. Especially our history in this city, in this country. Sometimes I think Britain thinks our history stopped in 1945, but as you know, it didn't.'

'I'm very well aware of that,' replied Mark. 'But the issue's more complicated.'

'I know it's complicated,' Ilse said. 'But you can help. Britain has copies of some of our files; the original card indexes were destroyed after the Wall came down, the ones that dealt with agents abroad. There's nothing of them here to piece back together. I don't really care how you came to have our files, but they belong here, they're part of our history, and we're asking you now, very politely, to give them back.'

'I think from the British government's point of view, it would set an unwelcome precedent to start returning every piece of someone else's history that we've come by over the years. And we're also worried that it's not just your citizens who are mentioned in these files. There could be unforeseen consequences for us. Not to mention national security issues.' Mark was saying what he was supposed to say.

'Yes, I know that.' He could see why Ilse had come as far as she had in such a short time. Everything for her was a competition. 'But what we would say is that it's about time that other countries took responsibility for the actions of their citizens, even if they betrayed their country. Look around here. Can you imagine what it is like to live with the knowledge that your neighbours, your friends, your teachers, even your own family might have informed on you? Never to be quite sure, and then to come here and look it up and find out that they did?'

Mark nodded. He tried to put himself here, among the residual smell of the cheap two-stroke engines of the Trabants and the brown wallpaper. Ilse continued. 'You are prone to think it's just us that have to understand our history. But you do too. If there are people in Britain who would have done the same, who did the same, you have the duty to know about it, to deal with it, even if it's not convenient, not quite "nice". Not just think it's something that happened to other people.'

Ilse let out a sharp sigh, and raised her chin high. Mark had a brief image of the girl she had been, finishing a performance with a flourish and a stretch of the arms towards the judges. She was convincing, but he couldn't stray too far from the line.

'I understand the point you're making,' he said in a soft, conciliatory voice. 'I genuinely do. You make it very well. And I agree with you that transparency is the principle that we should all be bearing in mind. However, this isn't a policy that I can change without further discussions at much higher levels than mine. I'll have some meetings about it when I get back. I'll tell them what you said.'

Ilse looked unimpressed. She shook her head.

'We've heard that before. Don't just have some meetings. Don't sound like one of those people who says it can't be done and I have to ask my superiors. We know what happens when people say that.' She looked around the room pointedly.

Mark got up from the table and walked towards the window, looking out at the huge complex of buildings that had been devoted to watching people and keeping them in line. He gestured to Ilse to follow him. She stood up and walked away from Louisa and her German opposite number, who were still sitting at the table. Mark spoke quietly.

'I'll do everything I can. I'm not just saying that. I think you're right.' Ilse stared at him closely, scrutinising him. 'I really do understand, for personal reasons. My father came from here. He was lucky, he got out.' He had never intended to mention that, but it seemed to be the only thing that would make her understand his sincerity.

'When?' Ilse asked.

'Before the Wall went up. Just before, a few days.'

'So you will do something?'

'I still can't promise, you know that. Nor could you, in my position. But I do understand why it matters.'

They turned back and walked towards the table. Ilse seemed to be retrieving a file from her own mental archive.

'Your father,' she began, 'is he Anthony Lucas?'

'That's it.'

'As in *Universal History and Barbarous Freedom*?'

'You've read it?' Mark was astonished. He'd never read it himself.

'Yes, at Yale. They had an excellent course in political theory. A very important text.'

'Thank you. It's beyond me, I'm afraid,' Mark said apologetically.

'I read somewhere that he was born in Germany but had lived in England for many years. You've talked to him about all this?'

'No, not really. He doesn't have much time for practical politics.'

'That seems a shame. I'd love to hear him speak.'

'Come to Oxford one day.' Mark extended an invitation that he didn't expect to be taken up.

'Perhaps I will,' replied Ilse cheerfully.

# 8

ALEX RUTHERFORD WORE a suit and tie to cross town, even though there was really no reason to any more. He felt that he would fit in better with the ebbing rush-hour crowds. He watched as other men and women in suits and overcoats held their passes up to doormen who acknowledged them, and zapped themselves into buildings with large glass revolving doors and bouquets of fresh flowers on the reception desks. Instead, he wandered around the plaza between the office buildings and watched a man drive a sweeping machine back and forth across the ice rink that was set up there for the winter. The machine's brushes made a jarring whirr, and Alex had a sudden and irrational desire to go ice skating. The rink wasn't yet open, and he couldn't skate, but he imagined for a moment that he could spin around on the ice in his suit and hope that the bankers in their offices above would look down on him and envy his freedom, as he envied them their work.

Alex found the cafe that James had described to him, and settled in to a table in the window. The waitress wasn't in a hurry to serve him, even though he was the only customer, and busied herself wiping the tables and rearranging the pastries before she came over to take his order. It didn't matter. Unlike most of the people she'd already served that morning with rushed coffees that they needed to have with them on their desks to start the day, he had nowhere to be except here. He decided that since that was the case, he would have a pastry as well.

He expected James to be late. He knew that James was

snatching a few illegitimate minutes away from his desk and that he begrudged Alex the time. He had been impatient, and didn't understand why whatever it was that Alex needed to talk about so urgently couldn't be discussed over the phone.

Alex was draining one coffee down to its last swirl of foam and contemplating another when James Rycroft hurried through the door. James banged his mobile phone onto the table and kept looking at it as they talked.

'What's this all about, Alex?' James asked, gesturing to the waitress. He ordered his coffee to take away, and she had to check that was what he meant to say. 'I've got a conference call with Hong Kong in fifteen, so I really can't stay.'

'It's work,' Alex began. 'My work. I'm in big trouble, and they might need to talk to you about it. I needed to tell you before they called you first.' For the first time, a look of concern crossed James's face. Then his phone rang and he answered it curtly.

'I'm in a meeting. I'll ring you back.' He looked back at Alex. 'What happened?'

'You remember that night out we had last time, with those friends of yours?'

'Sort of,' James said, 'it was a bit messy, as far as I can remember.'

'Exactly. And I lost my computer, which I shouldn't have had with me anyway, which is why the trouble. So they might want to ask you about it, to check my story.'

'God, your IT department are a bit heavy-handed, aren't they? Can the government not stump up for a new one?'

'It's not that,' explained Alex. 'I got it back, but, well, I lost something. Something that I really shouldn't have had with me.' Alex stopped. He had gone further than he absolutely needed to.

James struggled to translate this into his terms, but after a moment he looked as though he understood.

'Oh, I see. Client confidentiality. Market-sensitive information?'

'Similar sort of thing. Personal data.'

James nodded.

'We'd be done for that too.' He checked his watch. 'Which is why you're not at work now, right?'

'Right,' said Alex. 'Suspended, pending an investigation. So they'll want to talk to you. You talked to them once before, remember, when I started. There's nothing for you to worry about. You haven't done anything wrong.'

James didn't look convinced by that. He checked the phone again, swigged coffee from the paper cup, and said he had to run, that Hong Kong would be on the line. As Alex was saying goodbye, James turned back in the doorway.

'And you, Alex? Are you OK?'

Alex had already slumped his shoulders down as he watched James go. James must have seen the helpless look on his face, but Alex said as bravely as he could:

'Should be. I hope so.'

Alex watched James pick up his pace and begin to jog with a lumbering, rugby player's gait back to the office, pulling out his ID card with one hand and clutching the phone in the other.

The urge to go ice skating had gone, but Alex was still struggling to find ways to spend his time. He had found walking helped, so he turned in the direction of Moorgate and started to make his way through the unfamiliar streets of the City. He kept looking at his feet, almost as if the missing disk might suddenly appear on the pavement. One disk. One computer disk, shiny silver on the one side, white with lettering on the other. Lettering that, stupidly enough, said 'Secret'. All anyone who tried to read the disk's contents would see would be images of file card after file card. It wouldn't mean anything to most people. It astonished Alex more than ever that there was no back-up. When he'd told them it was missing, he'd asked whether there was another copy. All he got was a grim, impervious look.

He climbed a flight of concrete steps that raised him above London Wall and into the Barbican. An ancient church nestled incongruously behind the modern battlements. Alex didn't like it here, but he knew that if he followed the yellow line painted on the paving stones, he'd eventually find his way out, like a rat in an experimental maze.

It often occurred to him that there was too much newness in his world, and it made him uncomfortable. He preferred the time-worn and the familiar, the things that had survived, like the church that must have withstood the bombs only to have concrete towers encircle it. He passed the Museum of London, but decided that he had seen more museums lately than he could take in. Instead, he turned down the road towards St Paul's, climbing down another staircase to escape from the maze. Even here, things were changing. He made his way towards the river. The tide was out, and archaeologists in anoraks were standing in the river mud, measuring out squares to excavate before the piles for the new bridge were sunk.

Alex would have loved to piece together the past in that way, a way where all the hurt and the violence was safely distant. He'd progressed from his school, a noisy modern comprehensive that was already showing its age in the damp-stained concrete by the time he got there, to the calm of an Oxford college, and had always hoped to stay surrounded by books and muted footsteps in libraries. But he'd blown that. He was starting to think this was a pattern that would keep repeating itself.

The wind blew off the river and Alex hid his face deeper behind the collar of his black coat. His timing always seemed to be out: even though he'd only just started in the service when it was moved to Vauxhall Cross, he cursed the change as much as anyone who'd spent decades in the old places. No one liked the new building, which looked as though it had been put together by a giant child with a set of gaudy plastic bricks. It bristled with antennae and was shrouded in green reflective glass. Alex's desk was nowhere near the window, but he would often stand in the stairwell, gnawing on the rim of his polystyrene coffee cup, looking out at the river and the sedate older buildings on the opposite bank.

Those who'd been there longer talked wistfully of the days before the shiny new offices. It seemed more fitting that they should have worked in grey, anonymous blocks, in just the wrong parts of town. One of the few concessions to secrecy seemed to be that they'd made it so hard to find your way around the new building. You could barely find the front door unless you knew where to look, and once inside, you had to learn how to navigate your way from one room to another without the benefit of any numbers on the doors. You had to programme yourself to take familiar routes and not deviate from your habits. Perhaps that was the idea, perhaps the building itself was supposed to make your behaviour predictable. Another maze, different scientists.

He'd been relatively happy in that maze, though. He'd fitted in. Even when the work was routine and repetitive, as it some-times was, that was part of what he'd enjoyed about it. Take the last job, for instance, the one that had caused all the trouble. It was work that should have been done long before, probably even had been, though no one seemed to have the right records. There'd been some kind of argument between different depart-ments about who was in charge, whether it was them or the guys on the other side of the river. Alex hadn't much cared at the time. He'd just wanted to produce a respectable piece of work: neat, clear, complete; a grid with all the answers in their correct spaces and the omissions correct too.

'Can you believe it?' Graham had remarked one afternoon that summer, with disdain. He sipped tea from a proper cup and looked east towards the railway tracks. Graham's office had a view, but they were in the department that faced in the wrong direction. He rested his teacup in the saucer, and took a desul-tory bite of a flabby biscuit. He waved the biscuit in a dismissive gesture over Kennington.

'The old place. I went past it the other day, on the way back from the cricket. There was a sign up. A huge banner.' He sighed. 'Luxury apartments.' Each word gained extra syllables. 'Visit the show flat. I almost asked for a brochure and looked around,' he continued, 'but it was too much to be borne.'

It had been a few days since he had heard from anyone. He was to keep waiting. He would be contacted. Alex felt empty without his job. He had joined as a way of retreating from view: the blue postcard after he'd been rejected from the Foreign Office, as he'd been rejected from so much else, had offered him 'other opportunities' at a time when there didn't seem to be any. It had given him a safe berth. He kept walking along the Embankment, hoping that just putting one foot in front of the other would keep everything at bay. It was further than he remembered along the riverbank to get home, and his legs protested. The sky was flat and grey. He just had to keep going.

# 9

M OSTLY, ANNA REFLECTED, meeting someone for a drink after work didn't involve putting yourself through a scanner. She put her bag on the conveyor belt in front of the police officer and watched as its contents came up in outline on the screen. She rummaged in her pockets for keys and change, took them out and handed them through as well. The police officer, finding nothing untoward, smiled and showed her through into Downing Street.

Anna tried to look nonchalant as she walked up the street. Three reporters were standing in the road, in a line, mouthing words to themselves as they waited to go on air. Behind the metal barriers, their cameramen and producers stood adjusting lights and making phone calls. Anna stopped to watch them for a moment. They went quiet as Big Ben chimed six.

She realised that she would have to walk behind the reporters and into the frame of the cameras if she was to get to the door. It was a moment she would rather have had to herself, not one glimpsed by millions of people. When she'd spoken to Theo on the phone, she asked if he was sure she should come to the front door. Of course, he'd said. Why not? She understood now that he was trying to impress her. Well, he was succeeding. In which case, she wouldn't be precisely on time.

There were other people coming out of the black door now, leaving work, and it opened and closed regularly behind the correspondents as they gesticulated, making their points urgently. Anna decided to chance the walk across the road and up to the door, praying that she wouldn't trip on the pavement. She was just beginning to wonder whether she should knock on the familiar shiny black door when it swung open from the inside. The door was closed behind her, and another officer asked who she was to see.

As Anna waited in the entrance hall for Theo to come and fetch her, she tried to take in her surroundings: the black and white tiles on the floor; the portraits in gilt frames on the wall. A long corridor stretched away in front of her. At the far end, behind glass double doors, she could make out a couple of men in dark suits who looked as though they were arguing. The grandfather clock ticked as she waited; she paced the hallway and pretended to study the portraits. She wondered again what she was really doing here. Just going for a drink, she repeated to herself. Meeting someone useful. Seeing somewhere she wouldn't otherwise get to see, which was always good.

The double doors swung open and Theo appeared. He was with an older man, and they were still deep in conversation as they walked down the corridor towards Anna. They stopped just out of her earshot, aware that she was there but not wanting to include her.

So this was Robert Callander. Lord Callander, as she should probably call him. Anna doubted that she was one of the people who would get to know him as Bob. Standing next to Theo, he appeared short, but then so did everyone. Callander had untidy grey hair that swept back from a high forehead and gave him a professorial air. That must be partly what had led to him being known as 'the prime minister's brain'. From what Anna had read, though, his value lay more in his capacity for low cunning than for high-minded thinking. He nodded as Theo spoke. Anna could see that they had come to some kind of an agreement, or a truce at least, on whatever they had been discussing so fiercely. Lord Callander, battered briefcase in hand, was about to head for the main door. The police officer stood up, preparing to open the door, but Theo guided Callander with a hand on the shoulder towards Anna.

'Lord Callander – Anna Travers.' Theo made the introductions.

Anna shook his hand. Robert Callander appraised her, as though he was measuring her for something.

'The name rings a bell,' he said warily.

'She's a journalist,' Theo said, before Anna could.

'Aha.' Callander raised his eyebrows in mock surprise.

'And a friend of mine,' Theo added.

'A friend? How charming. I didn't think Theo here had friends, only interests.' Callander was pleased with this joke, and had obviously used it before.

'Palmerston?' replied Anna, recognising the quotation.

'Very good, very good.' Callander looked at her more closely. 'You want to watch this one, Theo. She's evidently much cleverer than you.'

Theo laughed, but his smile was forced. He let Callander leave first.

'So, what do you think? Have you been here before?'

'No,' said Anna, as calmly as she could manage. 'First time.'

'You start taking it for granted after a while,' Theo mused, 'but when you stop and look again it's still a pretty amazing place. It's like a rabbit warren in there.'

Anna struggled to keep pace with Theo's long stride as they walked back down Downing Street towards Whitehall. The reporters had finished talking; the cameramen were disconnecting cables and packing their gear away. Theo waved to one of the correspondents as he walked past, and Anna was relieved he didn't stop to chat.

'Can you slow down?' Anna asked as they turned another corner from Whitehall into the street that ran between the Foreign Office and the Treasury.

'Sorry,' Theo said. 'Can't help it.' But for a while his pace slowed slightly, as Anna asked him about his day. He was vague. 'Just, you know, very hectic. You can be asked about anything and you have to know what you're talking about. Get one word wrong and it all blows up into something big. Storms in teacups, lots of it, but they don't like it when that happens. It shouldn't happen.'

As if to prove it, his phone rang as they reached the top of Clive Steps. Theo moved away from Anna and leant against the plinth of the statue as he took the call, cupping his hand over his mouth as he spoke. He seemed animated, close to anger.

'Sorry,' he said to Anna after a few minutes, as he hung up. 'There are some hacks who just don't know when to stop. They just keep banging on and on about stuff that really isn't important, and that I've explained perfectly clearly anyway. They're idiots. Present company excepted, obviously.'

They reached a pub near the corner of the park. Anna was about to go into the main bar, which had large windows and was crowded with men who'd loosened their ties after work, standing with pints, watching football. Instead, Theo guided her to a set of metal steps outside that led to a downstairs bar. It was panelled with dark wood and there were partitions between the tables creating booths. Theo chose the bench that gave him the best view towards the door, as though he was expecting someone else. Anna wondered whether he didn't want to be seen with her.

He went to the bar and returned with a bottle of white wine. Anna was grateful that, this time, he'd at least ordered what she'd intended to drink, even if there was too much of it. Theo filled two large glasses almost to the brim, raised one in a toast, and started to question Anna.

'So, we don't see you around here much. Do you usually cover politics?'

Anna wasn't sure how to answer.

'Not as much as I'd like to,' she said. 'But I'm working on it. The by-election was a good start. They liked that.'

'Yes, I saw the piece. Not bad. And Lander won, though we would have liked him to do a bit better than he did. So not bad for us either. But you're not in the lobby?'

'No,' Anna replied. She wasn't sure how you joined the club

of political journalists, but she wasn't going to admit it. She sometimes asked herself whether one of the incumbents had to die first; it seemed as remote a prospect as her being appointed a cardinal. 'You should be,' Theo said. 'They could do with some new people.'

The conversation turned to mild gossip; people she knew, people who were well thought of by Theo, and those who weren't. Anna had been convinced until then that this world of rumours was not the real world, not the world she wanted to be part of or report on; but now she felt its enticements. She enjoyed the feeling that she knew things that other people didn't, of speculating in a currency that was still foreign to her. She enjoyed sitting in a wooden booth in the half-light with a persuasive man who bowed his head near to hers to exchange confidences, even if they weren't yet important ones. She even enjoyed drinking acidic white wine on an empty stomach, although she knew she might regret that later.

Anna wasn't sure how late it was when they were interrupted by someone coming up to the table. She had noticed how Theo kept watching the people in the bar, raising an occasional hand in acknowledgement to those he recognised. It had seemed on first glance like a great place for conspiratorial meetings, but Anna realised that this was the last place that you would come if you had a real secret to hide. Almost everyone in here wanted to look as though they had something confidential to discuss, but in reality also wanted to be noticed deep in discussion. It was the blonde woman, the one who'd had the clipboard at the hotel and had kept Anna out of the room with the prime minister. She beamed at Theo, but her mouth narrowed when she saw Anna.

'Julia,' he said, standing up to greet her with a kiss on each cheek. 'This is Anna. She's been asking my advice. Anna, this is Julia. We work together.'

'Advice?' Julia's voice was flat and heavy, the same way it had been when she'd told Anna she was sorry she wasn't allowed in the room. Anna had the same sense that she was trespassing on Julia's territory.

Julia and Theo quickly discussed something that Anna strained to hear, something about a meeting that was re-scheduled and an embargo that was lifted. She sensed, though, that this conversation was more a pretext than a message that needed to be conveyed. Julia turned away on her shiny black shoes and went back to sit with her friends on the other side of the room. She took a cigarette from a packet lying next to her phone on the table and lit it, raising her chin and blowing smoke high into the air. Theo watched her, then poured another glass of wine.

'Just work together?' Anna asked, feeling that she was being watched from the opposite table. Theo shifted in his seat and took a large sip of the wine.

'These days, yes. Which is . . . a bit tricky, sometimes.'

'I see,' said Anna.

'It's very intense,' he explained. 'You see a lot of people up very close. You work together all hours and you stop really knowing where one thing ends and another begins.'

The wine was almost gone and it seemed as though it was time to leave. Anna retrieved her coat, heaved her bag off the floor and walked across to the stairs, still under close observation. She imagined the critical gaze noticing how her cheap work jacket pulled awkwardly on her shoulder, creased by the habitual weight of her bag; how her shoes were flat and scuffed. Theo tipped his head slightly in a farewell to the table on the other side of the room.

They emerged from the underground bar into the dark evening.

'Which way are you going?' Theo asked. 'I'm heading for Green Park.'

'Green Park. Fine,' said Anna, who'd been meaning to go to Westminster.

They skirted the edge of the park, along Horse Guards

Road. Lights were still glowing through scrappy net curtains in the windows of the government buildings alongside.

'Do you work terrible hours?' Anna asked, thinking of the people still at their desks.

'Yes, pretty much,' acknowledged Theo with pride. 'It's very unpredictable. You can get called in any time and you have to go. I end up cancelling a lot of stuff. I'm a hopeless guest. But that must happen to you too, in your job?' He checked his phone to make sure he hadn't missed any calls while they'd been in the bar. There were none.

'Yes, sometimes,' said Anna, who wished she were more indispensable than she often found herself to be. The long train journeys and overnight stays in cheap hotels that her job required never seemed to have the great urgency and importance that she had imagined.

'All part of the fun,' said Theo, and he sloped a heavy arm across Anna's shoulders. Anna let his arm lie there for a while as they walked along. At first it felt awkward, as though she was weighed down by this extra limb that didn't belong to her. It was a gesture of easy familiarity from someone who she was not that familiar with, and she wasn't sure how to respond. She broke away as they waited near the traffic lights to cross the Mall, thinking how strange the two of them must have looked walking along together: Theo with his loose-limbed stride and she, her head somewhere level with his armpit, skip-hopping to keep up.

The path that led towards Piccadilly along the edge of Green Park was narrow and the street lamps cast intermittent pools of light along it. Anna was glad that she wasn't walking down the path alone, and when Theo slumped his arm across her back again, she wrapped her hand around his waist in return. His steps slowed to nearer her pace. Under one of the street lights he stopped and turned towards her, one large hand resting on her shoulder, holding her at arm's length and looking closely into her face.

'You're very lovely, you know.'

Anna laughed. This was half a bottle of white wine talking, and in any case she could imagine that he had said this to every woman, including Julia, probably in exactly the same spot.

'Thank you,' she replied, and started to walk on towards Piccadilly. They were nearing the lights and the hum of traffic, the brakes of buses creaking.

'No, you really are,' he continued, as though she had denied it. 'You should take a compliment.'

'I did. I said thank you.' Anna wrinkled her nose and thought that his trying to spin her really wouldn't work. 'That's very kind.'

'Not kind,' said Theo, 'true.'

They reached the steps to the passageway that led under Piccadilly to the Tube. Anna made to say goodbye, preparing to scurry towards the train home. Theo caught her briefly, a hand on each shoulder now.

'Are you going west?'

'North,' said Anna. She stretched up on tiptoe to kiss him on the cheek. She was moving her head away to brush his opposite cheek in farewell when Theo contrived to meet her in the middle, planting a kiss full on her mouth. Anna didn't pull away, but held there and was surprised to find herself returning the kiss. Words floated through her mind that now seemed very far away from her body. *Unprofessional* was the first word that she saw, as if written as a caption on a screen below a picture of her. *Crossing a line* was the phrase she saw next. Could you step back again from a line, once it had been crossed? She stepped back, as if to try. She said goodbye and almost ran down the stairs and through the hall towards the ticket barriers, fumbling for her Tube ticket. She turned and waved to Theo who stood outlined against the trees of the park. Then Anna set her face firmly towards the northbound platforms, leaning on the handrail of the escalator, and resolving not to look back again.

# IO

ANTHONY LUCAS WAS the only person sitting at a table laid for seven. The wine glasses caught the spring sunlight that shone through the wooden slats on the blinds and created striped shadows on the white tablecloth. The waitress had fussed over him, helping him to the table with such concern that he had snapped at her.

'I'm not so old that I can't sit down in a restaurant by myself.'

She had rushed away with an apology, but returned a minute later with the menu, and came back again after that, offering him drinks and a basket of bread. Anthony had ordered an aperitif, just to keep her away for a while.

Mark saw his father first through the glass of the large conservatory that formed the dining room of the restaurant. Mark was rushing down the road with Jack in a buggy while Emily drove around the side streets of north Oxford with Bella, trying to find somewhere to park. They were already fifteen minutes late. Jack was complaining loudly about being shoved hastily into the buggy. He wanted to walk; he wanted to walk everywhere, now that he could, but Mark was trying to tell him in terms that his son couldn't really understand that they were late for Grandpa, and that Grandpa didn't like people being late, and that besides, Jack still walked very slowly indeed. Nor did he have time for Jack to dawdle and look at every flower he passed, every bit of rubbish on the pavement, every bird and plane that had to be pointed at in the sky. He loved walking with Jack, but now was not the moment.

Mark was aware as he entered the restaurant that he was keeping up a running commentary on all of this out loud, ostensibly for Jack's benefit, but in fact he was talking to himself. The waitress showed them through the room to their table, relieved that someone had arrived to join the older man who sat on his own as the room had started to fill up with families and couples sharing Sunday lunch.

Anthony appeared to be somewhere far away by the time they arrived, looking through the glass at the trees outside and the road beyond. Mark worried that his father always seemed to look smaller each time he saw him, as though seen from a slightly greater distance than before. The green-brown tweed jacket that he had worn for as long as Mark could remember was starting to look bigger on his frame. Mark realised that it wasn't actually the same jacket: he knew that his father had several, all bought from the same gentlemen's outfitters, in his wardrobe, and that identical jackets had succeeded each other over the years. He thought of asking whether Anthony was eating properly, but he decided that was not a good place to start. Instead, he apologised for being late, and tried to bend Jack's chubby, recalcitrant legs in their blue dungarees into the high chair that stood at one end of the table.

Anthony reached over to take hold of his grandson's hand, clutching the small smooth fist in his fine, liver-spotted fingers.

'Hello, young man,' he said, and with his other hand reached for the basket of bread. 'Eat this, it's good.'

Jack didn't need more of an invitation, grabbing a roll and starting to worry away at the crust with his new teeth.

'He has a good appetite,' Anthony said. Mark was relieved that someone met with his approval.

Bella came skipping down between the restaurant tables, causing a waiter to swerve out of the way with a large tray of drinks. She was wearing new boots and purple tights that made her very proud. Emily followed closely behind, bearing the huge bag full of toys, beakers and supplies that accompanied them everywhere. Emily was always the one who made sure that the right things were in the right places. It was harder now they had to be in the constituency most weekends; Emily, Mark had discovered, wasn't above some subterfuge to persuade the children that their favourite things always made the journey with them. He was not to tell Jack, he had been sternly advised, that there were two Pigglies, only one of whom lived in London.

Bella ran straight up to her grandfather and threw her arms around him. Anthony put down his gin and tonic, kissed her on the top of her head, and ruffled her hair.

'Look at my boots, Grandpa,' she said, stretching her legs out one after the other to show him.

'They're beautiful,' he said, admiring them. 'You look very smart.'

Emily lifted Bella into a chair and handed her a colouring book and a packet of crayons. She was a careful child, and drew with a concentration that she didn't like to be broken. Mark had learnt the hard way that offering to help by filling in a space in a colour she didn't approve of, or worse still, going over the lines, was something that would make Bella very upset.

Emily turned to Anthony.

'So, did Mark tell you that he was in Berlin this week?'

Anthony nodded, and sipped his drink without replying.

'It must have changed a lot,' she continued. 'What was it like, Mark?'

'Very different,' he began. 'They're rebuilding everything, and refurbishing anything that they're not rebuilding.'

'Again,' muttered Anthony, and shrugged his shoulders.

'I think it will be better this time,' Mark replied. 'Some of the architecture is amazing. The new Reichstag has a beautiful dome, it's this sort of spiral with mirrors . . .'

'We'll see,' said Anthony. 'They've had too many grand plans before. They were never good. There was Germania. There was Stalinallee. Maybe it's time just to leave people alone without some big scheme to make their life better.'

'Have you thought of going there, just for a visit?' Emily asked. Mark tried to catch her eye, shaking his head slightly in warning. He'd had this conversation before. He looked to the waitress to bring the menus, hoping to avert it.

Anthony drew a deep breath.

'Emily, my dear, I left that place because it was a prison, and I wanted to live in freedom. Why would I go back to the prison, even if they have opened the gates now and let the prisoners free? It will still seem like the same prison to me. You are very lucky not to have to understand such things.'

Bella looked up from her colouring.

'Why is Grandpa going to prison?' She looked serious.

'He's not, lovely, don't worry,' said Mark. 'He's just talking about somewhere a long time ago.'

'In the olden days?' Bella asked.

'Yes,' said Anthony, 'Grandpa is from the olden days.'

They turned to the menus, and were starting to discuss whether they should order before the others arrived, when Rachel and Chris finally appeared, flustered and effusively apologetic, with an involved story about roadworks on the motorway and a diversion. Mark was relieved that his sister was for once less reliable than him, and suspected that the diversion story was cover for her having overslept.

Mark struggled to remember the last time he'd had more than enough sleep. Even enough sleep would have been an improvement. His nights were chipped away from both ends. There were the boxes and the dinners, the late votes where he spent hours sitting in his office or milling about in corridors, when he wished he could have been at home. Jack still often woke in the early hours, and often Mark found it hard to get to sleep again. Instead, he'd put Jack back to bed and get up himself, switching on the radio in his study and listening to the World Service, trying to get more of the work done. No matter how little he slept, it seemed there was always more of it. He'd promised himself he'd use the time better, come up with some of his own ideas, write articles about policy. Wasn't that meant to be why he was doing this, after all? But somehow it seemed that the ideas would not come, and the articles he supposedly wrote were drafted for him by someone else, for his approval, in words that were bland and hollow.

Mark was glad to see Rachel. His sister's presence always meant that his father softened, whereas when it was just him, they inevitably butted up against each other in argument. Anthony never seemed to criticise a building that Rachel had designed in the same way he would have taken apart an argument that Mark put forward, a policy that he supported. Chris hadn't been around for all that long, maybe a year or so, but Mark liked him too. He was a skinny, soft-spoken man who did something to do with the Internet that Mark didn't entirely understand, though Chris had often tried to explain it.

Emily offered to drive back to London, so Mark poured himself a second glass of wine. When they'd finished the roasts, and Jack had smeared chocolate ice cream all over the table of his high chair and was threatening to pull off the tablecloth with his sticky fingers, he was grateful that Emily suggested they all go for a postprandial walk through the Parks.

Anthony pulled a peaked black cap on to his balding head against the fresh wind as they walked along the path. Mark walked with his father as Bella ran on ahead of them, shouting back that she remembered this was the park with the ducks. Bella had secreted some pieces of bread from the restaurant in her coat pocket, and was deciding precisely how many she would share with Jack. Rachel ran along with Bella. Emily held Jack's hand as he toddled, and talked to Chris.

'I met some people in Berlin who were great admirers of yours,' Mark began.

'Really?' Anthony affected surprise.

'Yes, their minister had read your work. So had quite a few of the students I spoke to there. They had questions about it that I couldn't answer.'

Anthony didn't seem surprised by his son's inability to explain his work.

'I wanted to ask your advice about something,' Mark said. 'I'm not sure I should really be talking about it, so it mustn't go any further.'

Anthony shrugged.

'Who would I tell? Now your mother isn't here.'

'They want us – Britain – to return some files that we took. They would tell part of the story of who worked for the Stasi in other countries, in Britain. I think they're right, that we owe them the truth; but everyone here is telling me we need to keep them.'

'I see,' said Anthony.

'But what should I do? What's the right thing to do?'

Anthony walked on in silence for a while. They reached the edge of the duck pond, and Anthony pressed his hands together, his fingers forming a steeple in front of the bridge of his nose, his thumbs brushing against his lower lip. Ducks were swimming uncertainly in the water, staying close to the grassy rim of the pond.

'It's not as simple as that,' he said eventually. Mark dropped his head. It never was with Dad.

'Surely, though, in the interests of truth, of history, it's better that the information should be public. Don't people have a right to know?' Mark felt he was struggling. He got that sense he'd often had when he was younger, of being a slightly disappointing undergraduate who had presented his father with work that was insufficiently thought through and unclearly expressed.

'It's a very big obligation to inflict on someone,' Anthony pronounced, 'to tell people that they have a right to know something.'

'But surely they don't have to exercise that right, unless they want to?' Mark replied.

'They may not get that choice,' his father said. 'Think about it. Think of the people who find out about the people close to

82

them, their families, their neighbours. People may be happier without the truth. Do you have the right to deny them their peace of mind?'

'It's funny,' said Mark, 'there was someone in Berlin who said that, or almost that. The British ambassador.'

'He sounds a sensible man,' said Anthony. 'I know you'd expect me to say in theory it's all better, that truth is better than ignorance. In theory it is, but this isn't theory any more. So I can't really help you. Practice is too complicated. That's why I'm a theoretician.'

Mark knew the subject was closed. He saw that Bella and Jack were squabbling over the breadcrumbs for the ducks and went to mediate.

# II

IT WAS IMPOSSIBLE to walk down a corridor with Robert Callander without it taking twice the time it would with anyone else. This was particularly true on the long corridor that ran the length of the Houses of Parliament, where the carpet switched from green to red to tell you when you'd crossed from the territory of the Commons into that of the Lords. Everyone wanted something from him, even if it was just a greeting, a benefaction, or at the very least a nod of recognition. He was stopped by people he'd spoken with just the day before, who wanted to keep him updated on the progress of their discussions; he was stopped by people who hadn't seen him in months or years, who now felt it more urgent that they caught up with him and showed others that they knew him. He was stopped by journalists who wanted a quick word of guidance, a judicious piece of gossip thrown out for their use; he ignored other journalists who had displeased him, but they tried to stop him anyway, wearing the rebuff with pride. Others who wanted to appear important would charge down these corridors, papers in hand, as though they were needed urgently somewhere else, but Robert Callander had the luxury of really being needed, and of being able to choose where he wanted to be. He made a stately progress, and he knew everything that was going on.

Mark watched how Callander's air changed with each encounter: he could switch from bonhomie to disdain within a few paces. He was something to everyone, but something different to each. Mark knew that others worried which Callander they would encounter on any day or in any meeting; but now he felt confident in the warmth of Bob's approval, and noticed how that approval was reflected back at him from the people he passed in the corridor. And, he realised as he thought it, that he felt comfortable calling him 'Bob'. That must have meant either that Mark was genuinely included in the circle, or that he was one of those people who didn't know Callander at all, but claimed familiarity by using the nickname. Mark was fairly sure that it was the former.

They sat down to tea at a small table in the corner of an ornate room with a patterned ceiling and a chandelier that shone with mock candles. Mark saw that their arrival in the room was noted and remarked on by the other occupants. Bob Callander sipped at black tea that he had ordered with a slice of lemon. He was precise about which blend it had to be. Mark would have preferred coffee, but he drank tea out of politeness. It was something he'd learnt to do as a necessary condition of a political career. He had spent many years, before he'd been elected and since, sitting in living rooms and church halls, having cups of strong stewed tea pressed upon him by well-meaning constituents.

'He's very pleased,' Callander began. 'We're very pleased. It sounds like Berlin went well. I've heard you put in some excellent groundwork.'

'Thank you,' Mark replied. 'There are quite a few areas where I can see that we're all talking along the same lines. There are people there we can work with. Ilse Bernau's very impressive.'

'So I've heard.' Bob Callander never admitted to hearing something for the first time. He spread a scone with jam and looked wistfully at the dish of clotted cream. 'Better not,' he said, biting into the scone. Mark tried not to look too hard at the crumbs that dotted Callander's blue shirt as he spoke again, not waiting to finish the mouthful in case he lost the thought that had struck him.

'We're thinking that we need to use you more, in the run-up

to the summit. Have a few think pieces from you on the importance of the relationship, that sort of thing. We want to see you out and about a lot, get you some more airtime. You're fairly presentable and you can string a sentence together, not like some of them.'

'That would be great,' Mark said nodding, trying not to be over-eager, but without success. There were so many things he hoped to achieve, issues he wanted to bring to the prime minister's notice. But there was somewhere to start that seemed relevant, one thing that he might actually be able to do. 'There's one issue where I think a change would help, and which would play really well. Ilse Bernau raised the issue with me of the Stasi files – apparently we have them, files that would identify British agents who worked for them, and so far we've refused to give them back.'

Robert Callander munched on his scone without responding, so Mark continued. 'I think to give them back would show that we're serious about openness, about doing things differently. It would send a real message about change and transparency.'

Callander wiped his mouth slowly with a linen napkin.

'What's the FCO's view?'

'They don't like it. All I get from the civil servants are mutterings about compromising operational security, and it setting an unfortunate precedent in terms of national security issues. But it was more than ten years ago now, so I can't really see what harm it could do. What's the point in holding on to secrets about a regime that doesn't even exist any more?'

Callander weighed his answer carefully.

'I think this might be one where we need to consider the traditions of statecraft,' he began. Mark remembered that Callander was a professed exponent of statecraft. He had studied its practitioners, written about it, and now seemed to see himself as someone who would before long be portrayed in a gilt-framed painting like the ones surrounding them, hand on a globe and foot on a pile of leather-bound volumes. 'We shouldn't give up the information we have too readily. There might be consequences we haven't foreseen. And I think they have a point about precedent: what if the next country comes to us asking for their history back, and the next. And then wants to know what we have on them in the present day? Some of these countries may not have changed as much as you like to think they have.'

'But this isn't one of those countries,' protested Mark. 'This is Germany. The country I spend every speech calling our friend, our partner in Europe.'

'Of course, of course. I understand what you're saying. And I can see that for someone with your background, it's rather sensitive.' Callander broke off briefly, dabbing at the few remaining scone crumbs on his plate with a broad finger. 'How is your father, by the way?'

'Very well, thank you. Much the same as ever, you know.'

'The great man,' Callander mused. 'Always found him rather daunting, myself, in his quiet way.'

Mark decided not to admit that he often felt the same.

'But, as I say,' Callander continued, 'pushing too hard on this one is probably not the place for you to start. I think we'd be rather unhappy if it were.'

Mark took the warning. He didn't want the smile of bonhomie to find someone else to approve of, leaving him in the shadows of displeasure. He turned the conversation to something where he knew they would agree.

He was conscious of someone standing behind him, trying to catch Callander's eye. This was usual, but most people wouldn't have felt able to intrude onto their conversation. The tall figure leaning over him was Theo Sadler. As always, there seemed to be too much of him for the space available. Theo apologised for the interruption, and had to sink so low down to whisper in Callander's ear that he was almost kneeling next to the low tea table. Callander sent him away again, but Mark could sense that tea was drawing to a close.

Mark left the room uncertain of exactly how well he'd emerged from the conversation. He'd heard from his colleagues that that was often the result of a discussion with Bob Callander: there was praise, just enough to make you feel wanted and loved; but just enough criticism to make you feel that the affection could be withdrawn with ease. For now, Mark felt as though he belonged, in a way he hadn't since the early hours of the morning after election day, the moment the returning officer had announced his name as the winner. Mark Stefan Lucas, the duly elected Member of Parliament for the said constituency. Few people had yet asked much about the strangely spelt middle name, the unusual background. There might come a point when it was interesting, deserving of a profile, a talking point; for now, it was probably not worth drawing attention to. He walked down the corridor into the green-carpeted zone of the Commons. It felt slightly shabbier there, but more comfortable, like putting on a second-best pair of shoes.

Mark shuffled into the Chamber, stifling a yawn. His eyes ached with tiredness and he could barely read the speech that had been printed out for him. He leafed through the Order Paper and wondered how much longer he had to wait. He was all in favour of being held to account, but it didn't seem fair that he had to account for the government's policies when it was gone midnight and he'd been working since seven in the morning.

He'd escaped for a while, that was true, but he'd never heard Emily speak to him in such an ominous tone. If this was how she dealt with litigators, then it was no wonder they thought so highly of her.

'You will be back for the cake,' she had told him, her voice low and her words slow, threatening. 'There is no question about it. Do you want me to speak to the Permanent Secretary and the whips? Because I will. And if you don't, then my next call will be to Lucy.'

This was a standing joke between them, but Mark could tell

that this time Emily had meant it. Lucy was her best college friend: a divorce lawyer who was building a formidable reputation, often in high-profile cases which she wasn't supposed to talk about, but could occasionally be persuaded to mention after a few glasses of wine. Mark knew of several ex-husbands around Westminster who had Lucy to curse for their studio flats and lack of disposable income and furniture.

Because he did not want to incur the fury of Emily, not to mention Bella, or the phone call to Lucy, he'd left the office and taken the Tube home at teatime, cancelling a meeting and switching off his phone. He'd discovered that you could sometimes escape for a while if everyone thought you were in a meeting run by someone else: by the time different offices had spent an hour or two phoning each other to find out where you were, you could usually be back.

It was worth it to see Bella's face as she blew out the five candles, her cheeks puffed with serious intent. Her arm held Jack back as he tried to reach for the flames and his little mouth made raspberries as he tried to copy her and blow. She ripped the paper away from huge boxes, jumping up and down in exuberant delight when she saw the puppet theatre and the puppets that went with it. Mark sat cross-legged on the floor, resting a plate of cake on his lap as he applauded the impromptu puppet show that followed, all the while trying not to look at his watch, not to be working out too obviously when he had to leave.

Mark was doing his best to concentrate on the speaker opposite, while scratching at the trace of pink icing that he spotted on the left thigh of his trousers. Stewart Hale was a man who set Mark's hackles rising. His opinions on everything, even his appearance, seemed calculated to annoy someone like Mark, and Hale delighted in that. At least he was consistent: Mark sometimes thought that if he weren't sure what position to take on an issue, he would find out what Stewart Hale thought and decide to believe the opposite.

Hale always affected a pocket handkerchief in his breast pocket. Tonight's was turquoise, and, as ever, folded immaculately to a point. It coordinated with the blue striped shirt with a white collar beneath his three-piece suit. His dark hair, which Mark strongly suspected was dyed, was pomaded back from his forehead. Mark tried to focus on Hale's words, but found it hard. He mentioned sovereignty often; he quoted poetry, the kind of poetry they'd taught at Hale's school, but not at Mark's. Hale was notoriously long-winded, and Mark wondered what the point of this debate was supposed to be. It was notionally about Britain's position in Europe and her relationship with Germany; Hale was warning of dangers, but then he was always warning of dangers. Mark thought Hale was the opposite of a Cassandra: that his predictions were believed, but never came true. This was a little harsh, but he'd heard worse. He scribbled the thought down on the speech and decided to find somewhere to put it in his response.

Mark was starting to wonder whether Stewart Hale was deliberately spinning out his speech to make a point. The last time they'd argued – in a tea-room, rather than here in the Chamber – it had been about sitting hours. Mark had been complaining about the late nights and the hours of waiting around when he'd rather be at home with his family; Hale had fixed him with a pompous glare and told him loudly that it was his privilege to serve, and that he had no right to expect that duty to fall between nine and five.

'Why,' Hale had asked, rhetorically, on that occasion, 'do you do this, if not to serve?' Here in the early hours, Mark tried to answer the question to his own satisfaction. It was a vague answer: to change things; out of a sense of fairness and after years of watching things being done badly by other people. Because if he didn't do it, someone else would. Mark knew that he used to have better answers than this, more convincing and deeper-held ones that he had expounded on doorsteps and in meeting rooms for years without success before the success arrived. He was already forgetting what they were.

Then Mark suddenly realised he needed to listen more closely. Hale had moved on from his sweeping arcs of history and come onto something Mark hadn't expected he'd talk about. In fact, he hadn't thought Hale would know about this. He wasn't supposed to.

'Can the Honourable Member assure us,' Hale boomed, 'that any information on British subjects desired by Germany, however strongly, will continue to be held by the appropriate British authorities?'

Mark scribbled down more notes and flicked through his speech. There was nothing in it about this. He wasn't sure how he should respond. The best thing to do was to say nothing, or say something which sounded like an answer but on closer examination said nothing at all.

Hale's voice rose in a crescendo of outrage. 'Can he furthermore assure this House that any such information is and will be retained by those bodies with the respect and confidentiality that is correctly accorded to matters pertaining to national security?'

Mark looked around for someone to help him, someone who could drop him a quick note of advice or at least a reassuring look. Of course, there was no one. There were a couple of people on the opposite benches, one of whom he could have sworn was asleep at the back. On his own side, he was the last one remaining. It was nearly one o'clock in the morning and no one was listening. That, at least, was some consolation.

Hale wound up his speech with another portentous flourish and sat down. Mark heaved himself to his feet and leant on the despatch box, spreading out his papers in front of him. He trotted through his speech, grateful for the bland civil service language for once. He talked about partnership and cooperation, chucked a quick barbed comment or two in Hale's direction, and improvised an answer to the questions that had bothered him.

'I can assure the Honourable Member opposite that Britain treats our history, and that of others, with the greatest of respect and security. We do not take such matters lightly.' Mark invented his non-answer the way he thought he was supposed to. 'Of course, the Honourable Member will understand that I cannot comment here on matters of national security; and given his great experience, nor would he expect me to.' Flattery would help, with Hale. 'But I can assure him that confidential material does, without doubt, remain confidential, and that he can place his trust in those responsible.'

Mark sat down, with no more coherent thoughts in his mind than the longing for a car home and to be in his own bed, next to Emily. But, later that night, as he tried to sleep, from some-where came the intrusive idea that Stewart Hale, pompous idiot though he was, and wrong as he had always proved himself to be, knew something that Mark didn't.

# 12

ANNA LEFT THE morning conference in despond. If, as they said, you were only as good as your last story, then she clearly wasn't very good at all. Nor could she see that she had anything better in prospect. Her notebook, which should have held a list of ideas, contained nothing but unflattering doodles of the editor. She went back to her desk and looked at the blank screen of the computer and the phone that wasn't ringing as though she could will them into life, make them produce something for her.

She tried to clear a space on her desk free of old press releases and last week's newspapers. The newsroom was an unloved place where rubbish accrued in layers. She needed more coffee; the caffeine and sugar would start to make her head less fuzzy. She wanted to blame Theo for the fuzzy head, but really she had to take responsibility for that herself. It was becoming a habit, a very bad habit, and so was he.

Spreading out a newspaper as far as she could, she added one of the spare sections to a heap of think-tank reports and unread review copies of worthy books, picking up a pen so it looked as though she was working. She should have read it earlier, but she'd been late, making the morning's meeting only just before the door closed. Latecomers were not admitted. She held the pen over the page, looking for something she could circle, someone else's small story she could adopt, steal really, and follow up. Toddler eats cocaine. Couple found dead in house fire. Civil servant loses laptop. There was nothing there for her.

'Anna,' the editor had snapped at her in the meeting, 'what do you think?' She was not usually asked for her opinion. There were other people in the room whose opinions were there to be sought; opinions were what they were paid to have. This was a trap: a test to check whether she had been paying attention. She hadn't been; she'd been thinking about Theo's hand in her hair, about something he'd said and what it had really meant. It was lucky for Anna that things, this morning, connected. They'd been at a party, somewhere in Westminster, where the morning's story had come up in conversation. Anna recycled the opinion that she'd heard at some point in the evening, wondering whether to pass it off as her own or attribute it to an insider. She did both, stating it first as her own, backing herself up by claiming that lots of people in Westminster were saying just that. Well, the man at the party. Plus her. So that made at least two.

Swain, the editor, raised an eyebrow in grudging acknowledgement. She hadn't quite failed, that time. Before he could dig any deeper into her understanding, someone else took issue with what she'd said. Anna didn't feel the need to defend it; she was off the hook for now, though still hadn't overcome the general feeling of disapproval that seemed to hover in the room. Her mind drifted back to Theo Sadler. He was, after all, proving his usefulness.

The phone on Anna's desk rang, as though the willing of it to ring had actually worked. In the second between picking up the receiver and holding it to her ear, Anna entertained the fleeting hope that someone was calling her, out of the blue, with a real story. It was the woman on the reception desk downstairs; there were some people here to see her. Anna tried to think whether there was some meeting that she'd set up and then forgotten. Nothing came to mind. The receptionist asked if she should send them up; Anna decided that since she wasn't sure who they were, that might not be such a good idea. You never could tell who might have found her name somewhere and arrive with a conspiracy theory that they wanted her to prove, or an explanation of how the government was controlling their mind with radio waves which meant they had to wear a tinfoil hat. It was unlikely to be anything promising.

She left the half-empty coffee mug and the newspaper on the desk and took the lift to the ground floor. The couple standing there were hard to place. There was a young woman, slightly older than Anna, in her early thirties perhaps, and a man maybe five years older than that. They both wore suits, smart but not expensive ones, and flat black shoes. They could have worked in any office from an accountancy firm to an estate agents. Anna suddenly worried there was a bill she had left unpaid and they were actually debt collectors.

She pushed her way out through the turnstile by the reception desk and came forward to meet them.

'Anna Travers?' the woman began.

'Yes, hi,' Anna replied. 'Where are you from?'

While a man in a leather jacket and black motorbike helmet walked in the main doors carrying a padded envelope that he delivered to the reception desk, the woman took a few paces away from the desk towards the door and gestured for Anna to follow her.

'We're investigators,' the man began. 'We're . . . linked to the Foreign Office.'

Anna looked at them in disbelief, her brows pulled down into a frown. They did have a slight look of police officers about them. It was something about the shoes. She wondered if this was something to do with Theo. Surely they didn't run checks on people?

'Linked to? What does that mean?' she asked. As she asked the question, she realised that it was unlikely to get a straight answer. 'Do you have some sort of . . . ID?'

This was an even more stupid question. She had rarely dealt with people like this before, but she doubted that they carried a badge saying 'Member of the Secret Service'. That would kind of defeat the object.

To Anna's surprise, the man reached into the inside breast pocket of his suit and pulled out a business card. According to the card, his name was Nicholas Morden. There was little more information to be found there, just an official-looking embossed crest and a phone number that looked like a switchboard number. No organisation, no job title. Anna bent the card in her hand. The cream paper stock felt expensive, but, she thought, you could probably get these made up in any photocopying shop if you wanted.

'It's regarding Alex Rutherford,' he said.

Anna decided to show them in. She wondered for a moment whether it was the right thing to do, but she thought that even if they had any hard-won secrets lying around the newsroom, you'd be hard pushed to find them under all the crap. And she thought that Nicholas and his colleague were hardly likely to break out miniature cameras and start taking pictures of all the rubbish on her colleagues' desks.

She found a small meeting room in the corner, which was unoccupied. Though the room was separated from the newsroom by glass partitions, it too was scattered with crumpled newspapers and discarded paper cups. Anna sat down on one of the low seats. Nicholas and the woman sat opposite.

'When were you last in touch with Alex Rutherford?' Nicholas asked. If his name really was Nicholas.

Anna thought back. She remembered an excruciating dinner, Alex's uncharacteristic bluntness, and then silence. How long had she been in London now?

'It must have been maybe three years ago? Four?'

It was then that she decided that Nicholas and the woman, whose name, she was eventually told, was Clare, were definitely genuine. They were exactly like the people she'd met that one time before, the ones who invited her in to tell them everything she knew about Alex. That conversation had confirmed to her that she'd been right to leave him. She had been flummoxed by too many of the questions; there had been so much about him that she didn't know, even after two years. It wasn't the time or the distance from him, it was that she had never known, never thought to ask. She thought Alex had probably been right, though, to put her on the list of people who did know him best, despite everything. There weren't many people he was close to who he could have named on the vetting forms.

'Has he contacted you in any way?' Clare asked. 'Letters, phone calls? Even messages you didn't return?' She was a skinny woman with a stare that seemed to pierce through her glasses.

'No,' Anna replied. She was sure of that. He had disappeared from her radar. There had been no more postcards. She sort of missed the postcards. 'Why do you want to know? Has he done something wrong?'

'There's not very much we can tell you, I'm afraid,' said Nicholas. 'We're looking into a potential breach of the Official Secrets Act.'

Clare continued with the questions.

'Is there anything that's come into your hands that might have come from him, even indirectly?'

'Like what?' Anna was genuinely bemused.

'Information of any sort. Documents.'

She shook her head. She realised that she was getting into dangerous territory here. It was one of those concepts she had learnt theoretically and never yet had the chance to put into practice: that if someone had, hypothetically, given you, a journalist, a brown envelope full of leaked documents, you wouldn't admit to it, let alone hand it over. And certainly not to some people who turned up at your office unannounced, talking about the Official Secrets Act.

'Why is it you're investigating this, not the police?' Anna asked.

They looked at each other.

'We could potentially involve them at a later stage . . .' Nicholas began.

'But for now we like to keep things in-house,' Clare finished the sentence for him. 'So it's very important that you're straight with us right now. There could be serious consequences, otherwise.'

'I am being straight,' said Anna, prickling at feeling threatened for something she didn't know anything about.

'And have you heard anything about Alex that would give you cause for concern, through other friends, perhaps?' Clare pressed on with the questions as though she had a long list to get through in a short time.

'Because,' Nicholas continued, 'I'm sure you would be worried about him, if you heard that anything was wrong.' His questions were softer than Clare's, his tone of voice gentler.

'I'm sure I would be,' said Anna, 'if I had. But I haven't. And I told you everything you needed to know about Alex seven years ago. He is very honest, very loyal. There isn't anything more I can help you with.'

Anna stood up to show them out of the room. They looked at each other again, and then followed her.

'Can we take a phone number for you?' Clare asked. 'Home, maybe, or mobile?'

'No thank you,' Anna said. 'You can get me through the office. You found me here easily enough.'

'And you know how to reach us now, if you do hear anything from him?' Clare was certainly thorough. Anna supposed that she had to be, but it was becoming annoying.

'Thanks, yes.'

Anna made sure they left the building. She returned to her desk.

'Who were they?' asked Ashwin, who sat at the desk opposite. Anna and Ashwin were, on the surface of things, friendly, but the barricade of folders that had built up on the desk between them suggested the rivalry that lay beneath.

'Just, you know, some contacts,' replied Anna. 'Something I'm working on, long-term.'

'Go on, where from?' Ashwin persisted.

'Sorry, I could tell you, Ash . . .' said Anna.

'But then you'd have to kill me?'

'Exactly.'

He ducked his head back behind the wall of paperwork. Anna turned the earlier encounter over in her mind. At least, it confirmed something she had always assumed about Alex. When he'd asked her if he could give her name for a character reference, he'd said he was applying for the Foreign Office. It had surprised her, because it hadn't been what he really wanted to do; but then, there were plenty of people they knew who had never wanted to be tax accountants or solicitors either.

Alex had always been very vague about what he did, and the way things had been, she hadn't asked him about the details. They'd been in different countries, in different cities. It wasn't the sort of thing you asked on a postcard. There had been one awkward conversation: Alex had reluctantly called to ask her for a favour. Anna asked him, trying to make small talk, if he was going to be posted anywhere interesting, and he had just muttered that he didn't know. She supposed he could have spent the last few years out of the country and she would not have known.

She tried to picture Alex in various foreign settings, but it didn't quite work. She envisaged him in some African capital, full of half-finished concrete buildings and chaotic traffic, trying to keep cool under a ceiling fan. She thought of him attempting to keep his pale skin from burning in the sun. She switched the image to one of Alex in a Russian winter, wearing a heavy greatcoat, visiting the waxy Lenin in Red Square. This one was slightly more realistic, but still neither picture fitted with the Alex she had known. He was a reluctant traveller, at best; fond of temperate climates and places where civilisation was assured. They'd argued about it, and eventually there had come a point when they could no longer agree at all.

Anna sidled over to the desk where Dennis Neville sat. A rank of magazine files stood to attention on the front of the desk, filled with periodicals and tracts arranged in correct, chronological order. A scale model of a fighter plane defended the desk's perimeter. Defence and security were Dennis's professional territory, and he guarded it with eternal vigilance.

'Sorry to bother you, Dennis, do you have a moment?' Anna put on her most wide-eyed look.

Dennis sputtered and grumbled into motion above the pamphlet he was reading.

'Very busy,' he said. 'But go on, quickly, if you must.'

'It's about the Official Secrets Act,' Anna continued. 'I was just wondering what the maximum penalty is for breaching it?'

'Didn't they teach you that? Thought journalists were still supposed to learn law?'

'Of course. I could go and look it up. But I just thought you would have it at your fingertips.' Flattery would work. Flattery and Anna's long brown boots would work even better.

'Maximum two years in prison. Though it can end up more if you're charged with something else. Theft. Fraud. Misconduct in public office. Why? Someone leaked you something top secret?' Dennis laughed, as though this was vanishingly unlikely.

'No, no. It's just for a thing – a court case I might have to cover.'

'Which one?' Dennis snapped. 'Sounds like something I should be doing.'

'Oh, it's nothing big. Not really your sort of level. Anyway, it's all getting held up in legal argument so it may never happen. I just have to spend half the day waiting around in case it does.' Anna surprised herself with how easily she was making this up, and stopped before Dennis started demanding to take over the non-existent case.

Another image of Alex came into her mind – in a prison cell this time. She wondered how he would cope. He'd do fine with being away from the outside world, she thought, but he wouldn't be able to bear living in such close proximity to other people. It struck her suddenly that this was not just a figment of her imagination, that it might really happen. He would be destroyed by it. His parents would be destroyed by it. She didn't know what he might have done, but she couldn't conceive of Alex having deserved it. He must be all right now, less fragile; they wouldn't have hired him if he weren't fine. They must have done some kind of psychometric tests. But surely those kinds of tests couldn't predict how you would deal with that kind of pressure.

At lunchtime she went to the newsagents and picked up a slightly dog-eared postcard with a picture of the Queen on the front. All afternoon it lay on her desk as she wondered what she could write that wouldn't be immediately obvious to anyone who read it. After all, she assumed, they would be reading his post. And, she realised, she wasn't even sure where he lived.

# 13

THE WOMAN AT the front desk called everyone 'darling', from the prime minister down, greeting guests in her distinctive drawl. She already knew who Mark was, but then she made it her business to know who everyone was. She looked at him over her half-moon glasses before ushering him through the revolving doors into the newsroom. Mark was spat out of the doors into a large open-plan office with ersatz wood panelling on the walls, nearly bumping into a producer who was rushing to get through the doors in the opposite direction. She bashed the door switch impatiently, as though even a second's delay was going to ruin something vitally important, and with it her day. She huffed at the door's slowness, then looked up and apologised as she recognised him.

Mark was soon scooped up by another researcher, who marched him briskly down the central aisle of the newsroom, past ranks of journalists: some shouting into phones that they held between their ears and shoulders, their necks cricked sideways; others typing intently as they watched Parliament on TV screens, headphones immersing them in the Chamber that was in fact just across the road; others still holding animated conversations across the desks. One of the gossipers caught his eye and waved in a friendly manner. Mark wasn't sure he'd ever met the man, but he smiled and waved back anyway. Fortunately, the researcher swept him on into the broom-cupboard-sized studio that backed onto the main office before Mark had to try to recall the reporter's name.

The young woman busied herself with cables: she clipped a microphone onto the lapel of Mark's jacket. She clipped another cable to the back of his collar, and then wiped an earpiece carefully clean before handing it to him. He looked at the strange piece of clear plastic that was moulded to approximately the shape of the inside of an ear.

'You never know where they've been, do you?' he joked as he tried to fit the plastic shape the right way in his ear.

'Worse, I do know,' she laughed. Mark had an unpleasant vision of the earpiece being moved from one ear to another; he thought of his colleagues and his rivals, and the various waxy and hairy earholes that this plastic gadget had occupied. He tried to wipe the unsanitary image clear from his mind and focus on what he was supposed to be talking about.

'They'll be with you in about five minutes,' the woman said, retreating from the studio. 'If they're messing you around, come and get me.'

He looked at himself in the small monitor as he listened to a repetitive loop of music and a dull recorded voice telling him that he was being connected to the studio. His red tie was straight, his face wasn't shiny. His suit didn't look rumpled.

Mark had discovered that he was good at television. He had known he was good at making it; he didn't know he'd be good at appearing on it. He had not expected to enjoy being on this side of the camera, but he had found it easy to put into practice the tricks he had learnt from telling other people what to do over many years. He looked into the barrel of the camera as though he were looking into the eyes of a close friend, though he held the camera's gaze for a length of time that any friend would find unsettling. He had a knack for knowing when to smile and when to look gravely concerned; he could interrupt politely, answering only the question he wanted to hear. Most importantly, he could convey the message he was supposed to in twenty seconds or less, and not lurch off into ponderous subclauses.

The waiting, interrupted by occasional urgent voices telling him that they were coming to him next . . . really they were . . . two minutes now . . . allowed him to clear his mind. He tuned out all the distractions: the nagging questions about what it was, if anything, that Stewart Hale seemed to know; the piles of impenetrable documents he was supposed to understand before the summit; the perpetual question as to how well Callander and the rest of them thought of him today. Mark was glad he had shaken off Louisa at the office; he had managed to convince her he was able to walk down Whitehall and along Millbank unaided. He was happier doing these interviews on his own, without her standing over him with her colour-coded folder that reminded him of nothing so much as Bella's sticker-chart for good behaviour.

The interview went well enough for him to think he would have deserved a sticker. In any case, he knew that Louisa would be watching from the office. He was unfailingly positive about the initiative he was supposed to be pushing, he talked up the good relationships the government was building with its neighbours, he promised success at the summit, though not more than was realistic. Anyone reading a transcript afterwards would have found nothing they could disprove. He was retrieved again, detached from his wires. He followed the woman, whose name, he discovered, was Jenny, back through the office and along a tangle of corridors to the next studio. Jenny bounced along the corridors in jeans and red trainers: she never seemed to stop moving.

The only obstruction that blocked Jenny's path was the immovable figure of Hester Bradbury, who had just emerged from a radio studio, and was arguing with a producer outside the heavy studio door. Jenny shushed them, her finger to her lips, gesturing at the door. Hester and the young man stepped a few paces away from the studio to continue their argument. Mark could only catch a few words; the man, in the soft blue shirt and beige chinos that were like a uniform for him and his colleagues, was trying to persuade Hester to appear on camera. Hester folded her arms.

'I've told you, as I've already told several of your colleagues, I don't do television. Particularly not this twenty-four hour thing where I'm like a puppet on a string, talking to someone I can't see and can barely hear. I've spoken to the wireless, and I'm sure you have ways of cutting that up and putting it on the television somehow.'

'But our audience would really like to hear what you have to say,' the producer protested, without much hope.

'They can hear me on the radio. What you're saying is you want however few people watch you to see me, and I'm quite happy for them not to, thank you.' She pushed past him in the direction of the exit, seeming glad to see Mark in the corridor.

Mark watched the producer shrug his shoulders as she walked away.

'It's all very well for you,' Hester said to Mark. 'You suit that sort of thing. You look right. I look like a hefty old battleaxe, and even heftier on screen.'

'Surely not,' Mark pacified her.

'Don't be smarmy,' she said. 'I'd been meaning to talk to you.'

'What about?' asked Mark, while trying to catch Jenny's eye to see how long he had before he was needed on air again. She held up two fingers to indicate two minutes. Hester swivelled her head around, checking that no one else was listening.

'Stewart Hale is on the war-path. He's convinced you're hiding something.'

Mark shrugged and shook his head.

'That's as may be,' Hester continued. 'But he's like a terrier down a foxhole when he gets going. Doesn't give up until he's got his teeth into your leg. He wants to bring you before the committee. I'm telling him we can't just do it on some ill-founded hunch of his, but I'm not sure how much longer I can keep him at bay.'

Hester Bradbury did not give her advice lightly, and Mark knew that she was trying to help him. The last thing he wanted was to face her across a select committee room. For all that she was helpful now, once she took the chair of her committee she was notoriously unforgiving, whether questioning a political ally or an opponent. He didn't want to be questioned by Hester, let alone Hester flanked by Stewart Hale, and he didn't even understand precisely what it was they wanted to ask him about. It wouldn't look good to have the argument about giving back the files in public. Callander certainly wouldn't like that.

'Thank you,' Mark said as Jenny, impatient now, showed him into the radio studio. This was another thing to push to the back of his mind. Hester wasn't normally someone to take Hale's flights of conspiratorial fancy seriously. She'd known him too long for that. But she had the antennae to know when he had something useful to say, and that was worrying.

The green light above the baize-covered studio desk went on, and with it, Mark switched his mind over to his talking points. He answered the questions brightly and cheerfully, managing only to say what he was supposed to. He heard a tiny frustrated sigh at the end of the interview from the presenter, as he thanked him, that suggested he'd been so reserved as not to be newsworthy. Mark was grateful for that, at least.

Before he left the building, he spent a pointless few minutes being filmed walking down some stairs. He didn't complain; he'd spent enough time being the person beside the camera asking contributors to do far more stupid things than this. It was part of the grammar of television, a way to punctuate his comments, like a visual inverted comma. As he walked down the stairs past the camera, studiedly avoiding looking into the lens this time, he imagined the reporter's voiceover that would accompany it. 'The well-thought-of minister, Mark Lucas' or 'Mark Lucas, widely seen as one of the government's rising stars.' He realised it could all too quickly become 'the beleaguered minister, Mark Lucas' or 'Lucas, whose future is being called into question.' Mark hoped that the expression on his face was one of benign and generalised concern, not one of fear.

He walked the walk to the producer's quick approval – you wouldn't think it could be difficult to walk down some stairs, but Mark had seen people fail at even this – and then left the building.

# 14

ANNA SLID THE safety chain into its groove on the door and stood for a moment in the relative calm of her flat. Although the flat was small, Anna loved the glimpses it gave of the rooftops of north London and the tiny rectangle of concrete that passed for a balcony. All you could see now was the sodium-streaked sky that never grew completely dark, but she looked forward to sunny weekend mornings, when she would open the long window and sit on the wooden floor, drinking coffee and reading the papers, letting the spring sunlight stream into the room.

The light, the polish of the wooden flooring and the new-smelling white paint had almost sold the flat to Anna before the estate agent had to persuade her further. She believed what she had sometimes written herself in the paper, that this area was up-and-coming, that soon everyone would want to live here. From the balcony she could look towards more expensive roof-tops, the ones that rose up the hill in the area that had already up and come so far she could no longer afford it. Her parents, separately, had inspected the flat with her and expressed their doubts. Her mother turned up her nose at the smell of the kebab shops and fried chicken joints around the corner. Her father tried not to stare at the prostitutes who still occupied some of the nearby street corners; he did stare at the minicab offices, with their flashing yellow lights above the doors, as if the lights warned him the occupants would try to abduct his daughter. Anna had signed the papers, still gasped each month at the size of her mortgage, but knew this was a tiny square of London that belonged to her, and she to it.

She opened the door to the balcony and looked at the forlorn plants that had been struggling against the short days and the night-time frost. There was a spindly bay tree that had been a housewarming present; its leaves were turning brown at the edges. She watered the plants and rubbed the surface of the soil in a window box with a finger, wondering if the few bulbs she had planted might ever start to show signs of life. She turned to the other signs of neglect that needed to be remedied: she emptied flaccid salad from the bottom of the fridge and replaced it with freshly bought food from the supermarket; she took out the half-empty bottle of white wine and resolved it would only be used for cooking, the alcohol safely evaporated; she looked at the blinking light on the answering machine and decided against checking the message. It would only be one of her parents, complaining about the other.

Anna grated Parmesan over the chicken risotto she had cooked. It was something approaching the picture in the recipe book, a feat for which she congratulated herself. She carried the large bowl over to the sofa and ate, the bowl resting on the arm, her legs tucked up under her. Once the news had finished, she flicked channels on the television and wondered whether it was already too late to phone Alex's parents. She remembered that they went to bed early. It was a house where things were ordered and there was routine.

She found her address book on the shelf and turned the page to find the number. Patrick and Jennifer Rutherford lived in an Edwardian house in Putney; a house Anna had loved, the kind of house she aspired to. She remembered the black-and-white-tiled entrance hall, the light shining through from the coloured glass panels in the front door. The phone was on a table in the hallway, under old maps of London in gilt frames and etchings of street scenes. She realised it was such a long time since she'd dialled the number that its prefix had changed. She added the extra digit to her book. They would wonder why she was calling them now, after so long. Anna rang strangers every day, many of whom had good reasons not to want to speak to her, but this was harder. She tried to come up with a pretext, unsure of how much Alex might have told them about what was happening, even if they knew what he did for a living. Some kind of reunion, maybe?

She rang the number and waited. The phone rang for a long time before it was picked up.

'Hello?' The voice did not sound like Jennifer's. It was a middle-class, well-spoken voice like hers, but Anna remembered that Alex's mother had always answered the phone with old-fashioned formality, repeating the phone number back to the caller. This was a younger voice.

'Could I speak to Mrs Rutherford, please?' Anna asked.

'I'm sorry, they don't live here any more,' came the reply.

'Do you know where they live now?' Anna asked. She worried suddenly that they had died.

'I'm sorry, no.'

'I'm a friend of their son's. I'm trying to contact him. You're sure you don't have their new number, or a forwarding address?' Anna felt as if she was trying to wedge her foot in the front door of what was now this stranger's home.

'We're just renting. We got it through an agency. I really can't help you.' Before Anna could ask the name of the agency, the brusque stranger put down the phone.

Anna wondered how else she could find them, tried to recapture details of their lives that would help her track them down. Jennifer was a teacher at Alex's old school, that much she knew: there was a long-standing row between Alex's parents about state education versus private; it was one his mother had won. One Sunday lunchtime Anna had weighed into the argument without realising that she was going to draw the crossfire from two entrenched positions; Alex had shrunk back into himself as she held forth, clearly hating the way she had stumbled into a conflict he always tried to avoid. Patrick, a pale man who looked exactly as Anna imagined Alex would in middle age, worked for an oil company.

Suddenly alert, Anna quickly crossed the room to fetch her notebook from her bag. She wrote in it with a concentration that she hadn't managed in some time. *Jennifer – call school?* she scribbled. *Patrick – oil company? Which one? Phone books. Lettings agencies.* She tried to think who she was still in touch with, however sporadically, who might know where to find Alex, someone who wouldn't advise her against doing it, or ask why she wanted to. *Call James Rycroft*, she added to the list. She tried the last number she had for James, but there was no reply, and no answering machine. The rest would have to wait until the morning. It was too late to call anyone else, and she had resolved to have an early night.

Anna tried to think about Alex in the way the investigators were probably thinking about her: coldly, rationally. She tried to challenge the assumptions that she found herself making: she still saw Alex in London, despite her best efforts to imagine him elsewhere. She noticed how she imagined that he, too, was alone, before realising with a jolt that this might not be true, either. There might be a Mrs Rutherford, baby Rutherfords even, though surely not those yet. She drifted into sleep imagining the hypothetical new Mrs Rutherford, who appeared in her mind as a timid, studious blonde girl with glasses.

She was woken by her mobile phone ringing. She reached a clumsy arm towards the bedside table, where she always left it, charging up, in the half-hope, half-fear that she would be urgently called in by the newsdesk.

It was Theo. He wanted to see her; he was talking a bit too loud and a bit too fast. Anna let him talk for a while as she surfaced. Theo was using a voice she already recognised as his most persuasive tone, the one he used both on her and on the people at work he tried to flatter and cajole.

'I miss you,' he said.

'I miss you too,' said Anna, but she missed sleep more.

'I'll come to yours. I can be there soon. I want to see you.'

This was a rare concession; they usually ended up at Theo's – his life didn't much encompass anywhere without an 'S' or a 'W' in the postcode, SW1 for preference. It was a life that was rarely quiet or private; it seemed to be lived for a large part in a public space. She wondered what was wrong, for him to be calling her like this. He was usually the one who was elusive, the one who was too busy to meet and left things to the last minute. The trouble was, the last-minute invitations were usually enticing enough that she would go: a party she would never have been invited to; a private members' club she would never have dreamed of applying to; the kind of restaurant where you couldn't get in without booking weeks in advance. She saw a world that she would not see on her own merits, and once she was in it, Theo seemed proud of her, showing her off to the people they met as though she did deserve to be there. Those doors could quickly close again, she realised. It would be harder to get there for herself.

'Sorry,' Anna said eventually. 'I need an early night. I'll call you in the morning. I'll see you soon.' He made a slightly whimpering sound that didn't suit him, the sound of a child denied sweets. Right now, she thought that his presence, his exuberance would be too much. She was desperately tired, and she needed a night without his heavy limbs sprawling across her bed and his warm breath on the back of her neck.

Anna had been at her desk early, applying herself to her own private assignment with a thoroughness she had forgotten she could possess. Ashwin had nodded a grudging acknowledgement as he arrived at work, later than her for once; he'd hardly sat down before he was sent out again. 'There's always one more call you can make,' her grumpy editor at the local paper had told her, but many times she'd been reluctant to make it. It usually meant one more knockback; one more rejection. This time, one more call might just take her one step nearer to Alex. No one could take this assignment from her. She returned from copying down a list of P. Rutherfords in Scotland from the phone books that they now had on a computer disk in the cuttings library. There were more Rutherfords than she had expected. She found the news editor standing over her desk, looking irate that no one was there.

'When's Ashwin back?' Richard asked. He had the air of a sergeant major; Anna always felt she should sit straighter in her chair when he spoke to her, that she was being inspected and would not pass muster on some point or other.

'I think he's out all day,' she said. Richard appeared unusually distracted, and now slightly disappointed.

'They wanted him,' he said. 'But you'll do.' Anna heard the back-handed criticism long before she spotted the opportunity concealed in it.

'What for?'

'It's an investigation. We need someone to do the legwork. There's a meeting in half an hour.'

'Investigation into what?'

'It's a big project. Go to the meeting and find out.' With that, Richard left.

The list of Rutherfords lay in the notebook on Anna's desk. In half an hour she could call at least some of them. She picked up the phone and dialled a number in Aberdeen.

Anna was the last to enter the corner office, with its plate-glass window that gave onto rooftops and railway tracks. It wasn't that she was late – in fact she had been sure to arrive a couple of minutes early – but there had evidently been an earlier part of the meeting which hadn't included her. The seats around the editor's desk were taken.

She leant against a filing cabinet at the edge of the room, quickly aware that she had walked in on an argument that continued as though she were not there. The editor, Michael Swain, was pressing his fingers into his temples in exasperation.

Ian Phillips had contorted his long frame into one of the squashy chairs on the opposite side of the desk. He sat with one leg stretched out ahead of him, the other folded; the way his foot twitched showed he too was frustrated by the way the discussion was going. In the other chair, Dennis Neville was leaning forward, trying to make a point.

'I just think that if something looks too good to be true, then it probably is,' Dennis interjected.

'Remember the Hitler Diaries,' muttered Ian Phillips. 'None of us would survive something like that. The paper might not survive either.'

'Are you asking me to believe,' Dennis continued, 'that this has just landed in our laps for no reason; that even if it's authentic, which I very much doubt, that someone doesn't want it out there. We'd just be serving someone else's purpose, and we don't know whose.'

Michael Swain breathed out a sharp sigh.

'It is so like the two of you to get deep into the conspiracies before we've even looked at the basics. I know all the problems. We might be running a huge risk. We will no doubt get all sorts of flak from your Westminster friends, Ian. We'll probably get slapped with a D-notice or an injunction from some of your cloak-and-dagger mates, Dennis. But the way I see it is that this is why I get up in the mornings, this is why I bother. It has the potential to be a massive story, and if neither of you can see that without seeing all the reasons we shouldn't do it, then I don't know why you come to work in the mornings either.'

Swain leaned back in his chair, folded his hands behind his head and splayed his elbows wide, a gesture that demarcated his territory. This was where he was in charge. The two other men sat subdued. Anna shifted uneasily from one foot to the other. Michael Swain looked up and seemed to notice her for the first time.

'Which is why we need someone to do some very thorough groundwork on this. It needs to be double-checked, triple-checked.'

He stared at Anna, as though one long, severe look could gauge whether she was able to cope with the detail. Anna returned his stare.

'Yes,' she said. 'Can you bring me up to speed on what exactly this is?'

'This goes no further than this room, you realise?'

Anna nodded several times in quick succession.

'We've come by something that purports to be a copy of files from East Germany, Stasi files. They're the names and codenames of agents in the West, agents in Britain.' Michael gestured towards Phillips and Neville in front of him. 'I want these two here to concern themselves with standing it up, and dealing with the fallout we're going to get. It needs to be a bit higher level than just ringing the press office. I've got Foreign dealing with the German side of things. Your job is to go through it line by line and see what we can actually find out from it. Who these people are, or were. Where they live. What they have to say for themselves.'

Anna felt her pulse quicken as if she was about to start running a race that she hadn't trained for. She saw her two senior colleagues exchange glances, doubting that she was up to it and sceptical about the whole plan. The room suddenly felt colder. She had imagined that if an opportunity like this ever presented itself, that she would feel exhilarated, but instead she found herself terrified of the consequences of getting it wrong, gasping at the huge plummeting possibilities of failure that had opened up before her.

'The disk doesn't leave the office,' the editor continued. 'You don't make printouts and leave them lying around on the photocopier. You don't talk to people outside work about what you're working on. And even your colleagues don't get to hear about it before we're sure that we're running it. It will be round half the pubs in town in a minute. Do you understand?'

'Yes, of course,' Anna answered. She stepped towards the desk to pick up the padded envelope that held the disk.

'You do speak German, don't you?' Swain asked, offhand, as if everyone did.

'Um, conversationally,' Anna replied, hoping that a summer's exchange visit to Heidelberg and a GCSE would do. She didn't recall, though, any of the stilted characters in her textbooks discussing spies in East Germany. 'I worked on some stories like this,' she volunteered. 'In Prague. They called it lustration. Uncovering who the informers had been, I mean.' There was a slight nod from Swain that didn't encourage her to give him any more details.

As she sat at a desk just outside the editor's office, waiting to log in to the computer that she'd been told to use instead of her normal one, Ian Phillips approached. Anna smiled up at him, hoping for encouragement.

'I've seen you around in Westminster a bit, haven't I?' he asked.

'That's right, probably. I'm interested in politics. I covered the by-election. I'd love to come down there and talk to you a bit more . . .'

'Oh, yes, the by-election,' Ian cut her short. 'Just be aware that being interested in Theo Sadler and being interested in politics are not the same thing. And the main thing Theo Sadler is interested in is himself, and a close second, women. Not just you.'

Anna felt as though she was shrinking. She could not think of the words to reply.

'He won't hear about this story from me,' Ian continued. 'It's way above his level. And he had better not hear about it from you.'

Anna shook her head.

'No. No, of course not. I wouldn't—'

'I'd have no qualms about getting Swain to take you off this,' Phillips continued as though she hadn't spoken, 'or about telling him why. In fact, I have my doubts about you doing this at all.'

He gave Anna one last appraising glance before he wandered back across the office to commiserate with Dennis.

# 15

'SOMEBODY WARNED ME about you today,' Anna said idly. It was not something she had meant to say, and for a moment she thought Theo had not heard her. He was lying on his back, his eyes half closed. Anna looked at his eyelashes: they were long and black, almost girlish; they softened his face. Theo's eyes started open, the eyelashes flicking back in surprise. He had been listening, after all. He rolled onto his side and hoisted himself onto his left elbow.

'Warned you?' he laughed. 'About me? Who? Why?'

'I couldn't possibly comment . . .' Anna began.

'Go on, tell me,' Theo cajoled.

'I never reveal my sources,' she replied, rolling on her side to mimic his pose. She pushed her hair back from her face and then stretched her arm towards Theo's chest. Theo caught her wrist in his hand, his fingers easily encircling it.

'Not so fast,' he said. 'You don't get out of it that easily. And you always play with your hair when you're trying to avoid a subject. It's one of your things.'

'I'm not telling you,' Anna said, pulling her arm back towards herself. His hand followed with it.

She lay back again, listening to the CD that was playing. It was something she didn't recognise but was probably supposed to, a disaffected woman's voice singing over a soft electronic backing, the kind of music Anna vaguely knew you were meant to hear at sunrise on a beach after staying up all night. She only ever heard it here, in a flat somewhere off the Earl's Court

Road, where you heard the rumble of buses and late-night customers leaving takeaway cafes instead of the roar of waves. Over the music there came a loud clattering from another room, the exaggeratedly clumsy movements of someone who was both drunk and trying to be quiet. She heard something smash: a mug, a glass.

'Oh, fuck,' a voice said, forgetting to be quiet, and then, 'Oops, sorry,' in a stage whisper.

'Dan's back, then,' Anna observed. 'Sounds like he's had a good night.'

'Dan's always had a good night,' Theo said. He and his flatmate went back a long way, to their early schooldays, as far as Anna had gathered. 'The old reprobate. But you don't get to change the subject that easily. Was it a girl?'

'Was what a girl?'

'The person who warned you.'

'I will neither confirm nor deny that,' Anna said. 'See, the boot's on the other foot now, isn't it?'

'No,' Theo said, 'you're getting it wrong. Neither confirm nor deny means yes.'

'Or it might not mean yes. It means neither one thing nor the other.'

'So it's a bloke, then. Who said it, whatever this palpable untruth was.'

Anna scraped her fingers through her hair again, untangling it. 'No, still not telling.'

'And you're still playing with your hair,' Theo teased. 'So I'm going to list some names, and all you have to do is say yes or no. Or to make it really easy for you, you can just nod or shake your head.' He paused to come up with the names.

'Do you do that?' Anna asked.

'Do what?'

'Drop people in it like that?'

'It's been known to happen,' Theo said, shrugging his free shoulder upwards.

'No, I'm not playing that game,' Anna replied. She stretched out her hand again and placed it on Theo's chest. She pinched a coil of his chest hair between two fingers. He started to speak.

'OK, was it . . .' Anna pulled his hair sharply.

'Ow!' Theo exclaimed. 'That hurts!'

'I said I'm not playing,' Anna said. 'Try again and I'll pull somewhere else.' She stroked her hand further down his chest, onto his flat warm stomach and the trace of dark hair that ran up towards his navel. Theo reached his arm towards her hair and down to her shoulder, pulling her closer. The warning, and whoever had issued it, was forgotten.

As Anna had sat in the cavern of the wine bar earlier in the evening, watching Theo bump his head on the low ceiling with its peeling plaster, she had started to wonder whether he deliberately brought her to places that were underground, out of view. Wine bottles enveloped in years of dust lay in a caged alcove behind her and the walls were lined with yellowing newspaper front pages in frames.

'That's what becomes of it all,' Theo said, gesturing towards the newspaper cuttings with his glass of champagne.

'If we're lucky,' Anna acknowledged. She didn't want to talk work. Tonight, above all, it was important that she didn't mention it, that she didn't let the champagne lull her into talking too much, showing off, confiding in him. She had to put Alex, in particular, out of her mind. There was something she had been wanting to ask Theo, a gambit that she hoped would lead her away from here and now.

'Did you remember me?' she asked.

'You're Anna, right? Anna Travers.' Theo looked perplexed. 'At least you were when I went to the bar.'

'Very good,' Anna said. 'What I meant is, I met you before. A long time ago. But I don't think you remember.'

Theo lowered his black eyebrows in a look of deep

concentration, leaning his elbows on the table and resting his chin on his fists as he stared at her.

'Are you sure?' he asked. 'Because I'm sure I'd remember if we had.'

Anna took a slow, considered sip from her glass.

'I'm sure. At college.'

Theo shook his head.

'No, I'm sorry. I still can't.'

You were the editor of the magazine, weren't you? Trinity term, eighty-nine?'

Theo couldn't hide the look of pride that still came over him as he nodded in acknowledgement.

'And I submitted a whole load of articles to you,' Anna continued. 'Which you then rejected.' Theo pushed his hand back through his hair as though that would help his recollection.

'Were you there?' he asked. 'In the meetings? What were they about, the articles?'

'I can't even remember,' Anna shrugged. That wasn't true. She remembered them perfectly well, the badly written stories and her clumsy attempts to make them sound significant, but it embarrassed her now to recall them. Theo placed his forearm on the wobbly table and reached a hand towards Anna's.

'Did you look very different then?' he asked. 'Because if you'd looked like you do now, I'd have noticed you.' Flattery, his eternal tactic for getting out of things. Anna had learnt that Theo was a younger, adored brother of two older sisters; he must have acquired this skill young. She pictured her younger self, hunched in the corner of a student room in an unfamiliar college, beneath the reproduction film posters, as an argument raged that she did not manage to contribute to. It was like a scruffy rehearsal for the same kind of editorial meetings she went to now, the actors practising for the roles they expected they would soon have.

'You know, the same as most of us did. Big baggy jumpers, Doc Martens. A fringe halfway down my nose that I could hardly see out from under. Probably wearing some kind of affected beret. I obviously didn't make an impression.'

'I'm sorry,' Theo said. Anna was left unsure whether he was apologising for not remembering her, or for rejecting her work. It was the vaguest of apologies, and in any case it no longer really mattered to her.

'Everyone changes, I suppose,' Anna said, almost to herself. 'Though you don't seem to have changed much. If I'd known you when you were, I don't know, fourteen, would you have been just the same?'

'I'm not sure,' Theo said, gulping at the drink in his glass and nearly finishing it.

'What were you like, then?' Anna asked.

'I was a kid, I was at boarding school. It was all very sporty. Cross-country runs and that sort of thing.' He drained the rest of the glass.

'And you weren't?' Anna prompted. 'I've got it,' she said with delight. 'I think your secret is that you actually used to be a nerd. I bet you had copies of Hansard under your bed, stacked up in date order. You stood in the mock general election. Maybe even as a Tory. You were a little William Hague!'

'No,' Theo said, drawing the word out. Anna sensed an unusual weakness in him, and she was reluctant to let it go.

'You were, I bet you were. I'll ask Dan, next time I see him. I'll get him to show me the pictures. Particularly the one with the blue rosette. That might come in handy.' Anna thought she was pushing too far. She reminded herself to hold back, not to be overconfident, over-effusive. She took another small, slow sip of her drink and tried not to remember her younger self any more, not to make the connection with the person who was always there in her mind when she spooled through those days, not to think about Alex.

But in the flat in Earl's Court, as Anna sat up and pulled the duvet around herself, trying to resist the pull of sleep, she could not help but think about Alex. Theo seemed to be asleep already, his heavy left arm stretched across the pillow on her side of the bed. She was reminded of the narrow, lumpy beds in college rooms and the hours she and Alex had spent talking. It seemed they had talked from the moment they met; from the first week, when he, in his second year of Classics, had been assigned to show her, a new arrival, around. They had talked about everything, as they ate slice after slice of toast and drank so much coffee they could hardly sleep. They had talked about the books they had read and the ones they ought to have; about the ideas they were trying to understand and the world they felt they were watching from the edges.

A year later they had sat together in the back row of a crowded, darkened television room in college as the Berlin Wall came down, their view of the people scaling the wall and chipping away at it obscured by the heads of the other students, the voices of the East Germans and the astonished reporters half muffled by the constant chatter and debate in the room. The argument they had had during the weeks that followed was one of the things that started to chisel away at their closeness.

'This makes you afraid, doesn't it?' Anna had observed late one night, when they'd watched fireworks and celebrations on the news. She didn't understand Alex's mood: she was sharing the elation. These things didn't happen in the world she had grown up in; they never would, and there was no cause for them to. 'You don't like change,' she had pronounced. 'That's your trouble. But if there weren't change, if countries and governments and civilisations didn't come and go, you'd have nothing to study. You just don't want to be there when it happens.'

'You just don't know,' Alex had murmured. 'It could all go wrong. We don't know yet.'

'Are you going to say the thing about the French Revolution and it being too early to tell?' Anna asked. 'Don't say that.'

'I wasn't going to,' Alex snapped. He fell silent, and Anna did not continue the conversation that night. It was a conversation that she wished now they had continued. She wondered if he believed even more strongly, these days, that things were liable to go wrong with the world, and what secrets he might have seen to confirm that view.

It had become their routine to meet in the same sandwich shop, at a point halfway between the libraries where they each spent their mornings. One lunchtime in their final year, while more countries were collapsing and Desert Storm was raging, Anna arrived to find Alex already eating the same tuna sandwich that he always ate. He liked to order the same thing, he said; it meant fewer decisions to make, more space in his head for thinking about what he was trying to revise. Anna went to the counter, wavered for so long between the options that the man behind the vitrine started to tap the butter knife on the chopping board with frustration. Her sandwich eventually chosen, she carried it over to the high table where Alex sat looking out of the window onto the narrow cobbled street. Anna clambered up onto the barstool next to him, put the sandwich down and rummaged in her bag. She pulled out a newspaper from between the books and showed Alex the page where she had circled adverts.

'What do you think?' she asked. 'For next year? English teaching, or writing for the newspaper? Or both? If I were to get both, which is probably unlikely.'

Alex wiped mayonnaise away from his lips with a paper napkin and looked down at the blue biro circles.

'But they're in Prague,' he began. 'I can't think beyond the exams, let alone what happens after that.'

'Yes, I know,' Anna said with excitement. 'It's all happening there, apparently. It's like Paris in the twenties.'

'I can't go to Prague,' he said, his mouth still full of half-chewed sandwich. 'I'm interested in Roman *Britain*. All the places I want to study, all the funding and everything, they're here. I can't work in . . . whatever languages they speak there.'

'Czech. Or Slovak. Though Latin is still Latin, wherever.' Anna shook her head. 'I wouldn't expect you to. I know you want to stay here. But you could come and visit. I'd come back and see you.'

Alex left the remains of the sandwich on his plate. Anna would always remember the shocked, distant look in his eyes, as though she had become someone he hardly knew.

'Paris in the twenties,' he repeated. 'Why can't you ever be here, and now, in the real world, the world that you have?'

'Oh, whereas your world, your thousands of years ago world, that's real?' It was a cheap shot which Anna regretted as soon as she'd said it.

Alex pushed the barstool back, picked up his satchel of books, and put on his coat. He wrapped his scarf tightly around his neck and left the cafe. Anna sat in the window and watched him go from behind glass. Alex bowed his head against the cold outside and tucked his chin into the scarf. He did not look back at her. He refused to speak to her again, not even at the graduation ceremony.

Anna put her hand on Theo's shoulder and gently shook him awake. He muttered something in his sleep that she did not understand, words that didn't make sense. She pushed his shoulder harder. She cast a brief glance across him at the phone lying on his bedside table, switched on as always, and the pager that was there too. She wondered for a moment what she might find if she checked it, listened to his messages. Anna thought better of it: there might be things she wanted to know, but she expected she might also find things she probably didn't want to know. That was what Phillips's warning had meant, after all. Theo woke, with a blink and a snort.

'I have to get home,' she said. 'Got an early start.'

'Don't go,' he mumbled.

'Have to, sorry,' she said. 'You know how it is.'

'At least let me get you a cab,' Theo said, his arm fumbling for the phone on the table.

'It's fine,' Anna said, searching for her clothes that lay in dark heaps on the floor.

'Are you sure?'

'I'm sure.'

'Be careful, then.'

Anna crossed to the other side of the room, kissed Theo on his springy hair, and let him go back to sleep.

# 16

IT WAS THURSDAY afternoon and it was already later than Mark had wanted to be in the office. If he didn't get going before long, he would hit the worst of the traffic on the way to the constituency. So when Louisa in the private office told him there were people here to see him, he tried not to get angry with her. He didn't want to be one of those ministers he heard about with a reputation for a terrible temper and for treating their staff badly. Word got around in the civil service quickly. It had been a long week, though, and this was enough.

'Louisa, I didn't know there were any more meetings today. It wasn't in the diary. Sometimes you have to say no to people. It's part of your job. You can't keep over-scheduling me like this.'

She looked hurt. Mark wished he hadn't reproached her.

'I'm sorry. I wasn't expecting them either. I would have told you. They said it was important.'

She leaned over to him with a stage whisper. 'They're from SIS. I didn't think I could say no.' She showed them into the room – an older man and a younger woman. They looked just like any other officials, but they carried no papers. Mark indicated to Louisa that she should leave. The man began by telling Mark that he was concerned. Mark had days where he wanted, just for a change, to meet people who weren't concerned about anything, and this was turning into one of them.

'Can you tell me what this is about, please? Plainly, if possible.' He felt fractious and impatient.

It was the woman who replied. 'We're worried that you've been going further than your policy sets out,' she began.

'It's us who decide about policy,' Mark retorted. 'You're supposed to work for us, not the other way around.'

'We're not querying the policy,' she continued. 'We're happy with the stated policy. But some of your recent comments have been going beyond it, and we want some reassurance about that.'

'Is this about the German files?' Mark wanted to be sure that they were talking about the same thing, before he fell into some carefully laid trap.

'That's it,' the man said.

'This is precisely the kind of thing I knew I'd come up against. This is what I expected,' Mark began. He was about to begin one of the speeches he'd prepared in his head for just such an occasion, but he didn't have the energy to declaim it. 'To be honest,' continued Mark, 'I can say all I like about them, but if I don't have the bloody microfilms or whatever they are in my hands, there's fuck all I can do about giving them back. Though to be honest, if it were up to me, I would. Though you wouldn't, and everyone else I seem to talk to wouldn't. God knows why.'

They listened to his outburst in silence. Mark knew this wasn't the way a minister ought to behave. Please let this spook not say something like 'commendable honesty, Minister'. He didn't think he could take any more oblique, polite conversations.

'Well, if you put it like that, Minister,' the man replied, 'we can't give them back, even if we wanted to, so nor could you. Because we don't have them. Not all of them, anyway. They've been lost.'

'Lost?' Mark repeated, in disbelief. 'You can't just lose things, can you? Don't you have . . . I don't know . . . gadgets? Procedures?'

'Not as many gadgets as you'd think. But we do have procedures. And just like anywhere else, we have people, and they make mistakes.' This was the woman speaking now. She had a calming voice.

Mark blurted out more questions that they didn't appear to have the answers to, or else they were answers they were reluctant to share with him. They would not tell him who had lost the files, or how, or where they thought they might be now. They gave him stock forms of words about an internal investigation being underway, that there were currently no grounds to believe this to be the work of hostile forces. Mark thought that one was deliberately designed to send his thoughts in the wrong direction. Which hostile forces would want something like that, these days? Which hostile forces were left, anyway? This couple looked almost too young to remember the Cold War; they were probably still at school when the Wall came down, but they talked as though they had spent their careers staring through binoculars across barbed-wire fences. This was why these people needed to be brought out into the daylight; they were still living as though nothing had changed and they were all training their binoculars in the wrong direction.

When Mark had run out of questions to which they could provide unhelpful answers, he decided the meeting was over. They left, to rejoin the stream of civil servants finishing work for the evening.

Mark turned away from his desk and walked towards the window. He put his forehead on the cool glass and banged his head repeatedly against the pane.

Anna almost laughed each time she unlocked the drawer in the desk where the disk was kept. It was a pretty rudimentary form of security – she knew from experience that the desk drawers could be prised open with little more than a table knife and a bit of ingenuity. Mainly she laughed, though, because it seemed so impossibly unlikely that you would label a top secret disk with the word 'Secret' printed repeatedly around the rim of the disk's white label. Particularly to label them 'Secret' and then leave the files themselves unlocked, unencrypted.

Anna imagined that if someone had just written something

self-deprecating on the front – 'Holiday photos: Bognor Regis' perhaps or 'Annual expenditure spreadsheet: please return' – the files would never have arrived at the newspaper. She would not be sitting in front of this screen, her eyes aching, waiting for the disk to slide into its tray and for the computer to whirr and sputter into action.

Michael Swain emerged from his office as the computer was still firing up; he beckoned her inside. The editor looked at her with another of his penetrating stares that made her want to apologise before he had even asked her a question.

'What have you got?' he began. Swain spoke precisely and directly, and he expected answers in kind. He was not someone for small talk; it made him less at ease, rather than more. Anna had rarely spoken to him before she started work on the project; she was just starting to understand all this at first hand.

'I'm working through it,' Anna said. 'The only names I've been able to confirm so far are people who are already dead. One was a trade unionist, but not a big name. Someone pretty junior. There are some other names where I'm trying to find the right person – they're Browns and Joneses; it could take a while.'

Swain asked the name of the trade unionist and shrugged when she told him.

'We need more. We need it soon. I can't go with it on the basis of what you've got so far.'

Anna was persisting, though; she had no choice but to persist. She compiled a list and saved it on the computer. She had amassed a pile of reference books that she stacked around the edge of her desk – a *Who's Who* and a German dictionary were the bulkiest two and the ones she consulted the most often. She checked the names, she checked her wobbly translations. She made phone call after fruitless phone call trying to create connections between real, present-day people and the names in the files. She didn't list all this; he would take it for granted.

It was painstaking work, and Anna was torn between taking the pains it required and with rushing, skimming through the files in order to come up with what she knew they wanted. They wanted a scalp, someone people had heard of; someone whose name would sell papers when it appeared on the front page. So far all she had come up with were obscure officials, misguided students who had not gone on to become anyone of significance, and former Communist Party members who were either long since dead or impossible to trace. They could make something out of it, but it wasn't as big as they needed it to be. Anna longed to find someone with a distinctive name that leapt out at her, where there could be no possible confusion about whether the name in the file and the person she had to track down were one and the same.

'Do we think it's authentic?' Anna asked. 'What do Ian and Dennis say?'

'They're not getting anywhere with it either; though between you and me, I'm not convinced they're trying that hard. What do you think?'

Anna hesitated, framing the sentence in her head before she said anything aloud.

'I don't understand why someone would go to all the trouble of faking something like this without making it more obviously exciting. Without sticking big names in it where we'd see them straight away.'

'But if you were clever, perhaps you would, for precisely that reason? So that someone like you would think that?'

'But what would be your motivation? Whose interest is it in to create some fake files that we've never even heard of?'

Swain, unusually, didn't have a ready answer. Anna sensed that she had his grudging approval, but she wasn't sure it would last. She tried a question while it did.

'How did we get this, anyway?'

Swain just shrugged in reply. He had reverted to being enigmatic.

'A whistle-blower?' she persisted.

'Nice try, but I'm really not going to say.' Swain looked severe again. He pushed his hands through his close-cropped hair, though there was little of it to push back. 'I need you to come up with something more. Quickly. I want to go with it, but I can't unless you've got something solid. If you need help, tell me honestly, and I'll put other people on it with you.'

'I'm fine,' said Anna. If there was going to be credit for this, she wanted to keep it for herself. She worried that she didn't have long to come up with something more impressive, before they took the work away from her and gave it to Ashwin instead. She was sure he would be more systematic, more impressive, would find the kind of names they were looking for without appearing to flail so desperately.

She nearly told him then about the investigators, but she didn't want to tip Swain's mood back into dangerous territory. She thought of the business card they had given her, still somewhere in the debris of her usual desk, half hidden under some paper clips, Post-it notes and chewed pens.

Anna felt as if she was trying to piece together a huge jigsaw without being able to look at the picture on the front of the box. She couldn't get a sense of what exactly it was that she was trying to find. She laboured over the small details, as though she were building up a small patch of what might have been sea or what might have been sky, not knowing whether her ultimate aim was to complete a country landscape or an image of a storm at sea. She remembered a tutor at college once telling her disparagingly that 'Your problem, Anna, is that you can't see the trees for the wood.' He had been right, she supposed. She was happier knocking things into shape than working on them piece by piece.

As she tried to concentrate on the typescript on the screen, the letters blurred from the iterations of copying, a typewritten card that had become a microfilm and now an image on a screen, Anna's mind drifted back to stories she had worked on years ago. In Prague, the fun stories to do had been ones about newness and change: a bar that was opening, a theatre that was renovated and showing the plays it chose to for the first time. But there had been harder questions of how to deal with the past, questions of belonging that showed how the past couldn't just be glossed over with a fresh coat of paint and an optimistic smile. Anna had once accompanied an émigré who had returned to the country to try to buy back his ancestral home. Jan had a broad, square-chinned grin and looked like the well-fed Canadian he was, who Anna imagined had been reared on pancakes, bacon and maple syrup. His grandparents had left before the war. Jan was full of dreams of turning the crumbling, abandoned sanatorium that had once been his family's mansion into a luxury spa. He told Anna how it would attract visitors from all over the world, how he would revive his fortunes and with it the fortunes of the village where the house stood neglected among overgrown trees. She wrote the story then, with Jan's can-do quotes and his grand plans; the last she had heard, he had still been hiring expensive lawyers who spent billable hours in a variety of languages to argue the rival claims to the property. She had moved on before the case was resolved, never finding out how the story ended. There were so many stories where she never did.

Anna hoped that she would find out how these stories in the files ended: the interesting thing to her was why people had made the choices they had. It seemed so straightforwardly wrong now, but it couldn't have seemed like it then. That was the part she knew she would be able to do; she just had to get as far as finding those people and getting them to talk to her.

Alex would have been good at this. Alex loved detail, spotting how things fitted together, could tell instantly when something didn't fit a pattern or was out of a logical sequence. He could hold facts, dates in his brain in a way Anna never could.

Of course. Alex was good at this. This is what he did. This was what they had been looking for, the pair of investigators with their questions and their nasty suits. It must have been. Anna pressed escape on the document she was looking at and locked the computer screen.

She walked towards the window, feeling unsteady on her feet. Tube trains were emerging from a tunnel beneath the street; motorbikes hummed along the road. She saw the backs of buildings, the workings you weren't meant to see; the heating pipes and air-conditioning units. In the window of a building opposite, people were working at normal jobs; normal, dull, boring jobs. Every other day, she slightly despised them for working so routinely on things that, to her, didn't matter. Today, suddenly, she envied them. She was confronted with something which probably did matter, and she wasn't sure what she was doing.

Anna stood there for a while, until the floor no longer felt as if it was swaying under her. There was always another call she could make. The number had started to ring when Ashwin wandered by her new desk to ask if she wanted to come for lunch. She hung up the phone and clicked the document closed a little bit too obviously. She noticed Ashwin try to glance at the screen to see what it was she was working on.

'I can't do lunch today,' Anna began. 'I'm really sorry.'

'So what is it?' asked Ashwin.

'What's what?' she replied, though she already knew.

'This project you're working on.'

'I don't know if it's going to be anything, yet.' She tried to duck the question, but Ashwin easily spotted her politician's answer.

'Yes, you do. Because if it weren't, you wouldn't be working on it right here under Michael's nose where he can keep an eye on you.'

'It's really dull, honestly. It's something to do with Europe and defence, and they need someone to look through some hopelessly boring documents because Phillips and Neville are too busy eating lunch in posh restaurants in Westminster to do it themselves. What are you working on?' All of that was, broadly speaking, true enough.

Ashwin launched into a detailed description of the court case he'd been covering, how he hadn't managed to get nearly enough in the paper about it, how the editor hadn't given the story what it deserved. Anna commiserated with him briefly. That much they had in common: a shared feeling that their talents weren't being sufficiently acknowledged. When Ashwin left for the sandwich bar, having offered to bring her back a tuna mayo, she picked up the phone again.

It rang several times. She looked at the address she'd noted from the directory alongside the number – it was a house with a name, in a small town on the east coast of Scotland. She imagined a large Victorian manse with a view of grey sea and golf links nearby. Anna was about to put the phone down again when the receiver was picked up at the other end. She recognised the well-spoken, English-accented voice that answered, reciting the phone number she'd dialled.

'Is that Mrs Rutherford? Jennifer?'

'Speaking. Who's calling, please?' She sounded wary; either Anna's voice was not familiar, or it was.

'This is Anna. Anna Travers. How are you?'

'Anna. Good gracious. It's been a long time. Very well, thank you. And you? We keep seeing your name in the paper.' Jennifer was polite, but Anna could tell that it was a forced politeness, not a genuine delight in hearing from her. It would have taken a great deal to prevent Jennifer Rutherford from being well mannered, even to the girl who had run off, leaving the country and leaving her son heartbroken and fragile.

'I'm trying to get back in touch with Alex,' Anna explained. 'I've lost his address, and there's a college thing that we – our year – have been invited back to. One of the organisers asked me if I had his contacts.'

Anna tried to stop herself from talking too much. The more she added extra details, the more it sounded like the lie it was. There were two answers she was hoping for, and they would both begin with Jennifer saying 'Yes, of course.' *Yes, of course. He's right here. Let me pass you over. Or yes of course, here's the address, here's his phone number as well, do you have a pen?* She hoped it was the second; she didn't really want to speak to Alex. Not right now, not over a phone line that the spooks would no doubt be able to trace.

'Anna, thank you for calling, but I'm not sure I should give it to you. Not without asking him first.'

'Oh,' Anna said.

'I don't know whether he wants to be in touch with you. And I don't think he's very keen to go back to anything at college. You know that he was terribly disappointed when he left.' Anna knew that this, from Jennifer, was what passed for bluntness.

'I know,' said Anna. 'I'm sorry. But I would like to write to him, at least. Do you think you could pass on a letter, if I wrote it care of you? And then he could decide if he wanted to reply.'

'Well . . .' Jennifer hesitated. 'I suppose you could try that. I'll pass it on. But I can't promise anything.'

'Of course not,' Anna said. She listened to the address that Jennifer read out and checked it against the one she'd already copied down in her notebook. They matched. 'Thank you. How's Patrick?'

'He's very well, thank you. Enjoying the golf up here.'

'And Alex – is he OK? Is he still in London?'

'He's fine, as far as he ever tells me anything. He is in London, yes. He said something about having some time off work. I tried to persuade him to come up here for a holiday, but he didn't feel like it. I thought the fresh air would do him good.'

Anna believed that Jennifer would pass the message on; she wasn't the kind of person to promise to do something she had no intention of doing. Anna wondered, though, whether Alex would reply.

She still had the postcard she'd been meaning to send him. It was dog-eared now from being in her bag, and there were smears of newsprint on the white card, but Anna smoothed it out and wrote across the back. She sealed the postcard in an envelope and wrote the address in Scotland on the front.

# 17

THE YOUNG WOMAN holding up a sheet of white paper was obviously not the prime minister. Behind her on the wall were large portraits of women in sumptuous robes; she wore jeans and trainers. The camera lenses trained in on her anyway, tightening their gaze to bring her eyes into sharp focus, shifting slightly to gauge the precise shade of whiteness of the paper. She raised one arm, her hand indicating a point a few inches above her head.

'He's about this tall,' she said.

'Yes, I know,' a cameraman replied. 'What about the other guy?'

The producer, acting as stand-in, moved her hand a little lower. 'Shorter, I think. About here.'

The white double doors at the end of the long room swung open and the camera lenses spun on their tripods to catch the movement. The woman scampered away to take up her position next to one of the TV cameras. It was a false alarm. Julia Dyer walked into the room, her hair tied back and her blue shirt crisp. The photographers, the cameramen and the producers slumped as one with disappointment.

'It's just her, snotty cow,' one of the cameramen muttered under his breath as she marched towards them, but he smiled as she drew nearer, and asked if she could do something about the lights. Julia shrugged unhelpfully and said she'd see.

'How long are they going to be?' asked the woman in the trainers. 'They're running late, aren't they?'

'Ten minutes, maybe. I'll give you a five.'

'Maybe?' queried an older man who was still wearing his overcoat indoors. It was always cold back outside in Downing Street, the sun that shone elsewhere never penetrating the canyon between the buildings. 'We need exactly. Is there a problem we should know about?'

'No, no problems. Ten minutes, then. But watch for my signal in five, to confirm. And to check you know the ground rules,' Julia continued. 'This is really just a grip and grin, but with one question from each side. We haven't got long, and we won't take follow-ups. One UK broadcaster, one German.' There was a murmur of complaint from the print reporters who felt hard done by. Julia shrugged again, her habitual above-my-pay-grade shrug that still managed to carry with it an air of arrogance.

She retreated behind the door and they waited for her hand to be put through again, waving five fingers. The next time the doors swung open, the cameras whirred into life, tracking the prime minister and his guest as they walked across the parquet floor to the point on the Persian rug that had been prepared for them.

Mark Lucas and Ilse Bernau took a different path across the floor, at the head of a column of advisers and officials in near-identical suits who lined up against the back wall, out of shot of the cameras. Mark tried to keep up the small talk that had taken them out of the meeting room and down the corridors, but Ilse seemed to have gone silent. He wondered if she was awed by the setting, the history, then thought that was unlikely. She seemed to feel she was entitled to belong anywhere. Mark was about to lean on a table, but he glanced at the spindly antique mahogany legs of the table that held a lamp with a Chinese-patterned porcelain base and stopped himself. He took his place at the back of the room and tried to fold his hands away from where they might break anything.

Theo Sadler walked close behind the journalists, trying to catch a glimpse of precisely what the cameras were capturing.

He moved to the end of the line of reporters and tapped a stout, red-faced man on the shoulder of his suit jacket. He nodded; the reporter nodded and smiled back at him. Theo stepped to the side and took up a position just out of camera shot, but somewhere in the prime minister's eye-line.

Mark watched the prime minister and the German chancellor shake hands for the cameras. It was a practised move: the smiles; the eye contact; the heads turning towards the cameras and the smiles again. The motor-drives of the cameras chattered more quickly the more their faces grew animated. There were a couple of words he couldn't capture from the back of the room, words no one was intended to overhear unless they concerned the football, some slightly forced laughter, but Mark noticed that was as far as it went. They stood awkwardly side by side.

The prime minister pointed towards the man Theo had tapped on the shoulder.

'Jack,' he said, indicating that his would be the question.

Jack's was a short oration rather than a question, plump with subclauses and dotted with phrases from well-regarded pamphlets. Mark listened to it but still couldn't be sure precisely what Jack had asked. The prime minister bestowed one of his broader smiles on Jack and gave the answer he wanted to give, echoing the same friendly and diplomatic phrases. The other reporters rolled their eyes; there were other, sharper questions they would not now get to ask.

The chancellor pointed in turn to his favoured reporter, a bearded man with angular, wire-rimmed glasses. He spoke in faultlessly polite and fluent English.

'A question for the prime minister, if I may. Would you be able to tell us why the British government refuses to return historical files concerning Germany's recent past that are of great concern to many in our country? What progress have you made on this issue in your discussions today?'

The prime minister was still smiling but the smile no longer reached his eyes.

'Perhaps that's one for you, Chancellor?' He tried to deflect the question, unsuccessfully, and was forced to continue. 'Well, as I say, we've made huge progress on a great many areas today, we're building an excellent and, I hope, lasting relationship, but of course there are still a few areas that we hope to return to at our future meetings.' He pressed his hand gently onto the chancellor's shoulder, starting to edge him away from the reporters. The chancellor wasn't ready to be edged and interjected a short reply in German. Mark didn't catch every word, but it was basically something about having raised the issue at the correct – appropriate, maybe – levels, but how he was obviously aware of concerns at home.

'So, if that's all,' continued the prime minister, 'thank you all very much.'

With that, he propelled the chancellor towards the door, ignoring the attempts at questions that were shouted from the reporters who'd been ignored. A couple of them huddled around the German correspondent, asking for a translation. They scribbled down the comments in shorthand. Mark was swept up in the progress through the white doors. He hung back slightly to fall into step with Ilse.

'What was all that about?' Mark asked her.

'What do you mean?' Ilse tugged her jacket straighter.

'Your guy, asking that question?'

'He's not my guy,' she replied, turning to follow the convoy of suits down a staircase. 'Journalists ask what they like, you know that.'

'Sometimes,' Mark replied. 'And sometimes they ask things that someone tells them might get an interesting answer.'

'Do you think he got an interesting answer?' Ilse gave him a sidelong look.

Mark knew that he hadn't, but that wasn't the point. The point was that the question was out there with a space where the answer needed to be.

'You're not answering my question either,' Mark said, trying to keep his voice low enough and his smile friendly enough that he looked like he was just making conversation.

'Well, sometimes if you're not making any progress in private, these things need to be out there in public. We talked about this before,' Ilse said. 'You remember. I learnt a very useful English political saying once, "We must not let daylight in upon the magic."'

'That's about royalty,' Mark said, not willing to be outquoted by someone who'd learnt political institutions 101, or whatever they called it at Yale.

'Well, it's very British and it's very wrong,' Ilse continued. 'You need to let daylight in. And none of it is magic.'

When they reached the entrance hall they switched back into the polite, diplomatic conversation that was expected of them.

'So we'll see you at the lunch, then?' Mark asked, holding out his hand to Ilse.

'Yes, of course.' She shook Mark's hand warmly, enclosing it in both of hers. 'I'm looking forward to it. Is this what you call a banquet?'

'Not quite, I don't think. But it should be good.'

'I'll see you later.' Ilse turned to catch up with the rest of her delegation. 'Do what you can,' she said as she stepped out of the black door that was held open for her.

The handshakes finished and the door was swung shut again. Mark turned to walk back down the corridor, not entirely sure where he should be next and looking round for someone to tell him where he was needed. He felt foolish to have thought he would get a chance to show what he could do. When he saw Robert Callander's face he felt as though a dark cloud had blotted out the sunlight, leaving him standing in a rush of cold air.

'He's very unhappy,' Callander said. 'Very unhappy,' he repeated emphatically. Mark didn't know how he was expected to respond to this, but it seemed obvious that it was somehow his fault. 'Did you know they were going to have that asked?'

'Have it asked?' Mark hedged. 'Maybe he just asked it?'

'Don't be so naive. You know what their journalists are like. They're tame compared to ours. They don't spring things on people. It's all five honorific titles and would Herr Doktor Minister like to say something today.'

Mark thought he had no hope but to be honest.

'I didn't know.'

'Well, you should have. And you should have got that information to us before you left him standing there looking like an idiot and having to make something up on the hoof.' Mark stared at his shoes, feeling like he used to when he'd had to tell his father he'd got a bad mark in an exam.

'Well, I told you before they'd raised it as an issue. In Berlin.' It was a feeble defence, but he had to try.

'This is not what we wanted the message to be,' Callander continued, ignoring Mark's point. 'But what's done is done. Our only hope is that our hacks don't care about something that's firstly to do with history that isn't Nazis and secondly in a foreign language they don't speak. With any luck, they won't follow it up, if we throw them something else to gnaw on.'

'But what about the actual – the problem itself?' Mark suffered another look from Bob Callander that made him realise he was on the verge of falling further into disfavour.

'Our position remains unchanged.' Bob turned as sharply as his bulky frame could manage on his scuffed suede brogues and walked away. The conversation was over. Mark was about to tell Bob that the problem was bigger than he knew, but the corridor stretched between them like a chasm.

He checked that his jacket was buttoned and walked out into the street. He would smile and wave to the journalists and say nothing, and act as though nothing was wrong.

Mark had to show his face at the reception, however little he felt like being there. Emily was wearing the smile he recognised as the one she put on when she had to tolerate fools. Mark had to hold himself back from accepting the frequent refills of his wine glass he was offered, although he would rather have drunk them all down. Every conversation threatened to become an argument; there, too, he had to restrain himself. He was just beginning to wade into another debate, gesticulating to make his point, when Emily hissed at him. The music was loud – some new band that was supposed to exemplify British creativity – and he could hardly hear her.

'We need to go. I need to get back, and I'm fed up with getting back on my own.'

'I'll see you at the door,' Mark said, diving back into the room to find someone he could tell what a delightful occasion it had been. By the time he returned, Emily had collected the coats and her bag and was waiting in the entrance lobby, holding his coat out towards him. A cold draught blew in from the street as the front door opened and closed.

'It's not like you have to come to these things often,' he said, pulling out his red scarf from one of the sleeves of the coat and wrapping it around his neck. 'Not like the other wives do. I told them you had better things to do, work of your own. It's only sometimes I ask you to come. And none of them are as boring as law parties, that's for sure.'

'For you, maybe. Imagine it the other way round. Imagine everyone's always talking about who's making partner this year and the big case we won and no one would have the faintest idea if you were in the Cabinet, because they assume that all you do is make costumes for the school play, and they never ask you what you think. That's what it's like.'

'So don't come,' Mark said as they walked down the steps of the building and looked for the car. He couldn't see it. The street was busy with heavy, black diplomatic cars.

'That's not the point.' Emily followed him down the steps. 'The point is that I never realised it would be like this. That we'd never see you.'

'I never saw you when you were working late. All those all-nighters and trips to, I don't know, Frankfurt, Brussels.'

'That was before,' Emily continued. 'Before Bella.'

'Did you not realise this is what it would be like, being in government? Being a minister? It does actually matter, you know.'

'I know it matters. I just didn't expect it.'

'Didn't expect what, exactly?' Mark was angrier than he meant to be, and he knew it wasn't really Emily's fault.

'That they'd pick you. Now, or maybe even . . .' Emily stopped herself, but it was too late.

'You don't think I'm up to it?'

'That's not what I said.'

'But you don't, though,' Mark persisted.

'I didn't say that. And I don't think that. You're inferring something I never implied.'

'We're not in court now,' Mark said. 'Stop it.'

'And we're not in the Commons, either. I'm just saying what I'm saying. *You* didn't expect it. Not yet. You didn't even expect to be elected. And all this, so quickly . . . it takes getting used to, and it isn't easy.'

Mark was relieved to find the car. He had to peer in the window to check he'd found the right one. He opened the rear door before Dave, the driver, could look up from the book he was reading. Emily climbed into the back ahead of him, her face turned away. Mark stared out of the opposite window. The only sound during the journey home was the hum of the engine.

# 18

WHOEVER WAS WATCHING him was doing it badly, almost amateurishly, and Alex wasn't even making it difficult for them. For a while he had thought about leaving London, renting a cottage overlooking the sea and reading books. He had wondered about Cornwall. Somehow he had never been to Cornwall. Or maybe he would go and hunt for fossils in Dorset and look out to sea from the Cobb at Lyme Regis. He had experimented with a day trip to Whitstable, where he had wandered up and down the seafront, a sharp wind whipping at him. He stopped for a pint in a pub where he was the only customer apart from one old man with a grey fuzz of stubble, who wore his hat indoors. Alex couldn't tell whether the man was talking to himself or to his elderly Labrador. In the end, Alex wondered why he would waste the money they would not be paying him for much longer to stay there when he could stay in the comfort of the city, among his own things. There were few places more desolate than an out-of-season holiday resort. Alex had drained his pint, nodded to the man sitting by the unlit fireplace, and taken the next train back to London.

His routine now, such as it was, consisted of sleeping late and doing crosswords. He tried not to read the rest of the newspaper. He wished it was summer. Then, at least, he could have watched the cricket.

Alex stood at an angle to the window of his flat so that he was not visible from the street. He left the light in the living room switched off. The leaves of the plane tree outside were starting to emerge, green buds against the background of the peeling bark. A small figure in a dark coat walked along the pavement on the opposite side of the street. It was a woman with light brown hair, who seemed to be concentrating her attention on each house in turn, studying the door numbers. This was someone he hadn't seen before, and she didn't look like one of the usual crew.

His parents had tried to persuade him to come home. Alex's mother seemed to know that something was wrong; he hadn't told her the details, but she seemed suspicious. All he had said was that he'd taken a couple of weeks of leave. The house in Scotland, though, did not feel like home; it had never been his home. It was just another forbidding, windswept place.

Alex's parents were used to knowing very little about his life and what he did. He had never told them the truth about his job, either. You were allowed to, these days. Within limits, and within reason, Alex had been told. He had asked them what the limits were and what was reasonable. Your parents are fine, was the answer. Not your distant cousins or your most talkative aunt; not a subject for general gossip. Alex had still decided against telling them. It wasn't that they couldn't be trusted – his parents were eminently capable of discretion – it was just that Alex didn't want to burden them with having to keep his secrets. He didn't even know whether they would have approved, had he told them. He suspected that his father, pragmatic from years of trading in commodities that people needed, would have done; and his mother, who held on to a degree of idealism, would not.

As it was, they asked little about his work and he told them less. They knew that they couldn't phone him there, but they found it rather laudable that government departments didn't like you to take personal calls at the office. The only worry they expressed to him was whether he was happy. This was not what they had expected him to do, despite their relief that being something in the civil service meant at least a secure job and a good pension.

Alex stepped into the kitchen to make a cup of coffee. When he came back to his vantage point by the window, the woman reached the end of the block, looked around at the street names to get her bearings, and was turning back again. Her tread was determined, her shoulders were hunched forward as if she were walking into the wind, though Alex could tell from the tree that it wasn't windy. He was starting to change his mind about her. If she were watching his flat, she would surely not do it this obtrusively.

He looked along the line of parked cars to see if he could spot anyone sitting in any of the cars instead. He watched for delivery vans that did not appear to be delivering anything, for white vans whose drivers were unusually neatly dressed, their dashboards uncluttered with food wrappers or newspapers.

The woman stood on the pavement and pulled what looked like an A to Z out of a satchel-like handbag. She checked something on a scrap of paper that was tucked into the book and stepped out into the road, still looking at her note. Alex flinched as he saw her walk straight into the path of an oncoming motorbike that had turned the corner fast. He heard the squeal of brakes. Alex closed his eyes involuntarily as he waited for the impact of metal against flesh.

It did not come. Instead, he saw the woman jump back onto the pavement, her A to Z splayed on the road. He heard the motorcyclist curse her, his words indistinct from where Alex watched. She hitched the bag back higher onto her shoulder and held up her hands in a gesture that was only partly apologetic. The motorbike started up again and pulled away. Alex watched the woman lean forward into the road, more carefully this time, to retrieve her book. Her blonde-streaked brown hair fell forward over her face. She shoved the book back into her bag and pushed the hair back from her face again with a peremptory gesture. It was the way she grabbed the hair almost by its roots as she swept it back, as though she could make her hair stay where she put it by force of will alone, that Alex recognised.

She had found him. Alex was torn between wanting to carry on watching her and wanting to hide. It would be better to hide, but if he pulled the blind shut, she might notice. He backed away from the window, then dropped to his hands and knees and crawled beneath the line of the windowsill, feeling stupid and self-conscious, though there was no one inside to see him. He reached the other side of the window, nearer to the bookshelves. There was a chair there, within easy reaching distance of the books and the unfinished crossword. Alex hoisted himself up into the chair and, as he sat down, wished that he had brought the coffee cup with him from the table where he'd left it.

Alex tried to turn his attention back to the crossword, but he couldn't focus on it. He attempted to reassemble the letters of what was obviously an anagram, without success. As he scribbled the letters in a circular pattern in the margin, waiting for them to fall into their new shape, the doorbell buzzed. Alex ignored it.

He heard Anna's voice calling hello through the speaker. Alex held his breath for a minute, as though she might be able to hear any response without him picking up the receiver in the hallway. He counted the seconds as he waited for her to buzz again. It was two minutes before the buzzer sounded a second time.

'Hello, Alex? It's me.' She paused, realising that 'me' was no longer enough. 'It's Anna. Are you there?'

Alex sat as still as he could, though his leg twitched nervously. He pressed his hands down on his shin to try to control it. He would not answer. It would be dangerous to speak to her. He had opened her note, forwarded by his mother, one familiar handwriting enfolded in another.

Anna did not seemed to realise how serious this was. Even her handwriting seemed careless, thoughtless. Anyone would have been able to check and find out that there was no college reunion. He had torn the postcard up and scattered its fragments in dustbins he passed along the road that led towards the river.

He heard footsteps on the stairs. She must have tried the other doorbells and someone must have let her in: Anna had obviously learnt something from journalism, then. That, or from living in apartment blocks and forgetting her keys, as she probably still did. He would have to remind Mrs Baines, the elderly lady who lived downstairs, not to do that. Not for her, not for anyone.

He looked at the crossword again. The letters still would not shift into place. Alex heard the insistent knock, four times in quick succession.

'Alex, are you there? It's Anna. I need to talk to you. It's really important.'

For a moment he was tempted to move towards the door, but he stayed where he was. He was not going to let her hear even the slither of his feet in socks across the wooden floor.

She tried again: she had learnt some persistence, too.

'Alex, if you're there, which I'm sure you are, I want to help you. Please let me.'

She couldn't be sure he was there. Alex listened. There was nothing to reveal that he was: no lights; no radio; no rumble of machines running. He heard a fumble, a tear of paper, something being slid under the door. Then her footsteps moved away, back down the stairs.

Anna pushed the note, scribbled on a sheet of paper, under the door and listened for a last time before she turned away. There were no signs of life from inside the flat, but somehow she imagined Alex was there. The sweet-sounding old lady in the basement flat had buzzed her in, believing that she had a parcel to deliver for Alex. That, and a quick check through the junk mail piled up on the shelf above the radiator in the downstairs lobby, proved she was in the right place. Despite the boiled-cabbagey smell of communal hallways and the worn carpet on the stairs, she imagined this was a good place to live. There were high ceilings and tall sash windows that gave onto a tree-lined street, with a quiet square behind and a small church on the corner.

She wondered whether Jennifer had actually forwarded her postcard. She hadn't heard anything more from Alex's parents but James Rycroft had been easy to find: although the phone number she had for him was a couple of years out of date, it had only taken a quick call to the press office of the financial regulators to check which bank he worked at; after that, all she had to do was get past a rather snotty PA. She realised that a part of her had wanted to talk to Alex's parents again. James had been as gentlemanly as ever, though he sounded harried on the phone and didn't have time for small talk. As Anna had expected, he was still the kind of person who wrote Christmas cards and kept his address book up to date. Nor did he seem surprised that she had lost Alex's address. Anna didn't manage to get much more before James finished the call, polite but somehow abrupt.

'Have you seen him lately?' she asked. 'How was he?'

'A few weeks ago,' James had said. 'He didn't seem great, to be honest. Things not going too well at work, from what I could gather.' He wouldn't be drawn on it any more, saying he had a conference call and had to hang up.

Anna had surfaced from the Tube in Pimlico that morning, grateful for once that Theo lived on this side of town. She called in to the office to tell them that she was out chasing some leads on her investigation. As she stepped into the road, she had been thinking that this must have been where Alex's grandmother had lived. Alex had said she was a formidable woman, who had dropped broad hints about having been something at Bletchley during the war and had a taste for cigarettes and neat Scotch. Anna knew that she would never meet her now, knew how sad Alex must have been: although he was scared of her, he admired his grandmother, loved her too. Anna was startled by the motorbike that raced round the corner and nearly ran her over; shaken still more by the man who raised the visor on his white helmet, shook his leather-gloved fist at her, and called her a stupid fucking bitch.

Now she stood in the hall and pulled the latch on the heavy

front door open. There was a handwritten sign on the back of the door, which she hadn't noticed before, in neat angular capitals that looked like Alex's, reminding residents to please make sure that the door was firmly closed and locked behind them. That sounded like him, too. Anna obeyed his instruction: it was there for a reason.

She stepped out from under the portico of the front door and walked along the street, glancing back at his window. If he was gone, he was not long gone, or there would have been more post for him. Anna wondered whether other people had been here before her, watching Alex, whether they would be watching her too. Whichever way you looked at it, this was a strange thing to be doing. In the normal course of things, she would have called it doorstepping; others might have called it stalking. Normally, she would have thought that someone who pounded on the door of her college boyfriend, several years after the fact, was seriously disturbed. This was not the normal course of things.

Anna crossed a main road and rounded a corner. She was not really sure where she was going: the right thing to do would be to go back to the office, make more of the calls, find the people she was supposed to be looking for. She had lost her bearings in these streets of white-stuccoed houses with pillared entrances that all looked alike, the only difference seeming to be the black numbers, painted onto the pillars, that rose or fell in sequence along their pavements. They were interspersed with streets with small shops that looked as though they hadn't changed in years: dry-cleaners, little Italian delicatessens. There were still ranks of proper red phone boxes.

The street opened out into a green square, with a playing field and a half-timbered cricket pavilion on it. The Union Jack was flying from a flagpole beside the pavilion. It seemed incongruous in this part of town, more suited to a village green than a city square bordered by mansion blocks. It was the sort of place she knew that Alex loved. As she walked past the cricket pitch, a high trill of birdsong rose from the huge plane trees around the edge of the playing fields. She stopped to check her phone.

Alex heard the front door slam shut. He let out a long breath. Edging to the window again he saw Anna's back as she headed away, around the corner past the church. He felt trapped in the flat, as though he had been cornered there. He had to escape from the stuffy air and the room that he saw too much of most days now. Everything about it annoyed him: the furniture that had been his grandmother's seemed heavy and dated; the things that were his own were shabby and would never last long enough to date. He reckoned it would take Anna five minutes to get back to the Tube, if that was the way she had come. His minders didn't seem to be around. He could go for a walk.

He picked up the abandoned coffee cup from the dark wood coffee table that still looked wrong without Granny's onyx ashtray; the coffee was undrinkably cold now. Taking the mug into his tiny kitchen he sluiced the beige liquid down the sink. Then he shrugged on his raincoat, despite there being the hope of spring in the air, locked the door of the flat firmly behind him and headed down the stairs.

Once outside, he remembered some of the tricks he'd been taught in the early days when he'd just started work, on a course where he wandered around the streets of a mocked-up ruined town on an army base that stood for anywhere from Northern Ireland to Bosnia. He rounded the street corners by stepping out almost into the road, as though someone might spring out at him from the shadows; he swerved away from alleys and alcoves, looking into them as potential hiding places. Once or twice, he stopped to study noticeboards and shop windows with an air of deep concentration, as though he really wanted to check the date of the church fete or the opening hours of the dry-cleaners. He watched to see if anyone stopped in echo of him; no one did. He watched where others were going without them spotting him.

It was strange how these things came back to you, even though Alex had never really had to use them. There had been routine warnings from time to time about varying your route to work, being aware of your surroundings and all that. Alex never varied his route to work; he always thought it would have looked odder if he had. He took the most direct route to Vauxhall Bridge Road and walked straight along it and over the bridge, despite the noise and the rush-hour traffic. That way he knew what to expect, and knew if things were different. He had to remind himself that he wasn't going to work now, and didn't know if he would be again; his feet almost followed the familiar route by themselves. He had to force himself to turn away from it. He kept walking until he reached the cafe.

Here, at least, things were still the same. The black tiles on the outside walls were the same as they had ever been; the condensation settled on the windows with their green gingham curtains. Alex took his place at the queue at the counter, looking up at the specials chalked on the board above the kitchen.

The cafe was loud with conversations and the man behind the counter shouted out each order as it was ready in his deep voice. It was mid-morning, and almost all the seats were taken by men who had started work early and outdoors, returning here for a break and a fry-up. Men in fluorescent jackets, some still in hard hats, settled into the plastic seats and talked. Alex picked up fragments of conversations about football.

'Young lady,' the man behind the counter bellowed. The presence of a lady here, young or otherwise, was something that merited a special shout, even before she had ordered. Even elderly women were greeted as 'young lady', though they were rare customers. From the corner of his eye, Alex could see that the young lady was getting it wrong, trying to occupy a table before she ordered. There was a strict protocol here, and the regulars soon set her right, pointing her towards the counter.

Alex waited at the counter for the man to draw off dark tea into a plain white mug. He took the mug of tea carefully and picked up cutlery from a tray. Alex turned his head slightly more to take a look. There Anna was, incongruous in her office clothes, wide-eyed, dithering as ever over the menu. This wasn't her sort of place; it was his sort of place. But then again, he should have expected that she wouldn't go straight back to the Tube.

'Full English with two toast!' Alex's order was being called. He had lost his appetite.

'Full English, two toast!' the call came again, even louder this time.

If he walked away, he could never come back here. Even though he'd already paid, he could never face looking the man behind the counter in the eye again. He'd be the weird guy in the raincoat who'd abandoned a perfectly good full English, not to mention the extra toast.

'Thank you,' Alex mumbled, picking up the plate laden with eggs, brown-flecked bacon and sausage. Baked beans nearly spilled over the edge.

'You'll want this.' The man behind the counter held out a paper napkin.

'Yup. Thanks.' Alex took it.

'Alex?' Anna was standing at the end of the counter, waiting for the frothy coffee that the man was about to hand to her. He didn't look up, didn't acknowledge her. She could do the talking.

'Alex,' she repeated. 'It is you. It's me, Anna.'

'I know who you are,' he muttered eventually. 'What are you doing here? What do you want?'

'I need to talk to you,' she said as he started to walk towards a free table near the door, concentrating on balancing his over-loaded plate and the full cup of tea. She followed him and thumped herself down in the opposite chair.

Alex put his plate on the table and gestured to Anna to keep her voice down. He replied in a gruff, angry whisper that was partly muffled by the cafe's noise.

'Even you must realise by now that I don't want to talk to

you. I don't want to see you. I didn't reply to your postcard. I didn't answer the door. Can you not take a hint?'

Anna looked affronted by his anger, the way she had been that time before, in the restaurant.

'But I want to help you,' she said in a plaintive voice.

'Then stay away from me,' he retorted. 'The very fact that I'm talking to you could get me in all sorts of trouble. I said that I hadn't seen you, hadn't been in touch with you. If they find out that's not true . . .' Alex had said quite enough.

'Bacon sandwich for the young lady,' came the cry from the counter.

He watched Anna's back as she returned to the counter, looking away as she turned her head back to check that he was still sitting there. He regarded his plate, took a large bite of bacon and chewed it solemnly. The phrase 'the condemned man ate a hearty breakfast' bounced around, unwelcome, in his head.

'I told them I hadn't seen you either,' Anna continued as she sat down with her plate. 'It was true, then.'

'They came to talk to you?' It confirmed what Alex had expected. Anna lifted the bread from the top half of her sandwich and let ketchup trickle onto the bacon. She pressed the sandwich back together and nodded.

'They asked if you'd sent me anything. Like documents. I said you hadn't.' She paused for a bite of the sandwich and a swig of the coffee. 'I thought that was true, then, too.'

'What do you mean, thought?' Alex said. His voice took on its angry tone again.

'But you did . . . you have . . . I mean we got . . .' Anna seemed uncertain as to how to tell him. 'We got the disk. At the paper. With the files. The . . . German files. They were yours, right?'

'So they've turned up somewhere,' Alex said with a bitter laugh.

'Yes.' She spoke with a mouthful of bacon. 'But it wasn't anything to do with you?'

Alex didn't reply. He looked across to the two men at the next table. They were both in their late thirties, probably. They had short, neatly cropped hair. One was greying already. They were dressed as though they were going to spend a day walking in the hills: thick black fleece jackets patterned with zips and logos; those water-resistant trousers that were advertised as the kind explorers wore. Alex cast his eyes downwards towards their shoes on the red lino floor. They both had solid black lace-ups with a thick rubber tread. He tried to read the words on the security pass that one of them had swinging from his belt, but it was facing inwards. To Alex, they looked like detectives.

Alex pushed the corner of a piece of toast into the yolk of the fried egg. The yolk bled out into the orange of the beans. He looked up at Anna and shook his head.

'Listen, Anna, you can't ask me about this,' he said.

'About whether they're your files, or whether you gave them to us?' Anna replied quickly, trying to push him into telling her more.

He made the lower-your-voice gesture again, patting his hand downwards towards the Formica-topped table, though he knew Anna could never correctly calibrate her voice to her surroundings.

'I can't say,' he said, through a mouthful of egg.

'But if they are yours . . . were yours . . . what's in them? What do I look for? Who should I be looking for?' Anna was trying that new-found persistence again.

Alex shook his head in exasperation.

'I'm not helping you. I can't. You still don't understand anything, do you? You'll get me arrested.' He glanced across to the men who might have been detectives, or might just have been chartered surveyors. They didn't appear to be listening, but they might have caught the gist, if they were. Alex took a few more bites and then left the breakfast half finished on his plate. He swigged a large gulp of tea.

'Anna, you need to go now. And you can't tell anyone that you saw me.'

Anna's face was reddening, her eyes shining as though she was going to cry, but he didn't care. She bit her lip, pulled a note-book out of her bag, opened it to a blank page, and started to write.

'For fuck's sake,' he hissed. 'What are you doing? Just go.'

She tore the sheet of paper out and handed it to him across the table. He turned it face down without looking at it, or her, and waited for her to go.

'Please,' she said. 'I don't want you to be in trouble. That's not why I came. Keep it. Just in case.' Anna picked up her cumbersome bag and heaved it to her shoulder. She cast a glance at the remains of the sandwich, as though weighing up whether to take it with her. She turned and left without saying goodbye.

Alex felt the draught of air as the door opened, only looking up after he heard it close again behind her. An autographed photo of Stan Laurel, looking baffled and beleaguered as ever, seemed to stare down on him from the cream-tiled wall above. Alex thought he must have looked similar, minus the bowler hat, playing the fool. Another fine mess.

He picked up the sheet of paper with its frilled edge where it had been torn from the spiral-bound notebook, glancing at the phone number on the back. He crumpled the sheet in his hand until it was a tiny, compact ball.

# 19

IT WAS A day of postcard-blue skies and reflected gold from the sandstone buildings, but Anna had no time today for spires and gargoyles and nostalgia. The college she was looking for was off the tourist route, a few streets north in the Oxford of Victorian villas, barely announced to the outside world except with a small brass plaque on a heavy wooden gate in a wall. Anna grabbed the hooped metal handle of the latch and creaked the door open. Two tall students – a girl in a baseball cap and a boy in Lycra shorts and a college sweatshirt – followed her in, chatting to each other in American accents about rowing.

The entrance lobby was lined with noticeboards. There were lists of seminars and lectures, plays to see and rooms to let, but she was no longer entitled to distractions like these. She walked into the porter's lodge. 'Hi, I'm looking for Doctor Lucas's room, please.' This was a rare occasion where it was to Anna's advantage that she still looked as scruffy as a student, and the same age as a postgraduate.

The porter acknowledged her briefly, before turning back to arranging his sets of keys in a cabinet behind the desk.

'Out of here, down the corridor, third door on the left.'

'Thank you.' Anna made for the door.

'I'm not sure I've seen him in this morning, though. He usually collects his post by nine. Bit of a creature of habit.'

'Thanks,' said Anna. 'I'll try anyway.'

The corridor had a smell of musty books. It was lined with old college photographs, and as Anna walked along it she saw decades of students turn from black and white to colour, change from suits and gowns into jeans and T-shirts, add women and more shades of skin to their groups, grow their hair, grow in number.

The nameplate on the door read 'Dr Anthony Lucas'. Anna knocked and waited. As she listened for movement behind the door, she read through the titles of a list of seminars on eighteenth- and nineteenth-century German philosophy, full of some names she remembered only as outlines, other names she had never heard of at all. There was no reply. Anna knocked again. A woman emerged from the next office along the corridor. She had an angular face and greying hair loosely pinned back with what looked like a pencil. She gave Anna a critical look.

'Are you sure Tony's expecting you? He doesn't normally teach on Tuesdays. I'm not sure he's here.'

'It doesn't sound like he is,' Anna acknowledged.

'He might have meant to see you at home,' the woman continued. 'Perhaps you should check?'

'Maybe,' Anna said, looking at her notebook. 'Stratfield Road?'

'That's it.' The woman seemed impatient with Anna. 'Well, if he gave you the address, that's probably where he expected you to be. You'd better hurry. Tony's not very forgiving about lateness.' She continued down the corridor, an empty mug in one hand, her flowing skirt swishing behind her.

Anna was not in that much of a hurry; he was not expecting her. She might, after all, even have the wrong person. But Michael Swain was losing his patience with her now: he was threatening to take the story away from her altogether unless she came good. She had sidled back into the office after she'd seen Alex, hoping not to have been missed, hoping to have got away with chasing something that didn't work out, but he'd emerged from his office a minute later. The bang and wobble of Swain's glass office door was never a good sign; this was a slam that made Anna fear that all the glass panels might shatter. Swain emerged from his office in his shirtsleeves, a sheet of paper in one hand and a biro in the other. He thumped the paper down onto Anna's desk; it was a news agency story that had just dropped.

'This,' he said, as though Anna ought to know instantly what he meant. 'Did you see this?'

'I've been out,' Anna said, trying to buy herself a few seconds to scan the page. 'Chasing someone up.'

Swain took his biro and underlined a paragraph of the printed wire copy so hard that the pen almost tore through the page. He read the underlined sentences out with heavy emphasis, as if Anna couldn't read herself.

*Asked by reporters why the government refused to return historical files concerning Germany's past, the prime minister said there were a few areas that he and the chancellor hoped to return to at future meetings. The German chancellor told reporters that he was aware of domestic concerns about the issue.*

'It's only part of it,' Anna ventured.

'Of course it's only part of it.' Swain jabbed the biro into the paper. 'Which means this is even bigger. The Germans don't appear to know these have been lost, let alone found again. And the PM barely sounds like he knows what he's talking about. It's going to cause them big trouble, and we have to get it out there now, before anybody else does. So you had better find me something worth having, or I'll find someone else who can.'

'Yes, of course,' Anna nodded.

Swain continued his thought. 'The Berlin bureau say their government sources are up in arms about this, though Hugh in Berlin has a habit of making his sources sound a lot more important than they are. It's a bloke in a bar for all I know. The one good thing to come out of this is that Phillips is finally taking it seriously and is starting to do some decent digging. I need the same from you.'

It had taken much of the night. Anna had been working her way through the files systematically from the first to the last, ticking off each one as she tried to reconcile it to a real, current name. Late in the evening, staying awake on chocolate bars from the vending machine, the only one left in the office and close to giving up, Anna had skimmed through a series of files out of the correct order, skipping ahead on the disk, hoping for any name that she would recognise. It occurred to her that she should have done this first: look for the top line, look for what Swain needed her to find. There was one name. It was spelt wrong, but it was a start.

Anna had learnt that for all their diligence, for all that the secret policemen spent their days noting down the tiniest observations about the people they dealt with, they were often wrong about simple things: names, places, spellings. But then, they were writing down details of people in countries they would probably never be able to visit, places they had learnt about only in the abstract. Even their language was abstract, as though it didn't concern real people. One of the words they used was 'object': the object did this, the object said that. That must have made it easier for them: these people were not real people, real subjects of their own lives. They were objects, studied and typed up and recorded like data in an experiment.

The hedge in front of the semi-detached house was overgrown, rising above a low wall that bounded the tiny front garden. The curtains were open in the front window, but Anna couldn't tell whether anyone was at home. She rang the bell and listened for movement; eventually she heard a cough and a shuffle of feet. The light in the hallway was switched on.

Anthony Lucas opened the door. He moved slowly, with the gait of a man older than his mid-sixties, but his brown eyes were those of someone younger. He looked at Anna through his glasses with a slightly perplexed curiosity, as though he were trying to place her, then looked at his watch. He wore a cardigan of dark, mossy green over a checked twill shirt and thick beige cords that bagged outwards at the knees. He looked as though he was wearing the uniform of an academic, a costume he had adopted and never changed.

'Doctor Lucas?' Anna was tentative. She had mapped this conversation out in her head over and over again, but now she did not know where to begin it.

'Yes,' he replied. 'Did we have an appointment?'

Anna said that she didn't, and introduced herself. He nodded in recognition of the name of the paper, but still looked confused.

'Did you telephone? I think someone telephoned. Maybe it was you. Or maybe someone from the BBC, the World Service.' Anna hoped that no one else had phoned, at least not about this. 'There's something I'd like to talk to you about. Could I come in for a few minutes? Is it convenient?'

Anthony checked his watch again.

'It's not, particularly. I'm working. But now my train of thought is broken, so since you are already here, you may as well.' He held the door open and Anna stepped into a dark-painted hallway lined with pictures. They were mostly line drawings, portraits of children sketched out with a light hand, first as babies, later as cherubically chubby toddlers, then skinny kids with the illusion of constant motion. Anthony saw Anna look at the pictures.

'My late wife's,' he said. 'She was a very talented artist, though she never believed me when I told her this.'

'She was,' said Anna. 'You were right.'

'May I take your coat?' There was a formality about Anthony's manners, as there was about his voice. He hung Anna's coat on a rack near the door that looked as though it had, in the past, been used to bearing more coats than the two that hung there now: a tweed jacket and a trenchcoat. Above them were several hats.

Anthony showed Anna into the room at the end of the hall. It was a living room that had been overwhelmed by books. Dusty sunlight streamed in from the French windows that gave onto the garden. There was a gnarled apple tree on the lawn, still surrounded by last year's wrinkled windfalls.

'Would you like some coffee, Miss . . . I'm sorry, I've forgotten . . . your name again?' Anthony pointed her towards a high-backed armchair.

'Travers. Anna Travers. Yes, please. Just milk, no sugar.'

Anthony moved slowly towards the kitchen, his leather slippers scuffing on the edge of the rug. Anna put her bag down beside her chair and looked around the room. Two walls were lined with bookcases; they held a lifetime of books. There were titles in French and German on hardbacks whose spines had faded to paler shades than the rest of the dust jackets. There were heavy volumes of philosophy that had been much consulted, clothbound books with tarnished gilt lettering and pieces of paper, impromptu bookmarks torn from lined sheets, emerging from between the pages. Newer books were heaped on the floor in front of the shelves, glossy paperbacks and slim journals, the overflow of the system.

Anna could hear the kettle boil in the kitchen next door; she moved across to the desk by the window. Behind the piles of books and papers stacked there she saw a photograph in a brown leather frame: a holiday snapshot whose colours were fading. A woman and two children stood on a beach among sand dunes, with long wisps of grass blowing beside them. It must have been the early seventies: the woman wore an embroidered cheesecloth tunic. Her arms rested on the shoulders of a boy and a girl, the boy skinny and sunburnt in orange swimming trunks, the girl smaller, rounder-faced, in a red costume; the mother's hair was caught in the wind and she was laughing. The boy was maybe eight or nine years old – Anna was not very good at guessing the ages of children – and he and his mother had the same wide smile. Anna recognised it: she had seen it many times before. Mark's smile was still the same.

She heard the shuffle of Anthony's feet again and moved quickly back to the chair. Anthony placed the coffee cup delicately down on the coaster that lay ready on the table next to her, and sat down in the chair opposite. Anna pulled out a notebook and a pen, feeling as nervous as if she were about to read him an essay.

Anthony took a long sip of his own coffee.

'So, how can I help you?' he began.

'It's rather a tricky one,' Anna began.

'Tricky subjects are my speciality,' Anthony said, raising an eyebrow. 'Which one is this?' His light-hearted tone made it even harder. She had to tread cautiously enough that he didn't throw her out of the house immediately, but she couldn't be so delicate that she didn't get any answers.

'We – my newspaper – have been given some documents, some files. What seems to be your name comes up in them.'

'Can you be a bit more specific, please?' Anthony said, leaning forward. 'What sort of files?'

'They're files from the old East Germany, files the foreign department of the Stasi kept. Britain got hold of them after the Wall came down. There's an Anton Lukas, Lukas with a "k". Is that you?'

Anthony leant back again in his chair, folding his hands together carefully. He pressed his index fingers together to a point, his hands making the church and the steeple of the children's rhyme.

'This was my name, yes. I changed it when I came to this country, nearly forty years ago now. It was too hard for people like you to spell. But it was quite a common name there. So it might be me. It might also be someone else.'

'Could I ask when you were born?' Anna had to narrow it down.

'Nineteen thirty-five. May, nineteen thirty-five.'

Anna took a Manila folder from her bag and glanced at the top sheet of paper inside it. 'In Koenigsberg?'

Anthony nodded. 'Koenigsberg, yes. It is Kaliningrad now, in Russia. There's not much of the old city left. It was destroyed. You've heard of the bridges?'

Anna hadn't, but now was not the time for a history tutorial. She shook her head.

'I'm sorry, no. But that's what it says here, Koenigsberg. East . . .' She struggled with the copied typescript and the German for a moment. 'East Prussia. May 1935. So that sounds like it is you. And your middle name – is it Karl?'

'Indeed. So it sounds extremely likely that it is me,' Anthony acknowledged. 'But what are you really asking me? They kept files on almost everyone. You must know that.'

'Yes, of course.'

Anna was determined not to be deflected. She took another sip of the coffee. It was bitterly strong. 'But these are different. These are the files on people they were in contact with in Britain. People who were giving them information.'

'Spies. Use the word, if that's what you mean.'

'Spies.' Anna echoed him. 'Were you a spy? In Britain?'

'I did not spy for them.'

Anna wrote this down. She felt she was starting to get somewhere.

'But were you in contact with anyone who was working for the East German government once you were here?'

'That's . . .' Anthony thought about his answer for a long moment. 'You are familiar with the concept of proving a nega- tive?' He carried on regardless of whether or not she was. 'I may well have been, but you'll understand that would not have been how they introduced themselves.' Anna tapped her pen on her folder impatiently. She sensed that Anthony was twisting words, playing with semantics. The more she let him twist them, the less clear everything would become.

'There's a codename here: Krummholz. Does it mean anything to you?'

'Of course.'

Anthony got up from his chair with a sudden burst of energy. He walked over to one of the bookshelves behind him. He beck- oned Anna over. 'Look at this shelf. All these books. Some of them are mine.'

Anna looked at the books, but couldn't see how they were

relevant to what she was talking about. Some, as he said, had A. K. Lucas printed as the author's name on the spine. Anthony shook his head in disbelief.

'Where did you study? What did you study?'

'English. Here, in Oxford. I'm sorry, but I don't know what this has to do with what I'm asking you. I need to know about your past.'

'Ah, English. So you can read Beowulf in the original, but you don't know any philosophy. Or much history. So it helps you write journalism, but not understand what you are writing about.'

Anna shrugged. He was starting to annoy her.

'Immanuel Kant. A famous philosopher. I hope you picked this up at least, perhaps from some other undergraduates. We shared a hometown, though he managed to stay there all his life.' Anthony ran his finger down the spines of some of his books. 'I have spent much of my life studying his work.' That much she knew. It was in his *Who's Who* entry. 'Krummholz is a shortened version of the phrase for "crooked timber". It's a famous quotation from his work. "Out of such crooked timber as humanity, no completely straight thing can ever be made." He meant that people never behave perfectly, that freedom can always be abused if there is no higher law.'

Anna had brought the notebook over to the bookcase with her, but her notes made as little sense as he did. She scrawled *crooked timber – Kant quote?* Anthony showed her a piece of driftwood that sat on a high shelf. Anna hadn't noticed it before. It had a strange beauty; it was a curved branch that must have been tossed by the sea for years, its bark gone and the grain and knots of the wood polished by sand to a smooth, silvery finish.

'I keep this here,' he said, 'to remind me of the saying. To remind me that nothing is completely straight. And if it seems to be, then you have probably made a mistake somewhere.'

'But to get back to my question,' Anna said. 'Does that mean it is definitely you? That they used that name?'

'It is the kind of thing they would have done. They thought they were clever, some of them. Thought they had a sense of humour, too. Though that is one thing they certainly never had.'

'Straight or not,' said Anna, 'I need to ask . . . Did you ever work for the Stasi? Ever inform for them?'

'They would have known who I was,' Anthony replied. 'You couldn't be a student or work in a university without them knowing who you were, letting you have a place at the university or a job. But I left to get away from them, at very great danger to myself and others. I escaped to freedom with nothing. This country gave me my life, my family, my work. Why would I have done anything to put that all at risk again?'

'As you say,' said Anna, writing everything down now. He spoke slowly and her shorthand could keep up. 'People never behave perfectly.'

'So you are listening, after all. They don't, but we usually try our best.'

Anna sat down again and looked through the notes she had made on the sheet in the folder. She was about to start on more questions when Anthony spoke again.

'What do you plan to write about me in your newspaper?'

Anna drew biro circles on her notebook as she formulated her answer.

'I'm not entirely sure, yet. But it seems to be you that they have a file on. Are you absolutely denying that you were an agent for the East German regime, either once you came to Britain, or before that?'

'I was not working for them,' Anthony said. His voice did not change. It remained calm and gravelly. Anna listened for the hint of an accent, but barely detected one. She went through her list again.

'There are meetings listed here, dates.' She held out the top sheet to show him. She started to read some of them out. Anthony held his hands up, in a gesture that Anna couldn't place precisely as despair or resignation.

'Do you think I can remember meetings from thirty years ago? I told you, these were not people who would give you their name and tell you what they did for a living. There were always people who were not quite who they claimed to be: I had students, colleagues who came and said they wanted to talk about the old country, claimed to know people I had studied with. If I had no reason to teach them, I sent them away. Maybe some of them wrote this down and sent it to Berlin. I don't know.'

'And your son?'

This was the part Anna had left until last. 'Your son is Mark Lucas, the minister.'

'He is. But I don't see how this concerns him.'

'Have you ever discussed this issue with him?'

'Which issue do you mean?'

'That these files were held by the British government. That you might have been mentioned in them.'

Anthony hesitated.

'He never talked about me being mentioned.'

Anna suddenly saw a gap open up, the kind of gap that Anthony's caution and precise, wordy sentences normally wound tightly closed.

'So he did mention the files to you? What did he say?'

Anthony stood up. He motioned towards the door.

'I think I have said enough. I would like you to leave, please.'

Anna tried again. 'Your son, the minister, discussed this with you?'

Anthony was silent. He walked to the door and took her coat down from the rack, holding it out for Anna to put on. Anna grudgingly accepted it, sliding her arms into the sleeves. She had as much as she would get, and it was good enough.

He showed her out.

As Anna turned to go, she wasn't sure whether to say thank you. The normal formalities seemed wrong, seemed as if they were trying to fix something that was broken. She looked at Anthony.

'Please don't make any trouble for him,' he said. 'For Mark. I have seen plenty of trouble for one lifetime, but I don't want him to have to.'

There was nothing that Anna could say except goodbye. She could not promise not to make trouble for Mark. She knew that was exactly what she was about to do. Anthony closed the door behind her. She heard the key turn in the lock.

Anna hurried down the path, rushing now to get back to London, but waited until she was a suitable distance from the house to call the office.

Inside, Anthony picked up a small address book from his desk. It was bound in faded green leather and had numbers carefully written in it in pencil. He turned to a page and dialled a number he found there. He heard the long flat tone of a number that no longer existed. Anthony hung up, then picked up the phone again and called his son.

# 20

THE MEETING ALREADY seemed as though it had been going on too long. Mark eyed the plate of biscuits on the long table and decided against eating one. Instead, he swirled the last, cold sip of coffee around in the bottom of his white cup and drank it, placing the cup slowly back in the saucer and trying again to focus on what he was being told. He caught a disapproving glance from Louisa, who had started to learn when he wasn't paying attention. Mark made a scribbled note in the margin of a memo in front of him; the scribble didn't say anything. The senior civil servant opposite, a young man whose prematurely greying hair foreshadowed the kind of authority that he hoped in due course to acquire, asked Mark whether he agreed. Mark wasn't quite sure what he was agreeing to, but he said that he did. As he answered, Mark could detect the buzz of his phone. It seemed to be sending vibrations through his chair, but he wasn't sure exactly where they came from. The phone started to ring, and Mark fumbled for it before the ringing became too loud. He eventually established that the ringing was coming from his jacket, slung over the back of his chair, and he patted the navy wool until he found the phone in his inside breast pocket. He pulled the phone from the pocket, sliding it out over the orange silk flashes of the lining, and looked at the screen, increasingly conscious of the glares from across the table and the barely hushed hisses of exasperated breath.

Mark was surprised to see the black letters saying 'Dad' on the grey screen. His father rarely rang him at all, almost never on the mobile phone. He stood up and moved away from the table.

'Will you excuse me,' he said. 'I'm afraid this is important.'

There was a shuffling of papers and a glancing at watches, but no one demurred; Mark relied on the fact that they couldn't object. He walked to the edge of the room, turned his back on his colleagues and leaned against a wall.

'Hi, Dad. Is everything OK?' Mark was running through possibilities in his mind: his father was calling from home, so he wasn't so ill that he was in hospital; the worst thing would have been an unknown number and the voice of a nurse or a doctor, or a call from his sister, who was probably the one they'd ring first. Mark was used to people assuming that he wasn't available.

'Not entirely, Mark, no. I'm sorry to bother you.' His father's voice on the other end of the line sounded strange; Mark couldn't tell at first if the line was breaking up or if Anthony's voice was cracking. He moved towards the window to try to get a better signal before realising that his father sounded on the edge of tears.

'It's all right, Dad. What's the matter?' Mark made frantic hand gestures towards Louisa, trying to indicate writing. Louisa understood and brought him a pad of paper and a pen. Mark wrote *Sorry – family emergency – got to wind up – please apologise* on the paper and handed it back to her. Mark waved apologetically to the civil servants around the table as he left the room and tried to find a spot in the corridor outside where he could hear his father. Anthony was silent for a while before he spoke again; Mark paced the length of the mosaic-patterned floor, checking the phone was working.

'There was a girl who came to the house, this morning, just now,' Anthony began. These were not his usual thought-out sentences.

'What girl, Dad?'

'A reporter, a newspaper reporter. I wasn't expecting her, she didn't call, she just came to the door.'

'What did she want?' Mark was as confused as his father seemed to be. He knew Anthony spent too much time alone these days, but now he started to wonder whether his father was losing his grip on reality. Perhaps he should tell Rachel to persuade him to see a doctor; he would take it better from her.

'She had some questions about me, about my . . . my background.'

'That doesn't sound too bad, Dad. You've had an interesting life.' This sounded manageable. Odd, but manageable. Mark felt vaguely flattered that someone was interested enough in his family to want to write some sort of a profile. He could handle this. 'But they shouldn't really be coming to you without asking me first. They should have called my office. And they should have rung you before just turning up. Tell me who it was and I'll give their editor a call. It's not really fair on you.' Mark was about to head back into the room to collect another sheet of paper and take the journalist's details when his father continued.

'No, it wasn't so simple.' This sounded like Dad again – nothing ever was. Mark suppressed a sigh. 'She asked me some very specific things, about what contact I'd had with – the authorities.'

'Which authorities? Sorry, Dad, I really don't understand.' Mark could tell that his father was using euphemisms, being evasive, but he couldn't help him unless he explained what was going on in a way that he could actually grasp. He paced the corridor more urgently now.

'The old authorities, the East German authorities,' Anthony continued.

'Well, of course you had contact with them. You lived there. You didn't have much choice. It was a totalitarian state.'

'Mark, you are being obtuse.' His father was more brusque, more like his usual self. 'I mean the secret police, the Stasi.'

Mark's pacing had brought him to the top of a wide set of stone stairs. He sank down onto the top step and looked through the carved stone banisters.

'What exactly did she ask?' Mark said slowly.

'She wanted to know if I had worked for them, if I had informed for them.'

'But you haven't, of course you haven't. What did you say? You don't have to answer questions like that. You shouldn't have said anything.' Mark realised that he was gabbling. He looked around, down the stairs and along the corridor, checking whether anyone was listening. Ministers didn't sit on staircases.

'I told her that I was loyal to this country, that this country gave me freedom. It's the truth. But she showed me some documents; they were records they must have had about me. They looked real.'

'But you talked to her. You shouldn't have talked to her. You should have sent her away.' Mark felt that if he leant on the fluted stone banisters they would crumble beneath him, that he would fall from the top of the stairs to the tiles of the hallway below. He could almost feel himself falling, imagine himself lying broken on the cold floor beneath the classical wall-hangings and the cheerful modern posters saying what a great job the department was doing. The pictures of happy, diverse civil servants would smile down at his lifeless body from the walls.

'I'm sorry, Mark.' His father's voice was breaking again. 'I didn't know. She was polite and young and pleasant, and so I spoke to her. But I think I was very careful, very cautious.'

'It's OK, Dad. I'm sure it will be OK.' Mark was not convinced, but he knew that it was his father who needed the reassurance. He had to take charge, had to protect his father, and himself too. He became quick and practical. There were things that had to be done, and by doing them he could avoid thinking about the things that were more difficult, more elusive.

Still talking, he walked in the direction of his office. He needed to find out the name of the reporter, where she worked. It meant that the files had been given to her paper – there was no other way this could have happened. How they had come to be there was just one of the things he couldn't even start thinking about.

His father read out the details from a business card. The name was familiar: Anna Travers. Mark was good with names, good with remembering where he'd met people before. It was a quality that had always helped him so far. Mark loved the look of wonderment that came across people's faces when he placed them correctly; it made them feel important, made them feel that he was better than your average politician. Mark was sure that this ability had won him votes, the votes of the kind of people who organised village fetes and invited speakers and took part in things, the kind of people you needed.

Anna Travers emerged from a grey mist in his mind: a keen young woman shivering against the cold as she stepped out of a railway station, the one from the by-election. The one who'd been turned away from the meet-and-greet with the PM, after he'd invited her. He hadn't had time to feel bad about that then; he'd glimpsed her dismissed by Theo Sadler and thought nothing of it. It happened.

Mark couldn't remember the last time he had felt so bad about finishing a phone call with his father. They usually ran out of things to talk about before the conversation actually ended, and there was an exchange of pleasantries to mask the fact that neither of them had anything left to say. There was still so much that Mark needed to know, but he couldn't ask all of it over the phone, not when everything was pressing down on him like this. It somehow felt wrong to ask him even from inside this building, as though someone might be listening in. He hung up with a promise to come and talk to him soon, at home, and a warning not to talk to anyone else, to call him first, whenever it was.

Mark strode out of the office, not stopping to say where he would be. He wasn't sure himself, except that he needed to be away from the oppressive building and the people who occupied it. He crossed the courtyard, cluttered with parked cars, emerging from the security gates in the dark archway into the light of King Charles Street. He loped down the Clive Steps and crossed the road into the park. Normally, the spring flowers and the ducklings scudding across the lake filled him with well-being, but today he barely noticed them.

The phone buzzed again in his pocket and Mark was tempted for a moment to throw it into the lake, to scatter the ducklings and watch it sink beneath the pondweed. He answered. It was Louisa, reminding him he was due at a lunch in a restaurant somewhere in Pimlico, asking with a faint implied criticism whether he was already on his way there. He couldn't face lunch right now, and certainly not with the pompous political editor he was supposed to be meeting. The prospect of rich food, false bonhomie and the pretence that everything was fine was unbearable. Mark just had to be careful that his very absence didn't start some sort of rumour.

'I'm sorry, Louisa, I have to cancel. Can you call and tell him something urgent's come up. Anything that's not demonstrably untrue.'

Louisa sounded flustered, not wanting to be ill-mannered on Mark's behalf.

'But he'll already be there, or on his way. It's very short notice.'

'So it goes. He's been around long enough to know that. So call his mobile, if he has one. Call the restaurant and leave a message for him. I shouldn't have to tell you all this.'

He pressed the button to hang up. Mark put the phone back in his pocket, tried to breathe deeply and slowly, to focus on the signs of spring in the park, the daffodils emerging from their buds. The phone rang again; the temptation to heave it across the rushes at the water's edge and at the head of an unsuspecting Canada goose was even stronger.

The voice on the other end was female, hesitant but serious. Anna Travers introduced herself. She sounded as though she had spent a while planning what she was going to say. Mark looked around for a vacant park bench where he could sit down.

'I've just been speaking to your father . . .' she began.

'Yes, I know,' Mark cut her off. 'You had no business to be

doing that in the way you did.' He could hear her swallow hard before she spoke again. This was not in her script. 'It was perfectly fair. He knew who I was. He invited me in. Anyway, that's not the point I need to talk to you about.' Mark kept walking, cursing the tourists and the civil servants on early lunch breaks who occupied the benches where he wanted to sit, away from potential eavesdroppers.

'He's a private citizen,' Mark continued. 'You could at least have phoned to tell him you were coming.'

Anna ignored this.

'It's a matter of public interest. As you obviously know, I had some serious allegations to put to him. And I need you to comment on them.'

Mark stalled for time. 'I'm not going to do that now. I'll get back to you with something.'

'I need something before my deadline,' Anna persisted. This did not seem to be the girl from the by-election, the one who'd listened to everything politely and gone away when she was told to.

'As you say, you're making serious allegations here and they deserve a considered response. They need to go through the department.'

'This isn't a departmental matter,' Anna said confidently. 'This is personal. This is about your father. That's why I came to you directly.'

She was partly right, of course, but Mark couldn't be sure quite how much Anna knew that it was political, disastrously political. He couldn't give her the means to link it all together, if she didn't already have it.

'I'll get back to you,' Mark said.

'This afternoon. It needs to be this afternoon.'

Mark was almost at Buckingham Palace now. He switched off the phone and turned back towards Whitehall. The turrets of the buildings around Horse Guards Parade were framed in the budding trees. To him they looked sinister, despite the sunlight.

★

Edward Groves looked more disappointed than was usual. Until now, Mark had attributed that jaded expression to a feeling that, for a diplomat, communications was somewhat beneath him, and that he was biding his time until a suitable embassy became vacant, where he could get back to living the life he had signed up for. He looked as though he expected to be wearing a linen suit, to be driven in a car with a flag on the bonnet. Edward had obviously been persuaded that the modern diplomat needed to master the art of handling the media if his career was to proceed on the fast track that he had been promised. They must have been of a similar age; Mark sometimes envied diplomats like Groves their expectation that their lives and their careers would progress in predictable ways, that they could work out, if not precisely which country they would be in a few years from now, then at least which job they could expect to be doing. Mark felt now that he himself was the source of the disappointment.

Groves, a thin man whose suit hung loosely from his bony frame, had stood over Mark's desk, holding a red hardbacked notebook expectantly, until Mark insisted that he take a seat. It was an awkward conversation to begin. He told Edward that the matter was both personal and politically sensitive. The diplomat looked down at his jacket and made as if to brush an unpleasant smudge from his tailoring. When he caught Mark's eye again it was to give him another world-weary look.

'Quite how personal are we talking?' Groves looked as though he was mapping out a flowchart in his head, calling up some sort of official template for how to proceed. Affair: yes or no? If yes, then was there a security risk? If yes, then how quickly could Mark be removed before more damage was done?

'It's to do with my father.'

'Your father?' This was evidently not programmed in to the template. Wives, girlfriends, boyfriends and secretaries were all possible options. Fathers did not usually arise.

'He's an émigré – he came from the old East Germany. Before the Wall even went up.'

'We know that,' said Groves. 'It's not in itself an issue. If it had been, we would have recommended that you didn't have the job.'

Mark was irritated at being pre-empted before he had even begun the story.

'That isn't it. I know you know that. I filled out the forms. Something has changed.'

Edward listened, writing the date and Mark's name at the top of a page in his notebook, then waiting to see what he should fill in.

'He's been approached by a reporter,' Mark continued. 'She says, she claims to have documents that show he informed for the Stasi.'

'And did he?' Edward's matter-of-fact tone was disconcerting. It was the obvious question, the one Mark had answered to himself without wanting to contemplate a different answer. The one he hadn't even asked his father outright.

'No, of course not. I'm sure he couldn't have, wouldn't have.'

'Do you know that?'

'It would go against everything he stands for, everything he's ever said or written.'

'Yes,' Edward nodded. 'But can you be sure?'

'I believe it,' said Mark, after a long pause.

Edward's look suggested this was not an evidence-based answer that fitted his template. He moved on.

'When is she saying this happened?'

'I'm not sure,' Mark replied.

'Here, or over there?'

Mark shook his head again. 'Here, I think. But again, I'm not exactly sure.'

The blank spaces on the pages of Edward's notebook echoed the gaps that Mark had left. Mark saw that Edward could not construct a narrative from this; this did not give him talking points, the script that he needed to answer questions. Yet again, he was proving a disappointment, even though he was trying, as he always tried, to do the right thing.

'There's a bigger issue, more one for you,' Mark said at last. Edward clicked repeatedly at the button on the top of his pen. Now he might have something to write down. 'It's to do with how they came by these . . . documents, these files.'

'Well, that's assuming they are what they are claimed to be,' Edward replied. Now he was the one who was being cautious.

'It's possible,' said Mark. 'There are some files which we had—'

'Who do you mean by "we", in this context?' Edward interrupted.

'We meaning Britain, meaning HMG, meaning the intelligence services. We had them, but now we don't. They've been lost.'

'Lost?' Edward's was the same reaction that Mark's had been when he'd first been told this. 'We don't just lose things.'

'Apparently, we do. Someone did. And if a reporter has them, or part of them, it suggests to me they've been found. Or were never lost at all, just given to a newspaper. Sold, maybe.' Edward had not taken as many notes as Mark had expected. He looked fearful.

'This is not something I can deal with on my own,' he said, as though he were calling up that set of procedures again. 'There are a lot of different bodies involved here. I can't do anything unilaterally. We have to work out how to manage it.'

'But what do I do now? In the meantime?'

'You'll have to wait. It's a policy matter. It's not like . . . all that stuff.' Edward inclined his head in the general direction of the Foreign Secretary's office, a shorthand for the messy scandal of the previous year. Mark could see that Edward was getting ready to leave the room.

'How do I wait? They're calling me already, the reporter called me. I need to tell her something.'

'You can't say anything. There are a lot of other people who need to be consulted about this. I'm not sure I'm even allowed to know some of this.'

'What on earth does that mean?'

'Well, it sounds like this would be at a very high level of security clearance.'

'That's a ridiculous thing to say,' Mark retorted. 'You do know about it. I've told you about it. And if you don't do something about it by this afternoon then everyone in the country will know about it by tomorrow morning, when they read it in the papers. And you stand there saying you don't think you're supposed to know. It's a bit late for that.'

Edward looked puzzled. 'You think they're running it straight away?'

'That's what they told me. They want a statement by their deadline, this afternoon.'

'I don't think you mentioned that, earlier.'

'Well, I should have. You'll understand that I'm a bit distressed by all this.'

Mark was starting to realise something he should have understood long before: that Edward's job was not to help him. Edward's job was to make sure that things went smoothly, and if that wasn't possible, to eliminate whatever, or whoever, was causing the inconvenient bumps and potholes along the way.

'So you'll draft the statement?' Mark asked, his hope that this would happen rapidly fading.

'I need to consult a few people.' Edward's answer was non-committal.

'And if I just speak on my own behalf?'

Edward shook his head.

'I wouldn't advise it. But I can't stop you, and I'm sure you would have your ways of doing that, though you'd have to deal with the consequences.'

Edward snapped his notebook shut, indicating that his part in this conversation was over. He stood up again, appearing anxious to manage what was about to happen, wanting to give the impression that he was in control. He needed to get on with the process of smoothing the way.

Mark looked around the office. He had never even got round to replacing the pictures: they remained an incongruous mix of imperial heroes, tall men in red-coated military uniforms and breeches, with Colin Randall's choice of landscapes, some sort of bleak sub-Lowry splodges that must have reminded him of his constituency.

Mark picked up his phone and hesitated before switching it back on. There ought to be people he could call at a time like this, people he could rely on, but Mark struggled to think who they were. If he crossed Whitehall now and headed for the House, he could easily be surrounded by people: there would be dozens of other MPs he could have a coffee with or exchange a joke with in the corridors, but that was not what he needed now. The idea of walking into a tea-room terrified him. He could imagine a swirl of gossip starting to build around him, to buffet him, even though he knew they could have heard nothing, yet. Mark needed someone he could trust with his political life, and there was no one.

## 21

ANNA HADN'T EATEN anything since a greasy croissant at the station, but she had gone beyond the point of hunger. The congealed lasagnes languishing behind the glass of the cafe counter suggested that the few customers who came in didn't have much of an appetite either. This very unpopularity must have been why he'd chosen it. Anna took a table at the back and watched the door from across the low booths.

She was abrupt with the waiter, who was trying to lavish mock-Italian charm on her in the absence of any other female customers. It probably didn't work on the two builders occupying the seats nearest the entrance. As the waiter placed her cappuccino on the table with a flourish, Anna saw the glass door swing open and Mark Lucas enter from Horseferry Road. He kept glancing from side to side, scanning the room, checking to see if anyone had recognised him. This was not how Mark Lucas normally looked. The open smile was gone; his neck seemed to have disappeared into his shoulders. He sat down opposite her without his usual handshake. The waiter stood over him. Mark pointed to Anna's coffee and ordered the same.

The waiter raised an eyebrow and gave Anna a curious grin as he turned back to the coffee machine. He thinks we're having an affair, she thought. A handsome, furtive man in a good suit, meeting a young woman in an empty cafe. What else would you think?

'We've met before, haven't we?' Mark began. Anna nodded. 'The by-election. Freezing, wasn't it? My car broke down on the way back.'

He was still trying, even at this stage. She wasn't sure whether it was a calculated attempt to make her like him more, or just a conditioned reflex.

'I need to know . . .' she started, before Mark interrupted her.

'Can we just be clear,' he asked, 'what basis we're talking on?'

Anna hesitated.

'Lobby terms?' he continued.

'I don't . . . I'm not in the lobby,' she said. Mark seemed to take this as a statement of independence, rather than the accidental admission of ignorance that it actually was.

'This has to not come from me,' Mark said. 'Or I can't say anything. You'll get a "no comment" from the Foreign Office and a "no comment" from Downing Street and that will be it.'

'Sources?' she suggested. 'Friends of?'

He shook his head. 'Not even that.'

'It's understood that . . .?'

Mark stretched out his hands in a gesture of reluctant acceptance. 'I know that whatever I say, it'll turn into "this paper has learned exclusively", but I can live with "understood". I'll have to.'

Anna smiled, and then tried to stop herself. There was a charm about him that was unaffected. It didn't seem like something he'd been trained to do, but she had to make sure it didn't work on her. She opened her notebook to a clean page and smoothed the paper down, avoiding Mark's gaze.

'When did you know the files were missing?' she asked. He looked winded, as though he had realised in that moment that whatever he said now it was over, it was just a matter of exactly when it ended.

'It was . . . a couple of weeks ago. Two, three?'

'Can you be more specific?' Anna pushed. He shook his head. 'Before your trip to Berlin, or after?'

'After. Definitely after.'

She kept asking about the files, about what he knew and when, but she was getting little further. Either he really didn't know much, really hadn't asked much, which was bad enough in itself, or he wasn't telling her what he did know, or he was simply lying. Anna didn't always believe the journalist's mantra, that you should always ask yourself why the lying bastard was lying to you, but this time it was certainly a question worth putting. It seemed to work for everyone else. She changed tack.

'Why did you tell your father about it?'

'I didn't tell him.' Now Anna really did think that Mark Lucas was lying. Lying to protect his political career, lying to protect his father, maybe, but lying all the same. She flicked back a couple of pages in the notebook and read a sentence to him.

'Your father said: "He never talked about me being mentioned." So you did talk to him about the files.'

'You're getting it wrong,' Mark exclaimed. The waiter looked over the counter, hoping for a scene.

'How?' Anna did not want to be corrected. She thought of the swirls and knots in Anthony's piece of driftwood. Things may not be straight, but she still had to organise them in a straight line, and she had to do it by this evening.

'I never told him they had been lost. I didn't know, then.' Mark paused and sipped the coffee that had been cooling on the table in front of him. 'And I wouldn't have,' he added. 'I asked him for his advice, on the general principle.'

'What general principle?' Anna was impatient now. She looked at her watch. Michael Swain had reluctantly let her out of the office again, away from his supervision, on the promise that it was essential to the story.

'He's a philosopher,' Mark continued.

'I know. I've met him.'

'I was in the middle of negotiations, with Germany, about the files. And I wanted to ask about the ethics of putting that history, those secrets, in the public domain. Truth and reconciliation, you know. In general. As an idea.'

'What did he say?' Anna could feel herself being drawn into Mark's version of the story again. She had to resist the pull.

'He said that it was a big obligation to inflict on someone, to know the truth.' Mark hesitated again. He seemed to be holding something back.

'What did he mean by that?'

'I'm not sure I knew then.' Mark looked defeated. His eyes were tired and flat. 'Now I'm really not sure what he meant.' He took a long swig of coffee and started to shift in his seat, as though he was anxious to leave. Anna couldn't let him go, not yet.

'Look, sorry, I need some more. This is important. Did you know that he, your father, was mentioned in the files?'

'No. Absolutely not.' The answer came straight away.

'That's the truth? You really didn't know?' Anna leant back against the red vinyl of the cafe booth, trying to assess him from a greater distance.

'It's the truth. I promise you.' Mark gave her a long, imploring look.

'Because you've got every reason to be covering this up. Keeping the files secret. Not admitting when they've gone missing.'

Mark put his hands to his face in exasperation, his fingers splayed over his eyes.

'Anna, you're wrong. You're so wrong. That's precisely what I wasn't doing. I was arguing that they should be released, given back to Germany, made public there. I was overruled. Why would I be doing that if I had something to hide?'

There was a long pause. Mark rested his forehead on his hand, inscribing circles on his temple with his thumb. He looked up again.

'I have to go,' he said.

'No,' Anna replied. 'Not yet. One more thing. Was your father, has he ever been, a spy?'

'I don't believe it,' Mark said in a weary voice. 'I can't believe it. That would be the worst betrayal of all.'

Anna was starting to believe him, against everything she'd

been taught and picked up in every newsroom she'd worked in, and in every neighbouring pub. She started to think that maybe Mark Lucas was telling her the truth.

He stood up, edging himself out from the bench. He didn't hold out his hand to shake. She watched him go, saw him button up his suit jacket and start to turn back into a politician, into someone who could for now be seen walking down the street.

The waiter came over with the bill.

'He's married, isn't he?'

Anna said yes, without thinking what she was being asked.

'I saw the ring,' the waiter continued. 'Always a bad idea, darling. Trust me.'

Anna said nothing, but didn't leave a tip.

Ian Phillips led Anna at a brisk pace up a sequence of stairs and corridors she thought she would never remember. Before Anna could take in one panelled corridor, its Pugin wallpaper and its portraits, she found herself led through a door and into another. As she climbed a staircase lined with framed cartoons of Victorian politicians, always a few paces behind Phillips, she wished she had brought something to leave a trail with: some breadcrumbs, perhaps, or a ball of thread.

The office, when they eventually reached it, was even dingier than the newsroom: the walls were a dirty, nicotine colour, the paint was flaking and to reach the desks you had to negotiate heaps of old newspapers, Order Papers and copies of Hansard. It was only slightly redeemed by the view from the window: beyond the leaded ridges of the rooftop, the crenellations of the Palace of Westminster. The whole room shuddered slightly when Big Ben chimed.

Ian Phillips turned to Anna.

'So, I hear you think you've stood this up?'

Anna looked around the room, unsure as to who else might be listening. They shared the office with one of their rivals; at a desk by the wall, a stout man in tortoiseshell glasses was peering into his computer screen from a few inches away, stabbing at his keyboard with both index fingers as though he refused to accept the demise of the manual typewriter.

'Yes,' she said.

'Definitely?' Phillips was always sceptical, but this seemed like an accusation.

'I've got the father and the son.' Anna knew that Phillips had already been told who she meant.

'Both on the record?'

'The father, yes. The son didn't want me to say it came directly from him.'

'Everyone will know, though.' Ian shrugged his shoulders.

'I think he realises that,' Anna acknowledged.

'My problem is,' Ian began, before noticing that the jabbing two-finger typing had stopped, and that although the other journalist still appeared to be staring into his computer screen, he might also be listening in. 'Let's get a cup of tea.' He whisked Anna out of the room again and down yet another corridor, passing framed newspaper headlines from long-forgotten scandals.

As they entered another dark, wood-panelled room, he continued. 'The thing is, I'm getting flat denials from all my people. From Downing Street, from the Foreign Office. Officially and unofficially. So's Neville from his contacts. And these are people I trust, people I talk to all the time.'

'But look at what we know . . .' Anna began.

'What do we know?'

'That the files exist, and Britain has, or had them.' She started to count off a list on her fingers. 'The German minister said that, in public, in Downing Street. That what we have seems to correspond with what they're talking about.' She lowered her voice as they sat down at a table. 'Lucas admitted they were missing, though he claims not to know how it happened. Or that much at all, really, considering. Though he also says he didn't know his dad was involved.'

'And you believe that?' Ian Phillips stared at Anna over the frames of his glasses. Anna thought carefully before she answered.

'Yes. Yes, I do.'

He still didn't seem convinced. 'I'll go back to them,' he said. 'Them' meant Downing Street, as far as Anna could tell. 'But if they still won't give me anything, then I don't know what we do.'

Anna took a swig of tea, despite the empty buzz of caffeine that was already making her head pound.

'I can't see the problem,' she said. 'We have it.'

'You can't see the problem?' Anna felt as though Ian Phillips wanted to pat her on the head and tell her to run along. 'You have obviously never had the kind of phone calls I get every day. They shout at you. They swear at you. Which is all fine, it's what they do. We're all grown-ups. But then they just stop speaking to you altogether, which is worse. And this is going to be far worse than that. If Swain runs with it, which I'm still not sure that he will, you'd better hope you're right.'

As he looked at his watch, an amplified bell clanged at great length from somewhere Anna couldn't determine, drowning out all conversation.

'Division,' he said curtly. 'Better go and see what else is up.'

They walked back towards the office. Ian indicated vaguely how to leave the building, though Anna wasn't sure she would ever find her way back. The directions seemed to involve several turnings and a lift.

She found the lift, a narrow, juddering contraption that creaked as the doors closed, and descended a few floors. The doors opened onto a corridor she didn't recognise. Anna stepped out and turned left, before finding a heavy wooden door that was locked. She turned back towards the lift and tried another direction. A corridor lined with bookcases stretched away from her and she followed it.

Anna scurried along the corridor, head down, bag swinging over a shoulder that was starting to ache. Everything was starting to ache, if she stopped to think about it, though there was little time for that. Her head felt as though it was attached with taut steel cables. She reached her arm up to rub her neck where the leather strap of her bag chafed against her collar. A polished pair of black shoes approached her at speed along the green patterned carpet and she tried to swerve to avoid their oncoming owner, but she was just too late.

Anna was already apologising as her eyes made their way up a pair of grey flannel-suited legs, tracing an outline that became more familiar as she followed it.

'What are you doing here?' Theo said it in his usual jokey tone, but Anna detected an undercurrent of threat. She had to sound as though there were nothing unusual going on.

'Just dropping by,' she replied. 'They wanted me to have a look around.' She indicated with her hand in the direction she thought the press gallery must have been.

'Are they bringing you down here, then?' Theo said with approval. 'That would be good. I've always said so.'

'You have,' said Anna, allowing herself to look satisfied. Theo would take it as her acknowledging his good sense, perhaps his influence. He would think about it differently when he knew. 'It might happen,' she added. 'It's not definite.'

'Do you want me to talk to someone?' he asked. 'Mention you?' She shook her head.

'I'm not sure that would help,' she said, 'at this stage. They might take it wrong. But thanks.' It certainly wouldn't help, not now of all times.

'Do you have a pass, then?' Theo asked, running his thumb up and down the lanyard around his neck, which held a cluster of plastic ID cards that clattered together as he walked. It was as though the number of badges was a measure of importance. He had access to more doors than others did; he was accredited.

'No,' Anna said. 'Like I said, not yet.'

'Then you shouldn't really be here. Not in this corridor, not on your own.'

'Why not?'

'You need one of these.' He held out one of the badges. Anna shrugged.

'I was just on my way out.' A little bit of helplessness and ignorance would go a long way at this point. 'And to be honest, I'm not absolutely sure which corridor I'm in.'

Theo laid his proprietorial arm over Anna's shoulder and spun her round to face the direction she had come from. She realised that, for once, she knew more about what was going on than he did. He wasn't asking her about what she was working on. He hadn't been told anything yet. This was going on at higher levels than his, for all the ID tags he wore.

'Then I'd better help you find the way out. Carry on down there and you'll be behind the Speaker's chair before you know it and end up in the Chamber. And that's pretty much the main place you're not allowed to be. Though there are so many new girls around these days that probably no one would realise for a while.'

'Girls?' Anna corrected him.

'Women. Of course. Sorry.'

They walked on down the corridor, his arm still draped over her shoulder, emerging eventually into a vaulted space where dusty light shone in through leaded windows, beneath gilded patron saints holding up their hands beneficently. Theo stopped by a white statue of a forgotten politician.

'Here you are,' he said. 'Central Lobby. That's the way out.' He put his hands on her upper arms and pulled her in closer. 'Bet no one's ever kissed you in Central Lobby before.'

Anna flinched and stepped backwards. The lobby was full of people: a Scout troop being lined up by a teacher; a group of protesters in anoraks carrying petitions; MPs and their staff conferring in corners.

'Don't make assumptions,' she replied, making it a joke.

'Who?' he asked quickly. Anna shrugged her shoulders and tilted her head, as though she had something she wasn't giving away.

'I've hardly seen you, lately,' he continued. He did the big, puppy-dog eyes.

'I know,' said Anna. 'Sorry. Just got a lot of work on. I'll call you later.'

Before he could say anything else, she quickly kissed him on the cheek and strode off across the lobby, weaving her way between the petitioners and some errant Scouts who were staring up at the chandelier. She almost ran down the flight of stone steps that led to the final wooden door. A policeman smiled at her as she rushed through the archway and out into the street; Anna barely acknowledged him. She stuck out her arm for a taxi.

## 22

THE WHITE VAN pulled up with its wheels on the kerb, ignoring the horns of the cars streaming by and the bus drivers objecting to their bus stop being used as a parking place. The back door was flung open and a man inside heaved a heavy bale outwards. He leaned forward and dropped the stack of newspapers onto the pavement. The first drops of rain speckled the newsprint.

Anna waited for the stallholder to retrieve the papers from the rain and cut the plastic tape that held the bale together. He seemed to arrange the stack of papers incredibly slowly, lining up the edges precisely. He didn't read the headlines. As she waited, Anna looked at the magazines behind him. She didn't look for long; she had never noticed before that one prim row of respectable magazines scarcely concealed shelf upon shelf of porn, flesh overlapping flesh as the covers were arranged over each other at regular intervals. The stallholder, who wore a black woollen hat pulled low on his forehead, must have known his customers' tastes. That, after all, was the kind of thing that brought most people to King's Cross late at night.

She pulled three copies of the newspaper from the pile, dislodging the neatly arranged stack as she rejected the top, rain-flecked copy in favour of pristine ones beneath. The man held out his hand for the money, looking at her as though buying three identical copies of the same newspaper was a stranger fetish than any that might have been found on the shelves behind him. Anna pressed coins into the palm of his fingerless glove and he closed newsprint-smudged fingertips over them.

It was nearly midnight; she could have waited until the morning, but after a long night in the office and a quick celebratory drink just in time for last orders, she wanted to see it for herself. An image on a screen was nothing; she couldn't keep it, cut it out, send it to her parents. This was Anna's story and she wanted to be one of the first to have a copy of it in her hands. She checked the front page of one copy, reassuring herself that the story was actually there. There had been arguments taking place literally over her head as she worked: would it run; when; where; which edition? Anna was relieved: it was there, hardly changed, the word 'exclusive' in capitals, and her name. Admittedly, her name came third, after Ian Phillips's and Dennis Neville's, despite the fact that she had done most of the work and they had done most of the carping, but it was still there. Anna felt relief start to become pride.

She sheltered under the green corrugated canopy of the station and opened to the inside pages. There was more. Anna scanned the feature, the sidebars explaining the history, the images of the documents. Two faces looked out at her from the page: there was a half-profile portrait of a younger Anthony Lucas, with more hair and wearing a pair of large glasses, that looked as though it had been used for a book jacket or a citation for an awards ceremony, one tweed shoulder turned towards the camera. It must have been the only picture they could find of him. The second was of Mark, a shot of him striding along Downing Street, clutching documents, appearing purposeful and smiling the broad smile. The pictures were arranged on the page so that it looked as if Mark were running towards his father, unaware that they were about to collide. Anna felt as though a blast of cold wind had rushed at her down the Euston Road. She folded the newspaper carefully together, making sure it was only the sports pages that were exposed to the rain, and placed it carefully with the other copies in her bag. From somewhere beneath them, her phone rang.

Theo's name came up on the screen and Anna considered not answering it and running down into the Tube station, where she would be out of reach. She let it ring a few more times before she pressed the green button.

'Anna,' he snapped. 'Theo.' Not 'It's me.' 'What is all this . . . all this . . . bollocks?' His voice was heavy and breathy with anger. She didn't need to ask what he was talking about.

'I take it this is a work call, not a personal one?' Anna hadn't expected pleasantries, but she could at least try.

'Of course it's a fucking work call. What do you expect, with your name all over this crap?'

'It isn't crap,' Anna said, in the calmest voice she could manage. She was starting to shiver. She could hear Theo break off and talk to someone. There was the low hum of an engine turning over in the background. He must have been in a taxi.

'I'm not even going to start on all the ways this is wrong,' he said, though Anna expected that, before long, he would. 'We're talking to other people about that, to your editors. But you ought to know that it's very serious.'

Anna had always known it was serious. She also knew that his implied threat to go over her head was hollow. What Theo was mostly worried about was that this had gone way over his head, that she'd been working on something that he could have known about, and hadn't. That she knew more than he did and now everyone would know.

She remembered the way Michael Swain had insisted she come to the pub for a drink after they'd put the paper to bed: it was a rare privilege. He drank little these days; there was talk in the office that it had not always been like that, talk which it was well advised to keep to the lowest of whispers. He had ordered, pressing a large whisky on her without asking what she wanted, though in fact it was the perfect thing. The malt had an expensive aroma of damp Scottish earth. He gave her the appraising look which she normally dreaded, his eyes narrowing slightly as though to see her in sharper focus. This time he nodded.

'Good work,' he had said. Swain did not do effusive praise. Anna knew, though, that those two words meant more than several dozen from anyone else. At last, she had not been found wanting. She also realised that they meant he would defend her against any shouted invective, any threats, no matter where they came from or how high up.

'So since my bosses are talking to your bosses,' Anna said, trying again to duck the argument that was ultimately inevitable, 'I don't see why we're having this conversation.'

'Where are you?' Theo asked.

'Why?' Anna retorted. 'Just leaving the office, for what it's worth.' The small lie came more easily than she expected.

'Because we do need to have this conversation.' He was talking to her now as though she were someone who worked for him.

'Personal, or professional?' Anna asked.

'Both,' he said. 'Though I hardly think what you've done qualifies as professional.'

Anna nearly hung up on him then, but she wasn't going to let him have the last word.

'Don't . . . don't ever insult my work like that,' she said, drawing each word out. She jabbed her thumb at the red button and watched the display fade, then pushed her phone back into the depths of the bag and marched towards the Tube.

As she got to the bottom of the staircase, a uniformed man was pulling a grille across the entrance. Behind him, words scrawled on a whiteboard in marker pen told her that the last train had already departed.

'Can I just?' she said to the Tube man, hoping that he would let her through the gap in the gate, and maybe she could make the last train. He shook his head.

'Sorry. Too late. It's already gone.'

'Really? All of them?' He did not reply.

She turned away and trudged back up the steps, not looking forward to a journey on the night bus with the chucking-out-time drunks and the people who talked out loud to themselves or to God. This time, she deserved a taxi.

There was one, pulled up by the kerb, engine ticking over. Anna rushed over to it before anyone else could get there and leant in towards the driver's window. The driver slid the window down and shook his head.

'Sorry, love,' he said. 'Still got the meter running.' He gestured towards the back of a tall man in a raincoat who was standing at the newspaper stall. Anna looked over to the stall and suppressed a gasp. She looked around, not knowing which way to escape. She started to make for the bus shelter; she would get on the first bus, even if it was in the wrong direction. Or she would walk, fast, and keep walking. It was too late. Theo turned around and strode back towards the taxi, his long loping pace heavier than usual. He carried a stack of newspapers in his arms, tabloids heaped on top of broadsheets. He shouted her name across the noise of engines. Anna started to walk away, but he rushed towards her.

'I said I don't want to talk about it,' she started. 'And no one talks to me the way you did just now. I don't care how you get away with talking to other people.'

'You could have told me,' he said. It wasn't quite his plaintive look, but something close. To Anna, it just seemed like another tactic: bad cop, good cop, all in one body. It was too late for him to try to be charming.

'Of course I couldn't have told you,' she replied.

'Not everything,' he persisted. 'Just an idea, just a hint. A heads-up maybe.'

'There's no way I could have done that,' Anna repeated. 'You know that.'

'Well, it's too late now,' Theo said, dejected. 'It's a disaster. Is there more to come?'

'Stop trying,' Anna stonewalled. 'Why, what's going to happen?' If he could try it on, so could she.

For a moment, Theo couldn't help himself, the impulse to be the one imparting knowledge too great.

'He's gone, of course.'

'Lucas, he's gone already?' Anna suddenly wondered whether she should head straight back to the office.

'No, not yet. But he will be.' Theo stopped himself short. 'Anyway, I couldn't tell you. Now I know I can't trust you any more.'

Anna paused. 'I can't trust you either.' She was surprised how little emotion she felt. It was a statement of fact, nothing more. She was not sure, in fact, how far she had ever trusted him.

Theo turned back to the taxi which was still waiting, the red digits on the meter clicking up ever higher.

'I have to go,' he said. 'Have to deal with . . . all this.' He shifted the weight of the newspapers under his arm.

He climbed into the cab and slammed the door shut behind him. Anna detected a vanishing hint of aftershave over the diesel fumes in the space where he had been. In normal circumstances, there would have been a goodbye, there would have been a last enveloping hug from those heavy arms and a kiss, even a brief one, to acknowledge that there had been affection there once. This was a different game.

The indicator lights on the cab blinked right and the taxi slid out into the traffic.

# 23

THE NOISE OF traffic in the street seemed louder than usual: cars were parking, engines turning over. Mark stirred just enough to sense that it was barely light. The birds were already singing, but they rarely stopped these days; they were urban birds whose circadian rhythms were in tune with the street lights rather than the sun. It was too early.

Emily's ability to spring out of bed, instantly alert and with a good grace, was another of the qualities that he envied and occasionally begrudged her. She even seemed to thrive on little sleep, the way Margaret Thatcher was supposed to have done. One of Mark's blurry waking thoughts, as he tried to retrieve a corner of warm duvet and wrap it more closely around himself, was that perhaps Emily should have gone into politics instead of him. She was wearing a red T-shirt with a faded political slogan on the front, a top that had once belonged to him but which she had long since appropriated. She walked lightly across the floorboards to the window and whisked the curtains open.

'Oh my God!' she exclaimed, pulling them shut again so hard the curtain rail almost came loose. Mark sat up and switched on the bedside light.

'What is it, darling?' he mumbled, though he half knew already. Emily turned her back to the window as if by pretending she had not seen what was outside, it would no longer exist.

'What have you done?' she exclaimed. Her voice was one of a frightened, injured woman; not an Emily he had ever known. 'Tell me what you've done.'

Mark hauled his feet from the warmth of the bed and placed them on the cold floor. He felt unsteady as he walked the length of the room towards the window where Emily stood. He tried to put his arms around her waist, to feel her body inside the baggy T-shirt, but she pushed him away. Mark stepped towards the other of the two large sash windows and eased the dark-blue curtain away from the frame to reveal a sliver of the view.

The first thing he saw was a tall antenna stretching up from the roof of a white van, a cable coiling around it like a beanstalk around a bamboo cane. Next to that van was another, blue this time, with a satellite dish on top. A man in a black fleece was standing by the back of that van, unwinding bright yellow wires. A second TV truck was parked at the corner, a third drove past them down the street, obviously having arrived too late to get a good parking place. The street was full of cars he didn't recognise.

Mark held his breath, feeling that any twitch of the curtain would alert them to his presence. He looked again, hoping not to be seen. The photographers were milling about on the pavement, sipping coffee from paper cups and gossiping with each other. One or two trained their long lenses up at his window, but with a half-hearted air, as though they were just checking the light for now. A blonde TV reporter in a bright-pink coat paced up and down the pavement, looking down at a sheet of paper, reciting her words to herself. Occasionally she practised a hand gesture for added effect. Then she stopped, looked in the wing mirror of a van, and wreathed her head in a cloud of hairspray to fix her hard-set hair still more firmly in place. Mark looked at the alarm clock. It was quarter to six.

'Switch the light off,' he whispered to Emily.

'Why?' She wrinkled her nose at him.

'So they don't know we're here.'

'But I just opened the curtains, and then closed them again. They already know.' Emily was incontrovertibly logical. Mark switched off the light anyway, and sat back down on the bed. 'You have to tell me what's happened,' Emily said, moving towards the bed and sitting down, cross-legged on the end of it. Tears were starting to form in the corners of her eyes. 'Are you having an affair?'

'No,' Mark protested.

'It's that German woman, the one with the spiky blonde hair. The little minister with the snooty nose, from the banquet. Or Louisa. Is it Louisa? She calls you all the time. It's usually the secretaries.' She was no longer sounding logical.

'Emily, don't be ridiculous. This isn't like you. It isn't that.'

'Then what is it?'

'I'll explain,' Mark sighed. 'It's complicated. But it's not an affair. It's to do with Dad. And some other stuff.'

The green lights on the baby monitor on Emily's bedside table flared into life as Jack's wail crackled through the speaker. Emily pulled on a pair of pyjama trousers and rushed upstairs to him. Mark heard their chatter as Jack was lifted out of his cot. It was the one remaining, comforting sound of a normal morning. Emily carried Jack down the stairs and into the bathroom to change his nappy; he protested as usual.

A minute later he heard Bella's footsteps following them. She had heard that the rest of the house was awake and didn't want to be left out. Mark called out to her, wanting the reassurance of two unconditional arms around his neck and her clean, soapy, childish smell. She ignored him and trotted on down the next flight of stairs. Mark got up and went to retrieve her. He needed to shelter her from all this, even if he couldn't protect himself. She was too fast for him; before he could stop her, she had climbed onto the window seat in the living room and folded back one of the wooden shutters.

'Daddy,' she asked in the voice reserved for her most serious questions, 'why are there people?'

'Which people?' he asked stupidly, half hoping that it was one of Bella's more abstract queries, like 'Why are there stars?' She may have looked like Emily, but there were some ways in which she took after his father. Dad, he remembered. This would all be happening to Dad, too. Mark had called him again, last night, to warn him, but his father refused to leave the house, not even to stay with Mark's sister.

'Those people, out there. With lots of big cameras and all talking on phones.'

'Come here,' he snapped at her, sounding harsher than he meant to. She looked at him, puzzled. 'Close the shutter, lovely, and come to Daddy,' he said, in a softer tone this time. Bella complied. He led her back upstairs to the bedroom and, for once, let her bounce on the bed as much as she wanted. Emily brought Jack back into the room and he laughed loudly at his sister as she leapt up and down, her hair flying wildly.

'Whatever it is, why didn't you tell me before?' Emily asked. 'I could have done something.'

Mark didn't know what she could have done, except take the children away somewhere else and leave him alone to deal with this. Selfishly, he couldn't bear that idea.

'I didn't know it was really going to break, that they'd actually run it, until late last night. When I got back, you were already asleep.'

'You could have woken me.'

He could have done, but he couldn't bear to do that, either. He had come in late, drunk brandy downstairs with his music playing low so as not to wake the children, before going up and seeing her head on the pillow and her arms up, coiled as if to protect her face, and he couldn't bring himself to disturb her. She could at least have a peaceful night's sleep. He wouldn't make them all flee the house in the middle of the night, whatever it meant now.

'But I mean you must have known something was coming, before that?' Emily continued. 'How long has it been?'

Mark dropped his chin down towards his chest. 'I know,' he said. 'I should have. There are lots of things I should have done.' He would explain it all to her; she would help him make sense of it. First, though, he desperately needed a cup of coffee.

It was a couple of minutes past six o'clock when the phones began to ring. Mark had to stop Bella from answering; he left the machine to pick up the calls. They always seemed to wait until what they thought was a more civilised hour, not wanting to wake him; as though a quarter past six was a better time to have your life ruined than a quarter to.

Mark listened to the stream of voices: a polite, tentative girl who announced herself as calling from the *Today* programme and began her request by saying 'I'm so sorry to trouble you'; gruff male voices from newsdesks, rattling off the digits of their phone numbers too fast for anyone to be able to write them down; later, there would be one or two messages from colleagues, asking if he was all right. He would try to gauge which of them were genuinely concerned and which were merely nosy.

As for the rest: you're not sorry to trouble me, he thought, it's your job. And really, right now, a call from some relatively well-meaning girl which I am never going to return is the very least of my troubles. This was the penalty for having been approachable in the past: they knew his home number, knew his address. There were many times when he'd been happy for a radio car to be parked outside the door, when a friendly engineer would have rung the doorbell and shown him into the cramped space in the back of the van. He'd sit on a narrow bench, put on headphones and opine into the microphone.

Mark found his mobile in his coat pocket; the battery was fading and there were dozens of missed calls. It made a pathetic bleep and Mark decided to leave it to give up and switch itself off. He wished he could do the same. There were probably terse, insistent messages on his pager too, another list of numbers to call back, if he could ever remember where he'd put it.

Emily was about to take Bella and Jack down to the kitchen when Mark stopped her.

'They need breakfast,' she said. 'They can't not have breakfast.'

'Yes,' he replied, 'but they can't have breakfast with the entire press pack watching them through the window.'

Mark and Emily had loved their basement kitchen when they bought the house. As they'd wandered the north London streets looking for somewhere to buy, before Bella was born, they'd peeked into the similar basement rooms of house upon house, walking past the uncurtained windows in the evenings, when the lights were on, watching families sit together around tables; imagining their own future selves in the warm light that seemed to suffuse those apparently contented people. Now, the early daylight that would soon stream in through the railings would show them acting out a tableau of a happy family for an audience of journalists on the pavement above. Much good it did him now to live in the same part of town as the PM; much good had it ever done him. Whatever dinner parties and private meetings there were, he hadn't been invited.

'Breakfast upstairs today,' Emily decided.

'Upstairs?' said Bella, realising this too was something out of the ordinary. This seemed to be a day when the normal rules were not enforced, some kind of holiday. 'But what if Jack makes a mess? Jack always makes a mess.'

'It'll be fine,' Emily reassured her.

It was Emily who went into the kitchen, trying to stay close to the back of the room, trying to act as if the people outside were not there. They saw her, of course, and once they had seen there was definitely someone in the house who was up and making breakfast, they started to ring the doorbell, one after the other.

With Bella distracted by the delight of watching television while eating cereal, Mark tried to explain everything to Emily. Mark pleaded with her not to cross-examine him; he couldn't deal with as much scrutiny at home as he was going to face once he stepped outside the door. She listened, occasionally stopping to help guide Jack's mushy spoonfuls of breakfast closer to his mouth. Her first question was the same as Edward Groves's had been: what had Anthony really done? It was still the question Mark couldn't answer.

'What do you think?' he asked. 'You know him. You've known him for the best part of ten years.'

'On the face of it, I can't see it,' she replied. 'But then how much does he ever talk about the past – his real past, I mean, not history? He's hardly told you anything, apart from one or two stories about being hungry, which he's repeated ever since you were a kid.' She broke off for a moment. 'Bella, don't tip the bowl. It will go everywhere.' Mark noticed that his coffee mug was one of the campaign ones, from the election. He didn't think Emily had picked it out intentionally.

'You've always said it was because he didn't want to upset you, didn't want to drag up painful memories,' Emily continued. 'And I'm not saying there definitely are, but there might be other reasons, other things he wanted to keep from you.' It was her lawyer's brain, again, looking for evidence, looking for the obvious gaps in the story. 'So I think you shouldn't do anything until you know more.'

Mark shook his head. 'It doesn't work like that. There's no due process. They'll already have made up their minds.'

Emily wasn't going to let them stop her going to work. In the carapace of her black suit, the shoes Mark recognised as the ones she wore for luck during big cases, and slightly more make-up than usual, she was ready. Mark coaxed the children into their clothes, twisting arms into sleeves and feet into the right shoes.

'Are you sure?' Mark said as she prepared to open the door. 'You don't have to.'

'I do have to,' said Emily.

'I don't want you to feel like one of those wives being asked to put on a show, doing the loyal pose with your husband.'

'This isn't that, is it? I told you I'd never do that, anyway, when I married you,' Emily said. 'And in any case, I'm not going out there with you. Not unless you're coming out dressed like that. Which I wouldn't advise.' She pointed towards the old sweatshirt and running shorts Mark was wearing, the first things he had found when he got up.

'What about Bella and Jack?' Mark asked.

'I'll look after them,' she said. 'Send them out when I tell you.'

Mark hung back behind the door, shushing Bella, whose queries had not got answers that satisfied her, and trying to unfold Jack's buggy before strapping him into it. Emily opened the door and he heard the rattle of camera shutters and a cacophony of questions. Mark listened, trying to make out what Emily was saying. The cameras and the reporters fell strangely quiet. 'Mark will not be making a statement,' she said. 'I'm bringing our children out now to go to school and nursery, and I'd be very grateful if you didn't film them or shout at them. They, at least, are entitled to some privacy. Thank you.'

Emily cracked open the door again and whispered 'now' to Mark and the children. Mark pushed the buggy forward for her to grab, trying to stay out of sight; Bella went outside with a skip, swinging her book bag and barely acknowledging him to say goodbye. Emily was impressive, almost terrifyingly so, but Mark couldn't help feeling as though she were representing him as her client, rather than her husband. She was the solicitor appearing on the steps of the court, speaking on behalf of the accused. He heard Bella say 'hello' to some of the hacks in her bright high voice, heard some of them reply. The cameras remained silent.

He wished he had Emily's fortitude. Mark wandered back into the living room and picked up his half-drunk, tepid coffee. He looked out of the window at their back garden, a narrow strip of grass and paving stones with a few spindly trees. A rickety iron staircase led down from the ground floor to the garden below. Mark wondered for a moment whether he should just make a run for it, scramble over the crumbling back wall and into a neighbour's garden, emerge somehow onto another street where no one was looking for him. It wasn't a plan that stood up to more than a moment's scrutiny: Mark didn't think anyone in the houses that backed onto their terrace would welcome a fleeing politician, let alone usher him through their house and out of their front door, even if there were anyone in the house on a weekday morning. Not to mention the fact that 'Disgraced MP trespasses on neighbours' was an extra twist to the story he didn't need; this neighbourhood was rife with journalists and the odds were he'd end up in one of their gardens, treading on the daffodils of someone who'd find in their crushed blooms the perfect top line for that week's column. It was a problem of living in a terraced house that he had never had reason to contemplate before: there was no other way out.

Somehow, at some point, he would have to face them outside the front door. Mark plugged his phone into the charger. He would leave it a little while longer before he switched it back on.

The television was still on in the corner of the room. The Teletubbies were skipping around against a cloudless sky, scooting over green hills past fake flowers and docile rabbits. Mark changed the channel, reluctantly leaving the cheerful, primary-coloured world for the one that he recognised. The music switched from a catchy tune to an insistent, ominous thumping.

Then he saw himself: he was making the familiar walk down a staircase, into shot and out again, acting as though there were no camera there. Capital letters against a red background flashed up across his feet: *BREAKING NEWS*. He didn't listen to what the newsreader was saying about him – he could have written the script himself, and often had.

In the end, this was what his career came down to. He was just a man in a suit, descending a staircase to a landing, again and again and again. The ten seconds of film were repeated endlessly. Could those really be the only pictures of him that existed? After all that time spent turning up at the studios at unearthly hours, always available, always affable, almost always loyal.

There weren't even any of the other old standby pictures – him reading the morning's newspapers, him sitting at his desk going through important-looking documents with an air of high-minded concentration. Look harder, he thought, as if still giving some recalcitrant researcher instructions. There must be other ones, better ones. He remembered suddenly that this was no longer his problem. His mind was setting up strange diversionary tactics of its own, making him worry about trivial things as a way to avoid worrying about the big things.

The girl in the pink coat came into vision. She waved her hands in practised animated gestures and pointed to the house behind her: his house. He heard her voice twice, as if there was an echo, realising he could catch her words faintly as she said them outside his window, and then a few seconds later hear them louder on TV. Both times, Mark could tell that she really had nothing to say: she repeated a half-digested version of what was in the newspaper, hedged around with the word 'allegedly' and chucking in a few biographical facts about Mark himself. A world-weary presenter whose make-up strained to hide the bags under his eyes pushed the girl for some analysis: what did this mean? what were insiders saying? Her eyes widened slightly, giving her a fearful look, before she rushed through a list of people who wouldn't comment and then waffled something about the seriousness of the allegations. The girl standing on the pavement obviously had no insiders she could call on at dawn. The camera cut away and the presenter seemed to be trying not to roll his eyes.

Mark was already reaching for the remote control before Stewart Hale appeared; he nearly pressed the off switch as a reflex when he saw him, but stopped himself. He was evidently uncomfortable; he fidgeted with his earpiece and sat awkwardly in front of the image of Westminster on the screen, seeming to loom larger than the towers behind him. Hale wore a heavy suit in a narrow striped pattern which made flickering coloured lines jump across the screen, a strobing on the camera that was hypnotic and distracting at the same time. He could barely hide the excitement in his voice; his indignation was so intense it made the microphone pop.

'Serious national security issues raised,' he intoned, '. . . very profound questions for this government to answer.' Mark shrugged to himself. Hale said this all the time, about everything. The presenter asked Hale something to the effect of whether it really mattered, now that East Germany and communism were long gone. Mark watched Hale take a deep breath, puffing his chest full of air and outrage. He expelled it all in one angry response.

'This is about a betrayal of our country,' Stewart Hale began. 'This is about a cavalier attitude to top secret government information. This is about a minister who has neither the integrity nor the competence to be trusted with office. And finally, this is about a minister who has misled the House of Commons. How can you suggest any of that doesn't matter?'

The presenter, lost for a comeback, thanked Hale. Stewart Hale, Mark observed, had done something he had never before done in his life. It was the case against Mark, in the space of twenty lethal seconds. He had given a sound bite.

Mark muted the sound on the TV. He would have to switch on his phone. Upstairs in his study it was quieter; he could no longer hear the bored chatter from the pavement. He brought the phone with him, coiling the black wire of the charger in his other hand. He was delaying switching it on, and he knew that this too was inexcusable, this was making things worse than they needed to be.

Mark pushed the button on the top of the phone and watched it buzz into life, heard it hum its stupid little tune at him. It rang immediately, and Mark knew this was the call he had been avoiding.

'Where have you been?' Robert Callander didn't introduce himself. He didn't have to. Nor did he wait for an answer. 'We've been trying to get hold of you. How are we expected to handle this if we can't get hold of you?'

Mark muttered an apology, some half-sentence about the calls disturbing the children, and tried to suppress the thought that they were probably finding it easier to handle things without having heard from him.

'Well,' Callander huffed, 'you'd better give us an explanation.'

'Now?' Mark asked.

'Not now. We need you to come in.'

'What does he think?' Mark ventured. He was trying to gauge whether the decision was already made. Callander's claim to know what was going through the prime minister's mind was unrivalled. Sometimes he even seemed to know it better than the PM himself. 'He thinks it's bad. Very bad, on the face of it. But he's giving you a chance to put your side. Get here.'

There were still papers on Mark's desk. He picked them up carefully and locked them into the box, something he should have done long before. If anyone had seen this, it would have been yet another sign of his failings – vital documents left strewn across a table in full view of a window. Mark added the journalistic emphasis himself.

Mark was struggling to get his purple tie into a decent knot when he heard another car pull up outside. His fingers fumbled and the result looked too narrow and creased. He tugged at the loop around his neck to undo the knot and tried again. Mark cared about the tie. It was in an expensive, thick silk; he'd bought it with his first ministerial salary and it never usually let him down. After all, since these would probably be the last pictures of him anyone would remember, he may as well go out with the good tie. No point letting them mock him for looking shabby on top of everything else.

The engine of the latest car to arrive ticked over at a low pitch; Mark recognised it as the sound of his official car. Well, this morning it was his official car. By this afternoon it would be someone else's, unless he could somehow make things different. There was a rush of activity outside the door. Mark didn't look – to twitch the curtain was only confirmation, for both sides – but he knew they would be moving into place, knowing that a car meant a passenger, meant a door opening and him emerging.

Mark looked at himself for a last time in the mirror on the inside of the wardrobe door. He saw himself standing in front of the reflected rack of brightly coloured ties hanging from the other door. This was how it came and how it went. He still had roughly the same outline, the silhouette of a presentable man in a decent suit and tie, but the rest of it was gone. His engaging smile had fallen, his shoulders were no longer held so confidently, the reassuring gaze replaced with a tense mouth and an eyelid that was starting to twitch. But this was who he was now – the beleaguered Mark Lucas – and this was the man who had to go out there and face it.

In the hall, he checked his pockets as though he was leaving the house on a normal day, looking around for his keys and his wallet. He switched the phone back to silent before sliding it inside his jacket. Mark closed his eyes tightly before he opened the door, opening them again to see that it was all still the same. None of it was going to go away. He turned the key in the lock and pulled the front door towards him.

The noise surged around him. The cameramen hoisted their cameras higher on their shoulders and focused their lenses tightly onto his face; the photographers held their fingers on the shutters. Microphones were thrust towards him: foam-covered ones with logos, fluffy ones on long poles above his head or extended towards his waist. A radio reporter had scurried beneath the legs of the other journalists and crouched on the floor, headphones over her ears and her microphone held up as high as she could reach. They all shouted, a cacophony of questions and accusations that Mark could barely distinguish from one another. He tried not to look around, not to swivel his head from side to side or to catch anyone's gaze. They shouted his name and the title he still held, for however much longer: 'Minister, Mr Lucas, Mark . . .'

There were four steps down from the front door to the pavement; they had left the steps clear but clustered around the iron railings to either side, leaning on his car and that of the neighbours. Mark saw that he would have to push his way through to reach the Rover beyond them.

From among the garble of questions Mark could hear one gruff, smoke-filled voice shouting. The others were expecting the voice, knew the man it came from, and let him shout uninterrupted, because the absence of an answer was itself worth reporting; it was a ritual part of the occasion.

'Minister, are you going to resign?'

Mark looked straight ahead, concentrating on finding his way to the car and on getting into the back seat. He almost smiled at the fact that it was so predictable, that this was always, somehow, how you imagined it ending.

No, he thought, as he pulled the car door shut with a heavy clunk. I'm not going to resign. I'm going to be sacked.

Dave, the driver, was normally chatty, but this morning he observed a silence that Mark wanted to construe as sympathetic. He pulled the car away from the photographers who surrounded it gently, but with just enough determination to suggest that he'd be prepared to run over someone's foot if necessary. The lenses were trained on the rear windows of the car; Mark kept his chin level, staring somewhere ahead as they drove down the street. He didn't want to look as downcast as he felt. As Dave neared the main road, having left the journalists behind, he looked up into the rear-view mirror and caught Mark's eye.

'You all right, sir?' he asked.

Mark shrugged and moved his head sideways, indicating that he wasn't, really.

'Sorry, sir,' Dave said, easing out behind a double-decker bus and into the flow of traffic approaching the Angel. Mark could tell that he had seen all this many times before.

# 24

WHEN THE BUZZ of the doorbell woke Alex, he wasn't sure what it was, at first; by the time it sounded a third time he was starting to get annoyed. It must have been a mistake. He looked at the alarm clock that he no longer had much cause to use: it was ten to six. It was too early for a parcel, which in any case would certainly not be for him.

The room, at the back of the house, was cold, and the light had not yet reached this side of the building. Alex rolled over onto his side and hesitated before he stretched his feet out. Perhaps they would go away. He wasn't getting up for someone else's parcel, not at this hour of the day. The bell kept ringing, longer now each time, as though someone with heavy hands was leaning on it. He would have to get up, if only to tell them to stop. Alex unfurled his thin, pale legs, unhooked his brown towelling dressing gown from the back of his bedroom door, shrugged it on, and went into the hall.

He lifted the handset of the intercom and snapped into the mouthpiece:

'What do you want? Do you realise what time this is? It's not even six o'clock.'

There was a slow voice on the other end of the line, a voice that belonged with the heavy fingers on the doorbell.

'Alexander Rutherford?' it asked. He sounded as though he was reading something out.

'Yes?' Alex's voice was hesitant. No one called him that, no one since his grandmother had died.

'Metropolitan Police. We'd like to come in.'

Alex held the intercom away from his ear for a moment. Now that he was more awake, he was surprised they hadn't come before.

'Mr Rutherford?' the voice spoke again.

'Yes,' Alex said more quickly. 'Do you have some identification?' he asked, his training in suspicion overriding for a moment his instinct to comply.

'Of course, sir. We can show you, but you need to buzz us in.'

Alex pressed the switch and heard the answering click of the door downstairs. He didn't move from where he stood, only wrapping the dressing gown closer around himself and tying the belt. Two pairs of heavy feet trod on the stairs outside. Alex suddenly wondered whether he should get dressed before they reached the door of the flat. He reflected that it was too late for that now; that in any case, they would have to let him put some clothes on. Surely that was how it worked. When they turned up at your house before 6 a.m., without any warning, it wasn't for a friendly chat.

They knocked, and Alex took the chain off the inside of the door before opening it. There were two officers in front of him: one, a tall, uniformed man, stood a couple of paces back from his colleague, who was in plain clothes. The detective's hair was shaved close to his scalp and he was dressed in shades of grey and black; the practical, outdoorsy clothes of a man who didn't expect to be spending his day at a desk.

Alex noticed how as the detective stepped forward into the doorway the uniformed officer hung back and stayed on the landing, near the top of the staircase. He's there to stop me running away, he thought. Alex contemplated for a moment the idea of attempting to flee, of charging out of the door and trying to dodge the officer, who was roughly the same height and skinny build as him but no doubt stronger and fitter. He had an image of himself escaping down the stairs and out of the door, wearing only an old dressing gown, with boxer shorts and a T-shirt underneath. As he thought of this parallel self, stranded half naked in the street, with no keys and no money and probably a van-load of policemen waiting somewhere nearby, the vision came to an abrupt halt. The officer seemed to have the same realisation and entered the room behind his colleague.

'Mr Rutherford?' the detective asked. Alex nodded. 'I am arresting you on suspicion of breaching the Official Secrets Act.' While the detective ran through the form of words about not needing to say anything, Alex found the only thing he could think of was when he'd be able to get dressed. He was passive, waiting to see what happened next, as though this was all happening to somebody else.

Alex looked from one officer to the other, expecting someone to tell him what to do. They looked back, as though someone being arrested ought to know how they were supposed to behave. Alex worried that his passivity might itself somehow be taken to imply his guilt. Perhaps he ought to protest, with loud indignation, though he couldn't see how that would help either. After a while, he broke the silence.

'What happens now?'

'We'd like you to come to the police station with us,' the detective replied. Again, the politeness of invitations that could not realistically be declined.

'Can I . . .?' Alex looked down at his dressing gown and gestured in the general direction of the bathroom and the bedroom.

'Of course,' he replied.

As Alex turned towards the bathroom, the sergeant spoke.

'Do you have a computer, sir?'

'At home?' Alex said. 'No. No, I don't.' He could think of little he would use one for, if he wasn't working. Nor did he own a mobile phone.

The sergeant raised an eyebrow in slight disbelief.

'We'll need to look around.' He said it as though he was being shown the flat by an estate agent, not about to search it for missing official secrets and other incriminating information. He stepped into the living room and appraised it, scanning the bookshelves and the pile of newspapers on the coffee table.

That was when Alex flinched. He went into the bathroom and closed the door behind him, not wanting to see them start to move things, start to take things from their places. His quiet, orderly sanctuary was about to be disturbed. He imagined the books being turned upside-down and their pages shaken out, their spines cracked, put back in the wrong order if they were put back at all. He wondered whether they would send in those men in the white overalls you saw on the news, and then thought probably not. They were not looking for blood or fingerprints; it was not that sort of evidence they needed. It was evidence of words, evidence of thoughts.

Alex brushed his teeth more thoroughly than usual. He did not know when he would get his next chance, so he thought he had better take it now. He considered not shaving, but then thought he should do that as well, for the same reason. They could wait for him. He scraped the slightly blunt razor across his jaw, noticing that his face seemed thinner, though maybe rather less pale. It must have been all the time he had spent walking, even on those overcast days when the only thing that could have turned his skin a darker shade was the wind rising from the river. Alex had to take deep, slow breaths, trying to hold his hand steady so he didn't cut himself. He wondered who else's door officers might have knocked on this early in the morning. He tried to stop himself worrying about Anna.

Alex reflected that, in some ways, he was lucky. There were, he knew, other times and other places where it would not happen like this, probably even other people of his own time and his own country who were not treated in the same way. He would not disappear; there were forms of words that had to be adhered to and rights that had to be upheld. He would be ruined quietly and politely and according to due process, by people who called him sir.

The detective was waiting in the hallway as Alex crossed into his bedroom. He looked at his watch but didn't tell him to hurry up. Alex thought there must have been people waiting outside as well, in case he tried to escape. There was no way he could have got out of the bathroom: it had one tiny window, which didn't open, and an ancient air vent. Had the window opened, it would have given onto a narrow gap before a brick wall. His bedroom window offered nothing but a sharp drop of two floors onto a flagstone patio below.

Alex put on clean clothes: a pair of beige trousers, a blue shirt in some sort of soft denim, a grey V-necked jumper. He expected that wherever they took him, it would be cold. There was no point in wearing a belt; they'd only take it away. He found a pair of grey socks, pulled them on, and walked out of the room in search of his shoes.

He laced up a pair of scuffed brown brogues under the gaze of the police officers. Did they take your shoelaces as well? There was no point in wondering: all his shoes had laces, even the trainers that languished somewhere at the back of a cupboard. Alex picked up his raincoat, and he was as ready as he could hope to be.

He hoped more than anything that there was no one else watching, no photographer tipped off, no neighbour looking out of the window downstairs. Many of them, like Mrs Baines in the flat below, had known his grandmother and, though they had never had cause to complain about her grandson and his quiet habits, would be horrified to see policemen at the door of the building. The detective walked ahead of Alex down the stairs.

Alex's stomach lurched suddenly and he gripped the banister. He would have to tell his parents, he realised. He would get one phone call and he would have to call them, try to explain as far as he could what had happened, ask them to help him and find him a lawyer. He could already hear his mother's mixture of fear and disapproval that would be expressed more in the silences between her words than in the words themselves. Alex considered not telling them at all, but he knew that for once he needed someone's help, and he knew too that the only thing his mother and father would find worse than knowing would be their worry if they had no idea where he had gone. What, too, if they found out some other way? What if they saw him in that snatched photo he dreaded, in a newspaper, and he had said nothing at all?

Another officer in uniform was waiting outside the front door, standing at the foot of the steps in front of the pillar of the portico. There were two cars: a dark-blue, unmarked car parked in front of a patrol car. Alex was shown into the back of the unmarked car; the detective climbed into the front seat. The driver started the engine and the car pulled away. Alex turned to watch his home receding from view behind him, the front door left open and the officer outside standing guard.

## 25

A T LEAST THEY had avoided any more of the cameras. When the car pulled through the heavy black metal gates of Downing Street, the only faces looking through the windows were those of bewildered tourists, halted on the pavement by the policemen on duty, and a few civil servants on their way to work, who did not appear to register Mark with any undue interest beyond slight irritation at having to wait while the car was let through.

They didn't want him to be seen, though it was inevitable that someone would spot him, somewhere, and within minutes the ripple of the sighting would have spread. It was a relief that at least he didn't have to do the public, shaming walk down the street. Dave swerved the car away from the main door and towards one of the back entrances too smartly for any of the journalists waiting in the street to get a clear sighting of Mark. A young woman was waiting for him at one of the back doors, as if he were a parcel that needed to be signed for. He was shown up a dark, servants' staircase before he emerged into the light of the public rooms.

Everyone in the office seemed young, even to Mark. They were bright-eyed kids in their early twenties, some who looked as though they should still be at college. Probably all had been at college together, like the rest of them. A young blonde woman with her hair tied back in a ponytail offered him tea or coffee, using a concerned tone that she didn't sound accustomed to. Mark accepted coffee and the pretended sympathy that came with it. Two young men at the back of the office leant towards each other over their desks, whispering. One of them looked up over his wire-rimmed glasses before turning back to his colleague and nodding.

Mark had barely tasted the coffee – a bitter potion that must have been left stewing since the early morning – before he was called in. The impromptu Star Chamber that had been convened consisted of four men. The prime minister sat behind a large desk; his chief of staff lolled on a sofa, his legs outstretched; the head of communications leant against a panelled wall. Robert Callander perched on the curved arm of another green sofa that did not look as if it could take his weight for long. They had probably already made up their minds; there was only Mark to speak in his own defence, and he doubted that, however great his powers of persuasion, he would be able to alter that decision.

Mark was directed to sit down. He took a seat on the green sofa, sitting as far away from Callander as he could manage. The cushions were formlessly soft; Mark sank into them and he rested one arm on the sofa for support. He'd already been at an obvious disadvantage when he entered the room; the sagging cushions that left him far below everyone else's eye-line made it even worse. Mark noticed that on the sofa opposite was a copy of the newspaper with the story on its front page. He could just make out the top half of his own head above the fold. It seemed strange that it was what meant he'd ended up here, and yet he'd not actually seen the physical paper, read the words in print himself.

The prime minister looked across to his chief of staff and nodded, the judge to the prosecuting barrister.

'Mark,' the chief of staff began, his voice slow and sombre. Mark had never met Will Mason before, knew him only by reputation. He was supposed to have an intellect that people were in awe of, 'a brain like a trap' someone had told Mark once, but was also reputed to be glacial and distant. Just who you didn't want outlining the case against you, calling you by your first name as though he was your friend.

'We have a number of problems here,' he continued. Mason started to count them off on his fingers. 'Firstly, there's an obvious security issue.' He pre-empted the objection that Mark was about to open his mouth to make. 'Now, I accept that this isn't entirely your responsibility; it sounds like there have been plenty of system failures in the security services that we're asking them to account for. But once it was brought to your attention, we'd have expected that you raise it much more thoroughly than you did. We needed the wheels to have been put in motion on this much sooner.'

Mark looked across to Callander, who was nodding as he listened. How could he nod, when Mark had raised it with him, the man who was supposed to be able to make things happen.

'Secondly, Stewart Hale seems to think you misled the House.'

'That's Stewart Hale!' Mark exclaimed. 'He calls for everyone to resign, regardless. You can't go by what he says.'

'That notwithstanding,' Mason continued, using a word Mark rarely heard in conversation, 'he may have a point, this time. We looked back at the adjournment debate he's talking about. You said something about the files being kept with all due security.'

'Which I thought they were, at the time,' Mark replied. 'If I wasn't given the information, I can hardly be expected—'

'Thirdly,' Mason interrupted as he tapped his middle finger with the opposite hand, 'this is going to cause us huge diplomatic embarrassment, as I'm sure you're aware.'

Callander took up the thought. This was, after all, his professed area of expertise.

'It's going to cause us even more problems with Germany. It's obviously a terribly sensitive issue there, far more so than here. We've already had to smooth some feathers after the last meeting, when they brought it up in public, which was far from ideal.'

The arm of the sofa creaked as Callander shifted his weight.

Mark wondered why he was going over this again. He'd already had the lecture once before, after the press conference. He scanned the room and realised that although he was supposed to be the person they were addressing, they were actually only talking to each other. Mark Lucas and his job were only a minor part of the strategy.

'Now it looks as though we were deliberately withholding information from them. This is not what we need, with the summit coming up and everything else going on.'

Mark decided that he had to say something. He couldn't continue to sit here with everyone talking over his head, deciding his fate and not letting him do anything about it.

'I'd built up a good relationship with them. We were working on the issue of the files. I'd wanted to make more progress on it, move towards their position. But I was told that wasn't our policy. It would be harder for someone else to pick that up and start to repair it.'

Callander turned sharply towards Mark. The sofa creaked more loudly.

'Really?' His tone was withering. 'You'd like to set up a meeting with your dear friend Ilse Bernau and tell her that you've allowed a valuable part of their history to be lost, or stolen, or left on the top deck of a London bus then sold to the newspapers and put all over the front page? I can't see you getting on quite so well after that. I think she'd rather have someone else to deal with, someone who wasn't responsible for making quite such a mess of things.'

Will Mason was staring at Mark now. He ignored Bob's tirade, the elegant machinery of his well-trained mind processing something Mark had said earlier.

'You said you wanted to move towards their position on the files? You mean you believed they should have been released?'

'I did,' said Mark. 'It's a matter of record. It was my position at the time, but I accepted that wasn't the way we were going.'

'Why?' Mason asked.

'Why did I accept it?' Mark wasn't sure what he was driving at. 'Why was it your position?'

'My own personal view,' Mark began slowly, aware that he was about to appear to incriminate himself, 'was that in the interests of transparency, truth and reconciliation maybe, they should have them back. But as I say, I accepted that the policy wasn't mine to change.'

Mason looked towards the newspaper lying on the sofa next to him; as he did so, the press chief, Paul Norman, looked in the same direction. They both raised their eyes, acknowledging that they were thinking the same thing.

Paul Norman spoke first, another counsel for the prosecution wanting to impress the court. His voice was rough and he twisted a pen between his fingers where he obviously wished a lit ciga-rette could have been. He was a former journalist, one who believed nothing happened by accident; that there was always a design somewhere, if you could find it.

'Did you do this, then?' he said, moving round to pick up the newspaper. 'Give it to them?'

'Of course not,' Mark exclaimed. 'How could I have done? I never even saw the disks themselves, the files.'

'You could have got someone to do it, had them claim they'd been lost.' Norman either overestimated Mark's talent for conspiracy, or else it was a question purely designed to gauge his reaction. Mark looked at him, bemused. It wasn't even an accusation worthy of an answer. Norman realised that none was forthcoming, and changed tack.

'But you spoke to them? You obviously spoke to them.'

Mark shrugged. There was no point in denying it; they all knew the code, they all knew that the unnamed 'friends' were really Mark himself.

'After the fact,' Mark said. 'They came to me when they had it all. No one in the department would say anything to help me, you wouldn't even issue a denial on my behalf. What was I supposed to do?'

'You were supposed to leave it to us,' Norman replied, almost under his breath. 'We know how to handle things. We don't need you . . . freelancing.'

'And let you say nothing?' Mark continued, angry now at how little he counted for in all this. 'Ruin my reputation, ruin my father's reputation that he worked all his life for?'

'I rather think perhaps that was down to the good professor himself.' The comment came from Callander, who glowered down at Mark from his position above him. Mark had never been the target of one of Bob Callander's barbed comments until now, and this was the second in the space of minutes. He'd heard about how he could be vindictive, poisonous: how first there was jollity, an arm on the shoulder, a friendly word; the next day or the next week there would be nothing but an oblivious look; a further transgression meant venomous comments that were shared with glee by those who overheard them, in the bars and in the corridors.

The prime minister spoke for the first time, leaning in across his desk, resting his chin on his hands.

'And what about your father?'

Mark Lucas was suddenly the Cavalier boy in the painting, expected to condemn himself and his family under the gaze of those in charge.

'I can't believe . . .' Mark shook his head.

The prime minister inclined his head.

'I'm sure you can't,' he said. 'None of us can. I met him once, didn't I? I've certainly read a lot of his work.'

They had met, he was right. It was not the kind of thing the prime minister was ever wrong about. It had been years before, before Mark had ever thought of going into politics, an encounter Anthony still retold with faint surprise that the polite young man he'd discussed some ideas with had gone on to be anyone of importance.

This sympathy, with the gently tilted head and the recollections, was more disconcerting than the sniping from the others at the edges of the room. This was how it worked, though. He got to be the good cop, he was the one who could afford to be charming and seem benign. Mark was meant to be left with the impression that perhaps the PM wasn't such a bad guy, it was just those other mean, hard-nosed people around him who made him take the tough decisions. Mark realised this was intentional; it wasn't the people at the edges of the room, after all, who took the decisions.

'How is he?' the prime minister continued.

'I'm not sure,' Mark answered, conscious that this, too, didn't put him in a good light. He sounded evasive, as well as a bad son. 'I haven't been able to talk to him – properly – since this all really began.'

'Did you have any idea about this – about his past?'

So here he was, the little communist boy, his father's son, being expected to denounce him. Mark imagined himself as he might have been, in a utilitarian pair of grey shorts, with cropped hair that was still blond, a red Pioneer scarf knotted around his neck. He imagined the kind of questions there would have been in another place and another time: what does your father say at home? What radio stations does he listen to?

'From the conversations we've had,' Mark continued, 'he says he's never done anything like that. And I believe him.'

This was the least he could say. It was not all that brave. There was nothing worse that could happen than was already going to happen. Even if he wasn't completely certain in his belief, he had to express it with certainty. What else could he have answered? Yes, my father's quite possibly a traitor – but I'm not. Trust me, even if you don't trust him. Let him be the one who's disgraced, instead. No, he couldn't just leave it at that. Whatever the truth, it was because Anthony had left, become someone else from the Anton Lukas who had escaped, that Mark was who he was. He could not deny that, and whatever they found out now, Mark was still himself and not a Lukas-with-a-k, a British politician, not an Ossi trying to come to terms with a new world.

'Thank you,' the prime minister said, indicating that the conversation was almost over. 'I'm sure you realise we're going to have to ask you to step down. As Will said, we need to show that we have a grip on the policy, and we need to do it quickly. I'm sorry.'

'Not to mention how this looks,' Paul Norman added from the sidelines. 'Reds under the bed and all that.'

The prime minister shook his head slightly. He was trying to be gracious, and Norman's intervention didn't suit the tone he was taking.

Will Mason stood up and took the folder he'd been holding to the prime minister's desk. He extracted two sheets of paper from it and spread them out.

'We've drafted a resignation letter for you,' he told Mark. 'If you'd care to sign?' He looked around for a pen. The prime minister picked up his own, scratched his name in dark-blue ink at the base of one of the letters, and handed the pen to Mason.

Mark heaved himself to his feet from the low, uncomfortable sofa. He walked slowly towards the desk and didn't immediately take the fountain pen that was being held out to him. At least they could let him read what was in the letter first, given that he was supposed to have written it. He scanned the page: the usual platitudes. *Thank you for giving me the privilege to serve . . . with great regret . . . have been glad to play a part in building a constructive relationship with our European partners . . . my continued support for the successful policies of this government.* There was little in it that gave the reader any real clue as to what had happened, the events that had brought this about. His hand, holding the expensive prime ministerial pen, hovered over the paper. Mark wondered for a moment whether he should insist on some of his own words, but decided against it. What difference would it make now? He signed his name in the space that had been left for it.

# 26

IF YOU'RE GOING to be arrested for betraying your country
and taken to a police station, it may as well be a good one,
Alex reflected as the car pulled up on Buckingham Palace Road.
It was so close to his house that they could just as easily have
walked, but he imagined that detectives didn't like to frogmarch
their suspects down the street. Belgravia Police Station was new
and ugly, a modern office block with large windows grafted
onto a building that was solid, impenetrable red brick. As the
detective walked him up the flight of stairs to the entrance, Alex
suspected that he would find himself in the part without the
windows.

His mother was disarmingly calm when he called. It had taken
Alex a few embarrassing minutes to remember his parents' phone
number – the first number that came to mind was the one they'd
always had, in London. The new Scottish number would never
be imprinted on his memory in the same way. Jennifer had not
gasped, had not cried, but she had known instantly that something
must be wrong: Alex would never have called her at half past six
in the morning unless there was. She had switched from a confused
sleepiness into the usual tone of gentle concern she'd had whenever Alex had spoken to her lately, then abruptly to a professional
briskness, the kind she employed to deal with an unruly pupil.
She asked straightforwardly what had happened and Alex told
her, as far as he could. His mother assumed as a given that he
hadn't done it. She was stoical, practical. Alex wondered whether
she would cry later, when he could no longer hear her, when

she had done the things she had promised to do, like find him a lawyer. She said that his father knew someone, the daughter of a friend, who was supposed to be a good criminal lawyer.

'I need someone who really is good, Mum,' Alex chided her gently. 'Not just supposed to be. Because everyone's parents think their children are good at what they do. Even if it turns out that they're not.'

Jennifer managed a small laugh. This wry, self-deprecating Alex was the son she knew.

'We'll check,' she replied, 'and maybe ask for her boss, just in case.' There was little more Alex could say, and the custody sergeant was looking at him as though he ought to be finishing his call.

'I don't know when I'll be able to talk to you next, Mum,' Alex said.

'That's OK. I understand. Let us know, when you can. I love you.'

Alex took from her all the reassurance he could. He was relieved that she had stayed calm; she must have known, of course, that for her to seem upset would only make it worse for him, that the knowledge he'd let his parents down and that they were disappointed and distressed would make the hours ahead in a cell even worse. Alex already knew that being arrested was not what they would have expected of him. He hoped he would get the chance, sometime soon, to explain it to them.

It was cold in the cell, and Alex imagined from the smell that the person who'd spent the night there had been brought in to sleep off a heavy night of drinking and whatever else had followed. There was a thin scent of disinfectant overlaying an odour of vomit and stale alcohol. Alex sat down on the blue, plastic-covered mattress and stared at the yellow walls. If the last occupant hadn't already been feeling sick, the queasy acid tint of the paint might have been enough to send him over the edge. The tea they offered Alex was strong and tannic and it coated the inside of his mouth with a brown residue. It was a reminder that he'd had nothing to eat or drink since he was woken by the officers arriving at his door, nothing since the ready meal he'd heated up the night before. It was after seven o'clock now, and Alex could hear the streets outside starting to become busier, the usual rush of London on a normal day muffled by the thick walls. Alex wondered whether he should try to go back to sleep – there was bound to be a lot of waiting – but he doubted that he would be able to sleep on the slippery mattress unless he really had to, and in any case he wanted to know, as far as he could, what was going on around him. He was already vulnerable and afraid – sleep would make him more vulnerable still.

Kate Sheppard's suit was a hard outline of clean black against a white shirt. She was all monochrome crispness where everything else in the room was grey and grimy: the worn carpet tiles and the patterned upholstery on the hard chairs. Alex was shown into the room and sat down across the table from her. This was not the woman his parents knew: Alex established, awkwardly, that they were colleagues, but Kate was the solicitor on duty. Kate was anxious to get past the introductions. She asked what they had told him about why he was there.

'The police haven't really told me anything, yet. I suppose I can tell you everything – this is in confidence, isn't it?' Kate nodded. 'I work for the intelligence services and I lost my laptop – it was a while ago now. November. I left it in a taxi and when I found it again, the disk inside with a set of files on it was missing. There's been an internal investigation going on. I told them it was a genuine mistake and I hadn't given it to anyone. They didn't seem to believe me. But why they've arrested me now I have no idea.'

Kate leaned over and opened the black leather briefcase that she had placed on the chair next to hers. She pulled out a newspaper, unfolded it, and spread it on the table between them, the headlines facing Alex. She watched his face closely before she spoke.

'I expect this will be why.'

Alex's mouth was dry.

'Oh,' he said. 'I didn't know.'

Alex read through the story, looking at the pictures of the minister and his father. He recognised Mark Lucas; he was one of those new, enthusiastic politicians who seemed to crop up everywhere, always on message and skimming over the surface of things. One of those politicians who seemed to think that everything that was modern was inevitably for the best. The future, not the past. He had never thought about his connection to Anthony Lucas. The elder Lucas was a name in the files, Alex recalled. He could almost see the place in the grid where he would have fitted. He had a good memory for that sort of thing. He could visualise the other names, too, that slotted in around Lucas, that went in different columns, but he didn't see those names in Anna's article.

Kate was methodical and patient and talked Alex through everything. She explained what would happen next, what he should and should not say. She could not have been much older than he was; thirty, perhaps, but there did not seem to be much that could awe her. Once she realised that he understood what she was talking about, she changed her vocabulary to suit him. Kate recognised in Alex someone of a similar background, a well-educated man who she might have met elsewhere, under different circumstances. He was not the average kind of person who a duty solicitor was called out for first thing in the morning. As she bent forward to take notes, she tucked her dark hair behind her ears.

'There's one thing,' said Alex, 'that I think they're going to make a lot out of, even though it sounds more than it is.'

'What's that?' Kate asked. Alex thought she looked disappointed, as though he was not being straight with her. He couldn't bear to have any more people look at him that way. He ran his finger along the byline of the newspaper. A smudge of printers' ink came off on his fingertip.

'This journalist,' he began, 'the woman who wrote this.' Kate read the names upside-down.

'Anna Travers?'

'Yes. Anna Travers. I know her – well, we used to go out together, at college.'

Alex saw Kate's jaw clench. She wrote down Anna's name in block capitals in her notebook.

'And?' she asked.

'I hadn't seen her in years. And then she tried to get in touch with me again. She sent me a postcard.'

'A postcard?'

'Yes – it was one of the things we used to do. Stupid postcards, the more stupid the better. But anyway—'

'When was this?' Kate interrupted him.

'Not long after I lost the disk. I didn't reply.'

'How long after?'

'I can't remember, exactly. A few weeks. And she'd sent it via my parents, so it took a while to get to me. She wanted to see me.'

'Did she say why?'

'No.' Alex wanted to hurry her on. This was not the point he needed to get to. 'There was some pretext about a college reunion, but that wasn't true. Anyway, a while after that she obviously found out where I lived and tried to get me to talk to her, but I wouldn't. But then she found me in a cafe, and she wouldn't leave me alone.'

'What happened then?'

'She knew about the files, she said her paper had them. She asked me to help her understand them.'

'What did you say?' Kate seemed to be re-evaluating him; she had gone back to talking in the kind of very simple sentences you might use with a suspect who didn't understand the severity of what they were accused of.

'I said nothing. I told her to go away. I told her she'd get me arrested.' Alex looked around at the room and shrugged his shoulders. 'So, here we are. So they're going to think . . .'

Kate nodded again. 'Yes, I can see what they're going to think.

It's circumstantial, but still. You're going to have to try to be a bit more precise, about the dates when this happened. And I doubt she – Anna – will be of much help in backing you up.'

'Why not?' Alex asked.

'Because journalists aren't much help with things like this. It's a point of principle for them not to be cooperative. Not revealing your sources and all that.'

'Even if I'm not her source?' Alex replied.

'Even so.'

Kate pushed her hair back behind her ears again and folded her hands on the table. She looked directly at Alex.

'And what you've just told me is the whole story? Because I can't help you unless it is.'

Alex nodded. Kate closed her notebook and put the newspaper back in her bag.

## 27

'WE DON'T WANT you to take any questions,' Paul Norman had muttered. He'd been standing over Mark, peering over his shoulder as he typed on a computer that one of the kids in the office had reluctantly surrendered. Paul conferred briefly with one of his juniors, telling him that Mark wasn't going to be doing any interviews.

'Of course not,' he growled. 'Do they think we're that stupid? Putting him up to answer questions that none of us, not even him, have the answer to.'

Will Mason beckoned Norman over to him on the other side of the room. Mark continued trying to write the statement that he would have to read out once they'd all agreed on it. It was easier to write without someone watching every word that he wrote, then deleted, then wrote again; without Paul's smoky breath in his ear and the discontented rumbling noises that he made when Mark wrote something he didn't approve of. A couple of sentences later, Norman returned.

'There's been an arrest,' he said. 'So we're going to have to make sure you don't say anything that messes things up even more.'

'An arrest?' Mark enquired. 'Who?'

'The leaker,' Paul replied. 'Well, the alleged leaker.' He pointed to a sentence that he wanted changed again, something about an investigation being underway. Mark moved the cursor to the offending words and wiped them from the screen. There was so little that he was going to be able to say, and so much more that he wanted to say.

He found himself in the hallway for the last time, taking a final look at the portraits and the fine furniture. Mark could not envisage ever entering this building again. He had run the gauntlet of prime ministers on the staircase, enduring centuries of imagined disapproval. How many ministers, in that time, had failed like this? Dozens, hundreds? All footnotes of disgrace, remembered for a few weeks or, at worst, years, before being completely forgotten.

One of the young guys was sent out ahead to give the journalists a five-minute warning. It was the tall one with the springy hair, the one whose limbs seemed too big for his body. Theo Sadler. Mark wondered how he would ever find another use for being able to recall all these names. None of them would be wanting to recall Mark's name for much longer.

The police officer opened the door again to let Sadler back in.

'It's all fine,' he said to Mark, full of an incongruous exuberance. 'They're all happy.'

Mark raised an eyebrow. 'Good for them,' he said.

Sadler ran a hand through his hair, conscious that he had said something wrong.

'Oh, yeah. Anyway, I'll tell you when to go. And I'll follow you out.' He looked at his watch, beginning the countdown. Upstairs, they'd been starting to get nervous about the timings. They wanted this over and done with by the lunchtime news, to have control of it again before the newspaper deadlines. Mark had to surrender himself just long enough before the news that the statement would be there in time, but not so long before that they would be bored again and start asking more, and more troublesome, questions.

Theo Sadler indicated to the police officer that he should open the door. The black door swung inwards and the usual rattle of camera shutters started up. Mark straightened his jacket and stepped out into the street. It became strangely quiet. He had expected the shouting that he'd heard earlier in the morning, but now they knew what was coming and were waiting to hear him. Mark took his place behind the microphones that had been set up on stands in the middle of the road. The journalists were penned behind metal crowd barriers a couple of metres further back. He held one sheet of paper in his hand, the scripted words, but he was going to try not to look down at them. If he'd blown everything else, he could at least hold on to the fact that he was still good at saying the words he was supposed to say. Mark fixed his gaze on the camera straight ahead of him, its red light glowing above the lens, and began to speak.

As he spoke the approved words, he felt as though he were no longer there. Emily told him later that he had been flawless, not tripping over any words, or speaking too fast, or breaking down, but Mark could not have said himself what happened. Nothing broke his flow. The phrases that had been agreed on came out of his mouth; it was as if someone else had said them as well as written them.

He approached the end; he recited almost with feeling the lines about how he had been proud to be given the opportunity to serve this government, how he wished it continued success and would support it from the backbenches. It was the final formula that nearly got him: as Mark started on the lines about this being a difficult time for his family he could feel a constriction in his throat. As he spoke the concluding words, he felt as though he was coming back into himself, but he had to keep his real self at bay for a few words longer.

'And so I ask that you respect my family's privacy. Thank you.' He looked down as the clamour of questions rose again. They shouted one over another: was his father a traitor? Had he leaked the documents? Was he loyal to Britain? Did he know his father was a spy? Mark was not going to answer. Some of these were questions he could not answer, even if he tried. He turned his head slowly to the side, trying to see where he was supposed to go next. Surely they didn't expect him to walk down the street and out through the gates into Whitehall? They were cruel, but were they as cruel as that? Theo appeared at the edge of his field of vision and extended an arm out to the side, pointing towards a narrow gap in the railings at the far end of the street, that led to a set of stairs. Mark walked towards the passageway and the cameras followed him.

Once he left the security gate that led on to Horse Guards Road, he was on his own. There would no longer be any car to meet him, no one to tell him where he needed to be or what he needed to do. He looked to his left at the net-curtained windows in the grey-white bulk of the Foreign Office. Mark assumed that, right now, someone would be clearing his desk for him, packing up any belongings he may have left there into a crate. They would only need a small crate. There was a picture of Emily with Bella and Jack that he hoped he would get back in one piece. The papers that he was yet to sign would now await the signature of his successor; the decisions he had not yet taken would be taken by someone else. His traces would be swept away; in this, at least, the system could be relied on to work efficiently.

Mark looked in the other direction, towards Horse Guards Parade. He hesitated, trying to choose which way to take. He let a taxi pass, followed by a police motorcycle, and stepped out into the road towards the park. As he reached the other side, he started to pull off his tie. He rolled the purple silk into a neat coil and placed it in his pocket alongside his folded resignation speech. Mark undid the top button of his shirt. A swan came in to land on the lake, its heavy wings beating loudly. He walked on into the park, around the edge of the water. No one seemed to notice him. He had expected occasional knowing looks and whispers from the people he passed, but he did not see them. He felt like a private citizen again, an unofficial person surrounded by official buildings. Mark reached the edge of the park at the Mall. There were flags being raised along the route to welcome a visiting ruler: it was no longer his concern which country's flag it was or who represented it. He stuck out his arm and a taxi pulled up beside him. Mark Lucas, the ex-minister, went home.

## 28

A NNA WAS FIRST in the office, jittery with undirected
enthusiasm. She realised that she was no longer at the
centre of things. Her moment of glory had been noted, but
was already fading. The TV screen in the corner of the room
had been left on all night, unwatched. Anna went over to it
and turned up the volume. She watched Mark Lucas opening
the green front door of his Georgian terraced house and walk
out towards the cameras. He said nothing and got into a waiting
car. Anna thought perhaps she recognised the house, or at least
knew the neighbourhood. It was the kind of house she would
love to buy, one day, a few Tube stops closer to the centre of
town. She wondered how rich Lucas had to be to afford it,
before remembering that his wife was supposed to be some
sort of lawyer and probably earned far more than he did. She
tried to restrain her instinct to sympathise with him; it was not
how you were supposed to feel.

Anna felt someone standing behind her, also watching the
screen. Michael Swain gave her one of his stares and appeared
to decide that this morning she still met with approval. He
looked at his watch.

'Bright and early, I see. So, what's next?'

'You didn't need me to be there, did you?' said Anna, suddenly
worried that she should have been doorstepping Mark Lucas.

'No. No point, since you already got him. It'd be nice if you
can talk to him again, eventually. Keep on it. Not today, though.
Anyway, I sent Ash.' Anna looked at the screen to see if she

could spot her colleague in the scrum, but they had already cut away to another story.

'He'll be gone by lunchtime, won't he?' Anna asked.

'At the latest,' Swain nodded. 'So that'll be the top line. That and the fallout for the government. What I need you to be thinking about is where it goes next. We need to be a couple of moves ahead. I mean, is there anything more on the disk? Can you get any more names?'

'There might be,' Anna replied, rather reluctantly. The last thing she wanted was to spend another day hunched over that computer again, her eyes straining in the greenish light, while everyone else was out somewhere, chasing something happening now.

'And the trouble is,' Swain continued, talking more to himself than Anna, 'they're going to start making difficulties. They're going to want it back. The disk, I mean.'

'We're not going to give it to them, though, are we?' Anna asked.

'No, except under extreme legal duress. But you'd better see if we can get backups and maybe put some in a safe place, away from here. Just in case.'

Anna was despondent. The morning after her big triumph she was, essentially, glorified computer support. She walked over to the desk where the disk was locked in its drawer and prepared to switch on the machine. Swain moved away towards the glass enclosure of his office. Dennis Neville arrived in the office, red-faced and out of breath. It was not like him to arrive this early, and he had obviously exerted himself to an unusual degree. Neville normally sidled in late, complaining about how no one seemed to be able to run a transport network any more. His paunch heaved under his striped shirt as he tried to get his breathing back under control. He motioned towards Swain's office with a fleshy hand, trying to catch the editor's attention. Michael Swain emerged again into the newsroom.

'There's been an arrest,' Neville said. He sucked in a big gasp of stale office air.

'Of who? . . . Of whom?' Swain corrected himself. It was rare that a news story caused him to lose his grasp of grammar.

'The person they believe leaked the disk to us.' Neville sat down in an office chair.

'And they told you this?' Swain seemed surprised.

'I know. You'd think we'd be the last people. But it was someone I've known for ages. I think he wanted to let me know as a kind of warning.'

'What did they tell you, exactly?'

Dennis Neville puffed again as he heaved his bag onto the desk. It was a beige cloth satchel with a webbing strap that was designed to be used by anglers. He unbuckled it and took out his notebook.

'Male, twenty-eight years old. Employee of the intelligence services. Arrested this morning.'

Swain considered this information for a moment.

'Did they say where?'

Neville wiped his brow with a handkerchief before he answered.

'No. But I somehow got the impression it was London.' Swain raised his eyebrow at the 'impression'. This vagueness was not really good enough. 'And this was not from the police themselves, I presume?' Neville shook his head.

'Anna, get on to the Met. We need to get them to confirm the arrest. And if they won't do it via Scotland Yard, ring every police station in the vicinity of Vauxhall Cross and Thames House. Start with the nearest and move outwards.'

Anna hesitated; Swain started snapping his fingers.

'Twenty-eight?' she asked Neville. He checked his notes again and agreed. Anna turned to Swain, who was already walking away from the conversation.

'Can I talk to you for a minute?' she asked. 'In the office?' He grunted an unwilling assent.

Anna pulled the glass door closed behind her and ran her hand through her hair, twisting the hair between her fingers and tugging it away from her scalp.

'I think I know who he is,' she said.

'Well, that's good,' Swain replied, preparing to dismiss her again. 'Go and find him. Get me a name. The right name.'

Anna wasn't going to leave yet.

'The thing is . . .' she began, unsure how to continue, 'it's to do with how I know. You need to hear this.' Swain indicated the chair in front of his desk with the flat of his hand. Anna sat down, leaning forward and clasping her hands in front of her.

'I think,' she continued, 'his name is Alex Rutherford. I can't be absolutely sure.'

'And why would you think that?' Swain asked in a slow voice.

'I know him,' Anna said. 'Well, I knew him. I know that he lost some files, some official secrets. And I'm pretty sure that these are the same ones.'

Swain closed his eyes and pressed his fingers into his temples. This was what he did when he was about to be angry; Anna knew it did not bode well.

'I wish you people wouldn't come to me with your "impressions" and your "pretty sures". I need to know exactly what you know and what you do not. So let's be clear: what do you know?'

Anna tried to ignore the feeling of her stomach lurching as though she was in a faulty lift. She took a deep breath and tried to order her thoughts in the way Swain demanded.

'I know that Alex Rutherford, the Alex Rutherford who used to be a friend of mine, lost some files.'

'How do you know this?' Swain interrupted.

'Because some people came to see me. They were from the security services. They even had a business card. They wanted to know if he'd been in touch with me.'

'Anyone can print a business card,' Michael Swain mused.

'That's what I thought. But they seemed like the real thing.' He rolled his eyes again at the 'seemed like'. 'Anyway,' Anna continued, 'they asked if I had heard from him, but I hadn't.'

'And this was when?'

'Before all of this started,' Anna said. 'Before I'd heard anything about the files, I mean.'

'And why did these people want to see you, in that case?'

'I suppose because we were old friends from college, and I'm a journalist. I was one of his personal referees when they vetted him. I mean, they said he was joining the Foreign Office, back then. They must have thought that if he wanted something published, he could give it to me.'

'He obviously didn't give it to you directly, then,' Swain continued, plotting the events out in his head, trying to see where the gaps were in her story. 'Do you think he might have wanted you to have this somehow, indirectly?'

Anna shook her head. Swain would have made a better interrogator than any detective or spy she had yet met. No matter how much more trouble she was going to be in, Anna was prepared to tell him everything that she knew.

'No, because later, once I did find him, he was furious about it. He denied all knowledge.'

Swain made a gesture with his finger, turning it in circles towards himself, that indicated rewinding a tape.

'Run me through that again. You did find him?'

'Yes. I found out where he lives, waited for him. He didn't want to talk to me. He was livid, said I'd get him arrested.'

'You may have done just that,' the editor remarked. 'I hope you didn't do this all on my time, by the way.'

'It turns out it was part of the story, though.' Anna felt contrite. 'He wouldn't really talk about the files. The only thing he said was that he hadn't given them to us.'

'As you'd expect him to say,' Swain observed. 'Even if he had. Especially if he had.'

'Yes, but I know him. I know him well enough to know if he's lying. And the thing about Alex is he doesn't lie, he can't.'

'But he's a spy. He lies for a living.'

'Not him. He's honest. Far too honest for his own good.'

Michael Swain swivelled his chair around so he could look

out of the window. Anna wasn't sure what this signified: whether it was the calm before one of his outbursts of rage or just a chance for him to think without the distraction of her presence. She watched Swain's back and the set of his shoulders above the hard black plastic of the chair to see if she could discern any indication either way. He spun around again.

'You know what this means?' She didn't. 'It means you might be next.'

'Next for what?'

'In that if they've arrested him, they might arrest you.'

'But I haven't done anything illegal,' Anna protested.

'And if you're correct, neither has he. Which doesn't appear to have stopped them.' Swain wrote down a name and two phone numbers on a yellow Post-it note. 'This is the lawyer. It's Gerald. You'll have spoken to him before. If they come here, we won't let them in, and we'll make a very big, very public fuss about it. But if they come and get you at home, there's not so much we can do. In any case, you call Gerald.'

If this was meant to reassure her, it had quite the opposite effect. Anna wasn't sure she had the courage to be the poster girl for the cause. In fact, she was pretty sure she didn't. She bit her lip.

'I know we don't . . . reveal sources or anything, but . . .'

'But what?'

'Can we at least say, somehow, that it wasn't from him. The files, I mean.'

Swain's face softened for a moment. For the first time ever, he seemed to speak as a normal human being, even as a friend.

'Anna . . .' he began. 'At this stage, I would tell you, just between us, where they had come from. If I could get your friend off the hook by saying something to someone, I would. But the truth is, I have no idea how we got hold of them, so I can't logically rule him out. As far as I know, or anyone knows, they were handed in over the front desk in a Jiffy bag by a man no one remembers, who didn't leave a name.'

He snapped back into his usual persona.

'Now, go and get me official confirmation of who has been arrested. And another thing: if I thought for any reason that you had let secret service agents into my newsroom, business card or no business card, I would find any window that opened in this godforsaken air-conditioned place and heave you out of it. Understood?'

Anna understood very clearly; she tried not to look at the window and the drop to the street below. She left Swain's office and pulled the juddering glass door shut behind her. The TV screen was still showing Mark Lucas, on a loop. It cut to Downing Street, where a correspondent who had little new to say was gesturing with keen anticipation at the black door of Number 10. It did not take Anna long to find the duty sergeant at Belgravia Police Station who confirmed Alex Rutherford's name. Aged twenty-eight, of Pimlico, he agreed. Nearly twenty-nine, Anna remembered. It would be his birthday next week.

# 29

IT HAD TAKEN Mark so long to track down his father that he started first to worry, and then to wonder whether this capacity for concealing himself was something he had learnt a long time ago. The phone had rung out at home; there was no answering machine. Mark knew that it would take more than this to drive his father from his routine, so he tried the direct number for his office in college; there was still no reply. Mark left a message, despite knowing that his father never used the voicemail and would have no idea how to retrieve it. He called the porter's lodge, asking whether they'd seen Dr Lucas that day. They wouldn't tell him anything, even when he insisted that he was who he said he was, that he was his father's son. The porter on duty refused to answer his questions with polite disbelief.

'I'm sorry, sir,' he replied. 'We've had a lot of calls today, as you can imagine, and I've been asked not to give out any more information.'

Mark stopped himself from saying 'Don't you know who I am?' just in time. They didn't. They didn't believe he was who he said he was. And as of this morning, he was no longer anyone of importance, anyway.

He tried the other tactic that might have worked – asking to be put through to the man in charge. He didn't even get that far. The Master's secretary told him in far too cheerful a voice that the Master was in a meeting all day. Mark left his name and pointedly gave her the number of his office in the House of

Commons, in the hope that the fact he still had an office would prove his identity.

His office. Mark had been so disoriented that morning he had forgotten to check in with them again. He'd neglected the staff who would be sitting there, the phones ringing constantly, wondering what was going on and wanting reassurance.

Mark had been pacing up and down the room; as he reached the front windows he cracked open the shutters just enough to see who was still outside. A pile of discarded polystyrene cups was heaped on the pavement. The last crews and photographers were packing up; they'd stayed long enough to see him arrive back, to get the final shot they needed to round off the story. Disgraced ex-minister returns home. Tie-less, slump-shouldered, former golden boy closes the front door behind him.

Mark called the mobile number of one of the researchers, who answered it on the first ring. She sounded as if she had been crying. He was surprised there was anyone left who still had enough faith in him to have been upset by his resignation; he felt guilty for having let Amy and the rest of them in the office down, on top of everyone else. They were coping fine, she told him, sniffing slightly. We're saying no to everything, she added. Interviews and stuff. We thought that's what you'd want us to do. Mark agreed that it was. He thanked Amy for all her hard work, feeling the words rattle round like stones in his mouth. It was a stock phrase he hadn't meant to come out with; he couldn't find the right words to say something that he really meant, something that sounded a bit different. He detected uncertainty in her voice, between sniffs, as though she suspected his pat, meaningless expression was covering something up that she didn't yet know about. Mark tried again.

'I'm sorry, Amy, I really am. I've let you down. But you're doing a brilliant job, and you're going to carry on doing a brilliant job. And I'll be back in the office in a day or two, once things have calmed down. I'm not giving up, you know.' Mark could hear Amy suck in air harder, trying not to cry again. It was no good. She burst into tears, this time erupting in huge, childlike sobs. She tried to apologise through the weeping; he offered her the rest of the day off, if she wanted it, explaining that there was only one call that he wanted to return, if it came.

A new, long list started to come into his head, a list of all the other people who would also need to be reassured; the people in the constituency, the people who sat on committees and delivered leaflets and turned up in church halls on cold evenings on his behalf. It wasn't as easy as he had imagined: if he had considered it at all, he would have thought that resignation was a form of absolution; that he was gone and the slate was wiped clean. He realised now that it was not so straightforward. There would be people who had always mistrusted him – the guy from London who'd done nothing but work in the media – who now found themselves to have been right all along; there were others who might now find themselves in unexpected agreement.

It would have been better if he'd died, Mark thought. He wouldn't be here to worry about any of this. People would have to say nice things about him, even if they didn't mean them and had never liked him. He wouldn't have to face any of them, ever again. There would be a memorial service, and important people would come and speak of him as though he had mattered, and Emily would wear black, and the children . . . Mark snapped himself out of this indulgence as soon as he thought of them. Maybe it wouldn't be better, for them if not for him.

He wandered back upstairs to the study, took one of Emily's yellow pads and started to write a list of names of the people he would still have to talk to, have to placate and charm all over again, since he was, after all, alive. Once the names were on the list, though, most of them would have to wait.

The first thing was to find his father. Rachel didn't know where he was, either; she was worried for both of them. When Mark got hold of his sister she was on a building site, inspecting the progress of one of her projects. It was apparently an old office block being turned into flats. It was hard to make out Rachel's voice over the whine and clatter of machinery as she commiserated with him – she hadn't yet heard that he'd resigned, though having listened to the news in the morning, she was expecting it to happen.

'Did I tell you about this place?' she asked. No, Mark thought, wondering why his sister expected he would be interested now, of all times. 'Old secret service building, apparently,' she laughed. 'Six-inch-thick glass in the reception area and cellars that go on for miles. Took us ages to get them to give us the original plans. There's a sort of irony . . .' Mark agreed that there was, but wasn't in the mood to find it amusing.

'Have you heard from Dad?' he asked. 'Do you know where he is?'

'No,' she replied. 'I tried him in the morning, but there was no reply. So I don't know if that means he's at home, but not answering the phone, or gone somewhere else.'

'I tried the college,' Mark said, 'but they wouldn't tell me anything, not even whether he was in. What would you do, if you were Dad?'

Rachel thought about this for a moment.

'I think I'd stay put. He probably is in college, or in a library somewhere. Question is which one. He's probably gone to the most remote, quietest stacks he can find and will stay there till he feels he can come out. He probably won't even notice what day it is.' Rachel broke off to speak to someone on the site; Mark could hear her trying to make them wait.

'Mark, I've got a client with me, so I can't really talk. But I just want to know why you didn't warn us about this.'

'That's what Emily said,' Mark replied.

'Yes, I would expect it is. How's she coping? How are the kids?'

'Better than me,' he said. 'All of them are doing much better than me, at least they were at eight o'clock this morning. Emily is being magnificent, Bella just thinks everyone wants to take her picture, which she believes is no less than she deserves, and Jack doesn't care as long as he has biscuits.'

'And why didn't you warn us?' Rachel insisted.

'Because somehow I never really thought it would come to it, and once I did, I didn't realise how bad it would be, how quickly. I thought I could manage; I thought if I ignored it and put it off, it might go away.'

'Which has always been your problem,' his sister observed.

'Thanks for that,' Mark retorted. He didn't need anyone else to remind him of his failings, though his sister could always do so accurately.

'Mark, I've really got to go now,' Rachel said.

'What about Dad, though?' Mark insisted.

'About where he is? Or what he did . . . might have done?'

'What he did,' Mark responded. 'Do you think it's true?'

'I haven't read enough about it,' Rachel hedged. Mark could tell she didn't feel comfortable talking about it surrounded by other people. Her voice was lower and harder to discern above the building-site noise. 'It's . . . I don't know . . . it's possible, I suppose. There's so little we really know.'

'I know,' said Mark. 'Call me if you hear from him, won't you?'

'Of course,' Rachel said. 'And you. Take care.' Before she hung up, there was a thought that had come to her.

'You could try calling Martha.'

'Who's Martha?' The name wasn't familiar to Mark, and he usually remembered names.

'Have you not met Martha? She's his neighbour in college. A Slavonic philologist, whatever one of those is. She kind of keeps an eye on him, ever since Mum died. Brings him food, sometimes.'

'What's her surname?' Mark asked, wondering how Rachel had heard of this woman and he hadn't. There were even basic, everyday things about his father that he didn't know.

'I can't remember,' Rachel said. 'Ex-something, maybe. I'll call you if I remember. Got to go. Love you.'

It was thanks to Martha Exendine that Mark had found himself, a few hours later, pacing outside the entrance to the Ashmolean Museum, watching the open-topped Oxford tourist buses pass by, the guide over the loudhailer reminding him that it was the oldest museum in Europe. It was almost impossible, Mark found, to try to catch the eye of passing female strangers, and at the same time not to do so. Mark wanted to be found, but he did not want to be spotted by the wrong people. There was little he could do about it, though the jeans and frayed navy jumper he was wearing now made him look different from his old, public self. Martha Exendine would recognise him, and he had to stop trying to gauge whether every passer-by was a potential Slavonic philologist.

Martha, when she arrived, was unlikely to have been anything else. She stamped up the steps to the forecourt of the museum on clumpy sandals, her long, dark-red skirt swishing around her legs. She wore a shawl of some heavily woven fabric that was covered in red and green patterns. Mark made out images of birds and foliage in the folds of the shawl. Her grey hair was pinned high on her head with a rustic, wood-and-leather grip. To Mark, she looked as if she had walked out of the pages of a book of Russian folklore. Martha marched over towards Mark and gripped his hand.

'So, you're here,' she announced, without introductions. 'Glad you could come.'

'I had to come,' Mark said. 'We need to talk, Dad and I.'

'I'm sure you do,' Martha replied.

'How is he?' Mark asked cautiously.

'Remarkably calm, actually,' Martha replied. 'He arrived in college at the same time as usual, walked in from home just as usual.'

'Did he get a lot of . . . hassle?'

'He wouldn't really say. There was a photographer outside the college until he was shooed away by the bulldogs, the university authorities, you know. He didn't say anything until we had tea together, mid-morning. Then he said something about the bloody reporters outside his house, getting in his way. He still seems his normal self, though. Said that he's seen worse in his time.'

'Let me guess,' said Mark. 'That it wasn't the Russians who were coming, at least?'

'Something like that,' Martha nodded. It was a familiar expression from his childhood, though Mark wondered now whether it had always been said merely for effect. He was suspicious, for a moment, of Martha herself; why was his father, who had so often proclaimed his loathing of all things Russian, friends with her? Was she something to do with all of this?

As they talked, Martha had begun to sweep Mark back down the stairs outside the museum and around the corner. They entered another classical building. Martha extracted a pass from somewhere under the swathes of material that enfolded her and showed it, evidently explaining to someone who controlled the access to the building that she was bringing a guest. She beckoned Mark over to sign himself in.

Martha walked on, her heavy paces leading them up a sweeping staircase with a brass handrail. She had not explained precisely where she was taking him. They passed through a library, a high-ceilinged room with a gallery running around the top and books stacked tightly all the way up the walls. None of the students slumped over heaps of books looked up as they passed. Martha opened another door in an alcove and led him down another staircase. Rachel was right: he would find his father in the quietest, most remote of libraries, a sanctuary where he could switch out the clamour of the world around him.

'The Voltaire Room,' Martha whispered as she opened the door to a peaceful library with pale mint-green walls. White busts of, Mark presumed, Enlightenment philosophers, stood at intervals on the bookcases, casting impassive stares down into the room. He should have known this was where he would be.

Anthony Lucas was the only other person in the room. He sat at a long table, with a small pile of leather-bound books neatly placed beneath a lamp. As the door creaked open, he put down the pen he had been holding and looked up, scowling at the intrusion. He saw Martha first, then Mark. His face lightened slightly, but his brow was still knitted with anxiety. Anthony pushed his chair back and stood up.

Mark walked over to him, wrapping his father in an awkward embrace.

'You didn't have to come here,' Anthony said. 'You could have come to the house, later on.'

'I know,' Mark said, wondering why he always seemed to have done something wrong, even here. 'But I thought there might still be reporters there. I didn't want to give them anything new to say. Were there a lot, this morning?'

'Not so many,' Anthony replied. 'I think it bothered the neighbours, more than me. They kept ringing the doorbell, ringing the phone. There were even some at the college. So I came here.'

They were talking in whispers, even though there was no one else in the library. Martha was standing a few paces away from them.

'There's my office, down the corridor, if you need somewhere else to talk,' she offered, before stepping out of the room and pulling the door gently closed behind her. Anthony looked down at his books and seemed reluctant to move.

'They sacked me, Dad,' Mark began.

'Martha said you resigned. She heard it on the radio.' Mark was irritated by how his father never seemed to resist the temptation to correct him. He was always being marked down.

'Well, I didn't have much choice about it. So really, they sacked me.'

'I'm sorry,' Anthony said, clasping his son by the shoulder.

'It isn't your fault,' Mark replied, almost convinced that was true. 'It's to do with – how I handled it, or didn't handle it, as much as with you. I'd have had to go, even if it had nothing to do with you. You being involved made it happen more quickly.'

'I'm still sorry,' Anthony repeated. 'It's what you wanted to do. You loved it.'

'I did,' Mark acknowledged. 'Though I don't know that I was any good at it.'

'You were as good or bad at it as any of them,' his father answered. This grudging praise, to Mark, was enough.

'We need to talk about what happened, Dad,' Mark continued. 'Here, or in Martha's room?'

They both looked around at the room. There were no students there, only the blank marble eyes of the philosophers.

'Let's go to Martha's office,' Anthony said eventually. He stacked his books neatly, paper slips protruding from them to mark his place. He screwed the cap back on his fountain pen and tucked it into his top pocket, but left his file pad on the desk.

Martha happily vacated her small office, offering to make them coffee. The room was decorated with copies of doleful-eyed Russian icons. Mark had to clear a pile of books and papers and a patchwork cushion from one of the armchairs before he could sit down. He and his father sat almost knee to knee in the two chairs that took up much of the space in the cramped room.

'I need to know,' Mark began. 'I need to know why you're there, in the files. What you did.'

Anthony smoothed down the dark-green fabric of his trousers as he settled into the chair.

'It's complicated. I don't know how much I can really tell you.'

'Dad!' Mark exclaimed, exasperated. 'It's not always as compli-cated as you think, and I think by now I deserve an explanation. I'm not the only person you're going to have to explain this to. The Master, at the very least. The police, even. They could arrest you for this, prosecute you.'

'It isn't what it seems,' Anthony continued.

'Then why are you in the documents? Why did they have a codename for you?' Mark did not want to let his father get away with any more cryptic comments; he was tired of obfuscations and the twists of language. Anthony sat back in the low armchair and sighed. His eyes seemed distant, Mark thought. He was used to his father looking as though he was in a different place and time, but he was usually to be found two hundred years ago. He was not as far distant now.

'Before I left Germany . . .' Anthony began.

Mark thought this was the familiar beginning to a story he had heard dozens, if not hundreds of times before. How his father was a student at the university, how he had nothing and no one to stay for, how he was lucky enough to get out, by chance, just a few days before the Wall went up. Mark had often heard how Anthony had seen the people who were not so lucky try to escape by lowering themselves on bedsheets and curtains from high windows of the apartment blocks that looked out onto the West. Mark had later seen photographs of those people with their flailing legs and their desperate hopes and wondered whether his father really remembered the scene, or just the photographs.

The story Anthony was starting to tell was a new one, though, or at least a very different telling of the old. 'Before I left, I was in danger. I had once been a believer, when I was very young. There was nothing left after the war; I thought we could start again, should start again. So I joined the Party, because it gave me hope. Also, because it meant I could study, meant that I had a future. At first, it was like having a new family.'

Mark watched his father's face closely. He was not looking directly at Mark as he spoke; he addressed his words to the middle distance, as though speaking to an audience elsewhere in the room.

'But the more I tried to study, the more I realised there were things you could no longer say, books you were no longer supposed to read. You must remember, though, I had nothing else. I had no family left. So I hoped it could change. There was a while when I hoped it would.'

Mark realised that the story he heard before, was, like all family stories, a few moments, a few images, strung together in a pattern that had become familiar. He had rarely questioned them; they remained the stories he had heard in his childhood and until now he had seen them from a child's point of view. There was the story about having to eat raw potatoes dug from the ground with your hands; it was one Mark had heard almost as many times as he had failed to finish his supper and it had become something of a family joke. For the first time, Mark saw that story as he would see it now, imagined having to tell his own children to dig raw food from the fields they passed for lack of anything else to eat. He imagined his city-bred children having to work it out for themselves, because he was no longer there to help them. Mark realised how lucky he was never to have had to worry about his own survival. Whatever had happened to him, whatever would happen now that wasn't his own children starving or sickening or dying, could never be that bad. Mark wondered what compromises he would be prepared to make if his own survival was at stake; what his own younger self might have been willing to do.

'When was this?' he asked. Mark was trying to slot his father's story into the history that he remembered badly. 'Was that 1953?' All that Mark really knew about 1953 was the Brecht quotation that he'd used once or twice, without thinking too much about the events it referred to: the one about the government dissolving the people and electing another. He knew there had been demonstrations in Berlin, students shot. Anthony shook his head.

'There was fifty-three, yes. It was a terrible time. But then there was fifty-six, Hungary. The Russian tanks. That was when I realised that things would never change, and there was no point in hoping that they would. So that's when I first tried to leave,' he continued.

'And why didn't you leave then?' Mark asked. Anthony patted his hands downwards in a familiar gesture, meaning that Mark should slow down.

'This takes time,' he told his son. 'And you have time, now, for once.'

Mark inclined his head forward, his chin closer to his chest. He did have time. The only people waiting for him were Emily and the children; Emily knew where he was, and the children were not yet used to expecting him home. The cameras had gone, and as he'd left the house Mark had piled up the envelopes containing handwritten pleas for interviews that had been pushed through the letterbox and stacked them on the stairs, not quite ready to throw them away yet.

'So I went to the West – you could still go to the West, then, that part was easy. You just walked across. But then they had to process you. You had to go to a refugee camp, even though the last thing I wanted to do was stay in a camp. You couldn't just stay without going through the proper procedures.' Anthony laughed. 'It was the worst of all possible worlds: German bureaucracy, multiplied by three, for each of the Western occupying powers. You had a card that had to be stamped, dozens of times over with dozens of rubber stamps.'

Mark sensed that his father was wandering away from the story, but he hesitated before nudging him back on course. It was something he'd learnt in interviews, making documentaries. Sometimes you just have to let them talk, get to the point in their own way.

'So they interviewed you,' Anthony continued. 'They wanted to make sure you weren't being sent there by the East as a spy, that you weren't trying to infiltrate the West. They sent you to each of the powers, one after the other, going up in a building from one floor to the next. On the ground floor there were the Americans. I'd never met an American, but they were somehow just how I'd imagined them, big like cowboys. They offered me cigarettes and some black fizzy drink that I found out later was

Coca-Cola. I didn't like it. They asked me about things like military bases and railway depots, things I knew nothing about. They wanted to know if you had any useful information for them, you see. I obviously didn't, because they sent me upstairs to the British.'

'What were they like?' Mark asked.

'They were different,' Anthony replied. 'There was tea, of course, and they wanted to know about ideas, about what people were thinking and saying, not so much about military plans. The man I met called himself Patrick, though I suppose it wasn't his real name. He was a very charming man, very well educated. We talked about philosophy, about history. He was logical and reasonable and persuasive in a very empirical, British way. It wasn't all dialectics and theory, the way I was being taught. We talked for a while, in this refugee centre, somewhere in the West. Then they took me on to their headquarters, near the Olympic Stadium, and there were more conversations. Eventually they asked me to go back.'

'To go back? Why?' Mark interrupted.

'So that I would give him information about people I met, about the changes, about the politics and people in the Party. He convinced me that it was the right thing to do, even though it was not a thing that you would wish for everyone to do, that in this case I should do something for the greater good.'

It took a while for Mark to realise what his father was saying.

'So you stayed in Berlin as a British spy? That's what you're telling me?'

Anthony shrugged in acknowledgement.

'If that's the word you want to use.'

They were interrupted by Martha, who brought two mugs of coffee and cleared a space for them amid the piles of papers and journals on the table between their chairs. The long silence, hurriedly filled with too many thank-yous, made her sense that she had entered at an awkward moment. She withdrew, reminding them softly that the library would be closing before long, saying that they were welcome to continue the conversation at her house if they liked.

As she closed the door, Mark took a sip of the coffee, scalding his mouth, before he spoke again.

'Wasn't it dangerous?'

'I suppose it might have been,' Anthony said slowly. 'But you see, I didn't realise it then, not until after I left.' He looked towards Mark as he picked up his coffee, folding both hands around the green mug. 'They were different times. Everything was dangerous. Living was dangerous, saying what you thought was dangerous. If nothing else you might be killed by a stray bomb in the rubble or by an illness they didn't have the medicine to treat. I had survived that far, and most people hadn't: my parents, my brother. So I thought I was lucky, but if my luck ran out, and I just disappeared and was never heard from again, then it didn't matter to me so much.'

Mark could feel the beginnings of tears pricking his eyes. His father never talked about his family and what had happened to them; it was a conversation that had always been closed down sharply almost before it had begun. Mark remembered once being told with unusual ferocity how lucky he was to have a little sister, when he was about eight and tormenting the five-year-old Rachel by trying to pull her from a swing, insisting that it was his turn. Anthony had emerged from his study in a fury as they played in the garden. Mark and Rachel stood quietly, side by side, knowing that disturbing their father from his work was bound to have consequences.

'Be kind to your sister,' Anthony had shouted, before his voice dropped. 'You don't realise what it would be like to lose her. I had a brother, once, and he was lost. And for the rest of my life I would have given anything to have him back.' Mark had asked how he was lost; in his imagination his uncle had somehow been left behind, mislaid, like a fairy-tale child in a forest. His father had simply said 'he died', and would answer no further questions. Mark had been told then that he would know when he was older; when he was older, he still had not been told, and later still he stopped asking. The tears that he was trying to hold back now were not only for his missing uncle Stefan and the grandparents he had never known, but also because he could not help but imagine Bella losing Jack, losing him and Emily too.

'And then what happened?' Mark prompted. 'Why did you leave, in the end?'

'Because they told me that if I stayed any longer, I would probably be captured. There was an agent, a British man who had betrayed us all. Not the man I knew, someone else. So again, I was very lucky and I got out, just in time.'

'How?' Mark realised this was a question he had never precisely known the answer to. He had never known if his father had himself been one of the people jumping from the windows.

Anthony took a long sip of his coffee before he answered.

'Patrick said there was nothing they could do, that it was too risky for them. After all that I had done for them, I could hardly believe it, but that was how it was. But there were ways, if you knew the right people. I was lucky again – I did know some of the right people. They got me out in a car, under the seats.'

'How do you mean, under the seats? Just under someone's legs?' Mark could not believe that East German border guards would have been so lax.

'No,' his father explained. 'In the cavity beneath the back seats. They lifted the seat up and there was a space you could climb into, just. I was skinny, in those days. There wasn't much to eat.' Mark looked at his father's wrists holding the coffee mug. He was still thin – he had never been fat, but these days his skin had loosened around his bones where the muscles had weakened. Mark was about to ask what it had been like when Anthony continued.

'I remember the smell of petrol and the noise of the engine. The seats were red vinyl, but the funny thing is I can't remember the colour of the car. It was a dark colour, and it was night when I had to meet the people who would take me through. I was more afraid of suffocating than of being caught. I thought maybe it would be worse to die in the car than to be shot by the guards, but at least I still had the hope I would escape. I could feel every bump in the road – and in those days, in Berlin, every road was mostly bumps. I hoped every time the car slowed down that this was it, that we were crossing the border, and I don't know how many times we stopped and started. They told me later they had to be extra careful at every traffic light – they didn't want to be stopped for breaking the traffic laws. So when I finally got out, somewhere in West Berlin, my first memory of freedom is of feeling sick and of wanting the ground to stop moving beneath my feet.'

Mark, too, felt as though his inner ears were spinning and that the room was about to revolve. He was torn between wanting to escape from the confined space of the stuffy office and wanting to stay here for as long as it took his father to tell the whole story. He was afraid that if he broke off now, the story would never resume, and the door would slam shut again on the past.

'Why have you never told me any of this before?' Mark asked, standing up and hoping that the room would stop shifting around him if he held on to the edge of Martha's desk.

'I gave my word that I would not,' Anthony said, his manner more formal again. 'It was my duty, my obligation.'

'It was a long time ago, though,' Mark said. 'It wouldn't have hurt to tell me.'

'I promised that I wouldn't,' Anthony repeated. 'It was a promise that mattered. It was a promise that brought me here, and without it I would never have met your mother, there would have been no you, no Rachel; everything that mattered to me in the world. So I couldn't break it.'

'I need to hear the rest,' Mark insisted. 'Because I still don't understand why they would have records of you, once you were safely here. But we're going to have to go somewhere else now if they're closing the building. Maybe we can find somewhere quiet to have a drink.'

Anthony agreed. They left the office and returned to the library where Martha was waiting. Anthony sorted the books at his desk into piles and returned his notes to his briefcase. His movements, as always, were methodical and precise. Watching him, Mark thought, you would not know that anything out of the ordinary had happened that day. Things belonged in their proper places, and they were returned there.

## 30

OUTSIDE, ON ST Giles', a brisk wind was shaking the new leaves of the plane trees. Mark looked around furtively, checking that no one was lying in wait, as he stepped out onto the street with his father.

'Are you OK to walk?' he asked, knowing that he would usually be snapped at for asking. Anthony refused to be treated as an old man.

'Yes, yes,' Anthony said quickly, though without his habitual dismissiveness. Mark kept looking from side to side as he walked. Every tourist carrying a camera made him flinch. This was a photograph that someone would pay good money for: disgraced ex-minister and his disgraced father, side by side, in public view, conspiring. Mark tried not to imagine the headlines over the top, but they kept rushing into his mind in tabloid capitals. *Minister's spy dad: what did he know? The prof who came in from the cold*. That sort of thing.

They walked on, both rejecting the first pub they passed as too public, too touristy. You never knew who might be in there, they agreed, and it would be crowded, anyway. They kept walking north, hardly speaking. As Mark tried to understand what he now knew, and what he still did not, questions occurred to him that would not leave. What if this was still only one more layer of the story, and the truth lay several layers beneath? The car, the smell of the petrol: what if these were just details designed to distract him from getting to the next layer, the way the image of the people dropping from their windows had filled in the gaps in the old story?

He turned his head sideways and looked at his father as though he were someone he had never met before. Although he may have known Anthony Lucas for thirty-five years, Anton Lukas was a stranger to him. Mark saw a man of retirement age, walking along the street with determination, his woollen tie blowing in the wind and his hand gripping his briefcase. He was dressed as an English professor was supposed to dress, in clothes that he refused to alter or replace except *in extremis*. Perhaps if you wore a disguise for long enough, it was no longer a disguise. In the space of a few days, Mark had oscillated between admiring his father and despising him, and he still didn't know where on the scale the needle would come to rest.

They found a small pub on a narrow back street that was reassuringly quiet, with oak-panelled walls and one or two students wasting the end of an afternoon in a far corner. Mark gulped at his pint, hoping that the drink would start to soothe the day. He handed the other pint to his father and tried to resume the conversation where they had broken off.

'So once you were here, what happened?'

'First I had to go through the processing centre again, in West Berlin. This time they stamped all the right forms, they knew who I was, and when I told them I wanted to come to Britain, they stamped the right forms for that, too. I think perhaps they felt bad for having wanted to leave me there. They knew what could have happened to me. They helped me find a place to study; they had friendly people in some of the colleges. I met your mother. You were born. You know the rest.' Anthony appeared to feel the story had come to an end, but Mark knew it had not.

'I don't know the rest,' Mark insisted. 'If you'd left, why would the East Germans still have a codename for you when you were over here? How did they know where you were, or even who you were, at all?'

'So you think I was some kind of double, triple agent?' Anthony snapped. 'Are you doubting my story?'

'I don't know what I think,' Mark replied, though the return of his father's irascible side made him wonder still more. 'But you're telling me something different now from what I thought I knew for thirty years, so of course I have doubts.'

Anthony nodded.

'I suppose you have these questions. Given what's happened to you, after all.' He sipped the beer in front of him slowly and placed the glass back on the table. Mark watched a trail of foam make rings on the grain of the wood.

'When I left,' he continued eventually, 'it was real. I was genuinely leaving, I was in genuine danger. It was not some kind of trick. And so for many years, I heard nothing. There was no one back there who I could keep in touch with – that would have put them in danger. It was no longer home. They had no claim on me. Then a few years later, when you were small, I had people try to contact me under what I thought were false pretences. They claimed to have some kind of connection to me, to know people I had known. Someone in particular.' Anthony's eyes looked downcast.

'You mean East Germans? And who was the someone?' Mark noticed his father was becoming more cryptic again, now that they were in a more public place. Anthony waited a long while before replying.

'When I was still over there, I had a girlfriend. Her name was Christa. I had to leave without saying goodbye to her. It was for her sake – if she had known, they could have arrested her, sent her to prison, for helping me. I wished I could have told her I was going. I'm sure she realised what had happened.'

Mark looked at his father again, still seeing someone he hardly knew. He tried to imagine what his father had looked like then, realising what he had once known but had recently forgotten; that there were no photographs of a young Anton he had ever seen. Mark wondered how Anton the student, Anton the spy had looked, but got no further than an image of a skinny young man in thick glasses. He wondered who Christa had seen.

'Someone came to me one day, who said he had also left for the West, as I had done. He had come to England to study and he said he felt lonely, had trouble settling in. He wanted to be friends with me. So we sat in a pub, like this one, and he told me his troubles. And then one day he brought me a letter. It was from Christa. At least, he said it was from Christa.'

'Why would it not have been?' Mark asked.

'Wait,' Anthony said. 'It looked like her handwriting, but it had been a long time, and I couldn't be sure. I was suspicious. They had taught me how to be suspicious. I asked this man, Rolf his name was, questions about Christa, things he would only know if he had really met her. He seemed as though he really knew her. But at the same time I doubted him, I was afraid.'

'Afraid of what?' Mark was drinking now faster than he meant to; it seemed the only way to deal with what he was hearing. He wanted to get another drink, but didn't want to break the flow of the story. Worse than hearing the story was the chance that it might stop and never be resumed.

'Afraid that this was a trap. It seemed too obvious, too neat. So I waited, I tried to get in touch again with the people who had helped me to come over here. It took me a while; I went back to the academics who I knew helped them, but they were reluctant to put me in contact. I told them it was important, told them about Rolf.'

'And what did the letter say?'

'The letter . . .' Anthony cast his eyes down again, staring at the table and avoiding Mark's gaze.

'The letter from Christa,' he prompted.

'I know which letter,' Anthony snapped back. 'It said she had a son.'

'Your son?' Mark asked, almost in a whisper. His father nodded, a small, flickering nod. His son. Mark's brother. His half-brother. An East German half-brother, older than him. How old, exactly? Another version of himself, on the other side of the Wall. 'Was he . . . was she . . . was that possible?'

'It was possible. But I still wasn't sure if it was true.'

'But you found out? Did she have a picture? What happened when you wrote back?'

'There was no picture. That was one reason I was suspicious. Perhaps there would have been a picture, one day, but that could still not have been real. It could have been a picture of any baby, any child. I didn't write back.'

'Why not?' Mark surprised himself by exclaiming this. His father hushed him. The students at the back of the bar, jolted from their indolent drinking, looked around.

'Because my British friends, you know, told me it was most likely a trap. That Rolf was someone they knew about, someone they didn't trust. That the whole story about Christa was probably some kind of blackmail, and that even if it wasn't, it was a way to draw me in, to make me feel I had some obligations over there. That maybe even Christa was working for them, for the East German authorities. So they advised me very strongly not to have anything to do with her. I saw Rolf a few times, afterwards, and each time I told them, my British friends, what he had said. So I expect it is Rolf's reports that are in these files.'

'And you listened to them? Even though you might have had a son over there, even though they had left you behind when things got difficult?'

Anthony shook his head slowly.

'I still don't think you quite understand, Mark. I said that I owed them everything. You were a young boy, just started at school. Your sister was still a baby. I thought of the peaceful, stable life that you had, that I wanted so much for you. I somehow thought that if I didn't help them, they could take it away from me as easily as they gave it to me. Take away my passport, my citizenship. Your citizenship.'

'But it doesn't work like that, here,' Mark protested. 'That's the point, surely. That they can't; it's not just arbitrary.'

'You think that?' Anthony raised a straggly eyebrow. 'After

the last few days that you've had, you still think that?' Mark didn't reply. He needed another drink, now more than ever. He walked to the bar, turning back to look at his father as though he might run away, make another escape to avoid any more questioning.

The barman pulled the pints slowly. Mark watched the beer begin to fill the slanted glass, something familiar that today seemed strange, as though he was seeing it for the first time. The comfort of the routine had been snatched away from him. Mark understood what his father meant; it was something he must always have assumed, too, but had never realised until today: they could take it all away from you. They always could. You might think you were just the same, that you belonged here in the world of buildings that had lasted centuries and pints that were always pulled the same way, but if you hadn't been here as long as the buildings and the beer, you didn't really belong. Not when it mattered.

'Did Mum know?' Mark began, placing two pints on the table, although his father's first drink was not yet finished.

'Did she know what?' Anthony seemed to be stalling.

'How much of this did she know? About what you did, how you got out? About Christa?'

Anthony traced his finger down the side of his glass, avoiding Mark's stare. Mark concentrated on a small part of his father's face, trying to see his eyes where they weren't shielded by his glasses, through the gap spanned by the spectacles' metal frame. He might have been about to cry, but Mark couldn't be sure.

'Your mother knew as much as I could tell her without hurting her, without putting her at risk.'

'Which means what, exactly?' Mark regretted his sharp tone as soon as he saw Anthony's eyes grow more watery, a tear forming behind the barrier of the lens. It was hard to remember that he wasn't in that world any more, the world where the arguments were for public consumption, where he had points to score.

'She knew who I was, and where I had come from, and some of how it happened,' Anthony said in a small voice. 'I never lied to her. I could never lie to your mother. She would always have known it.'

Mark knew that was true, because he had often tried and failed. He remembered small lies: the smell of cigarettes he'd tried to mask with chewing-gum; the colouring crayons he had once stolen from his sister; the exam marks he had sometimes bumped up. She always did know. He wished more than ever that she were still here, now in his disgrace even more than before, in his triumph. Mark swallowed down the feeling that he, too, was about to cry; washed the emotion back with a swig of bitter.

'Of course,' Anthony continued, 'there were things I didn't tell her, which isn't quite the same. She knew that Christa had existed – I mean, that there was a girlfriend I had left behind. As you would expect, she didn't like me to talk about her that much. So I didn't tell her when they got in touch with me again. There was no reason to upset her about something I didn't know to be true.'

'But she must have known something . . . that something was wrong?' Mark remembered this, too, how his mother could sense the evasion that came before the lie or instead of it. Anthony raised his eyes towards the pub's yellowing ceiling.

'Perhaps she did. But I think she also knew when not to ask.'

The sky was darkening outside the rippled glass windows of the pub and Mark realised that he would have to leave before long. He wondered whether there would still be journalists waiting outside his father's house – his own old home, as he rarely thought of it these days.

'Will you be all right getting back?' Mark asked, changing the subject. 'The reporters might still be outside. Perhaps you should go somewhere else – Martha's, maybe?'

'She has invited me for supper,' Anthony answered, looking at his watch. 'But I'll sleep in my own bed, thank you. I've been thrown out of my own home by worse people than this, and I won't let it happen again.'

'Let's go, Dad,' Mark said softly, standing up and rounding the table. He offered Anthony his arm to stand; his father, of course, refused it. Mark held open the heavy oak door of the pub and ushered him through, then worried that he might be pushing his father out into an ambush. They might be here, they might have found them. The beer had blurred his thoughts so he wasn't quite sure which 'they' he meant. There was no one on the street who seemed to be watching either of them. It was dusk, and the warmth had gone out of the air.

'You should tell someone, you know,' Mark began as he followed his father's lead down a narrow street of terraced houses. He realised he didn't know where he was being taken. 'Tell them what you've told me.' Mark looked Anthony in the eye. 'It would help. It would mean there wouldn't be inquiries, by the police, by the university. Otherwise, I don't know what will happen to you. You could lose your job. They could arrest you, even.'

Mark realised it was unfair to frighten his father like this, but it was the only way he could imagine that might work.

'No.' Anthony returned Mark's gaze, unwavering. 'The people who need to know will be able to know, if there is such an inquiry. No one else needs to.'

'But it's an amazing story,' Mark pleaded. 'What about your reputation? Otherwise people will always have questions about you. You can clear your name.'

'You mean they'll always have questions about you,' his father retorted. 'You want me to clear your name. My reputation lies in my work. I know it's different in your work, and I'm sorry for that. But I'm still not prepared to break that trust, or for you to break it on my behalf.'

'What trust?' Mark replied. 'You trusted them. The trust was all one way, as far as I can see. What did you get out of it?'

In reply, Anthony waved a hand around ahead of him. Mark looked where the gesture led him: he saw a street of neat brick

Victorian houses, but he realised that the street alone was not what he meant. He meant this place, its stability, its peace.

'There were so many people who didn't realise what they had,' Anthony announced. 'But at least I did what I could.'

Mark let this go by for a moment, his mind already ahead of himself. He scanned the street as though someone might still be looking for them.

'It doesn't seem just,' Anthony continued, 'that you and I should be blamed. When there were other people who would have put all this at risk.' Mark realised that his father was not, as he first thought, talking to himself. This comment was addressed to him.

'What do you mean?'

'There were people then, students, my students, who believed the illusion. I tried to stop them making the same mistakes I'd made as a young man. Sometimes they went too far, they were getting involved in things that might put them or the country in danger.'

'In what way?' Mark wondered where his father was going with this; he questioned again whether he was spending too much time alone with his thoughts and whether those thoughts were as clear as they once had been.

'I couldn't stop them thinking stupid things, that was their choice, of course, though I could try to teach them to think better. But if I could stop them ruining their lives, then why not?' Something seemed to occur to him. 'Take your friend, your boss's friend. He had a funny name.'

'I don't know who you mean, Dad.' Mark felt some case study, some thought experiment, would only complicate things more.

'One of those silly English names, Scottish names maybe, that no foreigner can pronounce. It's like a test to see if you should be in this country.'

'Sorry, Dad, you're still not helping.'

'Colquhoun,' he said at last. 'Written *Colck-hoon*. Pronounced *Cal-oon*, or so they told me.' Mark shook his head. 'No one could pronounce it, not even British people, so he had to change it, later on, when he went into politics. It's funny, isn't it, how you have to have a name that people can understand, or apparently they won't vote for you. Even if it's a British name, one as old as the hills.' Mark wondered where this digression would end up. 'And even then they didn't vote for him, so they had to make him a Lord, and now he has all this unelected power. Sometimes I still don't understand this country.'

Mark tried for what he resolved would be one last time.

'Who do you mean, Dad?'

'Oh, you know who I mean. You're always telling me about him. Lord Robert someone, now. Callander, that's it. When I knew him he was Robbie Colquhoun. People like that were so young and hot-headed. They didn't realise what they might have been getting into.'

This was suddenly a story that Mark did want to hear.

'What did he do?'

'He was very radical, in those days. I used to argue with him: he was always talking about how things would become the revolution. He didn't seem to think it mattered that I had seen one and it wasn't how he imagined it would be. But that's only natural, to have dreams. It was when he wanted to go over there, to the East, and study, go on some "friendship visit" or whatever they called it, that I told him he was being a useful idiot. He didn't take that very well.'

Mark, knowing how Bob Callander reacted to criticism now, could well imagine it.

'But he still went?'

'Of course he still went,' Anthony replied. 'And I warned people here to keep an eye on him, find out the kind of people who got in touch with him. I don't think it's done him any harm.'

'No,' Mark agreed. Not yet, anyway. 'What do you mean, warned people? Which people?'

Anthony looked around the empty street, as though someone

might still be watching or overhearing him. They were approaching a corner, and he waited to speak until they had rounded it. A student cycled towards them; when he was gone, Anthony continued.

'My . . . friends. You know.' He shrugged. Mark understood.

'You informed on your students?' Mark said in a sharp whisper.

'That's a harsh word,' Anthony replied.

'But you did,' Mark insisted. 'Why?'

'Put simply, I wanted to stop people doing things they might come to regret.'

'I understand that. But it wasn't your choice to make, was it?' Anthony raised his palms to the sky.

'But that was their right,' Mark exclaimed. 'If I understand anything about what you've been working on all these years, that's the point. The freedom to think anything you like. That's the point of you being here in this country at all.'

'The freedom to believe it, of course. The freedom to express your ideas, absolutely. But acting on it in such a way as to damage the liberties of others, or even to damage your own future self that might not be so idealistic and naive, then no.'

'You've lost me with the future self thing, I'm afraid.' Mark was conscious of his father having slipped back into tutorial mode, but he had understood enough, for now.

They slowed down as they approached what must have been Martha's house.

'You know a wonderful thing?' Anthony mused as they stood on the pavement in front of the low garden wall and a sparse box hedge. The house was small, the front garden overgrown, the paintwork cracking. A large bicycle with a wicker basket on the front handlebars leant against the side of the porch.

He seemed distant again; Mark wondered which past he was entering now. 'The thing I had never seen until I came here?'

Mark shook his head, running through possibilities in his mind from the stories his father had once told him: bananas; oranges; the Houses of Parliament; the Changing of the Guard.

'The tide. I had never seen the tide. I had only ever seen the Baltic Sea, and there the water stays where it is. So when I came here, I went to the beach, and I watched the tide come in and rush out. I thought even the sea here is free to move. People wash up here, like driftwood on the shingle, and find a new home. So whenever we went on holiday, the family, I would think about that, about how lucky we were to see the tides of the sea, and to be standing safely on the beach, together.'

Martha must have heard their voices, as she opened the door before they had a chance to knock. Mark worried how much of their conversation she might have heard, whether she had been listening at the window or the door. She invited him in, but he refused. He needed to be alone, and to make his circuitous way home.

Standing in the porch, he hugged his father goodbye, not knowing what else to say. Mark muttered something about talking soon. Anthony turned and walked into the house, where a warm light shone. Mark watched the back of the man he had thought he knew disappear, and Martha pull the door closed behind them.

## 31

ANNA WAS STILL awake when her phone rang, though she'd
been trying not to be. It was just after half past twelve and
she was lying in bed, listening to the radio, hoping that the shipping forecast and 'Sailing By' would manage to send her to sleep
when nothing else, so far, had. The newsreader's calm voice
smoothed over the storms and gales as though they held no
dangers. Anna was still too alert to sleep; she had been watching
every news programme, listening to every bulletin, reading
between every line that every other reporter uttered to see what
she might have missed, what other people might be saying,
what angle they'd find next, what was being spun.

It was when she saw the first editions of the next day's newspapers, held up to the screen by a disdainful *Newsnight* presenter
at the end of the programme, that she realised one of the things
that was still troubling her. Most of the papers exclaimed the
fact of Mark Lucas's resignation; they showed him standing in
Downing Street or outside his house. He looked smaller than
Anna remembered him. The fact that a member of the secret
services had been arrested was, for now, the lesser story, and the
rival papers were behind on the details.

Anna had been asked whether she had any photos of Alex
Rutherford that they could use in the paper; she had half lied,
said there were none she could get hold of immediately. There
were some, in fact, in an album on her bookshelf, but they were
ones only she could have had, and she was not prepared to share
them. She suggested they try to find a college photo, an official

one in the records somewhere, giving them vague dates; so far, the picture library hadn't had any luck. Alex was represented by a black silhouette on an inside page. Anna realised, as she saw the pile of the morning's papers stacked on a studio desk, that he would not remain a silhouette for long. By tomorrow, his outline would have been filled in; if they didn't have a picture of him snatched outside the police station, there would be a young Alex in gown and white bow-tie, circled for easy identification, or there would be an equally young Alex in cricket whites, squinting into the camera. Alex would be in the public domain, and it would be her fault, and there was no way now of stopping it happening. If she could find Alex's parents, no doubt everyone else could too, sooner or later. They would be doorstepping Patrick and Jennifer. The circles rippled outwards, spreading the intrusion and the anxiety. It was beyond Anna's control now.

So when the shipping forecast was interrupted by the bleeps of electronic interference that presaged Anna's phone ringing, her first instinct was not to answer it. She remembered Michael Swain's warning: if in doubt, call the lawyer. Anna wondered whether it might be an angry call from Theo or one of his colleagues; she'd heard there had been several during the day, though they hadn't been directed at her. She was considered insufficiently important to be sworn at; it was a strategy of holding her in contempt designed to make her feel inferior, but it was one that scarcely bothered her. If being unimportant meant she didn't have to hold the earpiece away from her ear while an angry man channelled a spittle-flecked tirade into the other end of the phone, then so much the better.

Anna fumbled for the phone and looked at the screen. It was Mark Lucas. She had not expected to hear from him again, ever. She sat up as she answered it, pulled the duvet up around herself, and started looking around the room for a notebook and a pen. She hoped he wasn't drunk. Though half past midnight on the day you'd been forced to resign would be a pretty understandable time to be drunk. She hoped he wouldn't vent his anger at her.

'Sorry to call so late,' Lucas began. He sounded sober. He spoke quietly; Anna turned off the shipping forecast so she could hear him clearly. Somewhere out there, something was falling more slowly.

'That's fine,' Anna replied. 'What is it?'

'You didn't hear this from me,' he continued. 'Or friends of me or anyone anything to do with me, in any form of words.'

'Yes, OK,' Anna agreed. She got out of bed and went to the desk in the next room, trying to find a pen. She switched on the desk lamp and sat down, looking at the pad of paper in the small pool of light and waiting to take note of what Lucas said next.

'Do you still have the disk?' he asked.

'I can't really say,' Anna replied. She wasn't sure why he wanted to know; it was no longer his job to be trying to get it back.

'Listen, assuming that you do, this is just a tip, a hunch. It might be nothing. But there's a name you could look for, one you might not have recognised.'

'Go on,' Anna said, drawing question marks on the sheet of paper as she waited.

'Colquhoun,' Lucas repeated the name for her, spelling it out. 'Robert, also known as Robbie.'

'Who is he?' Anna couldn't remember if this was one of the names she'd looked at before, and drawn a blank with.

'That's who he used to be,' Mark Lucas continued. 'Until he started running for office, and was told he'd do better with a less posh name. He goes by Callander, these days. Still pretty posh, if you ask me.'

Anna tried not to let Mark hear her intake of breath. She wrote down *Colquhoun = Callander* on her pad, following the note with three question marks and surrounding the whole with an oval swirl of biro.

'How do you know this?' she asked, before he could ring off.

'It's a hunch, like I said. I can't say anything more. You need to check it for yourself.'

'Mark,' Anna said. There were more questions she wanted to ask him, but she wasn't sure which to ask first. Just asking him flat out if this was some kind of revenge would be guaranteed to end in the line being cut off. One question suddenly overrode all the others. 'Are you all right?'

'No,' he admitted. 'Not really. But thanks for asking.'

'Can I talk to you again, some time?' Anna persisted. 'When things have calmed down?'

'I don't think so,' he replied. 'Sorry. I've got to go.'

'Mark,' she tried again. This was not the thing she was supposed to say, but it was the middle of the night, there was no one else to hear it, and she was going to say it anyway. 'I'm really sorry. About your job, and everything.'

'Yeah?' he said. 'Really? Hmmm, thanks.' He made a noise that was half bitter laugh, half snort, and he was gone.

Anna folded the sheet of paper over twice and put it in the bottom of her bag. For a moment, she contemplated getting dressed and going straight in to the office to start checking it out; that idea passed quickly. If there was anything in it, this was going to be an even harder job, even assuming it wasn't a spurious, vengeful slander by a man who had every reason to want his own back. As she fell asleep, Anna came to think that was what it was most likely to be. She felt even sorrier for Mark Lucas: the man's career had been destroyed, probably that of his father, too, and his first thought was to try to drag others down with him. That was what politics did to you.

## 32

THE SHUNTING AND creaking of the cell door startled him; Alex saw the sodium glow of the street lights outside the window and realised that it was already dark, and he must have been asleep. He was not sure how much time had passed. He turned his head from side to side to straighten out the kinks in his neck from having slept sitting up, and swung his legs down towards the floor. When the custody sergeant told him he was being released, Alex had to ask him to repeat it.

The sergeant handed Alex back his possessions, sliding them out of a plastic bag; Alex buckled the strap of his watch back onto his wrist and put his wallet back in his coat pocket. As he put his watch on, Alex looked at his fingertips, still smudged with fingerprinting ink, as though he had been writing with a leaky fountain pen.

He asked Kate if she knew what exactly had happened. She also seemed slightly surprised that he was being released.

'It looks like they're on shaky ground,' she said. 'And they can't keep you here if they are.'

'What was all that about the taxi driver?' Alex asked. The detective inspector, Boyd, had grown more irritable during the course of the day's questioning. He kept asking Alex about the man who had driven the cab in which he'd lost the computer; Alex had insisted that all he'd seen had been the back of the man's head, and that he had been in no state to remember much about that in any case.

'So they think he gave the disk to the paper?' he asked Kate.

'Seems to be their line of inquiry, as far as I can tell. Though they seem to be having a hard time with that as well. Like I say, the newspaper won't tell them anything unless the police take them to court, and that could take a while, even if they go down that route.'

Alex hesitated in the doorway as he left. The blue-framed automatic glass doors slid back to urge him through. It was a clear evening and a half-moon was rising over the blocks of flats by the railway lines. He took a deep breath, grateful even for the exhaust-filled air of Victoria, where the coaches coughed diesel as they left the Coach Station and the trains shunted out towards the south coast from beneath the bridge.

He was about to head for the brick steps when he saw them; they seemed surprised to see him too, and they burst into life with quick movements. They were lounging at the bottom of the stairs and they were dressed as though they were prepared to wait, for a long time, in all weathers. The group consisted mostly of men, wearing waterproof jackets and talking amongst themselves. Alex noticed the stalk legs of tripods and a van with an antenna on the roof and cables trailing from its back doors.

Alex veered away from the steps that would have led him straight towards them, turned and walked down the ramp that led alongside the police station. He tried not to look up. If he didn't look up, if he ignored them, they might not know it was him. How would they know what he looked like, anyway? Alex hoped they would think he was a detective, a lawyer maybe, on his way home after a hard day.

A photographer, a tall, agile man in jeans and a black jacket, saw him and rushed along beside the ramp to get his picture. The camera flashed in his face and the photographer shouted his name, trying to get a reaction. The old *Great Escape* trick, Alex thought. Alex kept staring at the pavement, not looking around, not responding except to shake his head slightly, as if to say it wasn't him. Don't look up. Don't look guilty. The others saw the photographer and chased along behind, trying to catch up with

Alex. A cameraman ran up behind him and overtook him. The cameraman, his camera hoisted to his shoulder, turned to walk backwards. A red light above the lens was glowing. Alex guessed that meant it was working, that they were filming him. A girl walked back to back with the cameraman, her hand gripping the back of his jacket as she guided him away from lamp posts and the edge of the road. A young man shouted questions at Alex: was he Alex Rutherford? Did he leak secret government documents? Why did he leak them?

Alex didn't answer but kept walking, his gaze fixed somewhere ahead of his feet, near where the cameraman's feet now were. He came to a crossing and darted out into the traffic without waiting for the lights to change. A motorbike slammed on its brakes; a taxi hooted at him. He reached the other side of the road just before the oncoming coach had to do the same. The girl had hauled her cameraman colleague away from the kerb and the traffic; now they watched him from the other side of the busy road.

Alex looked from side to side, wondering how long he had before they caught up with him again. If he kept walking, he could be home in a few minutes; but if he kept walking, would they follow him all the way there? The lights were changing and they were certainly about to follow him across the road. He had to move quickly. Alex stuck out his arm for a taxi, walking on at the same time. He was lucky; a taxi pulled to a halt next to him and he jumped in. Alex gave the driver his address. He saw the driver's shoulders shrug at the short journey.

'You could walk that, from here,' the driver said, evidently regretting the bigger fare he might have picked up at Victoria Station.

'I know,' Alex snapped. 'I just don't want to.'

The driver nodded and pulled out into the traffic, making a U-turn to go back the way he had come. Alex sat as far back in the seat as he could, hoping the journalists wouldn't spot him. He could just catch a glimpse of the cameraman and his colleague arguing with each other as to who was responsible for losing him. Alex remembered that he hadn't taken a taxi for a long time, and then he remembered why. The driver, still with a bad grace, swung the cab into Alex's street and turned his head to ask him which door to stop at. Alex looked around as the taxi slowed and knew that he couldn't stop here, that there was no going home for now.

'Drive on, please,' he said. 'Don't stop here.'

'But this is the street you wanted,' the driver replied, as though his Knowledge was being impugned.

'I know it is. But I need you not to stop here.' The driver let out a long, exasperated sigh and accelerated away with a lurch.

They were here, too. There were people blocking the pavement in front of his door, more of the spidery black tripods, the cables snaking across the kerb, even a couple of step-ladders leaning against the railings.

'Where do you want, then?' the driver huffed. Alex pulled his wallet from his pocket and looked inside to see how much money there was inside: just a dog-eared fiver. He checked the meter. There wasn't much further he could afford to go.

'Double back,' Alex told the driver. 'Not back down the way we came, go round the block. There's a church on the corner. Drop me there.'

The cabbie drove on, tugging at the steering wheel so hard as he rounded each corner that Alex was jolted against the side of the cab. Outside the church, Alex handed him the tatty five-pound note without a word, receiving a sneer in return.

He entered the church and sat in a rear pew as if to pray. There was no one else inside, except for an elderly lady in a headscarf in the front row. He bowed his head and turned over his bunch of keys inside his coat pocket, as though fiddling with them would soothe him. If he had believed that praying would help, one of the first things Alex would have asked would have been that the taxi driver didn't drive back past the journalists on his doorstep, pick one of them up, and complain about the cheapskate who'd only gone from the police station to the church and had some strange reluctance to stop in that street.

It wasn't over; this was just a reprieve. He still had to go back to the police station, on the date they'd given him before he left. He could still be charged. It seemed like they were still looking for something, or someone; it just wasn't certain that it was him. It was the journalists, now, who were looking for him. Alex shifted in the hard wooden pew and tried to come up with a plan.

It seemed wrong to be in a hotel in London. Alex tried to remember, as he checked in to the hotel near the station, whether he had ever done so before; he couldn't think of any reason that he would have done. He gave his real name to the receptionist, partly because it was the one printed on his credit card, partly because he thought that even if people were looking for him, this was not somewhere they would try to find him. He didn't know how long he would be staying, but he hoped, as the woman told him the room rate, that it would not be long. He couldn't afford it to be. In the morning, he would decide where else he could go. She asked if he had any luggage to be taken up to the room; all that Alex carried was the plastic bag from the chemist's where he'd bought a toothbrush, toothpaste and a razor. Yet again, he'd forgotten to get something to read; probably because getting to the books at the station would have meant walking past the barricade of newspapers that he didn't want to see.

Alex crossed the lobby of the hotel in search of the lift to his room. A large group of tourists was milling about in the centre of the lobby, having returned from a day of sightseeing. Some of them still wore the clear plastic rain ponchos that you were given on the open-top decks of the tour buses. A group leader was instructing them impatiently, as though they were small children. Alex tried to work out which language they spoke; it sounded like Russian, though it might have been something else Slavic. It was still strange to hear Russian spoken in

London, Alex thought, a misplaced sound that you didn't expect and that jolted you with its unfamiliarity.

The only views in the room were the ones in pastel, framed on the wall to remind you that you were in London: a smudgy Houses of Parliament seen from the river and a Buckingham Palace that had been given a strange pink aura. The real view from the room was of the roof of Victoria Station, and despite the double-glazed windows, which did not open, Alex could still hear the brakes of the buses in the street below. Alex unlaced his shoes, sat on the bed, propped himself up against piles of scratchy, unnecessary cushions, and thought that he had better phone his mother. When Jennifer answered, she sounded out of breath. Alex asked her if she was all right.

'It is you,' she began, as though she had been in the middle of another conversation.

'Yes, of course it's me,' he said, wondering who else she had been expecting.

'I'm sorry, darling,' his mother said. 'Where are you? Are you still at the police station? It's just that there have been so many people calling that your father said I should stop answering the phone. I told him I couldn't, in case it was you. And now it is you, so that's a relief.'

'Who's been calling?' Alex asked, though he could guess.

'Oh, you know. Journalists, lots of journalists.'

'You haven't said anything, have you?' Alex said hurriedly. 'Because you really can't. Not even that I didn't do anything wrong.'

'I know, my love. I just say no comment and put the phone down. It's fine. But where are you now – what's happening?'

Alex's mother surprised him again with her ability to deal calmly with the unexpected.

'They haven't charged me with anything, at least for now. I don't really know what's going to happen next. But there were reporters waiting outside my house, so I didn't go home. I'm in a hotel.'

'They're here, as well,' his mother said. 'Quite a few. But they're not too bad. Quite civil. I made them tea.'

Alex was glad he had not decided to go there. His first instinct had been to run back to his parents' home; to go to King's Cross and take the sleeper and find his way on from Edinburgh in the morning. He had been halfway into the Tube station when he had thought of a good few reasons why this wouldn't work: he needed to be able to talk to the lawyer; it might look like he was running away; and, as he now knew, another house with journalists outside the door was no kind of escape. His mother was still talking, trying to reassure him. Alex apologised and said he'd talk to her again when he could, then hung up.

Alex tried several buttons on the remote control before he could get past the irritating message on the TV screen that welcomed Mr Rutherford and hoped that he would enjoy his stay. Mr Rutherford was not here out of choice and he did not expect to enjoy himself, despite the club sandwich and the half-bottle of wine that he had ordered from room service.

On the news, someone else was trying to fight their way through a scrum of reporters outside their house. Alex could barely make out the face, and he had missed the start of the story, but he realised it must have been Mark Lucas. The shot changed: Mark Lucas was in Downing Street, walking out of the black door to stand alone behind a cluster of microphones. He looked contrite and abandoned. He pronounced words that sounded as though they had been written for him by someone else and learnt by heart. Lucas walked away from the cameras.

Alex saw another man who had not expected his path to change, another man who had expected that if he turned up and looked right and did what he thought he was supposed to do then he would be rewarded for it.

Anthony Lucas's was one of the names that was supposed to have been redacted, would have been redacted if Alex had finished the job. Alex remembered the spelling, the confusion, the double-checking that had been taking him so long. He was supposed to be editing out the people they already knew about: the ones who had been on their side. It meant cross-referencing the German files against their own files, which were often scrappy, with omissions and handwritten scribbles. 'Operational reasons,' they told him, which Alex believed just meant there had been people out there in the field who were good at what they did, but rubbish at the paperwork.

Alex remembered the pressure he'd been under: every time he looked up from the screen it seemed to be because some boss, Graham or another one, wanted to know what was going on, and how quickly he could get it done. The guys across the river, the domestic guys, wanted the files back; they thought it was their job to track down the moles, however defunct they might have been, no matter that the country they were spying for no longer even existed. They wanted to claim the credit. Then there was the pressure from the politicians, who in turn were getting grief from the Germans about giving the files back to them. And then there were the people who were asking for other redactions for reasons of their own, things that weren't procedure. That was when the stress had got to him. He mouthed an apology at Mark Lucas, just as the ex-minister walked out of shot.

Two reporters appeared side by side in opposite halves of the TV screen; one in a darkened Downing Street, the other standing outside the police station he had not long left. The woman outside the police station was first, her image becoming larger as the man in Westminster disappeared for a minute. Alex was relieved that she seemed to have little to say – she too was reciting something as if by rote, saying that a twenty-eight-year-old man, believed to be a member of the intelligence services, had been arrested under the Official Secrets Act and questioned by police, before being released on bail. She looked slightly overwhelmed by what she was saying, afraid of getting things wrong, afraid even of the words themselves, that signified things beyond her complete understanding. That was a feeling Alex recognised too. 'Believed to be,' he thought. He liked that particular phrase. He too believed himself to be part of the intelligence services, though he wasn't sure exactly where he stood on that at the moment. Perhaps if he believed himself to be, then it would continue to be true.

# 33

ON THE MORNING of his twenty-ninth birthday, Alex woke up remembering that he was a year older, but having forgotten precisely where he was. The room was filled with an unfamiliar light, a blue-toned colour that swam through thin blinds. Everything in the room seemed pale and empty. It was certainly not his own room, nor the cell in the police station. It was definitely not the hotel; this was not the sort of dark-curtained place where you could forget that it was morning. There were expensively soft white covers on the bed and a floor of cold, blond wood. An orchid in a white pot on the bedside table might have been fake, had it not been starting to wither from lack of water. It was the room of a person whose life mostly took place somewhere else. Alex lay still in the hope that who that was would come to him before much longer.

His own watch, which lay next to the orchid and whose worn leather strap appeared to be the only old thing in this room, told him it was nearly nine. It slowly came to Alex where he was: this was James Rycroft's flat, and James was in Hong Kong or Singapore or somewhere. Alex got up to open the blinds, which revealed a balcony and a view of the river. If Alex stood towards the edge of the balcony and leaned over the industrial steel railings, he could just about see past the bridge towards the Tower of London. The tide was low this morning and Alex could make out the algae-covered blocks that bricked up Traitors' Gate.

When the phone rang, he thought it was unlikely to be

someone wishing him a happy birthday. Hardly anyone knew he was here. Alex let James's gruff, recorded voice on the answerphone tell the caller that James wasn't here right now, only picking up when he heard Kate Sheppard start to leave a message, asking Alex to call her back as quickly as he could.

'They want you to come in again,' she told him. 'As soon as possible.'

'Did they tell you what's happened? Am I going to be charged?'

'I really don't know,' she replied. 'They didn't give me much indication. But something is definitely moving. I wish I could tell you what.'

Alex pulled on one of the new shirts that he had bought; it still felt as though they, too, belonged to someone else. James had offered him the use of his clothes, as well as his flat, but the laundered shirts, stacked in their plastic packets with white cardboard folded under the collars, had been far too big, as Alex had expected they would be, and the banker's suits hung off his shoulders and hips as though they were hand-me-downs.

He moved through the ebbing rush-hour crowds, keeping his head down and rushing as though he were a normal commuter, inconspicuous. There were no reporters outside the police station that morning; they seemed to have given up waiting for him, their attention moved on to other things. Alex wondered whether they were still outside the house. He had been back once, sneaking in to his own home in the middle of the night. It felt as though that in itself was some kind of crime, though he had been told that it wasn't. He hated the emptinesses where things had been taken, the box of letters gone from the bookshelf. He had packed some clothes and a couple of books, scooped rotting food from the fridge into a plastic bag, and locked the flat closed again. As Alex dumped the mildewed vegetables and dried-out cheese into the litter bin on the street, he noticed the paper coffee cups that almost filled the bin. They meant the journalists had still been staking him out that day. He wondered whether he was still being watched by anyone else, whether they would observe that he had been there. There was a pile of handwritten envelopes in the hall that he had ignored, after reading the first one – an ungrammatical, scribbled request for an interview.

Despite the fact that the detectives had apparently been looking for him urgently first thing in the morning, when Alex reached the police station he still had to wait. He sat on a blue plastic chair among a few other unhappy-looking people – victims, he guessed, come to report stolen cars and burglaries – and unfolded the newspaper he'd picked up at the station.

There it was, finally. The story he'd been waiting for. He had the same sense of things elegantly slotting in to place that he had when he saw a well-made crossword puzzle solved, with the solution its compiler had intended. Nine letters, beginning with C blank L. It was an answer that had been a long time in coming.

Detective Inspector Boyd called him in and Alex folded the newspaper away.

He was in the same interview room with the bland walls and the four chairs around a table, but it felt different. A junior officer offered Alex tea or coffee, saying sorry that it was only from a vending machine and wasn't much good. The detective apologised for keeping him waiting. Kate Sheppard was shown in just after Alex – she too was apologising for her lateness and a delay on the Tube. Alex sipped at the coffee in its flimsy white plastic cup, swirled the half-dissolved granules on the top with a thin plastic stirrer, and wondered what was going on.

'I'm sorry to call you in at such short notice,' Boyd began. 'There have been a few developments.'

Alex waited to hear what they were. Kate, not prepared to wait despite her billable minutes, was more to the point.

'Is my client going to be charged?' she began.

'The short answer is no,' Boyd replied.

'What's the long answer?' Kate asked. Boyd took a long breath, as though the long answer would require all of the available air in the room.

'The long answer is that this has been a very politically sensitive case, as you'll realise. But the issue from our point of view – and the good thing from yours, Mr Rutherford – is that everything we have been able to find out has seemed to back up the story you told us. Some of the other . . . agencies involved don't seem to have done the basic legwork in any way that we can quite understand.'

Boyd rolled his eyes upwards, looking up to the floors above in silent reproach of his superiors and of the others, down towards the river. He leant in across the table. 'I don't want this to go any further, but I think your colleagues, and some of the people upstairs, were determined to find something more behind it. There's been a lot of political toing and froing that I don't like to get involved with. Things like this, official secrets cases, they have to go right to the top to get a decision. I just told them I have to go where the evidence takes me, and in this case, the evidence isn't there. Not regarding you, anyway.'

Boyd leant back in his chair. 'As I say,' he continued, 'the short answer is, the decision has been made not to press any charges against you. I'm sorry for any inconvenience.'

It was a bland, boilerplate apology, the kind of words at the end of a computerised letter or on the recorded messages you heard from call centres. Alex wondered whether the others would receive the same sort of apology; it had probably been more frightening still for a cab driver, a waitress, the man in the Lost Property Office to be suspected of something like this, something whose significance they would hardly comprehend.

Kate was full of indignation on his behalf. Alex only half took in the stream of words she came out with, but it seemed to include expressions like 'wrongful arrest' and 'compensation'. Boyd shrugged in response, unwilling to incriminate himself.

'There are forms,' he said. 'We'll see you have them.'

# 34

ANNA HAD ALREADY lost count of how many times, that evening, she had been asked how she had known. She practised different responses to the question: she raised an eyebrow, shrugged her shoulders, laughed the subject off or offered to buy the questioner a drink. As it started to become cooler on the terrace and they watched the tourist boats pass by under Westminster Bridge, she was beginning to acquire the nickname 'dark horse'.

Ian Phillips returned from the bar with another round of drinks; Anna took a token sip from her glass of white wine and left the glass on the table for a while.

'I know I've said this already,' he said, stretching his legs out alongside the table, 'but I can't remember a week like this, not in a long while.'

A stocky woman in a purple dress walked up behind him to the table. Everything about her was solid: her hair set into greying blonde waves; her breasts compressed by her dress into one large bolster. Hester Bradbury raised her pint glass towards Phillips in a salute.

'So, well done, I suppose,' she said.

'You just suppose?' Ian said, returning the toast.

'Well,' she shrugged. 'He was one of ours.'

'Anyway,' he said, waving his glass in the direction of Anna. 'Credit where it's due. Hester, have you met Anna Travers?'

Anna stood up and reached her hand over towards Hester

Bradbury. The MP had a handshake more forceful than most of her male colleagues.

'So, what led you to him?' Hester asked straight away; the question again.

'Luck and legwork,' Anna replied. Hester Bradbury stared directly at her, keeping hold of her hand.

'Nice answer,' she said, 'but I'm not sure it will be enough for the inquiry.'

'Leave her be, for now,' Ian interjected. 'There'll be time for that. Sit down. I want to hear what happened.'

Hester shifted herself into a wooden chair and hung her handbag from one of its arms.

'Bob took it very badly, as you can imagine.' She broke off, looking from Phillips back to Anna. 'She knows this doesn't go further, doesn't she?'

'I'm teaching her the rules,' Ian reassured her. 'She may be our dark horse, but I'm keeping my eye on her.'

Hester made herself more comfortable in the narrow chair. She surveyed the terrace quickly, checking that there was no one listening in from other tables nearby.

'Very badly indeed,' she continued. 'I heard there were tears. There was definitely screaming and shouting. Apparently he was claiming he'd been set up, that it was all a forgery designed to discredit him. He blamed everyone from the Russians to the Americans and most places in between. Particularly the French, for some reason that no one can quite fathom.'

'Well, why not the French?' Ian laughed.

'Yes, why not?' Hester took a long draught of her beer. 'Anyway, he demanded to see the head of MI6, though I'm not sure that C could find the time in his diary; he wanted MI5 involved as well. He wanted some kind of proof, he said.'

Ian leaned in towards her. 'He was firing off all sorts of lawyers' letters to us; threatened to sue us if we published anything. He was even calling it criminal libel at one point.'

Anna shifted her chair closer to the table, trying to catch

more of the conversation. She addressed her question to Hester.

'Do you think he was ever really . . . a threat? I mean, an actual agent?'

Hester gave her a thin smile that suggested it was a charmingly innocent thing to ask.

'That's rather what I've been charged with finding out, my dear. But without pre-empting the inquiry, and on the understanding I don't read this over my porridge, it seems he might just have been rather naive.'

'The thing is, these days,' Phillips added, 'it doesn't really matter. It's all about the perception. I heard that's what they told him, anyway. Word has it that Bob Callander said to the PM, "Well, at least I believed in something, even if it turned out to be on the wrong side of history." He told him better that than believing nothing at all!'

Hester laughed darkly. 'That sounds like someone has been embellishing things a bit for the sake of a good story. But apparently Bob maintains he was just a kid and he never knew who he was talking to. He just believed in the forward march of history, revolution and progress and all that, and got caught up in it. We'll see.'

Anna had watched Callander's furious, indignant statement in the Lords; it had been one of those moments that people told her came few times in any career. He had broken with every convention, said things she would never have been able to report if he hadn't said them in that privileged cocoon of red leather and gold. Even the peers who normally stifled snores from the back rows of the chamber, their heads lolling on the benches, sat upright, listening to every irate, bellowed word. Evenbetter had been the response from an elderly, waspish baroness, who had stood up after Callander had resumed his place, and quietly destroyed his judgement. She talked of having had the silent obligation to serve, and everyone listening had realised what she meant.

'Those of us,' she had said, 'who did not talk, when it mattered, and who understood that the lives of many people depended on it, will find it hard to understand the noble lord's protestation that he merely talked to people he did not know, in a place he says he did not truly understand, and thought that nothing rested on it. He may have been young,' she had continued, 'but so were we, during the war and after it, and nonetheless we knew the importance of protecting our country from its enemies.'

Afterwards, Anna had hovered in the Peers' Lobby and watched Callander charge through the gilded archway from the Chamber. He was breathing so heavily Anna thought he might collapse there in the entrance. She made a token attempt to try to speak to him, calling 'Lord Callander', trying to block his route; he batted her away with a fierce flick of his arm. He strode on, alone, into the corridor. Anna saw people turn and watch him, then turn their heads away, but no one came to talk to him, to commiserate with him.

She had approached the baroness too, and was rebuffed with glacial politeness.

'No thank you, young lady. I have said everything I have to say, in there. I trust you wrote it down.'

Anna had tried to speak to Mark again too, but with an equal lack of success. Once things had calmed down, sort of, she had tried to call him back. The phone would ring out a few times before she heard the ringing cut dead; Anna could guess that he had seen the number and rejected the call. She left a message, knowing that her call would not be returned. The third or fourth time she tried his number, the phone was switched off; later still, she heard a message telling her the number was unobtainable. She had wanted to thank him, to ask him again where the hunch came from. Something he knew, something he guessed, a lucky hurling of mud that simply stuck in the right place. Anna would never find out.

Once or twice, she had flicked through the list of contacts in her phone to Theo's name, her finger hovering over the green button, but she never rang.

The division bell summoned Hester and the other MPs away

from the terrace in a rush, leaving their drinks unfinished on the tables. The lanterns arrayed along the river wall of the terrace started to flicker on. Anna felt cold, and thought it was probably time for her to leave, too.

Ian Phillips looked along the terrace and up at the building behind. Anna followed his gaze, looking at the tracery of the windows, the sandy-coloured stonework, and the carved crests.

'So,' he asked, 'have you got the taste for this, then? Scented blood, and all that?'

'It's hard to take it all in, right now,' Anna said, drinking more of her wine in an effort to avoid answering.

'Because I think it's yours for the asking, right now,' Phillips continued. 'We'd like to have you down here.'

'Thank you,' Anna said. 'But aren't there a lot of people who must really hate me, Ian, after all this? There are certainly quite a few who aren't speaking to me any more.' She thought of Mark Lucas and his phone's flat dead tone.

'Oh, probably,' he replied indifferently. 'But you know, for every one who hates you because of all of it, there's his enemy who loves you for it. For every person who thinks you can't be trusted, there's someone else who thinks you're a great way to get things known. That's just how it goes.'

'And did you hear anything more about how this happened?' Anna asked. 'How it came to us, I mean? Could we still get arrested?' The office grapevine had gone remarkably quiet on the subject.

Phillips shrugged. 'Not heard anything either. It seems to have gone a bit quiet since all of this . . .' He indicated the Palace of Westminster, meaning the resignation and all the drama that had surrounded it. 'I think they feel they're on shaky ground to go after us too aggressively, given that everyone would just say they're trying to distract attention from Callander. Shooting the messenger and all that. There's the inquiry, of course. So we'll see.'

Phillips fidgeted with the pass on the red lanyard around his neck – it seemed to be troubling him somehow. Anna looked at the plastic tags and the red cord embossed with somebody or other's slogan in white letters, and suddenly wondered whether she did have the taste for it after all, whether she wanted to be attached, accredited, loved or hated by turns but just as easily forgotten again. A police boat bumped past on the river at speed, kicking up small waves in its wake that rolled towards the terrace. The tide was high that evening, the river full.

# 35

M ARK WATCHED HIS own face being shredded into ribbons, hundreds of times over. He picked up another pile of leaflets and fed them into the machine, which sliced and munched them until it was full. Logos and slogans were all julienned. A red light flashed on the top of the shredder, indicating that it couldn't digest any more. Mark opened the casing and tipped the tangle of paper, parts of his rearranged face, his promises, his speeches, into a black rubbish sack.

The constituency office was nearly empty now, ready for the new occupant. A new face would be pasted into the template and printed out on the leaflets, folded and stuffed into the envelopes. Others had offered to finish clearing up for him, but Mark felt it was something he had to help them do. He was the one who had left them with the hundreds of new envelopes that would need stuffing. He felt that if he stopped moving, stopped doing things, a huge inertia would overcome him, a coalescing of all the tiredness and all the weight of the last weeks. If he didn't keep moving now, he might never move again.

Mark tied the top of the rubbish bag and carried it out to the door. He looked around again at the office: it was a tiny place, a small shopfront with his name above the door in red letters and two old-fashioned desks with wire in-trays. The back room, scruffier and hidden from public view, was filled with photocopiers and leaflets and flyers, and a sink with a tatty kettle beside it. The box files in the front office remained for the next incumbent, containing the sheaves of problems to which Mark had attempted to find solutions: the tenants' homes with leaking roofs and patches of damp; the rejected visa applications; the complaints about waiting lists and lost letters to government departments. Mark thought that he himself had done very little to really help these people; he had sat and listened to their problems and then just signed the letters that his staff wrote for him. If anyone had really helped, it was probably the researchers who patiently drafted the letters, spent hours on the phone trying to get through to the council to get things solved, made the same calls again and again.

He dumped the final rubbish bag with the pile of others and went back to his old desk to collect a cardboard box. It held a couple of coffee mugs, a framed photo of himself with the prime minister, the one pen that he liked to sign letters with, and a handful of letters of thanks from the few people he really felt he had made a difference for. It was all that seemed worth keeping. He checked that the answering machine was switched on and then turned out the lights. He locked the door behind him and looked up again at his name above the door: Mark Lucas MP. That was him no longer. He balanced the cardboard box against his hip as he put the keys in a pocket. Mark looked at the photograph in its frame, what he could see of it under the mugs, at least, and bit hard into his lip. He'd been someone then, for a while. If he wasn't that person any more, the promising, smiling man shaking hands with another smiling man, he wasn't even sure who he was. He took the box to the car and locked the remnants of his political career away in the boot.

The others were waiting for him in the pub, an ugly, half-timbered place with patterned carpets and fruit machines that emitted loud jingles at intervals. Everyone complained about the pub, but it was the place they always went, and the complaints about the music, the microwaved food and the irritating machines had become part of its familiarity.

John Lander was at the bar. He waved to Mark as he walked in and gestured towards the beer pumps in an offer of a drink.

Mark protested that he ought to be buying the drinks, but John dismissed his protest and told him to put his wallet away.

'So, here's to the new Steward and Bailiff of the Manor of Northstead,' John said, raising his glass towards Mark. 'Do you get a certificate for that or something? A coat of arms?' Mark shook his head.

'Not seen it if I do. There's probably a scroll made from a dead goat somewhere with my name on, but it's not exactly something I'd want to put on my wall.'

It would have been easier, Mark thought, if you could just resign from being an MP, the way you could from any other job that didn't work out, but this was something they hadn't got round to modernising yet, and he doubted they ever would. So he had notionally been given an office of profit under the Crown, allowing him to step down. The irony was that you didn't seem to profit from it at all. Not unless you got paid in groats or farthings or something. Maybe there was a yard of ale in it for him. Emily had told him not to worry about the money; she insisted that she was earning more than they needed, that he would find something else he wanted to do, but nonetheless Mark still worried.

He could have carried on, he supposed. People had told him he would just have to wait his time, that people would forget, that he could work his way back, more gradually this time around. Callander's implosion had cast him in a better light; he was seen as the person who had, however inadvertently, revealed a supposed traitor. People who had been avoiding Mark had suddenly started speaking to him again once Callander was disgraced. Those easy reversals were one of the reasons he had decided to go; it was easier to bear the dark weight and the loneliness of the disgrace than the quick false smiles of those who seemed to like him again, for now.

John Lander started asking him detailed questions about wards in the constituency, about the people it was important to get to know. Mark had hoped he could just walk away from all of this, hand it over and forget about it, but there still seemed to be things he had to do. It was probably better like that, to cool down, to keep that illusion of movement for a while longer. Lander was talking too fast, Mark noticed, and his thumb drummed on the table as he spoke. Although Lander was still new, as the winner of the last successful by-election he'd been given the job of managing the campaign. It was a prize that came laden with warnings and hidden threats, that 'we' think you can do it, so make sure you don't prove us wrong. John had confided in Mark that he didn't feel ready for it, but Mark assured him that he was. Lander's diffident, detailed manner was serving him well. Unlike Mark, he obsessed about the small things. He noticed when things were starting to go wrong before they really did. He would get there, slowly and shyly, but probably for the duration.

Mark broke off from a detailed discussion of a planning application to knock down the town's damp concrete shopping centre when he saw that Lydia, the fifty-year-old secretary whose face was normally set hard, was looking up towards the door with a tentative smile and wide eyes. John Lander turned his head towards the door, then stood up with his arms outstretched.

'Our next MP!' he exclaimed. 'Congratulations.'

'Prospective MP,' Theo Sadler corrected. He pushed his quiff of black hair back from his face, lowering his eyes in an unsuccessful attempt to look modest.

'Let's not have any defeatism,' Lander urged. 'You're going to win, and I don't want to hear otherwise.'

Mark held out his hand to shake Theo's. Theo clasped Mark's hand so tightly he felt the bones press towards each other.

'I don't think Theo's a defeatist, John, do you?' Mark said. He looked towards Theo. 'Well done. It's a great place. They're great people.'

'You kind of have to say that, don't you?' Theo laughed. Mark stared at him, trying to gauge how facetious he was actually being.

'I don't have to say anything that I don't want to, any more,' he replied. 'They are great people. It is a great place. Don't ever forget that.'

'Yeah, of course,' Theo muttered. 'How much is your house going for, by the way?'

'Enough, thanks,' Mark said. 'Probably a bit big for just you, though. And it's already under offer.'

'I know,' Theo said. 'I'm not sure I want to be out in a cul-de-sac on the edge of town, anyway. There's a place I'm looking at in a new-build near the canal.' He turned to John. 'Do I have to get something before the election, do you reckon?'

'It would be better if you moved here, much better,' John acknowledged. 'Though you could just rent something, in case.'

There had only been one person at the selection meeting who had spoken against the consensus that Theo Sadler was the best candidate. Janet Wright had stood up and raised the glasses that hung on a cord around her neck to get a better view of the young man at the front of the room. She was grey-haired and wiry, and dressed as though she had just come back from a long hike across country. She was soft-spoken and sceptical.

'We've heard a good deal,' Janet began, 'about how well-connected Mr Sadler is, about how much he knows about Westminster and about Downing Street. We've heard very little so far about how much he knows about the constituency. Would he care to enlighten us as to why, after our recent disappointment, we shouldn't choose someone local whose main aim is to represent us in Westminster, rather than Westminster to us?'

There had been muttering and a little tutting. The meeting was overrunning and the result was foregone. Theo had prepared a reply to questions such as these that assuaged the rest of the room but didn't really answer Janet. He dredged up a distant connection to the place – a relative who had lived there once – and argued that knowing his way around the right places and the right people would allow his constituents' voices to be better heard. Janet took her seat again, resigned to the outcome, but shaking her head slightly as though she knew it would end badly, again.

Mark thought it was probably time to leave. Theo didn't need him, and John Lander probably didn't really need him either, whatever he said. He thought embracing Theo Sadler would be unnecessary, as he'd only just shaken the man's hand. Mark took a slight step back – Sadler was one of those people who always appeared to be closer to you than you wanted them to be. He settled for a matey pat on the shoulder.

'Good luck,' he said. 'Not that you need it. You'll be great. Hope I haven't left you with too much of a bad smell around the place.'

'Not at all,' Theo replied, moving closer to Mark again and wrapping his arm around Mark's shoulders. 'You'll be missed.'

The passive construction, Mark noted. Meaning I'm not going to miss you, but I want to give you the impression that other people might. Only not all that much. Mark had already given John Lander his approved form of words in praise of his would-be successor. A bright, talented man who would be an asset to the constituency and to Parliament. That was true, for the most part. It would also be true to say he was a duplicitous, ambitious, if occasionally charming, creep. He'd left that part out of the statement. Sadler would do just fine.

## 36

Vauxhall bridge was not one of London's best places to stop and watch the river. Four lanes of traffic rushed past, sirens screamed, lorries rattled over the bumps on the road. The red paint on the ironwork of the railings was flaking. Nonetheless, Alex stopped and he watched. A cold breeze rose from the grey swirling water. Below him, on the abutment of the bridge, he could make out the tarnished head of a bronze female figure. Alex used to know the sequence of the statues on each side of the bridge, as they marked his route to work. He was surprised how quickly he had forgotten this part of the routine. Which one was she? Alex craned his neck further over the bridge to see what the statue was carrying: it was a book, the bronze volume stained with birdshit. She was Local Government, pointing her finger and looking disdainfully downstream towards Westminster. The bridge was lined with the civic virtues, but most of the people who crossed it or passed beneath it had no idea they were there.

Alex cast a glance back towards the building he had just come from, wondering whether they were still watching him go. They had seemed to let him in reluctantly; he was escorted everywhere by a young woman who, though faultlessly polite, would not let him out of her sight. It was strange to be accompanied down the corridors he remembered by someone who knew them less well than he did; once, on the way to Graham Fletcher's office, Alex's escort had taken a wrong turning, and he'd had to correct her and show her the right way. She had seemed slightly offended by that, turning on her heel to take the lead again with a flustered apology. It was only once they'd arrived at the door of Graham's office that she left him, waiting outside the door until the meeting had concluded.

Graham Fletcher seemed hardly to have moved since the last time Alex had seen him in this office.

'Come in,' Graham called from behind the desk. Alex approached and prepared to sit down.

Graham eased himself slowly out of his desk chair and stood up, leaning forward and extending a slim hand towards Alex. Alex shook it and sank back into the chair facing the window. 'It's good to see you again,' Graham continued. 'There are a few things we still need to sort out, but I hope that shouldn't take too long.'

This was the Graham that Alex had been used to: the elegant, genial man who liked the finer things; no longer the hard, calculating operative he'd had a brief, unwelcome glimpse of. Alex shuddered to remember the room where he'd been interrogated. There was no other word for it. That's what it had been. This office, by contrast, was bright, the sun streaming in through the reinforced glass. Alex squinted against the light and held his hand to shade his eyes, then shifted his chair around away from the glare. He wondered whether this was calculated, another of Graham's tactics to make him feel ill at ease.

'Obviously it's unfortunate that events took the turn they did,' Graham said. 'I'm afraid we find it was all rather unnecessary.'

Alex tried to decipher this. This was a different kind of code, not letters in a book or a rearrangement of the alphabet. Graham was making Alex's arrest sound like some sort of minor social faux pas, as though Alex had been left off the invitation list for a garden party. Just like Detective Inspector Boyd had. This time, there was no Kate to do the talking for him.

'I can't go into too many of the details of the internal investigation, as the process is still ongoing.' He was smooth, evasive, as though he was reading from some procedural handbook.

'What do you mean, the process is still ongoing?' Alex asked.

Graham sipped from the cup of black tea which, as ever, was on his desk. 'We still have to formally conclude the internal investigation,' he said.

'Which, in plain English, means what?'

Graham picked up a biscuit from his saucer and turned it over in his fingers, examining it.

'Which, in plain English, as you put it, means you still lost the bloody disk, even if we can't prove you did it on purpose. The disk should never have left the office, the computer should only have left the office with authorisation, as you perfectly well knew. It's basic stuff, Alex. Trainee-level stuff. And things follow from that.'

'What things?' Alex said.

'Well, to put it bluntly, as you seem to want me to do, we need to be satisfied that you won't do it again.'

Alex stood up from the chair and paced away from the desk, towards the window. He turned back to face Graham. Now it was Alex who was silhouetted by the sunlight, and Graham had to narrow his eyes to see his face.

'Do you think I would go through all of this again?'

Graham seemed to be trying to study Alex's eyes as best he could.

'I'd like to think not,' Graham said. 'But there's another thing.' Graham indicated the chair. 'Do sit down.'

Alex folded his arms across his chest and walked slowly back across the room. He sat in the stiff, upright chair and frowned up at his boss. The sun had retreated behind the edge of a grey cloud, throwing Graham's face into shadow. He looked older than Alex had remembered him, his cheeks more hollow. For the first time, Alex wondered what impact the crisis had had on Graham: this was supposed to be his last job before retirement; he must have felt shamed that a career reputed to have been so successful in more hostile times and places was ending so shabbily here. He would still, no doubt, retire comfortably, with most of the quiet honours that he had the right to expect.

'What's that? The other thing?'

'Well,' Graham sighed, 'the, er, publicity that has resulted from this case is also unwelcome.'

Alex knew that. He wondered what Graham would tell him that he didn't already know.

'Your identity has been compromised,' Graham declared. That was the old-school way of putting it, Alex supposed. His face was all over the newspapers, was the more accurate, up-to-date version. His face outside the police station. His younger face, found in college photos. In the first he'd looked furtive, tired, his face in profile, turning away from the camera. The college photo made him look like a traitor from a previous age, a black-tied idealist in an ivied quad. An Oxford spy, for what it was worth, rather than a Cambridge one.

'It does make things rather difficult,' Graham went on. 'Though ways can be found around it, if you're agreeable.'

'Such as?' Alex prompted. He had spent so many years being agreeable; it felt much harder now.

'We might need to arrange a transfer, in the medium term. A different department, possibly a lower security clearance for the time being.'

'You mean I'd be demoted?'

Graham shrugged. 'I wouldn't put it quite like that. It would be a temporary measure. You'd have the same nominal grade, the same pension rights.'

Alex looked up and out towards the buildings beyond the office. The sun had emerged again and the light caught on the railway tracks by Vauxhall Station, fracturing into splinters of silver. When this had all started, he had thought he might be able to hold on to his old life, but he saw quite clearly what was happening now, and he was not going to let it happen. He was not going to go unobtrusively into a job that he didn't want to do, with a promise of a return to the higher grades of the service that would be postponed and postponed again, put down to factors beyond his control: the wrong position, the wrong timing. He no longer cared about nominal grades and pension rights. It would be more of the same, for as long as he could foresee.

'No,' Alex declared.

'It's all I can offer, I'm afraid,' Graham said. 'Things being as they are.'

'Then, no, thank you,' Alex said. 'I'd like to offer my resignation. Do I need to put that in writing?'

'Don't make a hasty decision,' Graham said. He picked up a pen and made a note on a pad in front of him. 'You're an intelligent young man. You have a good deal of aptitude. Your work has always been of a very good standard. It's a blot on an otherwise unmarked copybook. I'd urge you to consider this carefully.'

Alex had considered, and he told Graham as much.

'If you're sure,' Graham said. 'I can arrange for the paperwork. But perhaps take a day or two. Let me find out what other options are available.' Alex shook his head. He was as sure about this as he had ever been about anything.

'Have you contemplated what else you might do?' Graham asked. 'There are people, contacts we have, who might be able to help find you other opportunities.'

'Not yet,' said Alex. 'But thank you.'

Out on Vauxhall Bridge, Alex inhaled large lungfuls of diesel-filled air. It felt better than the air indoors. He hoped he would never have to enter that hideous building again. He hadn't had a chance to say goodbye to anyone, but he was relieved. The awkwardness of some kind of farewell drinks, warm wine and forced smiles, would have been dreadful. Alex knew that no one had been allowed to get in touch with him over the last few months, for obvious reasons, but he wondered whether they would have done, in any case. What if he'd been ill, away from work in some blameless way? None of them would have come, either. He did not miss them, and they no doubt did not miss him. They had probably talked about him, in the canteen, in the low voices that passed around privileged bits of gossip, but that didn't extend to caring how he was.

Alex glanced at the green windows again. They would be talking about him before very long, once his departure was quietly made known. As he imagined what they would be saying, Alex had the suspicion that this was what Graham Fletcher had wanted to happen all along. He had elegantly manoeuvred Alex into a place where he had no other options left, calmly offered him just too little, left it looking like it was Alex's own choice. This was what they had wanted him to do. Graham was good at this game, always had been. Better than he was perhaps letting on to his own superiors. Fine, if that's how it was. He resolved not to look back at the building again. Alex strode across the bridge towards the river's opposite bank.

## 37

A GROUP OF SCHOOLGIRLS in blue checked dresses sat on the floor of the gallery. They were maybe nine or ten, perhaps younger. Alex watched one of them trying hard to render the painting that she saw before her in pencil. It was an almost impossible task, but she kept working at it. Other girls in the group were not concentrating; they giggled to each other, swapped pencils, whispered.

A teacher called out a couple of names to silence the chattering girls. Meanwhile the girl who was drawing kept her head down over her work. Her light brown hair was pulled back into a tight ponytail. Alex noticed how the abstractions of the picture had become something concrete in her drawing; a pencil boat emerged more clearly from the swirl of snow. She had drawn a figure by the mast. It was funny how everyone could see in it what they chose to see, how everyone, not just children, felt the need to make the lines clearer and simpler, to make things real and figurative.

He tried to tune out the voice of the museum guide who was showing the children around. He knew what he saw in the picture and he did not need someone else telling him what to look for. He could see it for himself. Alex looked at his watch and wondered how much longer the tour would last, annoyed with himself for not having checked. They moved on just in time. The serious girl folded her drawing away into her exercise book and left reluctantly, hanging back from the group to take a last look at the painting. Alex had the room to himself. Their footsteps and their high voices retreated down the corridor before he heard someone trying to pass the group in the opposite direction, a voice repeating impatient 'excuse me's. Just wait, he thought. Be patient, if that's something you're capable of. You're not late. He would have stayed for a while longer.

Alex began to think that he had made another clumsy mistake, one that it was too late to escape from now. Perhaps he could just run away, down the other corridor, hide in another room until she had gone. He stayed. He hadn't come this far to bottle out now.

Anna rushed into the room, looking up from the postcard that she held in one hand. She scanned the walls, checking for the right painting, before she registered that Alex was already standing in the centre of the room. She slowed down her pace as she approached him. She looked well, her face more open, her green eyes clear, like someone who had just returned from a holiday. They stood awkwardly opposite each other; they always used to greet each other with a kiss on both cheeks, but that seemed wrong this time. Alex realised that, and he could tell that Anna did too. They sat on the bench that faced the painting, side by side.

'Thanks for coming,' Alex said.

'It's . . . of course I would come, if you asked me.' It seemed as though she had stopped herself from saying, automatically, that it was a pleasure. 'It's this one, isn't it?' Anna squinted towards the Turner seascape, comparing it with the reproduction in her hand. 'They all look a bit similar to me.'

'Yes . . .' Alex began. 'But about this.' He hesitated. 'There are ground rules, like I said.'

Anna nodded.

'I want to be clear about that,' he continued. 'Because, if I'm honest, I don't really trust you to keep them. But that's the risk I'm taking.'

Alex's voice was barely above a whisper, though there was still no one else in the room.

'There are some things I can tell you,' he said. 'As long as you promise not to use them. And as long as you keep other people, other journalists, away from me.'

'I don't know what I can promise,' Anna said. 'I'll do my best about calling people off. But the rest . . . it depends what it is you're telling me.'

'Don't try and go all high-minded on me,' Alex said. 'Promise, or I'll leave now and there will be nothing.' Anna moved to get her notebook from her bag, which lay on the bench between them. Alex stretched out his arm to stop her. 'You can remember it. Don't write it down.'

He turned back towards the painting, not meeting Anna's eyes as he spoke, though he could tell she was still watching his face.

'You know that they've dropped the charges against me?' That much, at least, he had already seen in the papers, though you would have to be looking hard to have spotted it. Alex found it in one of those columns down the side of the page, between a house fire in Norwich, no one hurt, and a survey on eating habits conducted by a chocolate company.

'Yes. I'm so glad. It's great news.' Anna's voice was conciliatory.

'Not great enough to make the front of the paper, though.' Alex surprised himself with the hard undertone to his words.

'I'm afraid not,' she said. 'It was a big day. There was that shooting.'

This was how the world moved on, then. Something worse happened to some other people, far away, and things drifted away from him. He was no longer interesting. Alex saw that there was little point in having asked Anna to call people off: she would not need to. They were, for the most part, already gone.

'It was kind of a big day for me, too,' he said.

'I'm sure. I'm sorry.' Anna seemed to be worried that she was saying the wrong thing. 'I mean I'm not sorry they were dropped, obviously. I'm sorry about how it all happened.'

'We'll come to that,' Alex said, keeping his face towards the painting.

'Look at me,' she pleaded.

'Why?'

'Because I want to tell you I'm sorry, and I'd rather do it to the whole of your face.'

Alex kept his shoulders facing forward and turned his head a quarter turn, a calculated compromise between what she asked and what he wanted to do. He gave Anna a sidelong look, ready to turn back at any moment.

'I am sorry,' she continued. 'Not just for you being out there, your name, but for how I've behaved towards you. Please tell your parents I'm sorry too.'

Alex turned his head slightly further in Anna's direction, assessing her sincerity.

'I've lost my job. Well, technically, I've resigned, but they didn't leave me with much option.'

'Are you sure?' she asked.

'It's a hard thing to be unsure about. I signed the resignation letter.'

'I mean are you sure you don't want me to do something about it? We could make an outcry, have a campaign, try to get you reinstated? Since you didn't do anything wrong, except lose a computer, which could happen to anyone.' Anna spoke quickly, her idea inflating as she talked like a balloon that was destined to burst.

'Over my dead body. I've had enough outcries. And anyway, I don't want to go back. They said I could stay, get shunted sideways somewhere until the fuss had died down, but I don't want to be. This will always be on my record. I don't want to do it any more. In any case, it's a bit more complicated than that.'

'More complicated how?' Anna was wrinkling up her nose in the way she always had done when she was struggling to understand.

'Do you know what this is? Alex asked, indicating the painting in front of them with his chin.

'A snowstorm at sea?' Anna offered.

'Well done, you read the caption. Top research.' He almost laughed, despite himself. This was both old Anna and new, eager to please, wanting to learn but bluffing to cover the gaps in her knowledge.

'You know I'm not great with paintings,' she replied. She inclined her head to one side as if doing so would help her see it better.

The picture was streaked with lines of grey and white, sea and snow merging into the same spiral that revolved around the canvas. A darker curl of brown paint, reflected at the bottom in the moving waves, marked the smoke emerging from the small steamboat at the centre of the image. Even the horizon was tilted off its axis. The ship's mast was spindly, bowed against the wind.

'So you'll have read the bit where it talks about an elemental vortex,' Alex said. 'The story is that Turner actually went out there, on the boat, into the storm, tied to the mast. If that's true, the thing is that he chose to do it. He wanted to be out there in the middle of it.'

'I know,' said Anna. 'You never did.'

'It was worth it for him,' Alex continued, 'because he got this out of it. Turner got something – we all got something – that was worthwhile and would last, and is still here a hundred and fifty years later. Something that was worth being lashed to the mast for, despite all the dangers.'

He turned to look at Anna, who was staring hard into the painting, as though trying to make out a figure at the centre of it.

'Sometimes these things are worth doing,' he continued. 'Sometimes you have to.'

She turned her head sharply towards him. Her eyes were wide in disbelief. Alex indicated that she should be quiet. He surveyed the gallery again: they were still the only people in the room.

'You didn't! Why?' Anna asked.

'Because people should have to answer for themselves and the choices they make. You can't just reinvent yourself and intimidate other people into making excuses for you. At least, you shouldn't be able to.'

'Callander?' Anna whispered.

Alex nodded. 'All those hours, days, going through this stuff, knowing the history of how people's lives were ruined. It didn't seem right that some people had to account for themselves and others didn't.'

'But when I saw you in the cafe . . .' Anna began.

'For their benefit,' Alex said. 'In case. Which is why I'd better not say too much more, now. You never know.'

'Just tell me how.'

'They teach you that stuff. How not to be noticed. Like you didn't notice me delivering the package. That was a close call. Pretty bad timing, as it happened.'

'And you were prepared to take that risk, Alex. Why my paper, out of all of them?'

Alex was silent. She stared at him.

'For me?'

'It's taken you a while to figure that out, hasn't it?'

Anna fell quiet for a while, looking at the painting again.

'Behind the boat, look.' Alex looked. 'There's a bit of blue sky. The storm will blow over. There's hope, there. He put the hope in it too, not just the vortex. He could see that, in the middle of it all, from the deck of the boat.'

Alex turned to watch her. She was staring hard at the picture and didn't return his gaze. For once she seemed totally absorbed in something outside herself. She had stopped fidgeting and sat still, becalmed, her hands folded in her lap.

'What's happening to the disk?' Alex wondered aloud.

'Oh,' Anna said, 'I'm not sure. We were getting quite a bit of hassle about it, legal threats and stuff. There was talk about chopping it up at one point. They don't tell me all of it. Last I heard, the editor had some plan to give it back, hand it in at the German embassy with a big photo of him shaking hands with the ambassador. Though I'm not sure the ambassador is so keen on that.'

'They should give it back,' Alex said. 'There are other people who might need to know. Maybe in a less dramatic way. It's their truth, their history.'

'You're right,' she nodded. 'What about you, though, Alex? Even if they aren't going to come after you. You still don't have a job.'

'They'll help me find something else. Go back and study, the way I always wanted to. They still have people they can have quiet words with, apparently, even these days.'

'But I thought that was . . . a problem, because . . .' Anna stopped midway through the sentence. 'Because of your bad degree', was the unfinished thought that Alex inferred. 'I need to answer for myself, too, don't I? For the person I was,' she continued.

'It might help. You never have.'

Anna stood up and took a few paces towards the painting. For a moment, Alex wondered whether she was about to leave. She turned back again and sat down on the bench awkwardly.

'I was pretty vile, wasn't I?' Alex didn't contradict her. 'I suppose I was trying to create this sort of image of myself, the woman with the world at her feet. And I thought that kind of woman didn't cling to people from the past, no matter how important they were. I didn't realise what it would do to you until it was too late.'

'I wasn't the past,' he said.

'I know,' she replied. 'I'm sorry. It was heartless just to tell you I was going. Especially when you still had exams to finish. Awful.' Her shoulders slumped and she stared at the floor. It was the beginning of what Alex had wanted to hear.

'So what do you do next?' Alex asked. 'Where do you go from here?'

Anna didn't answer immediately. She seemed somewhere distant, out at sea.

'You mean me personally, or work?'

'Whichever.'

'There are lots of things they're offering me. They wanted me to stay here, stay in Westminster. But I want to go somewhere else.'

'Like where?'

'Somewhere different. Somewhere harder. They call it putting hairs on your chest. Small wars and earthquakes and all that. But that's not how I see it.'

'And you probably don't want the hairs, either.'

'Exactly. I just want to be somewhere it's clearer, more obvious. Not so subjective.'

'I don't think there's anywhere like that,' he warned. 'People are just as complicated, anywhere in the world. You're not just running away again, are you?'

'No. I'm not putting it very well. It's just that after Lucas, after Callander, I don't want to report just stuff that happens in rooms, if you know what I mean.'

'You're going to save starving orphans, is that it?' Alex worried that this was another of Anna's schemes coming on, another balloon that she was puffing up before it floated away with her inattention.

'Don't twist my words, Alex.'

'No, that's your job.' He was trying to resist these barbs, but they kept coming. If he didn't try to keep this tendency under control, he could see himself in a few years' time, becoming waspish and embittered, his comments dreaded by his students. It was a glimpse that marred the otherwise peaceful and undisturbed future he imagined. Perhaps he could learn to let his guard down, sometimes.

'Fair point,' Anna replied. 'It's not that. I just want to go somewhere, see what I can see, do what I can do.'

'Win all the awards you can win. Get a suntan and a promotion into the bargain.'

'That's not it. Really it's not. But believe that if you want to.'

Anna stood up and shrugged her bag back onto her shoulder. Alex moved to stop her going, blocking her path towards the door.

'When do you go?' he asked.

'I don't know, yet. I don't even know where it'll be. A few weeks, a few months.'

'Can I see you again, before then?' Anna nodded. 'But there's still a lot I can't talk about,' Alex went on. 'Things I can't tell you. And I need to be able to see that I can trust you with what you already know. I still have to be careful.' That caution was a habit that would take a lot of unlearning.

'Yes.' Anna held out her arms to hug him. Alex stepped forward and clasped his arms tight around her back, feeling the black wool of her jacket. Her shape was familiar, the smell of her hair the same, although these were never the kind of clothes she used to wear. She leant her head in towards his chest and onto his coat. Her back heaved a couple of times. She was crying, but trying not to. He stroked her hair, kissed her on the forehead, and let her go.

There was a damp patch on his shirt where her tears had been. She stepped back and wiped her eyes with the back of one hand. He noticed a black smudge of mascara on her hand and another below her eye.

'We can't leave together,' he said. 'Because of . . .'

'OK,' she said. 'Who's going first?'

'You go,' Alex replied. 'I could happily stay here all day. You still have things to do. Go on.'

Anna was hesitant, lingering by the painting.

'Off you go,' he urged. 'I can find you. And in any case, I know you know where I live.'

# 38

I T WAS WHEN they got out of the taxi on Gendarmenmarkt
that Anthony stopped so suddenly Mark was afraid his father
was going to collapse. The taxi driver slammed the boot of the
beige Mercedes and Mark handed him a clutch of Deutschmarks.
He turned to look at his father and saw his face pale, heard his
breathing irregular. Mark grabbed Anthony's elbow tightly,
clutching the rough wool of his tweed jacket with a sudden,
intense fear that this had all been too much. After everything
they had been through, perhaps this shock of returning was what
would overcome him. Mark silently urged him not to be ill, not
to die. He felt that this, too, was his fault. Just because he
had to find something to do, a project to keep himself busy, to
keep up that illusory momentum. It was at his constant urging
that they'd eventually decided to come.

'Are you all right, Dad?' he whispered. The fact that his father
was not pushing him away, telling him not to make a fuss, was
even more worrying. They stood close by one another, the bags
next to them on the pavement. Mark listened for his father's
breathing; it seemed, after a pause that was too long, to come
normally. 'What's the matter?'

They were in front of the hotel. A commissionaire in a black
suit waited by the entrance, hovering uncertainly by one of the
ornamental trees that stood on either side of the doorway.
He, too, seemed to be weighing up whether he should call
someone to take the bags in or be calling an ambulance. The
hotel was newly opened, converted from what had once been

an apartment block. Anthony turned to face away from the hotel and waved his arm towards the square. The doorman took a pace nearer, in case he was needed. Mark tried to gauge whether the arm-waving was some kind of symptom of a heart attack, like clutching at your chest. He remembered reading somewhere about shooting pains running down your arm being a bad sign. Which arm was it supposed to be, again?

'This,' he said. 'All this.'

'All this what, Dad?' Mark said. 'Do you need to sit down?'

'None of this, nothing was here.' Anthony indicated a classical building in front of them, dotted with statues and topped with a dome whose gold bosses caught the sunlight. 'That was a ruin, burnt out. The dome had fallen in. Even when I left, there was still nothing here. Not a tree, hardly a building. Just rubble.'

Mark tried to see what his father saw; it was hard. What he saw now was a square in a city that was hoping to become rich, or at least to give the impression that it had forgotten some of the hard times it had fallen on. There were trees in leaf and expensive hotels; on the corner they had just passed there were restaurants with green awnings and tables on the pavements. It was difficult to say, any longer, which was an old building and which was a replica. He tried to look more closely: he saw that the trees were spindlier than you would expect them to be, because they had not been here long, and the apartment blocks that looked as though they had been there a hundred years were built from materials that were perhaps only twenty years old.

'Nothing is how I remember it,' Anthony repeated. 'I remember this place, but not like this.'

'Is that good?' Mark asked.

'Perhaps it is,' Anthony said. 'Perhaps it is. The place I knew is gone. But then I start to wonder whether I really remember it at all.'

The doorman motioned to a porter, who brought an elaborate luggage trolley that encased their scuffed bags in a gilt cage.

★

In the morning, they stood on the same pavement as another taxi was hailed for them. A pendant, a turquoise eye on a blue glass background, hung from a beaded chain on the taxi's rearview mirror, staring at the two men in the back seat. The taxi driver looked up into the mirror, then turned back to his passengers to ask them where they wanted to go. Mark found his accent hard to understand; he hesitated.

As his father spoke, Mark sat in silence, overcome with a strange, dislocated feeling. He caught the gist of the conversation; it was something about how his father spoke good German, the driver asking where he'd come from and whether he'd been to Berlin before. It was all phrasebook stuff, the kind of thing Mark could follow. What he had never heard before was his father speaking his own language to a stranger. The words came easily, but his voice seemed to have a sharper edge to it, the sounds rougher. In Mark's childhood, it had been a language that was never spoken, only read and heard sung. Some of the old books on Anthony's shelves were in Gothic script, full of letters with strange flourishes, the 's's pointing downwards like daggers on fragile, browning pages, that Mark, leafing through, found sinister and hard to read. Mark would hear the words of operas drift up through the ceiling from his father's study to his bedroom, unclear in any language. Sometimes a phrase would escape out loud from his father's lips, an old saying or a rhyme from a children's book that had no exact translation; when Mark was much younger, he would have asked what it meant, but later he stopped, never having got an easy answer. Once, Dad had said something to him in the wrong language by accident. Mark had started, asked him what he'd said. His father had looked shocked too, not having realised which language he was speaking. He always dreamt in English, he said. There was a hidden part of Anthony that still lived in his language, but it was private to him, and not to be shared.

Anthony told the taxi driver only that he'd been to the city before, but he hadn't been back in some time. He didn't say that he'd lived there, or when, or why he hadn't. There must have been hundreds, thousands of stories like this, so many absences and so many reasons. The taxi driver, Mark thought, said something along the lines of the place having changed a lot. Anthony agreed; it was not a statement even he could easily disagree with. He lapsed back into silence and looked away from Mark, out of the window.

On the threshold of the brown, pebble-dashed office block that they reached, Anthony hesitated. Mark held open the glass door and tried to usher his father inside; Anthony held up a cautionary hand. Mark looked puzzled.

'Nothing good comes of these places,' Anthony said. 'Nothing good happens in places like this. Places full of bureaucrats and forms and rubber-stamps. They're all the same.'

'This is different, surely,' Mark urged. 'This place is about trying to undo what the others did wrong. Come in.'

'Sometimes, you still talk like a politician,' Anthony muttered as he stepped inside.

It had taken them months to get this far; there had been forms to fill in, identities to be proved, weeks of waiting punctuated by faxes and phone calls. Mark had tried to hurry them along, to plead exceptional circumstances. He was rebuffed: the phone calls and faxes were apologetic but said the same thing; that there were many thousands of people in the same situation, all waiting to be allowed to see their Stasi files, and that Herr Doktor Lucas and Herr Lucas would have to understand that many of them had to wait. At last, a fax came that said the correct documents had been found, and offered an appointment. Anthony had still been reluctant.

'Why not just wait longer, wait until I'm dead,' he'd told Mark, deadpan. Mark had sighed.

'Because it won't make sense, without you. There will just be names, and cover names, and stories that I won't understand. I need you to be there.' Mark guessed that his father's reluctance was skin-deep, that whatever he might not have wanted to know or to remember, his intellectual curiosity and his desire to see unseen documents, to go back to the original reports filed on him by the original agents, would overcome it.

Anthony clutched his briefcase more tightly as they presented themselves at the reception desk. Identification was requested, and produced; visitors' passes were stamped and presented in return. As they were shown down a corridor, Mark started to understand why Anthony seemed so anxious. He could imagine this is what these places had been like, even then: cold corridors with cheap lino floors and pale institutional paint; a stale, sweaty smell.

Frau Hartmann showed them into a small office, invited them to sit down with formal politeness. Perhaps she had already read his file, or perhaps she detected something in Anthony's manner of speech, but Mark understood her to say that she could tell he hadn't been here in some time.

'Yes,' Anthony acknowledged. 'It will be forty years, very soon.'

She placed a beige cardboard folder on the table between them. There were numbers stamped on it, original numbers and new numbers, the word 'Krummholz' in neat print script on one of the lines.

'This is the first file,' Frau Hartmann began.

'The first?' Mark asked as he looked at the thick folder. She nodded, switching into English for Mark's benefit.

'There are several more, from several departments. Doctor Lucas was obviously a person they found significant.'

Anthony ran his finger along the edge of the cardboard with the gesture of someone used to old documents, who knew how to approach them and felt comfortable lost in them. He took out a notebook and pencil from his briefcase and laid them beside the folder. Now it was Mark who felt nervous. He twisted his fingers together as he watched his father open the cover of the file. As his father set to work he tried to read over his shoulder.

'What have you found?' he asked after a while. 'Is there anything about Christa, about the child?' About his possible half-brother, who may or may not have existed. Who may or may not be still alive, could even have been someone they passed in the streets of the city.

'Not yet,' Anthony said. 'You have to be patient. This will take a long time.' Mark should have known better than to interrupt him at work.

Later, they walked out in the early evening light, skirting the cranes and the hoardings that were bringing the other buildings back from their pasts. There were buildings that still bore the marks of shrapnel, jagged pieces torn out of the brickwork. There was an unspoken agreement between them that they should walk, breathe air that was not musty with years of smoke and secrets. Mark offered to carry the briefcase that was now heavy with the weight of photocopied files.

On Bebelplatz, they stared together into a glass square set into the cobbles which they had almost walked over before they saw it. Beneath their feet, rows of white bookshelves stretched away into the ground, an empty library that stood as a monument to missing books, missing stories, and the people they had belonged to. A plaque set into the paving reminded them that this was the place where books had been burned, back in the thirties, where people had gloried in the destruction of knowledge, where the destruction of people would follow. The monument gave Mark a sense of vertigo as he stood over the empty white room, as though he could fall into it and be trapped there. He looked up, following his father's frame from his suede desert boots upwards, past the familiar cords, the jacket and tie, to his face. The white light from the memorial was reflected off his glasses; it made it hard for Mark to see Anthony's eyes, but he thought his father might be crying. Mark wondered which missing volumes he was thinking of, but there were so many.

Even after a long day of working their way through the docu-ments, there were still the gaps that it would take time to fill in, black rectangles where names had been redacted. His father was better suited to the work than he was; Anthony understood the slow processes of logic and deduction, the occasional calculated leaps that would make the connections and make sense of it all. Mark thought that all he had been good at was pretending the gaps were not there, presenting a flawless whole to the world even where there was not one.

As they moved on, crossing the square in the direction of Unter den Linden, Mark's phone rang. It rang so rarely now that he almost ignored the sound, looking round for someone else whose phone it might be. It was Emily, asking how the day had gone. As they spoke, Mark could hear Bella clamouring to be able to speak to him. Emily put Bella on. She spoke in a high, excited voice, wanting to tell Mark everything about the prize she'd won at school for the painting she'd done. It was a painting of their house, she said, and the whole family, and Daddy at home.

'I'm glad you're at home a lot now,' she said. 'When are you coming back? Is Grandpa with you? Can we get a dog?'

'Soon,' he replied.

'The dog soon?' Bella squeaked.

'I'm coming back soon, I meant. And yes, Grandpa is here, and we're having a nice time. Ask Mummy about the dog.'

Mark remembered the clasp of her warm hand in his as she had skipped to school alongside him the morning he'd left, talking constantly about her drawings, her teachers, the eggs in the classroom that would soon hatch into chicks, and the things her friends had told her. She had run into the classroom without looking back at him or saying goodbye. She had no idea that without her, without Jack, it would have been hard for him to look forward to the days ahead of him, that without a tousled child jumping on him first thing in the morning, urging Daddy to get up, the mornings might have slipped away until lunchtime. The parents at school smiled at him more often now. Mark realised that very few of them had known who he was; their wariness was just of a change in the routine, of an unfamiliar dad they couldn't place.

Mark reminded himself that whatever else had happened, he was lucky. Bella and Jack were lucky. They had him and Emily. The children had each other. He could not imagine a world in which they would have to find their way across a country, alone, hiding from soldiers in barns and abandoned houses and scavenging for food. They would never have to make their lives from nothing, create their own stories with no one to help them and no one else to remember what they had seen. Mark said goodbye to Emily and went to catch up with his father, who was ahead of him, approaching the main road. He decided he would get Anthony to tell him the whole story this time, from beginning to end, and if his father wouldn't write it down, then he would. Not for himself, but for them, for Bella and Jack. Even if they were too young to know it yet, it was their story too.

At one of the new-old restaurants near the hotel, they passed under a red canopy and waited by a velvet rope as the maître d' checked a list on a clipboard, sucking his teeth and looking at his watch. After much consideration, he showed them to a small table by a marble pillar. This was one of the restaurants that was not ersatz: the pillars and the ornate tiles had survived war and communism; the new clientele were the politicians and film directors and artists of the city, living the excited, optimistic life of the new capital.

Anthony sat down on a red velvet banquette. As Mark sat in the chair being pulled out for him and unfolded his white napkin, there seemed to be heads turning in the room. He pulled in his chair, placed the napkin back on the white tablecloth and kept his head down. The attention could not be for them, Mark thought. This is a place where they would not know him. He felt his chest tighten with a sudden anxiety that he might be wrong again. Maybe his story had made the German news, too. Perhaps someone had recognised him. Maybe here, they would think he'd done the right thing. Mark followed his father's gaze to see if he was watching what was going on.

The maître d' had rushed away from their table, back towards his post at the entrance. He returned ahead of a tall woman with long, dark hair and impossibly slender legs who glided across the tiled floor on dramatically high-heeled shoes. She was shown to a better table with a flourish of unfolded napkins, the menu presented to her like a precious object. It was a large table, laid for six; she was obviously expecting friends. A blond man with steep cheekbones followed a few paces behind her and took his seat at the table. The other customers in the restaurant looked towards her and then quickly looked away again, leaning in to their companions and whispering. Mark did not recognise her, but people here did. The waiter confided in them later that she was an actress in a TV series, that the man was an actor too, but they'd not been seen out together before.

Mark had ordered half-a-dozen oysters, and they both ordered the Wiener schnitzel, the house speciality, to follow. The waiter drew the cork from a bottle of white wine and poured two glasses. He and his father had just clinked their glasses to each other across the table when there was another interruption. Mark swallowed an oyster and was starting to regret his choice of restaurant, reproaching himself for his desire to eat somewhere that people came to see and be seen. He would have to restrain himself in the future, learn to live more quietly. A grey-haired man was standing by his shoulder. Mark left the remaining oysters in the silver tray, shimmering on their bed of ice, and wiped brine away from his mouth.

'Sorry to interrupt,' the man said in perfect English. 'I didn't expect to see you here.' He was English. He wore a double-breasted suit whose buttons strained over his stomach. His wife stepped to the side to allow a waiter to pass between the tables with a platter of seafood. Mark suddenly placed them both and stood up to greet the ambassador. He wasn't sure whether to take 'I didn't expect . . .' as an implied reproach, a diplomatic way of saying he should have been informed.

'Sir Malcolm,' Mark began. 'How lovely to see you.' Mark found it easy to switch back into professional mode. 'I'm sorry, perhaps I should have let you know we were coming. I didn't think I needed to, now I'm . . .'

Malcolm Caudwell finished the sentence for him. '. . . a private citizen? No, of course not.'

'I'm so sorry,' Mark continued. 'I must have, we must have caused you a huge headache. You were very helpful. You had some wise words, when I was here.'

'Well, there was something of a headache, as you put it. Though I'm sure you yourself weren't entirely the cause of it. Smoothing these things over is what I'm here for, after all.' Mark wondered what he said in private, in his despatches back to London.

'I've been out of touch,' Mark continued. 'What happened, in the end? To the source of the problem, so to speak?'

Sir Malcolm took a discreet glance around the room.

'I understand it was returned, eventually. To my German counterpart in London. To end up back here.' He sighed. 'Which, I suppose, is probably for the best.' The ambassador looked towards the banquette where Anthony was sitting.

'I'm so sorry,' he said, with a politeness born of years of practice. 'We haven't been introduced. Malcolm Caudwell.' Anthony placed his napkin on the table and rose from his seat, leaning awkwardly across.

'This is my father,' Mark said. 'Anthony Lucas. Doctor Anthony Lucas. Dad, this is Sir Malcolm Caudwell. He's the British ambassador here.'

The two elderly men held out their hands. They shook hands formally, carefully. Mark wondered what the diplomat's calculations were, what he knew and was not saying. He watched to see how quickly he would try to move away. Instead, he did not rush away, despite the crowded restaurant and the press of busy waiters, the table and the guests that awaited him. The two men stared at each other and clasped one another's hands for longer than politeness demanded. Anthony pressed his other hand over the ambassador's right before he released his grip.

'Sir Malcolm,' he said, 'it's an honour to meet you.'

'Anthony,' he replied. 'Doctor Lucas. Likewise. An honour and a pleasure.'

'Are you staying long?' Lady Eleanor said. 'We would love to meet you, properly, if you have the time.'

'We're here to look up Dad's file. He left here a long time ago, before the Wall.' Mark and the ambassador's wife looked at the two men, how they seemed to share something. 'I expect it's you that have the busier diary. But perhaps we should.'

An impatient waiter appeared by the table, wielding two plates of Wiener schnitzel. Sir Malcolm and Lady Eleanor withdrew, letting the waiter put the plates down and turn them towards Mark and Anthony to best effect. Mark looked at his father again. He seemed younger, a man in the same place in a different time. He inclined his head towards the departing diplomat, as though he had a hat that he were tipping. Anthony picked up his knife and fork and cut into the schnitzel, taking his first bite. He said nothing. Mark, too, started to eat. He would get to the stories, little by little, one piece at a time, even the ones that were not in the files. He hoped that they would have enough time to finish. There was a whole room of bookshelves to be filled with the stories that had not yet been told.

# Acknowledgements

I would like to thank my agent, Rebecca Carter at Janklow and Nesbit, and my editor, Mark Richards. I'm also grateful to Rowan Coleman and Faber Academy, and my fellow alumni, for their encouragement. And huge thanks to all of my family, especially Gareth Williams, for believing in me and in this book.

**From Byron, Austen and Darwin**
to some of the most acclaimed and original
contemporary writing, John Murray takes pride in
bringing you powerful, prizewinning, absorbing
and provocative books that will entertain you
today and become the classics of tomorrow.

We put a lot of time and passion into what we
publish and how we publish it, and we'd like to
hear what you think.

Be part of John Murray – share your views with us at:

www.johnmurray.co.uk
johnmurraybooks
@johnmurrays
johnmurraybooks